Night Skins

TALL TALES OF A BLACK AMERICAN PRINCESS

BOOK 1: GENNA

KD BLADE

INK BLADE BOOKS, LLC

ISBN: 979-8-9870470-1-9

Cover designed by KD Blade

Edited by Richard Shealy

sffcopyediting@gmail.com

SFFCopyediting.com

Published by Ink Blade Books, LLC

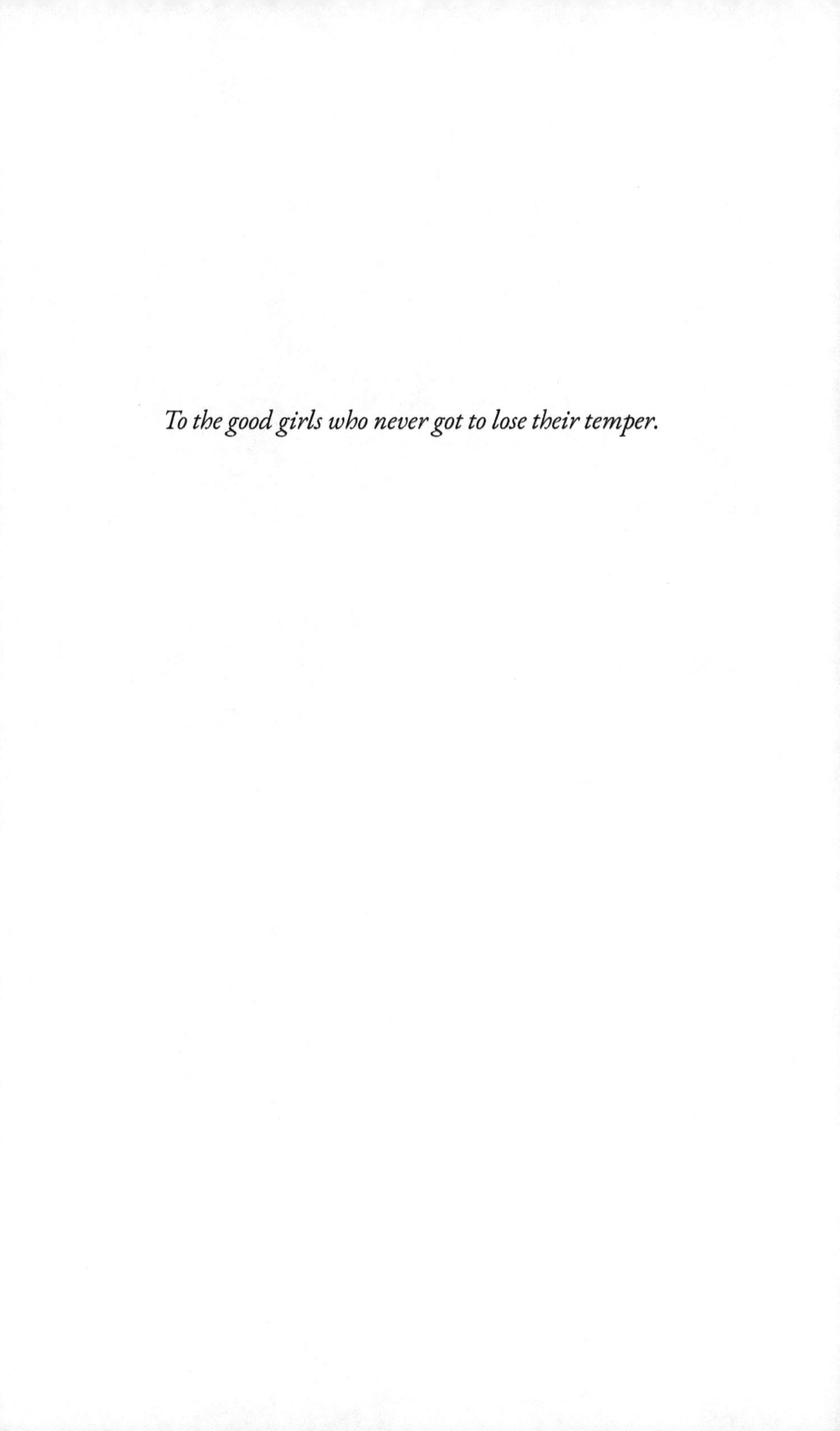

To the good girls who never got to lose their temper.

One

Keesha liked to run alone at four in the morning. Her headphones nestled in the shell of each ear. Her luscious brown skin glistened with sweat. She wore nothing but a sports bra and booty shorts. The impact of each stride made her big juicy butt-cheeks and wide hips jiggle. Her micro-braids were gathered up into a high ponytail with a pink folded bandana on her hairline.

Man, Keesha was hot. Look at those boobs bounce. She didn't look like the mother of three. Not with a body like that. She barely looked thirty. But that's what they say. Black didn't crack.

She rounded a long, sloping curve. The soles of her coral-pink New Balance sneakers flashed as she picked up the pace. Her long legs were like a gazelle's as she flung herself forward. Her face scrunched in concentration as she strained against gravity.

Ainsely followed Keesha through the quiet subdivision. She hadn't noticed him. Not yet. But she would. When he wanted to get close enough to see her eyes get wide and hear her breath lose its steady rhythm.

He knew her route. The places where the shadows were a little darker. The screen of untrimmed hedges. The clump of bamboo that expelled a cloud of mosquitos if brushed. It had taken longer to find the right place to grab her than he expected. That was part of the fun. Each hunt had its difficulties. That sweetened the reward.

Keesha had been a track star in high school. Ainsley liked to watch her then too. He would hide under the bleachers to sketch her and the other girls on the field. His comics about their sexy lesbian adventures were so much better than real life. He got good at drawing boobs and butts. But no one ever wanted his comics. They said that his stories were weird and boring.

He even went to Japan to become a manga artist only to get the same critiques. His dream of having his own cult hit hardcore anime were smashed. No one cared about his art. Why should they hire him? He was just another horny nerd jerking off to his own sketches. They told him to get a job. To finish college. To find something else.

Heartbroken and humiliated, he went home to America. He stopped drawing. He dropped out of college. He became a Realtor to make a quick buck like his dad. He made a lot of money.

Meanwhile, Keesha went to Carnegie Mellon University on a full scholarship. Big deal? She got pregnant. The slut. She married her high school sweetheart. It was shotgun wedding. She got divorced three years later. Keesha never remarried. She was now a single mother with three kids from three different men. She never went anywhere but from Sweetwater into Pittsburgh.

She bought a house in his subdivision of Moon Township. He remembered when they poured the cement of her three-story McMansion. He knew where she put her kingsized bed in her bedroom and which bathroom was her favorite. He knew that she always locked her doors and windows. He hated her big ugly dog that snarled at him that one time he tried to pick the lock.

This was his domain. He was the king. He gave her a good deal on her house. Who was she to say no to him?

She had looked at him like he was a bag of wet trash when he approached her at the Sweetwater country club. She didn't remember him from school. She didn't want the drink that he'd already paid for. She wouldn't even talk to him. She was mean. She had no right. He had more money than some mid-level COO at a no-name startup company. She was a slut who couldn't keep her legs shut. She probably wasn't a good mom, either.

Keesha took a left at the cypress trees, heading for the long series of stairs built into the steep mountain face that divided the poor section of the subdivision from the wealthy side. Ainsley hurried to his hiding place where his things waited. The grass and brush were wet against his clothes. He tried to hide his breath as he puffed up the incline. He had to stay quiet. He grinned as she jogged up the first flight of steps.

She never noticed him in the boxwood bushes. Or the narrow deer path obscured by curling ferns behind it. The path led through a thicket of ivy-wrapped oak trees and down an indented slope to a fissure of earth where the roots spread like a lattice net. The ground was smooth and soft underneath from catching rain runoff. It was an easy channel to drag a body.

The first time he took a woman, Ainsley had rushed it. He saw Laurel in the Giant Eagle grocery store parking lot. Her Steelers shirt was stretched so tight across her big boobs that it was a marigold sign from God. Laurel looked like an almost-girlfriend who had dumped Ainsley after he refused to give her cunnilingus. He grabbed Laurel and took her into the little copse of trash and trees between the grocery store and the public high school football field. He buried her body under a pile of dead leaves. Then he ran.

That had been fun but too fast. He was thrilled and guilty and waiting for someone to point a finger at him. No one did.

The second time was sloppier. Chelsea wasn't supposed to die that quick. He hated her for fighting back and making him a necrophiliac. He wasn't a pervert freak. That time he had to go on a six month business trip to Taiwan to make sure no one noticed.

The third time, he did it right. Gisselle looked like a hood-rat version Keesha. He took his time and it was glorious. Whatever was in that bottle he bought in Taiwan worked wonders. She was wet and wild and willing after the injection. He should have bought more. There were no police reports either. Gisselle simply disappeared without at trace.

He was glad he had practiced before Keesha. Now he knew what he was doing. He was ready. Everything was perfect.

Sweat caught in the stubble of his neck. He scratched it absently. He reminded himself to shave after he showered. To wash his hands instead of keeping the smell of pussy juice under his fingernails like last time.

Here Keesha came. This flight of steps was the longest. She would be staggering and swaying by the time she reached the landing where he waited. Her fatigued muscles from taking the stairs too fast as she always did would slow her reaction to his grab. A sharp punch to her jaw would keep her quiet. Then the injection in the meat of her big booty. He could already feel her in his arms. Her slick sweet sweat. The soft bounty of her breasts. He couldn't wait to chew on the crotch of her running shorts.

He took the syringe and bottle out of his tool bag. He filled the plunger to the limit. He tapped on the syringe to clear the bubbles.

A sound. Soft. Quick. Paws on grass. Fur against bracken. The wet animal pant.

Ainsley looked around with irritation. Some stray dog was about to ruin everything. Then he stared, too stunned to even scream. His eyes were at war with his brain. His vision ping-ponged around features that were neither human nor lupine.

The werewolf had black fur so dark that it swallowed the faint pre-dawn light. The monster's ears were pressed back. A ruff around the broad shoulders stood up like a bristling cape. The long muzzle wrinkled back as a mouth crowded with sharp teeth opened wide.

The werewolf had no smell. There should have been a smell. Like wet dog. Or an animal musk. There was nothing but the forest and his own sweat.

The werewolf cleared the distance between them in one powerful leap. Ainsley woke from his horrified fascination. Under the thick fur the werewolf had a pair of breasts!

He turned to run but the boxwood hedge was a wall. Hard impact knocked the syringe out of his hand with breath stealing strength. Teeth clamped on the back of his neck. The furred weight pressed him down. He pushed, heaved, tried to throw the werewolf into a tree. He was bigger. Heavier.

He expected a rush of pain. The wet tear of his throat being ripped out. A frenzied rush, like an attack of a wild dog, savage and awful, but mercifully brief. For the animal snarls to shake his brain inside his skull. But the werewolf was quiet. Focused on the kill. Her breath whistled against his ear from a cold wet nose.

He grunted like a bull floundering in mud as her claws sank into the wattle of sweaty stubble, tearing open tender vital arteries and the muscles of his sides. His boot got tangled in a strap and he knocked his tool bag over. He scattered coiled rope, rolls of duct tape, the second needle, the bottle, his favorite hunting knife, the extra knife, and a bottled water into the bushes. His boot slipped on the metallic wrapper of the mint chocolate granola bar he had brought in case he got hungry. He lost his balance and fell to one knee.

Ainsley grabbed for a knife. The werewolf knocked him onto his ass with a clawed backhand across the jaw. Pain ricocheted up his tailbone when he landed on a rock. The werewolf hauled him backwards down the deer path by the neck. The tendons on his throat and his back were a symphony of agony as they tore under the strain.

His fingers cringed away from the werewolf's face at a warning shake and snarl. His feet kicked divots into the muddy ferns. His fingernails scraped on tree trunks as he was dragged down the slope. His hands tangled in vines that were actually poison ivy and stinging nettles. The narrow channel between the roots perfectly caged his struggles. He spread his legs and arms wide. His head was dragged downward. The oversaturated ground crumbled around his shoulders. The soft growls and sharp tugs pulled him deeper. Then stuck. His belt had snagged on a root.

He had laid a black tarp down at this part of the channel. Just past the werewolf's big feet was the gag, a pair of rolled socks, and zip-ties looped into handcuffs lined up in a row.

He was prepared. He had planned. He was trapped halfway inside the channel.

Rocks kicked and scattered. His arms pressed against his sides. His fingers slapped his thighs. His head was wrenched sideways. He stared at startled worms wiggling back into the disturbed earth. An earwig scuttled over his eyebrow, up his hair, and back into the dirt. Loose change, his phone, and a switchblade that he had forgotten about fell out of his pockets as he kicked up at the air. He lost his balance and flopped backwards. The small of his back was a starburst of pain. His body was unused to flexibility. He was unable to pull out of his inversion. His belly was bruised and scraped. Blood rushed to his head. Veins raised along his early patterned bald spot. His black baseball cap was misplaced as he was dragged into the channel. He was well and truly stuck upside down.

The werewolf pulled him deeper into the channel. The dull insistent *twang* of his belt against the roots stopped. Strong clawed fingers inspected his position. The werewolf had him where she wanted him. Trapped upside. He couldn't breathe. The inexorable pressure of teeth on his throat and the back of his neck slowly increased. The werewolf was in total control. No waver of muscles straining. The toe claws sunk through the tarp and into the smooth earth below. The tail tucked between muscular haunches as she pulled downward.

His lips were made of rubber. His pale skin mottled. Red turning blue. Eyes bulged from internal pressure. He could only see dirt and the edge of fur until his vision blurred. The wet, squelching gurgle as he tried to breath around teeth crushing his throat. His tongue flapped, licking air that would never reach his lungs. He jerked and bucked and pushed. His torso was a balloon straining to pop. His chest was a vise of agony, trying to breathe. He needed to *breathe*!

He was frantic for a miracle, mewling denial at the werewolf's existence and his impending death. Wouldn't someone save him?

Then the pressure relented. The werewolf let go. Ainsley inhaled, desperately, loudly. Relief filled his throbbing body. Wonderful, glorious, orgasmic air!

Teeth broke the connection between his brainstem and his spinal column with a wet snap. His corpse jerked and flailed as it died. His khakis stained with urine. Excrement mounded in his briefs.

The werewolf ripped the beleaguered skin of his throat. Her claws peeled back skin. Her teeth bit and tore. Her tongue licked. Her throat gulped. Her mouth slurped.

Blood dribbled out of his gaping mouth. His eyes were dull and empty. His head was broken further and push out of the way while the tight network of tendons were chewed off of the verte-brate. The clavicles were broken with teeth and pulled out to get better access to the chest cavity.

Beyond the bushes was the fast stomp of scuffed running shoes ascending a cement staircase. The faint music from headphones.

Perspiration glistened on Keesha's skin. Her arms pumped. Her teeth gritted. The landing was in sharp relief against the blue dawn.

"Come on, girl, one more step. One more step!" Keesha reached the top of the staircase that led to the bigger houses in the subdivision. She pranced in a weary circle. Her fists punched the air in victory. "Yeah, bitch, yeah! You did that shit!"

Keesha ran home, tired but exhilarated. She was proud of herself. She was ready for the day.

～

Blood spilled over fur as Genna pushed her muzzle deeper, then pulled out the tops of the lungs. However, it was mostly rubbery tubes. Vital but not particularly flavorful.

Well, she had wanted to experiment with her kill.

Her prey had provided his own medical scissors. It was easy enough to unzip and cut his jacket and shirt away from his belly.

This was why she called eating sexual predators her 'Happy Meals.' They were fatty, easy to hunt, and came with their own toys. He had already picked a good hiding place that was perfect for an unhurried meal.

She pushed her muzzle deep into the torso, digging past the intestines, angling under the ribcage to get to the liver. She slurped and chewed, delighting in the rich iron flavor. Liver was her favorite organ. Especially when it was fresh. Blood pattered on the tarp.

She left the lower half of his body untouched. His sex organs stank. Gross. Had he ever gone to a doctor to get treated? Or did he think those festering sores would magically go away? He clearly did not care or maybe even enjoyed passing it on to his victims.

Well, not every meal was perfect. Humans were disgusting, disease-plagued creatures.

Werewolves could eat anything because their healing ability combatted illnesses that plagued dogs, humans, and wolves. They were very hard to poison or kill. Silver was an allergy that only hurt some werewolves just as some vampires had no problem with crucifixes and holy water. Genna was immune but her coyote caution kept her alive. Hubris killed the unwary.

Vampires turned into ghouls when they didn't take blood diseases seriously. Ghouls filled the hospitals, hospices, cancer treatment centers, and senior living facilities. Genna had a theory that ghouls had evolved to feed on that cocktail of diseased blood and medicine. Katie said that ghouls were a lower class of vampire. They were Turned not born.

Katie McBride was an elitist. Her snobbery was inherited. She was born a vampire princess from a long line of vampire queens.

Her mother, Mimi McBride, and queen-grandmother, Pipsy Montgomery, were worse. They believed in purity of blood and monsters. Anything Turned by a bite was inferior. Ghouls were barely above revenants.

Genna was a werewolf princess. Her high-born pedigree was twice as old as the McBride vampires. Genna did not know any werewolves by name. They avoided her when she tried to interact with them. The werewolves hunted humans in more densely populated areas than Sweetwater. Genna had to use Katie as her hunting partner. A werewolf and a vampire hunting together was embarrassing and weird but since they were both princesses and extremely lethal, any haters disappeared without a trace.

Both Genna and Katie preferred wild game to humans. White-tailed deer had their problems, but genital warts and chemotherapy weren't some of them. There was an abundance of wild pig in Sweetwater Forest. They helped the environment by eating invasive species.

Katie tracked Keesha while Genna ate. She stayed far enough back from the high fence so the pitbull inside would not smell her. She thought about eating the entire family while Keesha jogged up the steps of her side porch, unlocked the door, turned off the security system, entered the foyer, and locked the door behind her. Keesha did not remember that one time Katie glamoured her into an impromptu tour of the house. It would be easy to step inside. But Genna got mad when Katie did not stick to the plan. Not the fun kind of mad, either.

Genna was a better hunter. Katie knew she would have been caught already if she didn't have Genna around to yell at her about leaving traces behind.

Besides, Genna was a gourmand. Katie ate better, fuller, and with more variety than if she hunted by herself. Katie liked to eat, not plan. When she stayed in the mansion with Mimi and Pipsy, she had to eat last, lick up the dredges, or drink from the swimming pool. It was full of blood but Mimi always peed in the pool. Who wanted that?

By the time Katie returned to the kill site, Genna had eaten her fill. Katie smiled at the half-filled bucket set under the corpse to catch spills. She rubbed against Genna's back. "Aw, you're so thoughtful, Iffy. I love you. I'm so excited that we're getting married."

"I will never marry you, Katie," Genna said as she stood up and licked her muzzle clean. She stepped clear of the corpse and Katie's undulations. She transformed completely into a black coywolf, a coyote-wolf hybrid. She loped away, as fleet and as quiet as a shadow.

"The engagement party is tomorrow. You need to work on your vows," Katie called after her, but her fangs were already extended. They were long and hooked like a viper's. Her nostrils flexed. Her champagne-pink hair flared like a cobra's hood. She lunged at the corpse.

Two

Iphigenia 'Genna' Bellwether's engagement to Katelynn 'Katie' McBride was glamorous but unremarkable, except for the fact that same-sex marriage had only been legalized in Pennsylvania the day before their engagement party.

The lavish event was at the Phipps Conservatory, an indoor botanical garden full of tropical plants and glass art. Strategic lighting illuminated the glass building so that it glittered like a palace made of diamonds.

Protesters and LBGTQ+ activists shouted on either side of the blockaded road. A red carpet stretched like a long crimson tongue from the street into the main awning. Local celebrities and the social elite in their couture finest milled along the illuminated gardens. The engagement party was crowded with paparazzi. The decorations and table settings were thousands of dollars. The attendees shook hands, took selfies, and made deals while guzzling expensive champagne.

Katie McBride was pale, thin, and all smiles in rose gold, champagne pink, pearl white, and antique lace over nude skin. Everything she wore was glamorous. Her bridal gown was hand-made. Thousands of white sequins and pearls on her dress were sewn to look like snake scales. She laughed as she flirted with the well wishers, a glittering tiara caged her pink hair.

Unlike the Met Gala, this was Pittsburgh. Everyone wore black except for Katie. Including Genna, the other bride.

Genna was tall and regal in black. Her abundant curves were exaggerated by elegant corsetry. Her strapless black charmeuse dress was like spilled ink, ravens wings, and pure midnight. Diamonds sparkled like stars along her floor length crushed black velvet cape. Her handmade black lace veil was dotted with jet beads. Her bouquet flowers were red roses and red spider chrysanthemums so dark that they looked made of blood and matched her lipstick. Her crown was purple tanzanite. Black pearls strung along the tines of her crown like spiderwebs. Her black curls were strategically pinned to spill down her bare back like a soft waterfall. Her jewelry was silver and platinum. Her tan cleavage was brushed with gold and purple glitter. Her long eyelashes and black makeup were fluted with gold and silver and copper. She looked sculpted out of polished gemstones and shadows.

Genna did not smile. Her dark smolder and poise wrapped silence around her. The ambient golden glow from expensive and beautiful lighting hidden among arches of white flowers enhanced her intimidating beauty. Her stillness reinforced the nickname of Genna the witch queen.

Genna watched the McBrides from the top of the stairs. It was a balmy spring evening. The night air was gentle against her skin. Her feet did not ache. They were numb from Botox injections. Everyone wanted to see her Stuart Weizmann diamond-encrusted Cinderella heels. The same ones were worn to the Oscars by Alison Krauss. They looked better on Genna. A beautiful contrast against her brown skin and the black fabric of her gown. Thanks to a prank from Katie last year, Genna's feet pictures made a tidy fortune for foot fetishists.

She ignored the grinning comments muttered from the envious and the doting as cameras flashed. They were here for the McBride party not for her.

The McBrides always hosted the best parties. Fortunes were made and lost at the Halloween, Christmas, New Year's Eve, and Easter parties hosted at McBride Manor. The whole summer was one nonstop orgy. No one cared that people died at the parties.

There were drug overdoses in the driveways and suicides in the bathrooms. There were bodies found discarded in the pickle ball court bushes, buried in the golf course sand traps, and hanging from the street lights that lined the long driveway.

Genna thought it was a win to have the engagement party in Pittsburgh instead of at McBride Mansion but here Pipsy was, kibitzing like a normal person. The evening glow was kind to her pale face. She looked like a six-foot-tall version of Audrey Hepburn from *My Fair Lady*. The enormous black-on-black floral hat, ruffles, pinstripes, and bustled train did not seem so ridiculous when the humans were dressed in their noir spring finery. All of Pipsy's minions wore drab versions of similar attire.

Pipsy Montgomery was the matriarch of the McBrides. The public had no idea that she was a three hundred-year-old vampire. Her wealth and media control embroidered a narrative that she had refused to take her husband's name when she married the oil tycoon Tom McBride fifty years ago. She came out as a lesbian after her husband's mysterious suicide. Her backroom influence pushed the governmental bills legalizing same-sex marriage into a reality.

It was difficult, but Genna stayed still for photographs. First by herself then with her family posed around her, careful of her long train. Then her so-called wedding party, then her friends, then work colleagues. People she had known all of her life crowded on the platform tiers for a picture. There were members from Jack & Jill, Links, Alpha Kappa Alpha, Girlfriends, and other Black sororities, fraternities, and groups. There were well-known civil rights activists, professors, ministers, politicians, boardroom giants, businessmen, and council members. Everyone wanted to be seen.

"It's only an engagement party," her mother told her soothingly between photos. "Smile."

Genna did not glare at her mother. People said it was an engagement party. They said it over and over again. But Genna knew that tonight was the wedding.

The whole point of the engagement party was a conqueror's strut. Even the protestors stoked Pipsy's bloodless smiles. An energy vampire thrived on drama. The uproar and the scandal only increased her notoriety. Rumors of wild debauchery the likes of Caligula were reinforced by the puritanical fury at her unrepentant attendance at the Sweetwater Presbyterian church. The tabloids caught her son Donnie with one underage girl after the next. Her daughter-in-law Mimi was photographed lying on a bed of naked young men. Their son Kyle died in a childhood accident, drowned in the pool. Katie the bride was as wild as her parents. No one could believe that her marriage to Genna was anything besides political.

Genna's family wore modern haute couture. They were reserved and dignified. They had never been ostentatious. Their brown skin had its own way of standing out. The Bellwethers had been wealthy and Black for four centuries. It was a feat in itself. If her family had not been glamoured until their eyes turned iridescent, they would have loathed this much publicity.

This wedding was the merging of two dynasties. The Bellwethers and the McBrides.

Genna kept her body relaxed. She held her bouquet. A black wood paper fan hung from her wrist. Closed, it appeared to be a simple accessory. She had practiced with the fan for a solid twenty minutes. Open. Shut. Open. Shut. A lifetime of ballroom dances and debutante balls taught her the etiquette of the fan. The wood was heavy and two feet long. The paper was reinforced. What was printed on the paper was important. She had to wait for the right moment.

Katie flounced up the steps to join Genna on the platform,

radiant with triumph. "Oh, my love, isn't this wonderful? Everything is perfect. You're perfect. My beautiful bride!"

Genna did not answer. Katie did not notice. She was too busy flirting for the camera.

Genna's Glamazons, her beauty team, bustled around her. They gave her a sip of water through a straw. They flared her cape, and added more glitter and dusting more foundation. Katie's team fluffed her gown, added more lipstick, and gave Katie a bouquet of dusky pink roses and pearls. They layered the long French lace train of Katie's gown and veil over Genna's to form a heart. Genna stared at the fabric heart as bright lights flashed and random people shouted at her to look their way.

She slipped the fan into her hand. Then reached down to grab a firm hold of the charmeuse, black velvet, and black lace. She yanked free of Katie's lace. Fabric rippled like a flamenco dancer's skirts. The sound was loud. The sudden movement drew attention.

"I will never marry you, Katie!" Genna proclaimed, haughty and dismissive.

Everyone in earshot gasped with scandalized delight. Everyone loved having a front row seat to drama. Cameras flashed faster.

Katie stopped smiling. Her blue eyes were empty as glass and as predatory as a snake's. "What do you mean?"

"I will never marry you, Katie," Genna repeated, pointing the fan at her. "Or your disgusting father."

"You have to marry me. You're my bride!" Katie lunged at Genna. Her sparkling nude and diamond manicure turned into glittering claws. Gone was the cutesy glamor girl. Here was the monster, the true Katie, screaming like a banshee. Her jaw was wide, so wide. Her fangs extended but Genna was the only one who could see them.

Genna pulled the bouquet back and opened the fan in Katie's face with a sharp *crack*, loud like a gunshot. Katie recoiled, confused by the sudden noise and eclipsed vision. Her hands were still wide and grasping. Genna closed the fan and clubbed Katie across the face with her real strength. Katie fell down the tiered platform, tangling in her own veil as she bounced to the red carpet.

Genna stood at the top of the stairs, glaring as Katie fell. Her lips were tight. Her closed fan was held sideways like a sword. Her other hand clutched the bouquet like a shield. She was a full figured queen framed in golden light and arched white roses.

She pointed her fan at Donnie McBride, who smirked by the bar. Her shapely lips twisted into a wintery sneer. "I'll never marry you, either, Donnie, you disgusting pedophile!"

She flicked the fan after Katie, mired in finery. The fan contained the actual annulment documentation, already signed. Along with a restraining order.

Genna's security team, resplendent in tailored black-and-silver brocade Tom Ford suits, formed an armored escort. Four men gathered up her train and veil carefully into a satin lined bag for Genna to hold while they carried her down the platform on a chair.

They hustled her to the street while other bodyguards formed a human wall to keep the red carpet clear to the street. A chauffeur in black with a silver monocle and a silver handlebar mustache pulled up in a black six-wheeled Nautilus. The vintage car was decorated with silver filigree and rococo with lavender leather interior. Genna climbed in. Her guards adroitly tucked her petticoats and cape out of the way as they closed the door.

She hurled her bouquet at the crowd of photographers, the black pearls and lace arcing through the air as the Nautilus peeled out. A crowd of women rushed from all directions. They elbowed each other and screamed as they fought to catch the bouquet, further hampering the paparazzi's attempts to follow Genna's escape.

More of Genna's personal team hustled her family into waiting black Range Rovers ignoring the white limos that the McBrides had provided. Then the guards got in their own cars and drove after them, running interference for anyone trying to chase.

Katie screamed Genna's name. Her hair was wild. Her tiara was askew. Her makeup was a smeared mess, a fake eyelash ripped off. She tore her veil and her delicate lace dress trying to untangle her legs. She chased Genna's Nautilus until she was stopped by other people, who did not want the jilted bride to get hit by a car.

Genna felt Katie's scream in her blood. Her vampiric influence hauled like fishhooks in her skin. Genna leaned forward, grimly fighting the glamour. Fire in her veins burned. The wind caught her eyelashes, forcing her eyes wide as the blockade and the protesters whipped past.

"Is the plane ready?" She demanded.

"Yes, ma'am. All gassed up and raring to go," the chauffeur said. "I must say, that was one hell of an exit. If you're gonna be a runaway bride, do it in style."

She did not smirk at his approving harumph. Instead, she wrapped the veil around her shoulders like an oversized scarf. She kept the crown on.

The black cars sped in front and behind. Every light turned green for the Nautilus then red for her pursuers.

She hoped everyone in her family was in their cars. She had to get them in their planes and across the Atlantic Ocean to Barcelona. A large body of water would break the spell the McBrides had over them. They would be angry when they woke up. Running away was only the first part of the plan.

A year ago, Genna had refused Katie's proposal the same way she refused anyone who asked for her hand in marriage. She slammed the door in Katie's face when she showed up at her college apartment. She ignored Donnie and Mimi's hungry leer. She thought nothing more of it. Then Genna's mother told her that the McBrides had different parenting styles and not to expect much help from Katie. Genna saw the iridescent gleam of enchantment in her mother's eyes and knew that her entire family had been compromised.

Genna stayed quiet. She did not cry. She read the fine print. It was an arranged marriage with her family's wealth as the dowry.

The rage was hard to suppress. Just because Genna could rip Katie's face off did not mean she should. She needed a plan. She needed to save her family and their money. She was alone.

Genna bought two planes and a bunch of businesses in what appeared to be a flurry of nuptial bliss. She had not wanted to buy prisons, housing redevelopments, horseshoe-crab farms, and other morally gray companies, but desperate times called for desperate measures. She needed enough money to declare her own financial and legal independence. She made peace with the enterprises she purchased. She hired a team of lawyers that were capable of taking on her family and the McBrides during the annulment proceedings. She prepared for a long and brutal battle. She gathered her strength. She waited and struck.

Smacking Katie with the fan was a signal to her loyal team of Glamazons to buy and sell stock. The flurry of strategic purchases would hamstring the McBrides from immediate financial retaliation.

It didn't matter how ancient and powerful the vampires were. The McBrides were going to learn not to come for Genna's family.

Three

No one believed in vampires, but that didn't make them any less real. Or maybe it was a preservation tactic. Humanity would always be afraid of the dark.

The McBrides called themselves vampires to exploit pop culture. Some parts of traditional vampire lore applied, like their inability to enter a place unless invited. They fed on blood, vitality, and emotions. They could mesmerize and control the physiological reactions in their prey. They could stand in sunlight. They could transform into enormous snakes.

The truth was old and unvarnished. The McBrides were monsters that preyed upon humans. They wore human skin. Vampires, especially old ones like Pipsy Montgomery, had money and no morals. A vampire's bride did not survive her wedding night. Genna would be sucked dry, turned into a mindless revenant, and all of her family's assets would be acquired by morning.

Or at least that was the plan.

Katie wept into Genna's abandoned bouquet. The petals caught her tears of betrayal and rage. She was a picture of tragedy. Several dead women who had tried to claim the bouquet for themselves were quietly carted away.

There were more photographs of Katie with her mother and grandmother. Three shockingly young and beautiful pale women. Though there was no mistaking which one was Pipsy Montgomery. The McBrides' assistants and staff formed a human wall around the three vampires.

"Katelynn, stop sniveling. It's unbecoming," Pipsy said, her feet entirely hidden by ruffles. She glared after the disappearing Nautilus. She sucked on her teeth. "Iphigenia is gone."

"Pipseee," Katie said, clinging to her grandmother's narrow hips. "She's supposed to marry me. I can't believe she left me. She can't do this to me. She's my bride. I love her."

"Calm yourself, my darling," Pipsy dabbed her tears away with a lace-covered handkerchief. Katie sniffled and leaned into her grandmother's touch.

"How dare she do this to us," Mimi snarled. She wore a tight slinky black Versace dress with white trim. "She won't get away with this. The Bellwethers will pay."

One of the on-site manager's assistants picked up the fan. She tried to fathom how the engagement party that was supposed to make her career had gone so horribly wrong. She numbly opened the fan. She read a few sentences.

"What've you got there?" someone from the paparazzi said.

The assistant cowered in front of the horde of camera lenses. The fan was snatched. Photos taken. Someone read a few lines aloud with glee. "It's an annulment. An annulment! The wedding's been canceled!"

They sounded like grackles and seagulls fighting over spilled fries. Mimi stomped over and clawed a man in the process of snatching the fan away. He yelped, holding his bloodied wrist. Mimi swept back to Pipsy and Katie, reading with growing outrage. She shook the fan. "What is the meaning of this? She's annulling the marriage to Katie *and* Donnie?"

Three sets of narrowed blue eyes focused on one ruddy tanned man in a Mariano Rubinacci three-piece mohair suit.

Pipsy took the fan from Mimi. She read the folded paper. Genna had been thorough. She used plain and explicitly detailed language, unlike Donnie's weaselly attempts to have her married to him instead of his daughter.

Pipsy slapped the fan closed in her palm, squeezing it with fury. "Iphigenia found a loophole."

"What? How!" Mimi exclaimed.

"You mean she really didn't want to marry me?" Katie wailed.

"Donnie," Pipsy hissed.

Power flexed through the gardens. The flames flickered out. The cameras swung toward the flowers, the dinner guests, everyone but the vampires. The humans forgot all about the McBrides. The music played. Servers bustled around with trays of food. Humans sat at the tables and ate with blank-faced intensity. They ate fast, responding to Pipsy's hunger. Food and drink spilled on silk and sequins and linen. Others were inside on the dance floor. The live music playing a fast but old version of "I Put a Spell on You" to amplify Pipsy's spell.

Mimi added her own flavor. The protesters and activists started to fight each other. Across the street, students in the University of Pittsburgh and the Cathedral of Learning began to fight, cry, fornicate, or eat. Cars horns blared. A traffic jam clogged the roads. Adults wrestled free of safety belts to get out of the cars and fight the assholes who had just rear-ended them. Babies and children screamed.

Katie's tears and wails caused animals to flee. Birds flew fast to get away from the Phipps Conservatory. Some bounced off cars and buildings in their haste. Squirrels, rats, raccoons, and stray pets got hit by cars as they fled on foot. The humans chasing their runaway dogs got hit too.

Donnie stood in the nexus of angry silence. He straightened his tie, annoyed. He had thought that being in public would save him. Except it was night. Pipsy was angry. Mimi was embarrassed. Katie was upset. They never worked together. Not in concert.

Usually, they were at war. He could get what he wanted by playing all sides. No there was no protection.

"Explain yourself," Pipsy commanded.

"Same-sex marriage wasn't legal in Pennsylvania until yesterday," Donnie said with the trace of a whine.

"You signed this for Katie," Mimi said. "You signed as her legal guardian."

"Daddy?" Katie said, on the edge of a hiss.

Donnie shrugged. "It's nothing, sweetheart. She's lying. You're still a child. You're barely twenty."

"According to this, the legal age of adulthood in Pennsylvania is eighteen," Pipsy said. "Iphigenia had filed and achieved legal and financial independence from her own family. She is entirely free of their influence or ours." The fan creaked under the strain of her grip. "She has also filed a restraining order against you, Donnie. And Katie. The same with litigation. What is the meaning of this?"

"You were going to marry Iffy instead of me?" Katie's strangled screech drew more attention. More photographs. Another flex of power from Pipsy made the cameras swing away again. "Daddy, how could you? She's *my* bride."

"Oh, come on, Katie. She's just your first bride. It's not a big deal," Donnie said.

"Sounds like someone wanted a new wife," Mimi said.

"Whatever, bitch. We're divorced. You're not getting anything from me. I'm the only male McBride. Out in the real world, you three have to do what I say. I'm the head of the household."

Pipsy smacked him across the mouth with the fan, breaking one of his veneers. Donnie toppled in the loose-limbed, limp-armed, head-lolling descent of the concussed. His hard landing was not helped by his temple connecting to the cement.

"She is mine!" Katie pounced on her father, her teeth extending. She bit him through his suit. Donnie struggled, feebly batting at the air.

Mimi stomped him in the balls with her sharp Jimmy Choo heel. Pipsy stopped her with the edge of the fan.

"No, this is Katie's kill."

"After everything he's done to me. I deserve this," Mimi said, though she did not bare her teeth at Pipsy.

"Katie is my heir, *daughter-in-law*." Mimi flinched at the dismissal. Pipsy took the fan apart, reading the other pages. "Donnie stole her bride. Katie has the right of first kill."

"Why did he ruin everything?" Mimi said, gesturing at the engagement party. "We had them."

"I know my son. This was always his plan. I knew he wanted the Bellwethers' fortune, but I did not think he would take their firstborn daughter, too. His greed exposed our strategy. Iphigenia exploited a loophole he made with his own incompetence. Now she has slipped out of our hands."

"We'll get her." Mimi frowned, surprised by Pipsy's acknowledgement. "They won't get far."

"I can feel the Bellwethers' connection fraying. Clever of her to use their own planes. By the time they cross the Atlantic, they will be free and forever immune of my hold. When we look, we will find that she built the escape into the flight plans and frayed our connections in plain sight. Truly, Iphigenia is a formidable wolf. So rare in their kind." The vampire queen seemed cooly amused instead of furious, like a chess master outmaneuvered by a novice.

Mimi longed for her mother-in-law's approval. To hear the coveted compliments given to Genna Bellwether for humiliating them in public filled Mimi was insecure rage.

"She had help," Mimi seethed.

"Yes, she did," Pipsy neatly put the fan back together. "And I know who."

Donnie had stopped flailing. All of the skin in his face sagged in on itself. His eyes shriveled like pale grapes. His gums pulled back away from his teeth. His fangs were yellow from cigarettes and coffee. His nostrils folded in on themselves. His mohair suit deflated. The jewelry fell off his wrists and fingers. His skin turned to sinew, then frayed. Then disintegrated into dust.

Katie rocked back, her skin blushed pink, rubbing her throat.

Pipsy walked over the suit that had been her son. Katie leaned her chin into Pipsy's long-fingered grasp. "Thank you, Pipsy. I feel better."

"Go enjoy your party, my darling. Don't you have several dresses planned for tonight's festivities? Have a wonderful time."

Katie giggled and bounced to her feet. She hugged and kissed Pipsy. "I love you!"

Then she flounced off.

"Clean that up," Pipsy said, waving a hand at the suit as she followed Katie.

Mimi glowered. She had dreamed of draining Donnie to dust for years. She loathed her daughter for stealing yet one more thing. She snapped her fingers.

One of her many boy toys trotted up. "Yes, baby doll?"

Mimi looked him over. The boy toy had a different color of hair, brown instead of strawberry blond, and was twenty years younger, but he was close enough. She reached into her Hermès purse and pulled out her perfume. She spritzed him in the eyes with Chanel No. 5 as she cast her spell. "Put these on. You are Donnie McBride. Eat. Drink. Fuck. Everyone who sees you will see my fucking ex-husband."

"Yes, baby doll." The boy toy took his clothes off without a hint of self-consciousness. He donned the suit, the jewelry, even though it did not fit his hands. If the dark blue fabric seemed a little dusty, he would say that it was from the cigar ash of a great Cuban. Then reach into his pocket and offer a monogramed gold case of cigars.

"Throw those rags away," Mimi commanded.

"Yes, baby doll." The stand-in Donnie bundled his Armani suit into a ball and placed his loafers on top. He walked off to find a trash can.

Mimi brushed her dress. She decided it was time she too had a fashion change.

The spell broke apart. Normalcy drifted back into the party and the surrounding area like a fog. Tomorrow, there would be reports of someone from the McBride wedding party pouring some kind of aphrodisiac inhalant into the party fog that had caused a mass carnal rush in everyone in a five mile radius.

Those McBrides really knew how to throw a party.

Four

Genna made sure the scandal of the annulment
did not go the way the McBrides planned by deploying one
picture taken at her seventh birthday party.

A photographer made his fortune publishing Genna's child-hood fight with Katie McBride. He had lain in the grass, taking action shots of two little princesses fighting in the flower garden as if capturing a football game. He was excited to use his telephoto lenses to get the white stone turrets and ramparts of Genna's new castle as the backdrop.

The iconic photo forever connected to any Google search of Genna Bellwether was her child-self's face frozen in a howl of pure screaming murder. Thin lines of blood dripped down her face from the rock Katie had used to split her eyebrow open. There was blood on Genna's lavender ballgown and Katie's pale blue dress. Their tiaras, hair, and petticoats were a whirlwind. Their pretty faces were scrunched in snarls.

The photo caught Katie on her back arching upward, arm mid-swing with a rock. Genna stabbed Katie in the belly with the broken half of the golden scissors she had used to cut the ribbon strung across the front door of her new castle. Genna thrust down with both hands around the large looping end of the scissors. The metal edge caught the light. A straight line down to Katie's belly. The ruffles and petticoats hid the scissor's purposefully rounded and kid-friendly tip.

Several adults were in the background, shouting and running to pry the two little girls apart. Other little girls dressed as princesses cheered while hugging kittens and puppies.

The story behind that photo was a prologue to the perpetual struggle between Genna and Katie.

Genna had caught Katie eating a kitten from the petting zoo during her birthday party. Genna hit Katie in the face with the scissors like she was swinging a baseball bat.

Schrodinger the kitten would never recover. Nor could he die. Whether born or newly Turned, baby vampires were a lot like newly hatched vipers. They did not know how to control their venom. They put all of it into their bites. Schrodinger and Genna both got bitten in the scrum. Katie's venom caused the magic in Genna's blood to ignite like wildfire and lightning. Schrodinger got a full dose of Genna too.

Attempts to hide the real photograph only drew more attention. Arguments of fake news. The photo was in direct conflict with the belief that sweet little girls only cried and pulled hair. Not actively tried to kill each other.

The wedding media was on Katie's side. Katie was the victim. Genna had broken her heart, leaving her at the altar. Genna was the crazy violent one.

Except the damning picture remained. Even after the original photographer had a tragic car accident. It became a meme. A little Black princess caught trying killing a White princess. *Slay Queen* and *Never send a dragon to do a princess's job* and *No I'm the fairest!* kept the picture alive.

The town of Sweetwater had nothing to say to the paparazzi about Katie McBride and Genna Bellwether. The gawking masses found to their surprise that no one wanted to talk to them.

"They're a couple of rich bitches who think they're better

than everyone," the inquisitive said. "What do you think about that photo?"

"Let sleeping dragons lie," the townspeople said.

The paparazzi tried bribery, except everyone in Sweetwater was rich or depended on the wealthy for a paycheck. They tried the churches, except the two families were major donors to every religious organization in the community. They tried high school classmates and teachers. They ran into a brick wall.

There were plenty of rumors about Belle and the Bride. Sweetwater residents had a superstition that was akin to the townspeople who lived near Dracula's castle. They knew that magic and monsters were real. Wild magic did not show up on camera. It had to be experienced. They had survived that fateful birthday party as children. They went to school with Genna and Katie. They attended the same church, ate at the same country club, and lived like small animals trying to avoid their predatory attention.

White and pale-coated animals went to Katie in the desperate hope that she wouldn't eat beloved and expensive pets. Or play too hard with their kids. Or sleep with their husbands or wives or siblings. Or visit their parents in nursing homes, hospital, or rehab. There were a lot of reasons to keep Katie's cheeks pink and rosy.

Meanwhile, every black dog, cat, horse, bird, and even goldfish found its way to Genna's property in the hopes that lightning or mysterious fires would not burn their houses down. The reclusive Genna Bellwether was seen rescuing a litter of kittens born in a storm drain or carrying a puppy out of a hoarders hovel. She knew who abused, poisoned, or killed animals and those people died hard. And if a townsperson was kind to animals, leaving out water or birdseed, if they were ever lost in Sweetwater Forest, a cat would lead them to Bellwether Castle, the one place the McBrides could not go.

The slanderous posts against Genna were taken down. Every company and business or random speculating internet troll got a knock on the door. An army of lawyers in tailored suits were deployed to cease and desist all inquiries.

The ambitious and stubborn drove up to the top of the mountains, locally called the Heights. They snuck into Sweetwater Forest that surrounded Bellwether Castle and McBride Mansion. They ignored every warning as local bullshit. They were determined to uncover the real story. Those people didn't come back.

Only the birthday picture remained. The image was a lot like St. George slaying the dragon.

Five

WHEN THE BELLWETHERS ARRIVED IN BARCELONA, Genna put her family on a fleet of yachts she had bought to circumnavigate the globe. She dressed them in anonymous loose black and navy blue clothes. Their hair was stuffed under baseball caps. Their faces were hidden by black masks and sunglasses. She had body-doubles on several boats speeding off in different directions. Others flew, took trains, and drove a series of luxury cars to various remote locations. She knew that the McBrides would hunt those people down. She paid each body-double a fortune and hoped that they survived long enough to spend it.

When her family were in open international waters, having switched to a beautiful yacht, the iridescent enchantments finally cleared from their eyes. Their desire for answers was loud as they sat in the lushly appointed brown leather stateroom.

"Iphigenia, what is going on?" her mother demanded.

"This feels like a kidnapping," her brother said, joking but not joking.

Genna stifled the urge to cry. She was happy to hear them sound like themselves again. Their eerie smiles and pleasant compliments had been nearly as bad as Donnie's covetous leer.

She told as much truth as she could. "Donnie McBride

planned to marry me instead of Katie. He set it to start at that fake engagement party. It was written in the wedding contract. I was supposed to be his second wife. Then he'd take over our family businesses. All those contracts you signed gave him full access to everything."

"What do you mean everything?" Her sister said.

"I mean *everything* everything." Genna had tablets with the contracts for them to read. They took the tablets but stayed focused on her. By their expressions, they did not believe a word of it.

"This is bullshit," her brother said.

"It's not. I've annulled it, but we need to lay low. If they couldn't get me, they'd go after you three. I've fixed it so they legally can't but that doesn't mean they won't try."

Her brothers were loudly disgusted. Her sister's jaw was tight. Her mother paced like a caged tiger.

"It's not an annulment if you haven't been married." Her father frowned at the tablet. "You haven't been married, have you?"

"No, I haven't. I call it an annulment because I nullified everything they did." There was a magical component to every legal sheet of paper binding her family to the McBrides that had to be meticulously defused and obliterated but they didn't need to know that. The Atlantic Ocean and time were the best remedy to dissolve what Genna couldn't but only if they listened to her warnings.

"Please don't go on land," Genna added, a warble of insecurity escaping her control.

Her family scowled.

"I have things to do," her sister complained. "I have a life, you know."

"I'm sorry. I want you safe, okay? You should be able to do everything you need to from the yachts. Please don't go in person to any meetings for at least a month. Stay on open and international waters. I have to go."

"Whatever," her sister said, but she would do it. Genna knew she would. She could smell her fear.

"Where are you going?" her father said, striding after her.

Genna stopped him with a hug. "I love you, Dad. I'm so glad you're okay."

He hugged her back. "Oh my wonderful daughter, you were such a beautiful bride."

"Thanks, Dad."

"You're going back to Sweetwater, aren't you?" Her mother said, frowning in the doorway.

"Yes, Mom. I can't leave the horses."

Her mother nodded. That she understood.

"You need to be safe," her father said.

"I will be," she said. "I promise. I love you."

Genna did not let her mother coax her into having a family dinner on the yacht. She did not answer any buzzing phone calls or pointed questions from her Glamazons or assistants. She climbed into a smaller and faster yacht and sped away. She took a different plane to fly to Martha's Vineyard, an island off the coast of Massachusetts.

She swam in the water at Inkwell Beach. The water was brackish. Full of human stench. Her feet brushed sea grass and sand. The current pulled her towards open water. She kept swimming until the last of the McBride enchantments washed off her skin, stinky and clotted like old mayonnaise. Only then did she swim inland.

Genna climbed up the shore. She lay in the yellow sands, panting and naked. Broken shells pricked her skin. Sea foam tickled her feet but she was too exhausted to move. The gentle thunder of waves on the sand lulled her into the dazed joy. It was great to lie still. For a moment, the world was not in constant motion.

Months of planning and sleepless nights spent worrying over every detail. The escape was flawlessly executed. The McBrides were fooled. Her family was free. Her triumph would have felt better if she were not so exhausted.

A dark-skinned woman walked over, holding her large floppy straw hat on her braids. "This isn't a nude beach, honey child. There are children here."

"The current stole my bathing suit," Genna said, blinking at the seagulls overhead and the shadow from the woman standing between her and the sun.

The woman offered Genna a red towel. Genna missed, trying to remember how to use fingers. The grit of sand along her breasts and between her butt cheeks itched.

The woman smiled as she spread the towel over Genna from chin to knee. "You were swimming a long time, honey child. I was worried that the ocean had swallowed you up."

Genna blinked blearily. The face swam into recognition. Steel gray hair braided into a loose crown. An old-fashioned cotton blouse. Khaki slacks. Round shoes. A denim blue apron so long and voluminous that it was often mistaken as a dress. The weight of the blanket was a familiar black fur opera cloak.

"Miss Bootsie? I thought you couldn't leave the forest," Genna said. "What are you doing in Martha's Vineyard?"

"The Inkwell is still the Inkwell." Miss Bootsie smiled at her and the other brown-skinned people on the beach. "There are still Black spaces that remain when others are forgotten. I used to come here a long time ago."

Miss Bootsie sat down and folded the cloak conservatively across Genna's legs. Genna rolled like a beached whale. She rested her head on Miss Bootsie's lap. Her long black curls looked like seaweed clotted with sand. She exhaled as Miss Bootsie's gentle hands stroked her head and neck.

"It's good to see you," Genna mumbled.

"Rest, honey child," Miss Bootsie said, "You have done enough."

Genna had not told Miss Bootsie what she planned but little got past the boo hag.

"It worked," Genna said. "They're as safe as I can make them."

"Yes they are," Miss Bootsie dusted sand off of her jaw. "You saved your fire for when you need it. You waited. Then struck!" She chopped her hand into her palm. "I couldn't be prouder."

"It feels like a decade since Donnie enchanted my parents. I didn't actually sleep."

"He has glamoured them for twenty years, honey child."

"Twenty years?"

"Ever since you were born. You did well. You are strong, Iphigenia."

The awful magnitude of her words made Genna want to throw up. She did not feel strong. Her lips trembled. She swallowed hard. Keeping her eyes open was a herculean effort. "The next phase of the plan is to stay on the island for a few months but I want to go home. I've only been gone a day and it feels like too long. I want to sleep in my bed. I don't care how mad Pipsy is."

"Then we shall return to the forest." Miss Bootsie spread her cloak over them both. The shadows swallowed Genna but it was a gentle darkness, soft as homespun cotton.

Genna woke up on the pullout couch in Miss Bootsie's cottage. She tried to get up but found herself too weak to do more than turn her head.

The old television was on. The whine of a VHS tape player was an ambient noise. Miss Bootsie sat in her chair, eating a bowl of freshly made kettlecorn. The movie *Sister Act* played raucously loud. Whoopi Goldberg was in a nun's habit singing.

Katie's screech as she banged her knuckles on the door had woken Genna up. "I know she's in there, Miss Bootsie. You can't hide her from me. Let me in!"

Genna glared at the door. "You locked her out?"

"I can't hold her long." Miss Bootsie smoothed the cloak

more firmly over Genna's shoulder. "I can only take you this far, honey child. You have to get yourself to the castle." She lit a candle inside a mold of a black glass wolf with a match. She set the candle in her palm. "Concentrate. Find the path in the shadows that only you can travel."

Genna stared at the wolf. The flame. The darkness under the figurine along the contours of Miss Bootsie's hand. It was hard to concentrate but Miss Bootsie was right. She did know how to walk through shadows. The key was to get out of her own way.

Genna sank into the shadows between the cloak and the pullout couch. Then rose out of the mattress in her big bed in the highest room in the tallest turret of her castle. Her bed linens were welcoming soft reds, blues, purples, and greens. She had collected the patterned pillows and goose down comforters from overseas. The blackout curtains were partially open. A beam of moonlight had reached the bed.

The room felt musty. Dust motes floated in the moonlight. She wondered if her family safe. She exhaled. She got out of the bed and opened the window to let fresh air in.

Genna expanded her awareness through the castle. She felt every floor, wall, and ceiling. She traveled along the furniture and paintings and curtains. Through the food in the pantry and the saltwater in the Olympic-sized pool. She sniffed the plants in the solarium and greenhouse. She drifted across the rose maze, the floral, herb, and decorative vegetable gardens. She floated over the garage full of cars then out to the animal graveyard behind the garage, and the forest beyond. Her awareness brushed along the tall grass of the pastures as though through her outstretched hands.

She paused to greet Sekhmet by the stable as she swept over the pastures and the other buildings in her property.

Sekhmet's head was the remains of a statue taken by Genna's ancestors during the Napoleonic invasion of Egypt. They had brought the statue back to France in pieces. The rest of the body was lost in transit. The head was used as a mounting block, a boot-blacking station, and an auction block. The black boot polish had sunk into the lion's snarling face, preserving the sandstone. Everyone forgot it was from Egypt. They simply liked the lion's head.

The mounting block was a family heirloom. It was the perfect height. It was moved from stable to stable. Genna's mother brought it to Sweetwater. No one was going to take Sekhmet back to Egypt. She was part of the family.

Genna's awareness spread into the stables, the kennels, and animal pens. The horses, dogs, and cats woke as she petted behind their ears and the underside of their chins. Toto the Carin terrier barked and Grim the Bouvier Des Flanders woofed in greeting. Pirate the jersey rooster squawked. Black Beauty, the pregnant Friesian mare, who everyone called Bibi, nickered in greeting.

Grim was a grimhound. He was a Bouvier des Flandres mix. He looked like a black curly-haired Wookiee. Genna had found him in the forest, tangled in barbed wire. She rescued him from Katie. He bit anyone who wasn't her.

Toto looked exactly like the black Cairn terrier from the *Wizard of Oz*. Saving her had been more difficult because Toto was clamped to Katie's throat. Prying the little fuzzy ball of indignation off Katie had got fangs in her forearm. Katie hated Toto.

Pirate was an enormous black twelve-pound Jersey rooster. He was the sole survivor of an attempt to raise chickens near the McBrides. He lived in the greenhouse.

Genna moved on, tracing all of the buildings. The old mansions where her family used to live until she bought them. She had turned them into apartments for medical staff. Her outreach program to improve mental health and reduce stress by giving doctors, nurses, and janitorial staff horses to ride, dogs to walk, and cats to socialize was only at its beginning stages but so far seemed to be working.

She continued on, down the trail mouth and into the forest. The tree branches rustled as she floated on the wind to Miss Bootsie's cottage.

Schrodinger was hunting in the forest. Schrodinger was the same kitten Genna and Katie had fought over as children. He was now an enormous Maine Coon cat. He had black fur with brown and yellow stripes in the bottom layer, which gave him the image of a moving shadow in the forest. He was also a traumatized vampire cat. A byproduct of getting a full dose of Katie's venom and Genna's rage. Thirty-three pounds of fur and fear. He purred and rubbed against Genna through the shadows.

The cottage had odd bone-white brick and a clay roof that was yellow as old fingernails. The mortar was a dark brown. Knowing the cottage was made from bone, dead flesh, and blood was different than seeing and smelling it. Yet the building was as familiar as Katie's screeching tantrums.

The door was reinforced wood. The shutters closed. Miss Bootsie refused to let Katie in.

Leave her be, Genna thought.

Katie sensed Genna's presence and spun around, her fangs extended. "Iffy, you can't do this to me. You're my bride. Get out here right now or you'll be sorry!"

Genna retracted her awareness back into her property. She sighed and settled deeper into the bedding.

She was home.

The castle was the only place the McBrides could not enter. No Katie knocking on her window or laying in her bed. Crazy ex-girlfriend was only the tip of the iceberg. Vampires interpreted *no* as *try harder*, which meant Genna had to keep fighting. She needed new ways to build fortifications and fight.

She snuggled under the blankets and pillows. Sleep first. Then it was time for brunch at the country club.

Six

GENNA COMBED AND FLAT-IRONED HER WET HAIR INTO her usual Aaliyah look. Soft, swooping bangs low on her eyebrow and large black curls down her back that bounced with each stride.

Miss Bootsie loved to brush Genna's hair straight. She would flatiron it, pull it straight with a boar hairbrush. She put different ointments made of beeswax and honey and sunflower oils. Miss Bootsie's hair products were gritty and weird. The odd smell was penetrating. Genna disliked how her hair lay like a dead pelt after being hot-combed. Her mother hated the smell of Miss Bootsie's hair products.

"She means well," her mother would say, then Genna would be subjected to another round of hair care.

As a compromise, Genna shampooed off as soon as she got back to the castle. When she kept it curly, Miss Bootsie frowned and picked up the boar hairbrush.

When she tried to cut it short, the hairdresser called her "dyke" in front of everyone in the salon. Katie turned that rumor into cannon fodder. Genna was yanked out of a closet she did not know she was in. She was Katie's sacrifice. That way, when Katie came out as a lesbian, it wasn't even news.

When Genna's hair was straight and long, no one bothered her.

She darkened her eyes to full black. She painted her lips a heavy purple. Her silver Balmain pantsuit rippled sensuously along her curves. She knotted a black Salvatore Ferragamo scarf with red and purple poppies around her throat just in case Katie tried to bite her. She chose a pair of vintage chandelier gemstone earrings. The teardrops of peridot, pink sapphires, purple amethyst, rubies and tourmalines sparkled inside the silver chains.

She clogged her fingers with rings.

One ring was the spiral cross section of a seashell from Aruba. Another was a silver-pronged ring from Norway, a modernist take on a pair of moose antlers. A two-hundred-year-old silver-and-turquoise ring from her family's silver mine. And four gold-cast rings from Ghana. They looked like starburst or insect cocoons. Conical prongs jutted from different directions. She bought four because they represented great wealth and were in the style of sixteenth-century Akan royal regalia. They also looked like a set of spiny gold knuckledusters when worn together with the other rings.

She chose a silver Cartier watch. She stacked bejeweled bracelets and necklaces, by David Yurman, Mikimoto, Foundrae, and Bulgari to balance her hands and her pantsuit. The point about layering gemstones and precious metals was to have fun.

She smiled at herself as she added another layer of mascara to her fake eyelashes. Could her Glamazons do it better? Yes, but they were compromised. When she was home, she let her curls bounce around her head in a wild mane. Today, she needed to be fully armored and glammed out. No smudges. Her foundation was flawless.

She walked down the spiral staircase in a worn pair of red Air Jordan 1 High 'Chicago' sneakers. She carried her Dior boots in one hand and a black Birkin purse in the other. The castle was too damn big for heels.

She crossed the covered stone bridge that connected the castle to the garage. The bridge between the castle and garage had many uses. It had the same architectural stone and latticed cement as the garage and the castle. Expansive double-paned windows gave her a scenic glass view of the forest and garden. It was convenient way to keep the grass clear, and reach the cars in the winter without dealing with snow.

The garage was a warehouse filled with cars, vintage and new. It was enormous and well appointed but ultimately a dumping ground for barely driven cars. Her family were not car people. It was one of those things that everyone collected. The castle housed leftovers from the car phases that Genna went through after she turned sixteen. There were matching pairs of cars that her dad bought for himself and his wife. There were specialty cars that were won in a business deal and kept in the garage like a deer head mounted on a wall.

Genna went to the custom made eight-speed purple 1969 Mustang Boss 302 waiting in the front row. It was her favorite car and a birthday gift to herself. Her Mustang was unique.

She had watched a show about an all-women's car shop. They started because their female friends complained about how difficult it was to be treated well at a car shop. Their hardships of getting a business off the ground, be taken seriously as lady mechanics, and their passion for cars inspired Genna. She researched muscle cars. She picked a Mustang, because she liked horses, but bought a few others to see what she thought. She commissioned the company to work on all of her cars. The Mustang was the only one she kept for herself.

The Mustang's airbag system required a full reconstruction. The purists were offended by its modifications but she liked it. Every inch of the Mustang was painted in some overwrought detailing, snakeskin here, feathers there, ribbons along the grill and taillights. The black leather interior had violet piping. There was purple leopard print on the ceiling with roses and skulls and scorpions. She had told the women to do anything they wanted on the detailing, no matter how outlandish. She wanted the girliest muscle car. They surprised her by making it beautiful. It matched her personality from the rims of the white wheels to the custom-made silver hood ornament of a horse running against the wind.

The Mustang was a ridiculous ugly-beautiful car full of color in a world bleached a hateful bone white. It was loud when every electric car was as hushed as silk spread across bare skin.

The silly purple Mustang was also an armored car. There were others, of course. The standard big, black, and intimidating Escalades and Range Rovers. The Mustang had everything, too. As well as reinforced armored lockboxes for storage and an air tank if she ever needed to hide inside the trunk.

She felt safest in the Mustang. She drove it through Sweetwater because sometimes it paid to advertise her presence. There was less chance of getting pulled over too. Outside of town, she had plenty of more-conventional cars but the Mustang was the most driven car in the massive garage.

She drove down the long, scenic driveway. It was lined with towering oaks. Their green boughs created a lush, arched corridor. Older trees native to Pennsylvania, oak, maple, and elm crowded the tree-line. The manicured front lawn was dotted with dandelions. The wind whipped several seedpods as she passed, the sunlight caught them for a moment. The flowers in the flower gardens and the sculptured topiary were in bloom. The maze entrance was twin walls of pink peonies, blue hydrangeas, magenta rhododendrons, juniper, and italian cypress trees trimmed into spirals.

The castle sat upon the top of a mountain. The architect had been inspired by the Bahá'í Temple in Chicago. He used uninteresting building materials to make a beautiful place. The exterior was white stone and cleverly poured cement in geometric patterns that looked like lace. There was enough quartz in the cement that the castle appeared to be painted in glitter. Anything that wore out was easily replaced. The castle had four turrets and forty bedrooms.

Genna had renovated the interior but the outside always remained the same. It was too beautifully made to change. She loved craftsmanship.

Even though Genna could and had traveled around the world, the castle felt the realest. She had worried that Katie would hire someone to throw eggs at the facade or rob the place. Sure enough, there were reports of break-ins. Only, they found nothing but smooth stone. The precious artwork was locked down in the underground vault. The rooms were sealed behind cement. The library was fireproof.

The paramilitary security team she had hired to live and quietly patrol the interior, captured and dealt with intruders. The smokehouse and refrigerators was stocked with bodies. Identifiable features, hands, feet, and heads went in the incinerator at the funeral home and animal shelter. The teeth and bones were ground into bone-meal and scattered in the rose maze. The rest were fed to the four hog and livestock farms she owned in West Virginia.

The security building was a small fortress in its own right. Genna found it more secure and safer for the staff if they lived in expensively appointed barracks instead of commuting. There was less chance of being eaten by the forest.

She was aware that inside of the gates the castle, the nine mansions, the smaller secondary buildings, and the farms operated like an autonomous fiefdom in all but name. Genna had spent enough time saving people from the forest and the McBrides that she accepted the role as its queen. There was always a bribed mercenary trying to infiltrate her staff to hurt her, steal stuff, and ruin things that could not be replaced. She tried to be a benevolent and hands-off ruler. Everyone had top tier health insurance, child care, vacation, four day work weeks, and high speed internet. Most of the employees and residents were women. The castle ground was primarily a safe space.

Candidly, Genna wished the staff's acceptance was not so damning. There was always a polite impenetrable wall between herself and her employees. They believed that every rich person who lived in the Heights was crazy and weird. Anyone who tried to be normal was the real danger. Genna letting her freak flag fly indicated that she was just an eccentric rich girl who was out of touch with reality but had a good heart.

A security guard opened the wrought-iron gates. The Mustang purred through the covered entrance. Genna shivered as she drove through the magical security system.

The invisible barrier was powerful and direct. She had created it when she banished Katie and all of the McBride vampires from her seventh birthday party. It covered her land like a soap bubble. The forest fed it, growing conifer trees along the brick wall. Genna had built the guard post wall just inside the perimeter. Revenants were electrocuted when they tried to test the boundaries. Yet another reason her staff was paid to stay on site.

On the opposite side of the road stretched the rolling mountains of Sweetwater Forest. She drove into the green shadows, one blind curve after the next, until she reached Backbone Road.

There was only a short stone wall to demarcate the edge of the narrow steep-sloped road carved into the mountain's face. A solid wall of mossy slate to her right. A sheer drop-off to her left. Old trees reached up from far below. The emerald-green gloom was darker than usual as the rain clouds thickened.

She took the scenic route through the forest. Over the stone bridges, the water running high along the mossy arches. Her feet danced on the pedals, shifting gears, letting the delight of driving ease her mind. She never drove the Mustang enough.

Backbone Road led through the Heights and down into Sweetwater proper. She passed one picturesque red brick colonial mansion with beautifully landscaped lawns after the next. The average house was at least two hundred years old. Some had gothic architecture and others were hypermodern boxes bursting with ultra-modern technology. It was easier to clean blood off of stone and glass than wood.

The country club's golf course, tennis courts, pools, and

gardens dripped from the morning rain. Die-hard athletes in damp sportswear tried not to skid on the slick tennis courts and turf out their golf balls in the clotted sand traps.

A few glanced her way at the Mustang's gas-guzzling growl. She did not need to see their noses' wrinkled in disapproval to feel it. Royal purple was a clown color for a vintage car. The envious annoyance from the townspeople when she stopped at the country club for breakfast was familiar. Some were personally offended by the blue snakeskin and other ridiculous designs along the body and nose. Others loathed that she drove the Mustang and not them. A few assholes dismissed the Mustang as a pony car. She needed something heavy like a Dodge Challenger or an Impala to be really into muscle cars. If she were someone else, they would have flocked to her garage. Instead, they turned and hunched away.

Sunday brunch at the country club was its usual level of standardized opulence. Every town had its diner. In Sweetwater, that was the country club. The attendants opened the high double doors for her so there was no interruption in her relaxed stride.

She sat at a table by the window, looking out at the hydrangea gardens. The omelet and cranberry mimosa were delightful but lacked flavor. No one liked spice around here.

She enjoyed the live harpist playing Vivaldi on a raised stage among potted tropical plants.

Katie was across the room, holding court in her favorite corner. Her champagne pink hair matched her Oscar de la Renta dress. The rest of her minions wore Easter-egg pastel Chanel, tweed, and pearls like the basic bitches they were. Their immaculate makeup hid the bovine vapidity of their expressions. She had drained so much of their vitality that their foundation no longer matched their sallow skin. The only difference between a vampire and rich bitch were the retractable teeth in Katie's vagina. Several of her girls wore lambskin kid gloves to hide missing fingers. Katie ate her entourage when she felt peckish. Yet there were always more volunteers excited to expose their throats. Genna had given up on trying to save them. They died believing that Katie would Turn them into a vampire if they were good.

"Why, Iphigenia Bellwether, how delightful to see you back in town. We thought you had run off." Mimi McBride stalked away from the bar. She wore a daffodil Prada dress that was a little too tight and a little too slinky for Sunday brunch.

Mimi's smile was always slightly too long and slightly too wide. Rumors of a bad facelift replaced the truth. The older a vampire was, the more snakelike her features as the seams of her mouth slipped farther into her cheeks. Pipsy had false scales that looked like cheekbones and operated like door flaps when her mouth distended. The scales retracted into a ridge to protect her eyes as her eight fangs extended. Katie was still too young. She only had a single set of fangs. Mimi was the daughter-in-law. She was Turned instead of born. Her fangs were thin and brittle. She tried harder but she lacked the same ethereal beauty of Katie, currently glaring at Genna.

Katie left her entourage to join her mother. Genna's posture tensed slightly but stayed seated. Mimi and Katie stood close but not too close. The three gracefully squared off.

Those eating at the other tables in the banquet room watched the McBrides as mice watched rattlesnakes. The harpist plucked nervously at her strings while hiding behind the harp's filigreed body.

It was High Noon in the country club.

Genna ignored the vampires and poured herself a refill of coffee from a silver tureen. Katie blushed, seeing the insult in the elegant way Genna held her bone china tea cup and the dangerous glint of her rings when they twinkled in the chandelier light.

"You left me at the altar, Iffy," Katie said. "You broke the glamours."

"Donnie is a disgusting pig," Genna said.

"He's dead now. Car accident."

"I'm still not marrying you. I told you and you never listen."

Katie stepped closer, angling her head so her hair fell into a pink curtain. Her perfume of ambergris, peonies, and daffodils was cloying and comforting. Her voice slid like silk along Genna's skin. "I love you."

"You bad dog," Mimi said at the same time, shouldering Katie aside. Her voice was like a donkey's bray. It shattered Katie's siren call. The perfume scent vanished.

Genna sipped her coffee with a small smile.

"You're so boring, Mother," Katie said, flicking her hair over her shoulder as if the enchantment had never happened. "A wolf is a wolf. Never a dog. That's why I love her."

Mimi turned to hiss, furious to be upstaged by her daughter, but Katie had already flounced back to her table. Mimi glared at Genna but the moment had passed. Mimi stalked away, smoothing the wrinkles on her hips as if the banquet room was a catwalk. Genna watched them as she drank her coffee. The humans around them whispered of scandal. A few photos were taken with phones. The harpist played with rushed relief.

Genna finished her meal. She ignored entries of false friendship to spread gossip from neighboring tables. She slid back into her Celine leather trench coat. She tipped the Black valet generously and got back into the Mustang, whose friendly purr cheered her up.

She chewed on her worries like a piece of gristle stuck in her molars as she drove up Backbone Road. Being seen was the point of coming to the country club. Both sides raising their swords. Declaring war. She was not sorry. She was not running away, either. If the McBrides had a problem, they could get over it. There would be consequences, predicted and unknown.

What happened after a bride said no to a vampire?

Her phone buzzed in the cupholder. She ignored it. One of the perks of driving a vintage car was its lack of technology.

The foliage on a blind curve hid a group of women on horseback. The equestrians glared in disapproval of the Mustang's loud engine messing with the bucolic splendor. Their thoroughbreds and quarter horses flicked their ears and swished their tails. Genna owned the forest they were in. This area was so commonly trespassed that she found it was easier to ignore than fine.

After ten more minutes, she reached the tall stone gates with the lions' heads built into the pillars. The gate opened with barely a creak. The perimeter spell burnt up several minor curses clinging to her psyche and clothing like burrs. She sighed in relief as she drove the Mustang up the driveway.

The castle was her home and she missed it.

INSTEAD OF PARKING IN THE GARAGE, GENNA trundled down the grass-lined lane between the two wings of her pastures. Her horses grazed and swished their tails against ambient flies. There was a marked difference between the leased horses and her own herd.

Percherons, Clydesdales, Shires, Friesians, Belgians, Vanners, and more. Her mother loved the big herbivores. Genna favored drafthorses too.

The prudish equestrians of Sweetwater liked the sleek, long-legged, and performance-oriented breeds. Working horses were unrefined and too monstrous for the show ring with their big muscles. Making them jump was intimidating, not graceful movement. Horses were supposed to be light as the wind. Not able to tow buildings. They never wanted their horses socializing in the pasture, either. What if one of those monsters ate an Appaloosa or a big soup-plate hoof stove in the ribcage of a fine-boned Arabian?

Never mind that feisty Arabian horses picked fights like chihuahuas. The tough little horses were capable of jumping over a Clydesdale's back and kicking it in the face along the way.

Still, most people bought their horses like they bought yachts and mansions: to display wealth. They never rode them or trained them. It was safer all around to keep personal herds separated from the professional. Less complaints. There were lots of stables, more glamorous and established, but the horses at the Bellwether Stables were healthier.

Genna's mother had a gift for animals. She could heal anything. She was a neurosurgeon until her success in medical business took her off the surgery floor. She was a hobbyist veterinarian with a big heart and even bigger budget. She had a lot of stables across the world. Her children were deeply entrenched in the business of horse-trading by proxy.

Genna parked the Mustang under the awning. She walked up a short flight of steps to a porch and knocked on a door. She looked inside of Miss Bootsie's apartment. It was empty.

The family had renovated the stables with a lavish attached apartment that was the size and layout of the cottage. It was built for Miss Bootsie's comfort as a part of castle's renovation. There were several apartments for the stable hands, but this one was exclusively hers.

Miss Bootsie was probably in her cottage in the woods.

Genna took her boots off and put them in the Mustang. She put her jewelry in a black fabric bag in the glove compartment. She walked barefoot down the trail mouth into the forest.

The green shadows were hot. The whine of mosquitos and squish of mud under her feet became pleasant.

Her skin folded from human to wolf. Her black fur swallowed the sunlight. The transformation felt like a sneeze. She was agitated. Usually, a Clothed Turn was smooth. Her Balmain suit frayed. Silver fabric scattered like confetti.

Genna turned back into a human. Crouching naked, she clicked her tongue against the roof of her mouth, aggravated by the devastation. Sometimes the clothes got destroyed, no matter how many times she practiced a Clothed Turn.

She reached into a small stone chest that was kept in the bushes under a mulberry tree for exactly such occasions. She unlocked the combination lock and opened the plastic wrapped basket. Inside was a tiny black dress. Nothing special. Only a ready-made Prada. Not even good fabric. Mostly Lycra. She put that on and searched the basket. No shoes. Not even a pair of sandals.

Damn. She had forgotten to replace the footwear.

She gathered as much of her destroyed couture as she could find into the basket. She was glad she had taken her jewelry off. Except the gold-and-diamond family ring. It never had a problem transitioning because it had its own magic.

Genna did not try to Turn again. As punishment, she walked in human shape, the basket balanced on the top of her head. The way she had practiced her posture as a child. Straight back. Relaxed shoulders. Her mother claimed that textbooks were better because they slid out of alignment when jostled by an uncouth step.

Robins, mourning doves, and other birds flitted overhead. Blue jays and crows argued. Squirrels and animals got on with their own business. Genna's skin itched from mosquitos. Miss Bootsie never got bitten. Genna might have been born in Miss Bootsie's cottage during a thunderstorm, but these were not her woods.

The trees got older the deeper she walked. The trunks were tall like the support beams of a cathedral. Sunbeams streamed through the green shadows like eyelashes of a giant demigod. Spiral of flies danced inside each beam over ferns. Goldenrod and other plants smeared pollen on her dress. The mud and rock along the creek squished between her toes. She carefully navigated the algae and mossy rocks and climbed up the slope on the other side. The water level was low. The forest was waiting for more rain.

All of this would be easier to traverse with four legs, but Miss Bootsie was strict about littering. She could sew the clothes back together and remind Genna how to keep the threads intact. There would be another lecture about leaving traces behind. Annoying but friendly.

Miss Bootsie's cottage was in a glen. The tall grass was cut down as though recently mowed. The windows were dark. Genna set the basket down on the porch.

Well, if no one was home, she could go for a run. She took off the black dress to be safe. She turned into a coywolf then loped through the tall bushes.

The forest knew she wasn't a coywolf. The birds got quiet or flapped above the canopy. The animals scurried in their burrows. Silence filled the canopy. She tried to blend in. That was one lesson that was difficult to learn. Still, it was too sunny and too nice. She loved running through the forest.

Seven

Miss Bootsie York lived in the cottage in the woods. She wasn't cuddly or particularly nice or gentle. She was right and old and had views so archaic that it was stifling. Genna called her *grandmother*, seeing no difference between the two regal ladies she was related to and the elderly woman who lived in the woods by her stables.

Miss Bootsie was a boo hag, a skin witch. Her opera cloak was made of different kinds of living furs. She could change into all kinds of animals but preferred bears.

Her people had lived in the forest between Genna's castle and the McBrides' mansion since before Sweetwater was a summer home for plantation owners and robber barons. Her father was York, the slave explorer owned by William Clark. He was called 'black as a bear' and over two hundred pounds. This meant Miss Bootsie was roughly two hundred years old.

She protected the town of Sweetwater from the McBrides. The townspeople called her a witch. They blamed her for the things that the McBrides did. Yet she endured and stayed. Those same haters knocked on her door when they had lost hope. Someone had to stop the monsters.

She had taken care of Katie and Genna since their birth. Genna's siblings never found their way to the cottage. Kyle, Katie's brother, was not dead, only too grotesque to be around polite society. He lived in the McBride mansion's pool room.

Miss Bootsie taught Katie and Genna how to change their skin when they were children. Genna leaned how to Turn into a coywolf and Katie into a snake.

"Why is no one in my family like me?" Genna said. "Why am I the only one who can see what Katie is?"

"You are something they are not, honey child. That doesn't mean you don't love them or they don't love you," Miss Bootsie said, steamrolling the cranky whine. "Your great-grandmother put her power into this gold ring. To never forget. You haven't. Not for generations. We are all connected. Magic manifests in ways that suited each personality and circumstances. We are all Night Skins."

"I'm a Night Skin too?" Katie said.

"No, you're a McBride vampire," Miss Bootsie said sharply. "A vampire is an unnatural thing."

"Unnatural?"

"I change into a wolf when I get mad enough," Genna said. "What about your cloak? We're more like Katie than we are like other people. We're not exactly human."

Miss Bootsie gave Genna a look that warned she was standing on her last nerve. "A snake ain't nothing but a snake."

"I don't understand," Genna said. "How come no one else can do what we can?"

"Much that was has been lost," Miss Bootsie said loftily. "I have never met anything like you, but that is not uncommon. Many Night Skins shed their skins to pass as human. They squashed and swallowed their magic. They married humans and had magic-less babies. That happens enough times and the magic drains away. Or it's put into objects, like your family ring." Her hand drifted over to Genna's right hand to hover over the gold ring on her fourth finger but never touched it. "Your family's legacy is in the gold you wear. It is not gone. It lives in the blood, the skin, and the stories we tell of those before. All of the stories and peoples are not lost. They hide."

"Then I can learn to be like you," Genna said.

"I'm a boo hag, honey child," Miss Bootsie said. "You are something else."

"I can turn into a wolf," Genna said irritably. "How is that different from a boo hag? You're still quilting skins together, aren't you?"

"When I wear skins, I am that animal. I hold their memories in my heart. I sing with them. I sew my life with theirs. That is not the same. I taught you how to be a wolf to contain your anger. As a child, I was afraid that you would burn yourself out. As a wolf, your anger can be teeth and claws and fur. You can attack and kill. You can hide and be still. You learned control because you understand what danger is but you are not a wolf. Do you understand?"

"Yes, I do," Genna said glumly.

"She's still your mammy," Katie said.

Genna kicked Katie's fangs in.

"Stop fighting you two," Miss Bootsie said, prying them apart.

"Don't you call her that!" Genna snarled, fighting the transformation.

"She's mine, too," Katie said, mouth bleeding as her fangs regrew. "Pipsy spanked me when I called her my grandmother."

"You girls need to do something about that anger," Miss Bootsie said.

"Why? It's fun." Katie hissed at Genna who growled back.

Miss Bootsie had two glass hollow figures. One of a snake coiled up. One of a howling wolf. She poured the wax into them. Lit the candle wicks. Let them burn. She tapped the glass with her nail. "You see this. What happens if I burn a candle at both ends? Do you think it lasts longer?"

"No?" Genna said.

"What happens if I drop it in the fireplace?"

"It burns up?" Katie said.

"What happens if the fire takes your little body? Do you think you'll last long?" She tossed the candle in the fireplace. They watched the wax melt over the coals and logs. "That's your body when you lose control. You melt like that Barbie you put in a microwave."

The girls squealed, grossed out. They both remembered what happened to Barbie and the microwave.

"Not my skin," Katie said, "I get scales. I'm the brightest fire!"

"You think someone won't come along and put your fire out if you keep burning? You think Donnie, Mimi, and Pipsy are going to save you if someone comes with a bucket of water? I can tell you what your daddy did to my Sable's original skin. That's why you learn to keep your fire in your skin. Or someone will snuff you out."

Genna was horrified. Katie looked down at the melting wax. "Is Sable dead?"

"No, I made Sable into the wind to fly far away with my sunshine girl. She will never return."

Genna and Katie glanced at each other. They were often compared to Naomi, the sunshine girl.

"If she's air then she doesn't have a candle," Genna said. "Maybe she's like a kite on a string?"

"Yeah, how hasn't she burned out?" Katie said.

Miss Bootsie glared down at them. She became terrifying, as big as a great mountain about to stomp on them with boulders and bury them under a landslide. Both girls did not back down. They stood, waiting for answers.

Katie was used to being terrified. To her, it was as normal as breathing. And Genna was old enough to understand how rich and powerful her family actually was. Her knee bowed to no-one but God. Miss Bootsie couldn't scare her.

"I still think Naomi isn't real. Or she burnt up. Or she's nothing at all," Genna said. "How do you know Naomi is better when you've never met her? Naomi isn't Cinderella. I am way too beautiful to be the ugly stepsister."

"Yeah, I'm Cinderella," Katie said.

Miss Bootsie yanked their skins off and tanned their hides with a cane. The girls wailed and fought and cried. Then Miss Bootsie threw them back into their skins and sent them home, sniffling and rubbing their reddened skin.

"My sunshine is better behaved than you two!" She slammed the cottage door shut.

The girls walked through the forest.

Genna scuffed the moss on a rock, growling softly to herself. It was weird to feel inadequate to this glowing perfect girl who danced in sunshine, had long hair, no acne, and was the prettiest. "She always does that."

"We're too damn old for spankings," Katie hissed.

"You figure out a way to keep her from doing that, then let me know."

"There is a way. We kill her."

"That's not a solution, Katie. That only means someone else who's a boo hag can do the same thing to us. There's very limited information on skin witches. The best I can find is putting black pepper, cayenne, and salt in the skin. But since it's *our* skin she's taking, it's not a solution."

"Well, if you can't find it, then no one can."

"We need to grow a thicker skin so strong that she can't make it into a quilt."

"Yeah, she can't take Pipsy's skin."

Genna snapped her fingers. "I got it. We need a look. Like armor. Pipsy looks like Audrey Hepburn all the time. It's like a shell. Mimi looks like someone stretched out Sarah Michelle Geller."

"Oooh, I've got to call her that sometime."

"We need a look. Something that's an anchor. They have to look like us."

"Someone famous."

"Like Aaliyah," Genna said, thinking about her current crush. The R&B singer Aaliyah was beautiful, tragic, and taken too soon. She was edgy and feminine in *The Queen of the Damned.* She had the same skin tone and black hair as Genna. Her makeup and hairstyle were achievable though at thirteen, Genna already had bigger boobs and, well, everything.

"I'll be Charlotte La Bouff," Katie said.

"The blonde from *The Princess and the Frog?*"

"Charlotte and Tiana should've gotten together. She should've killed that frog."

Katie's gross brother Kyle transformed into a poisonous toad instead of a snake. Genna did not like amphibians because of Kyle.

The girls went home. Their glam and wardrobe teams were instructed to reproduce the Aaliyah and Charlotte La Bouff looks. They practiced at school and at home. Their looks hardened into armor. Then sank into their skin.

Genna mastered Aaliyah's look until she could do it in her sleep. Genna's mother believed in the philosophy of Black supermodels like Leomie Anderson. *Always do your own hair and makeup.*

Genna kept researching what a boo hag was. She learned about skin witches by paying attention. There were scraps of information hidden in the margins of books like *Uncle Remus, His Songs and His Sayings: The Folk-Lore of the Old Plantation* by Joel Chandler Harris.

The Middle Passage, slavery, and the Trail of Tears had stories about skin witches. The various ways people were stripped of their culture and dignity had caused a transmutation. The magic of Black people was hidden in the blood and the skin. Some remembered the old ways. The magic of air, the earth, the fire, the water, and the shadows were in their blood, in the curl of their hair, and in the soles of their feet. They were able to hear the songs, dance in ring shouts, and call to the ancestors.

But many people forgot themselves in order to survive. They shed their history in exchange for better camouflage or because remembering was too heavy. The terrible burden of race was a daily struggle to survive. Different philosophies on what was worth remembering changed over time. The price of looking back was knowledge. The wish to forget was never truly realized. Their skin kept the stories. Their blood flowed with memory. Their hair stayed curly. Their noses stayed broad and their lips were as full as their bodies.

Boo hags could read the history in living flesh and blood. Other witches and magical people could do plenty with dead flesh. However, to sew the living skin into quilts without killing the host was a special skill of boo hags. They rode their victims like horses. They birthed nightmares. They preyed upon the slaves because all of that skin, filled with suppressed love, rage, and pain, was a delicious magic. The boo hags had access to millions packed together. All they had to do was reach out. It was too much of a temptation to resist.

Boo hags stalked the plantations. They fed with abundance, glutting themselves, and learned secrets from the continents of Africa, the Americas, Europe, Asia, and everywhere there were humans. The boo hags had sewn skins since there were people in caves. They told stories. They remembered when others chose to forget.

The older a boo hag was, the harder she was to find. She, and she was usually female, because in an emergency, a boo hag put her power into the baby in her womb. Died so the child could live. The memory in the skin. A mother's love baked in. Her faith that with time, the child would learn to listen.

It was difficult to read about such abject racism and exploitation but Genna persisted, compiling her field notes in a private journal. She discussed her findings with Katie, determined to teach the vampire social grace that defied Pipsy and Mimi's personal beliefs. Miss Bootsie did not help matters. Her favorite Disney movie was *The Song Of the South* which was based upon those Uncle Remus books. The boo hag remembered when it first aired. She loved Br'er Rabbit and the stories.

"Do you think she's the skin witch in the Uncle Remus story?" Katie asked, tapping on a copy of the book she had stolen from the library.

"Or it's someone she knew," Genna said.

"I could be a boo hag. I've got an ancestral connection to Sweetwater forest."

"You'd have to shed your skin and stop being a McBride. That means you wouldn't be the heir to the throne. No more power. Just skin magic."

Katie grimaced. "Yeah, no thanks."

The next time Miss Bootsie got mad, both girls glared at her, braced for the attack. Their feet apart. Their hands clenched. No fear. Only fight.

Miss Bootsie raised her eyebrows. Not an admission of defeat but a grudging acknowledgement. "You've been practicing."

Perhaps as a reward for growing a thick skin, Miss Bootsie told them a story how she met Pipsy Montgomery.

Miss Bootsie was a girl-witch just growing into her birth skin. She had been washing herself off in the river. Her menstrual blood had attracted the vampire's attention. She had been too young to be afraid when Pipsy Montgomery slithered up the Ohio River bank as a giant cottonmouth snake.

Miss Bootsie remembered Pipsy's big sharp smile as the snake arched up. "The water here tastes sweet. Your blood does too."

Then the vampire shook herself off. Her scales became a giant dress with layers upon layers of gingham petticoats. She became a rich White lady in a muddy antebellum dress and a burnt wide brim straw hat. When her dress touched the ground, she unleashed thousands of vampires she had carried from her plantation in the Devil's Punchbowl. She had swum up the Mississippi River from Natchez, Mississippi, escaping Sherman's march across the South during the Civil War.

Miss Bootsie didn't talk about the massacre to her people or how she survived. There was no record of how Sweetwater really came to be. Her anger and pain was in the silent way she folded socks, like she was peeling the skin off of skulls. Even Katie kept her mouth shut when Miss Bootsie got quiet.

That was Miss Bootsie's way. She was always there. She was in the woods. She always had answers.

Genna knew that she was not a boo hag.

Eight

GENNA WOKE UP IN HER BED AND STARTED RUNNING. She was scared like she had never been scared before. Angry like she had never been angry. The night air was too heavy, too still, and too old. It pressed down against her eyes like a blindfold. It stoppered her ears like wax. It tried to squeeze her lungs and scratch down her throat.

Something was wrong in the woods. Something about Miss Bootsie. A cry for help from someone who'd lost their voice screaming.

Genna did not change out of her loose jersey t-shirt and pajama pants. Her bare feet slapped carpet then stone as she ran through the castle, out of the greenhouse door, and into the night.

The horses were quiet but shaking, locked in place. The dogs whined, high-pitched. The other mansions around the property had the lights off. Maybe they couldn't hear the drumbeats. Maybe they couldn't smell the smoke. Or see the fire in the woods.

There were worse things than Katie McBride. Worse than her mother Mimi or her father Donnie. Pipsy Montgomery had made her move.

Genna ran, as though through a heavy fog. She trusted her feet instead of her eyes. She ran for the silent scream. She found Bibi in the shadows. She sprang upward, grabbed a mane that became a horse that became a gallop.

The darkness's hold ripped. All of the animals were suddenly able to move, bark, howl, whinny, and crow. Bibi charged into the midnight forest toward orange firelight. The trees bent like the rib cage of a snake.

Genna knew the way. Genna did not stop. Genna did not slow down when she reached the clearing. She did not look at the fire, or the candles with human skulls set in a circle on white stones.

Miss Bootsie was on her knees. Her shoulders sloped. Blisters formed on her burnt skin when Pipsy held the fur cloak over the flames of a wood burning fire pit. The witch's hair frizzled tight against her raw scalp. Her clothes burned off her sagging body. The vulnerability of aged breasts hanging down to the dirt. The strain of her exposed spine as Pipsy's fury pressed her face to the ground.

"Do you think you've won, Boostie?" Pipsy hissed. "After all this time, you still defy me!"

Pipsy's severe green dress covered her from neck to ankle. Too tight for knees. Just fine for a thick black snake tail coiled under her as she arched over the boo hag.

Katie was on one side of the ring, holding a black bullwhip like it was going to bite her.

"Punish her, Katie!" Mimi commanded, outside of the ring. She held a vodka bottle and a lighter by the cottage door. "She humiliated us!"

"Do I have to?" Katie whined, her eyes averted from Miss Bootsie. She was looking right at Genna as Bibi erupted from the forest in a blur of speed.

Genna snatched the cloak out of Pipsy's hands then leaned to the left. Pipsy reared back.

Bibi spun, dodging the snake's bite. The horse was the best at barrel racing despite her size. She loved the trick turns. Dirt and grass clots kicked up by her hooves. Genna's arm stretched out, reaching over the skulls. Bibi's long legs stretched, moving faster as Genna hauled her tighter.

Miss Bootsie sat up. Her hands lifted as if in prayer or perhaps in denial. It didn't matter. Genna's arm hooked hers, yanked her sideways, and pulled her astride. Bibi completed the circuit and charged back the way she came.

Katie leapt on behind Genna. The whip in her hand. Arms around her waist. She hugged Genna tight. "Let's get out of here!"

Genna focused on forward. On the branches that swung low, clawing. The roots tripping. The ground opened like mouths. Genna focused on only the part of the ground Bibi touched. Not what chased. Not what shrieked. Not the heat of flames.

The mulberry trees. The boundary between her part of the forest, but it could be any tree, any illusion; nothing mattered. Miss Bootsie's thin breath. Her boneless slump against Genna's chest. "Protect the cloak for my sunshine girl."

"Don't you dare. Don't you dare. Don't you dare." Genna yanked the cloak tight.

Katie's thin, strong hands and tail held on to them both breathlessly tight. "She's not going to make it, Iffy."

Genna grabbed Katie's tail and wrenched it free. "Fuck off."

"Iffy!" Katie's pained screech as she lost her seat.

Genna saw the low branch, as thick as a steel girder, and ducked. The branch brushed her back and hit Katie in the stomach. Katie lost her grip on Genna and Miss Bootsie. She fell sideways. Mimi missed, grabbing Katie instead of Genna. Katie and Mimi hit the grass, their bodies elongating in snakes. They tangled in a fight, distracted by their personal animosity. Pipsy roared behind them but could not break up the fight.

Bibi galloped on.

The trees opening up. The bracken was a lighter shade of dark. The dead yellow grass in the ditch that lay between the forest and the pasture looked as deep as a canyon and as treacherous as a bog.

Bibi's muscles bunched, preparing, speeding up. Genna leaned forward, hugging Miss Bootsie and the cloak tight, and bracing herself. In one burst of power, Bibi leapt. She drifted over the canyon, over the bracken, over the roots, over the gopher hole waiting to break her leg, over the dead grass, the sucking mud, and over Pipsy's numerous illusions.

Bibi landed in pasture. The hard impact almost knocked Genna off her back.

Miss Bootsie popped like a water balloon. Blood soaked Genna's front. Bibi's back. The cloak. Blood from Miss Bootsie's ears, her eyes, her nose, her pores, her back. Genna coughed, accidentally swallowing the blood in her mouth. She squinted at the pasture while Bibi galloped up the long slope, legs pumping to get away from the forest and up to the castle.

Yet the farther the horse ran, the smaller Miss Bootsie became, shriveling in on herself. In her panic, Genna had forgotten that Miss Bootsie could not go up to the castle. She could go no farther from the forest than the stables.

Genna leaned hard to the left, squeezing tight. Bibi skewed sideways, turning to the stables. She jumped over the fence. Then it was a straight shot down the thoroughfare to the unlit stable. Bibi slowed down to a bumpy trot. The horses whinnying their greeting and upset from their stalls. The dogs barked in their kennels.

Miss Bootsie coughed up another gout of blood, wet and tarry. Genna tightened the cloak around Miss Bootsie as best she could while on horseback. The boo hag was no longer leaking and shriveling. Genna slowed at the mounting block. Bibi was well trained enough to stop by a thigh squeeze command.

Genna slid off her back. She landed with both feet on the mounting block. She swung Miss Bootsie into her arms, wrapped in the cloak.

Genna carried Miss Bootsie into the stable to her apartment.

Magic opened the door. Genna strode through the living room, into the bathroom. Miss Bootise was light, terribly light.

Genna set her down gently in the bathtub, cloak and all. She turned on the water. She grabbed aloe from the window garden but could not figure out what to do with it. Her mind was a whirl. Genna knelt next to the tub. Tears flowed freely. Her hands searched Miss Bootsie's face, her chest, the cloak.

"What do you need? Tell me what to do."

"Honey child." Miss Bootsie looked so small. The cloak was changing colors. The fur turned red.

"Tell me. I can fix this."

There was so much blood. Yet none of it drained into the bathtub, magnetically attracted to the cloak. Genna saw streamers worming along the ground. She looked back. A long line of blood streamed off of Bibi, who was halfway into the door, ears flicking. The blood on her coat hurried to the bathtub.

"I did something wrong, didn't I?" Genna said.

"You said no." Miss Bootsie sagged sideways.

It sounded like a joke. "Surely, someone has told the McBrides no."

"No, honey child. No one says no to their kind. Not for long. I couldn't be prouder."

Genna touched foreheads. "She hurt you. I thought you were safe."

"This isn't your fault. I burned my candle up getting Sable and Naomi free of Pipsy. I knew the next battle wasn't going my way, but I'm glad I saw it. You changed the game, honey child. No one's ever refused to be a McBride." A tight nod. "Mighty fine."

"You can't go. I-I won't let you."

"Take the cloak. Protect it. Give it to my sunshine." Miss Bootsie's thin hand grasped Genna's. "Don't be afraid of love, honey child. People are out there. People who'll accept you for you."

Genna gritted her teeth as she felt Miss Bootsie wandering

away from her skin. "Stop talking like you're not going to be here."

Miss Bootsie snapped back into her skin. A gruff smirk. "Don't worry. I'm not dying today. It's not my time. I've still got a little something-something. I wouldn't give Pipsy the satisfaction of being the death of me."

"You better not." Genna tried to smile instead of weep.

Bibi lowered her face down to lip Miss Bootsie's head. Sweat added a shine to her black coat. Miss Bootsie leaned against the horse's jaw. "That nightmare Bibi's carrying. You'll need to go get him yourself. Protect them."

"I will."

A soft brush of fur. Grim the black wolfhound. Toto the black Cairn Terrier. Pirate the rooster. Bibi the black horse. Schrodinger the cat leading a horde of black cats down the stable aisles. Meowing as they jumped into the bathtub.

"Protect my guardians," Miss Bootsie murmured, "They keep the forest and my magic."

"I will."

Genna had known they were special. Now she knew why.

Miss Bootsie pushed Genna's hands back. "Go get your parents now. I'll be ready by the time you come back. I'll still be here. I promise."

"No wandering," Genna said, moving carefully around the animals. She tried not to step on anything as the forest entered the stable.

Genna had to watch her feet. She stayed pressed against the wall. More cats. Ravens and crows and bats. Black skinks. Lynx. Bobcats. Coyotes. Foxes. Boar. Deer. Skunks. Possums. Raccoons. She made it to the back door of Miss Bootsie's house. Opened it and was nearly trampled as more animals poured in.

The stench of animals. The noise of restless movement, underfoot and overhead. Bats and owls flew under the lintel.

She let the dogs out of the kennels and the horses out of the stalls.

She edged carefully along the side of the stable. Then flattened herself as an enormous black grizzly lumbered past. Silver dusted his muzzle like powdered sugar.

Genna stared at him, incredulous. "York?"

The bear paused. Grunted. Then pushed himself inside the apartment door.

The stream of animals seemed too numerous to fit into the house, but there was no sign of stopping. It dwindled as Genna got farther from the stable. She walked up the leased side of the pastures. She needed to run but instead she kept a purposeful stride. There were cars but she had no keys. Nothing but black grass all the way up to the castle. She realized she had nearly walked to her parents' old mansion. She was used to them being there, even now. She hopefully checked the building for a lit window. Nothing. No one.

She so desperately wanted someone in her family to have the same instincts.

The castle was a bastion of normalcy. She had to trudge up to her bedroom turret because only her personal phone had the authorized group family emergency contact number. Sometimes, having a giant castle was a pain in the ass.

HER PARENTS DROPPED WHAT THEY WERE DOING. HER siblings did too. The stable was surrounded by cars by the time Genna woke up from an exhausted sleep. She was roused by her baby brother. He greeted her with a grim smile. "It's time to wake up, Sleeping Beauty."

Genna looked around her bedroom, blearily. "Oh, shit. I fell asleep! How is she?"

"Miss Bootsie's okay. She said you got her out of the woods and stabilized. The cameras saw it too. Though it was weird to see a stampede of cats like some kind of reverse Pied Piper."

"You feed enough strays, they follow you." Genna yawned,

rubbing her shoulder that clicked and popped. Her legs and seat were a collection of bruises from riding bareback.

"Schrodinger's gotten big and fat. That fuzzy monster's still scared of men. He saw me and the poor thing ran."

"He's afraid of everything. Katie's a shit pet owner. I thought rescuing would fix him, but some things can't be fixed."

Genna's baby brother prodded the leg of the footboard with his boot. "Hey, come on. Get dressed. Everyone's here and you smell like you rolled in a swamp."

Genna creakily stood up. "I'm glad you're all here."

He gruffly patted her shoulder. "You did good, sis. Real good. After all the crazy shit that went down at the engagement party, I didn't know why you came back. Now I'm glad you did. You were worried about her. She would've been alone. I feel like such an asshole."

Genna raised an eyebrow. "Are you mad at me?"

"I wish you'd told me the plan instead of throwing me into a car like a sack of potatoes. But whatever. Hurry up."

GENNA DISLIKED THE CAREFUL WAY MISS BOOTSIE walked. Back in the cottage and the forest, she strode around fine, but as long as she was on the property, she minced and always wore the cloak.

"It helps my balance," Miss Bootsie said. "My skin knows where it is when I wear it."

The stable apartment was renovated. A smaller bed with arm rails. A walker and cane accessible bathroom and kitchen. Genna suspected Miss Bootsie used them in private but never when anyone was around. That was fine. What was important was the guardrails could take her weight. The edges of the furniture were rounded. The carpet were padded and soft.

Miss Bootsie hated modern technology past VHS tapes and vinyl records. That was easy enough to accommodate too. The

VHS player's ambient whine was as much a part of Miss Bootsie as the smell of candles and fur.

The living room had a wall of shelves full of VHS tapes, books, and vinyl in easy access to several comfortable recliners. Her long black opera cloak was spread over her legs. It did not matter that it was July. She never sweated.

Genna's family left. Genna stayed close. Miss Boostie allowed Genna to drive her to the Sweetwater Cemetery.

The blue sky was decorated by patchy clouds. Dragonflies danced over the headstones. They walked along the pathways past headstones and obelisks. They stopped at the Tuskegee Airmen Memorial. They sat on the granite benches next to the memorial.

Genna set down the bouquet of flowers she had picked from her garden. She had tied them neatly into a bundle with a strip of muslin and twine. It had taken all morning to get the right flowers then make them into the bouquet while Miss Bootsie critiqued each blossom.

Miss Bootsie traced the names inscribed in the large black granite. She refused to say which one was her husband.

She had many men in her life. Many children. Except she only mentioned one, Sable.

"Sable was my last child. It feels like they were my only child." Miss Bootsie said. "You remember the ones that are Night Skins. The others fade, like flowers. Or fall like leaves. You watch enough of your children wither and they lose importance. Birth doesn't feel like hardly nothing at all."

Genna sifted on the wet granite bench. The thought of giving birth even once was revolting. The fact that Miss Bootsie had birthed and buried so many children that she lost count was horrifying. Genna kept her feelings to herself. "So Sable was a boo hag like you? What was that like?"

"Sable abandoned their original skin. They stopped answering to Rosabelle or even she." Miss Bootsie closed her eyes. "You have a word for what Sable is now. Transgendered. But back then I thought they were just being stubborn."

Genna grimaced. "Isn't it easier to be a transgendered boo hag because you keep changing bodies?"

Miss Bootsie shook her head. "Every boo hag goes through a phase of hopping from skin to skin. You want to try out being male, female, short, tall, round, thin, dark or light. You need to see what it's really like to live that way."

"You'd be okay if Sable passed as a White man?" Genna said, astonished.

Miss Bootsie gave her a look.

"Sorry," Genna said.

"A boo hag must settle into a body, whatever that body is." Miss Bootsie continued, "Hopping skins uses up our power. You can't defend yourself. Sable didn't listen. I thought it was a phase. I warned them that there would be trouble. They weren't being careful. I forgot that I was once young and foolish. It's hard to be tied to one skin when you can be anything or anyone."

Miss Bootsie pressed a hand over the engraved names. "Donnie McBride found my Sable's original skin. He chewed it up and sucked it dry. Then he filled it with pain and his seed. Sable was too weak to fight back. Male McBrides have stingers, you know."

"I'm sorry." Genna said.

"He even glamoured Sable into thinking that he loved them." Rage passed like a storm cloud across Miss Bootsie's expression. "I gave Sable everything in me to change their pain into sunshine. Then I put my beloved child and their unborn baby into the fire to cut their connection to Sweetwater. I burned their skins and made them into wind. They are safe from my enemies but I will never see them again. That's why all that's left is what you see. This old woman in the woods."

"You're still here," Genna said urgently. "We love you. I love you. You're family."

Her small sad smile was awful. "Thank you, honey child."

Genna stared at the green grass under her Doc Martins. Her pants were soaked from the stone bench.

Miss Bootsie had told her Sable's story before. But this time the repetition was urgent. As if this was the last time. Miss Bootsie was draining away like water slipping out of cupped hands. The harder Genna squeezed the more Miss Bootsie lost. Genna tried to stay perfectly still.

Nine

Nothing could scream like a horse in agony. The enormous painted Shire reared, his hooves trampled his own guts. The torn skin made worse as he kicked. Blood and viscera slopped around the cement and hay. The deafening boom of a rifle fired in a closed room. The heavy crash of the dead Shire.

"Get the Shire on the wagon," Genna's mother said, checking her rifle. "I want a full autopsy report by tonight. I want to know who did this."

"It was the vet, Dr. Bellwether," the farrier said. "I'm sorry. I saw him driving like a bat out of hell. I thought he had some emergency surgery."

"Find him!"

It shouldn't have been possible. No McBride was allowed on the property, but the horses were dying. The stable was full of awful screams and vomit. There was blood on the ceiling and crossbeams. Several drafthorses had gotten a leg stuck kicking their hooves through the stall walls as they thrashed on their backs like cockroaches. Each horse was capable of dragging cars, houses, and dead trees. Now they were dying from vampire venom. They were a danger to themselves and everyone near them.

Genna's mother tried to save all the horses. She ran from stall to stall. There was too much venom. The horses were too big. In too much pain. Trapped in death throes.

Genna focused on Bibi who had gone into early labor from the venom. All alone. Genna kept Bibi calm. She turned that stall into an island of tranquility. She let the noise and death become background. She did not have much to use. Only a few ointments and big pieces of aloe. The hard drugs and big equipment were needed for the rest of the stable. Genna made do with what she had. She risked getting kicked or crushed as she slid her hands inside the whimpering horse up to her shoulders. The baby was in the wrong position. The blood and effluvia as she clawed and hauled on the amniotic sac seeped into her clothes.

The night pressed in. The umbilical cord was purple-black around the baby, crushing him. Blood. So much blood. Bibi's thin wails were getting weaker. Genna kept her hands gentle and scent confident. There was enough fear and rage outside the stall. She had to put that into the ground. Keep it away from the horses.

She went into the shadows. She found Bibi and the baby. The death curse had wrapped the baby's back hooves up by his head. It coiled tight around Bibi's heart and lungs. Its fangs were sunk into their bodies.

Genna grabbed the curse by the tail. She yanked it clear of the horses and whipped it high and hit its head on the mounting block.

Thwap!

The curse went limp and transformed into a black snake.

She grabbed the snake by the neck. She pinned the snake's mouth open, squeezing it hard. Eight fangs extended. Green venom dripped out. The snake wiggled, pain rousing it, but Genna held it tight as she milked the venom out. The liquid slid down the contours the snarling lion's face. It looked like Sekhmet was weeping with rage.

The venom changed color as it dripped off the mounting block and onto the ground. Genna cupped her hand, catching the anti-venom. She smeared it on the baby's face, around his eyes, nose, mouth, and ears. She did the same to Bibi. The mare and baby roused. She coaxed them to lick the anti-venom off of Sekhmet's face.

A soft hand touched her back. Genna felt an echo of the heart attack that knocked Miss Bootsie flat on her back as though she'd been kicked in the chest by a horse. The snap of a skin being shed. Miss Bootsie stood behind her, refusing to be seen. She spread the cloak across Genna's shoulders. "Well done, honey child."

Genna's tears mixed with the anti-venom but she kept feeding the baby. "You told me you were okay. That you wouldn't give Pipsy the satisfaction."

"It wasn't Pipsy."

"Katie." The hatred she tried so hard to keep at bay flared bright orange and purple lightning. Over Sekhmet and the horses. Into the cloak. "She killed you. I'll kill her!"

"That won't change nothing," Miss Bootsie said briskly. "A snake ain't nothing but a snake. It's their nature. I put her in my pocket. I knew better."

"Wait, drink this. You'll get better."

"You didn't make that for me. You made it for the little nightmare. He needs every drop."

"You can't die. Fight this."

"Two wolves live in your heart, Iphigenia. Love and hate. The one that's strongest is the one you feed." Miss Bootsie's voice was fainter. Her spirit wandered into the shadows. "I love you, honey child. Protect the cloak for my sunshine girl. Don't forget to feed the nightmares. They're yours now."

Genna wept but she kept feeding the horses anti-venom. She diverted her pain away from them. She tried desperately to be kind and gentle when she wanted to rage and tear things.

The snake fought and wiggled in agony as Genna wrung it dry. Then it shriveled back into a bullwhip. The same one that Katie had held. Genna had accidentally brought the whip onto her property in the chaos of the rescue. She wanted the whip to burn up. Instead, her fury hardened it into smooth leather. It became hers, too.

Bibi and baby were made of shadows, smoke, and fire. The mare struggled back to her feet. The baby could not stand, wobbling and confused.

Genna picked him up and put him across her shoulders. She walked out of the shadows. Bibi followed, unwilling to leave her baby.

They stepped out of the shadows and into the stable, returning to their skins. The screaming had not changed but the inside of Genna's head was filled with fire. The bullwhip lay over Genna's shoulders like a stethoscope. The heavy handle and the thin tip tapped her thighs. Horseflies fell out of her hair, dried and dead. The baby was sticky. A cloud of horseflies had settled across his body, teeming in his ears, nostrils, and the crust of his sealed eyes.

Genna took the Chanel scarf covering her hair off, dipped it in the water trough, and wiped him clear. Then she wrapped the scarf around his little face. Bibi was also covered with flies. She swayed, legs filling the stable. Genna hastily picked the baby up, put him across her shoulders again, opened the stall door, and stepped out so Bibi had room to stand.

"The foal." Genna's mother stopped in the middle of the corridor, staring at the baby. "It's too soon."

"He's okay. Bibi's okay too," Genna said. "I'm getting them out of here."

Her mother was not listening. She stared in wonder at Bibi mincing carefully out of the stall. Then she rushed to the mare, wrapped her arms as wide as they would go around the horse's broad neck. She clung to Bibi like she was the only real thing in the world. Bibi bent her head down, nickered softly as she pressed her chin against her back. Her mother's broken little sob filled Genna with so much grief that she wanted to scream.

Her mother never hugged Genna like she hugged the horses. Not because she didn't love her daughter. It was simply not their way. Affection was easy with animals. They could talk about anything and nothing as long as there was an animal involved. Genna wished it were not so complicated. Except wishing changed nothing. She was as much an agent of her own isolation as they were.

Her mother took a deep breath, petting Bibi's mane as she stepped past to nudge the baby. "Get them out of here, Iphigenia. They're your responsibility."

"I'll take them up to the castle. I'll make the greenhouse into a temporary stable. I'll move the cars out of the garage so we can have the survivors recover there."

A ghastly little shake of negation. "Don't worry about the garage."

Genna walked out of the stable down the long, wide channel between stalls. The stable hands and vet techs and everyone on hand, paused to watch Genna and Bibi pass. The stable hands not actively wrestling the horses stared up at Bibi like she was an angel come from heaven. A few caught their breath in a quick sob.

"She's walking? She had the baby?"

Funny how Genna could hear anything. How the screaming and the buzz of horseflies had turned into ambient noise.

Bibi did not need a bridle. She walked next to Genna. The flies followed but diffused as they stepped out of the shadows and into the sunlight. They walked past the mounting block. Dust clotted Sekhmet's still-damp features. The pitted muzzle. Genna had not realized that Bibi's stall wall was right next to the mounting. She paused. Pressed her hand on the black sandstone.

"Thank you."

She wiped the mounting block clear. She took the scarf from the baby's head. Then she lay the scarf down flat. She coiled the whip carefully on the top of the scarf. The woven leather lost its gleam. The scarf frayed. They disintegrated into black dust. The wind sucked the flakes away.

Genna and Bibi trudged up the grassy lane. The baby's sticky weight bounced on her shoulders. The sunlight was so bright.

The mowed grass was soft under her boots. The swish of Bibi's tail. The persistent flies. The blue summer sky had circles of turkey vultures. The trees were full of ravens arguing with crows. Other birds. Other animals. Everything that Miss Bootsie left in her care.

If Genna were a real wolf or coyote then she would howl. Instead her grief was filled with silence.

She focused on the path ahead. On the baby's heartbeat against her neck and the clop of Bibi's hooves.

They walked past Miss Bootsie's apartment. The curtain was drawn across the window. Miss Bootsie's body was laid on top of the bed. The cloak spread neatly over her body like a blanket. The black side up. The red side down. The oversized hood over her face.

Genna's mother had already cleaned and dressed the body. She had not told her daughter. Not ready. Perhaps believing she could spare her. Perhaps knowing Genna already knew. Her strange daughter who had brought her favorite horse back from the dead. Who had saved a foal who should have been a stillborn.

The echo of rifle shots behind her. This was the first time Genna's mother had ever given up. Or perhaps that was the lesson.

Sometimes, the best death was a swift one.

Genna had not saved Miss Bootsie from Katie or Pipsy or that circle of skulls. She had only prolonged the inevitable and gotten all of her horses killed in the process.

"Don't interfere in affairs that don't concern you again," Mimi said in a shadow between pine trees beyond the property line. "You're not a part of the forest."

"I was born in the forest. Right in that cottage you tried to burn. You screwed up, Mimi. You can't burn the cottage or the forest. That's why I could get through."

Mimi hissed but she would always be the weakest. Brittle and vicious. Genna was covered in anti-venom. Her horses were now immune.

Genna trudged on.

The swallows and other birds danced along the pasture. The dragonflies zipped past. Genna and Bibi reached the trees by the castle. The flower gardens were in full bloom. Birds chirped inside the boxwoods and mugo pine bushes.

The castle staff had gotten the call from her mother. They bustled around, moving potted plants, stacking blankets, and preparing the sun lit glass greenhouse for the horses. Pirate the rooster strutted and flapped. He immediately began snapping up horseflies, grooming, and pecking. Other birds darted out of their perches. The cloud of flies was decimated by the time they entered the greenhouse.

Genna bathed the baby in warm water. Then Bibi. Needing to check everything to confirm that there was no infection or bites. Bibi nudged her meaningfully. She wanted to be with her baby. Genna backed away. She watched Bibi groom him.

"Lunch is ready when you are," one of the chefs said. He glanced at her black gore soaked Black Lives Matter t-shirt.

Genna numbly showered. She dressed in Birkenstocks, black bike shorts and a *Foxy Brown* screen-printed t-shirt. She came back downstairs.

Her mother sat at the dining table with a weary smile. She was dressed in a black sheath dress and black kitten heels, far more formal than Genna.

"I can go change," Genna said, turning for the staircase.

"No, it's fine. Sit."

Her mother wore a new necklace. A single mustard seed inside white glass on a gold chain. Miss Bootsie's necklace. On the back of Genna's chair was the fur cloak, neatly folded.

"She wanted you to have it." Her mother's voice was as dry as driftwood. "The apple crumble should be done by the time we finish eating."

They lunched on peanut butter stew with handmade clover rolls. Genna guzzled several cups of iced cold brew coffee. The chef spread chocolate frosting on double-layered yellow cake.

Genna made it through the first bowl of Miss Bootsie's favorite meal before she started weeping. She kept eating. Her mother dabbed her eyes.

After they ate too much her mother asked Genna to go on a drive with her. Genna obeyed. They sat together in the back of a black Porsche Cayenne in a fog of grief. Genna held the cloak, absently petting it.

She was surprised that the driver took them to an airfield. Her mother nodded as the car parked next to an airplane hanger.

"You said you liked the Dassault Falcons but you wanted a real mattress in the back. We have redesigned the interior to fit a king bed."

The Falcon stood proudly in its hanger. Sunlight gleamed on its silver wings.

Genna stared at the plane. She fell in love. She walked up the stairs into the interior. The beige and pearl white would have to go but she could feel the future as she ran her hand along the plush stuffed seats. "I love it. Thank you."

Her mother clasped her hands and sat down. Genna sat with her, attentive. "The planes we flew after your annulment both had malfunctions. The crew and the security guards are in critical condition or dead. The Nautilus was also found in pieces."

"I'm sorry."

Her mother reached out. They squeezed hands. "Right now they're building a pyre for the animals. It wasn't only horses that were targeted."

Genna gulped, remembering the spiral of turkey vultures. "I see."

"That was Katie, wasn't it?"

"Yes, Mom." Genna loved her but could not resist. "Because you said yes to Donnie when you should've said no."

Her mother frowned severely, back straight even in defeat. "Isn't there anything we can do?"

Genna stroked the gold ring. "Never forget."

"Your father and I have talked. I don't think it's safe for you here anymore. You can come back, but it's time to fly, Iphigenia. Finish college online and abroad."

"I'd like to take Bibi and her baby with me. I don't want to leave them behind."

Her mother nodded. "I agree. We'll talk to a broker—"

"I'm not selling the castle."

Her mother frowned. "Iphigenia, it's not safe."

"I'll go but I'm coming back. It's the only home I have."

"That's not true. You can get a new castle. Start a new life."

"I'm keeping the castle." Genna leaned forward. "Sell me everything connected to the McBrides. I'll deal with it. You need to be free of this. I love you but I can't do what I need to do if I'm worried about you all. Stay away from the castle. Stay away from the McBrides." She took an unsteady breath. "Stay away from me."

"You're our daughter."

"I know it doesn't look like it right now, but I know what I'm doing. I love the Falcon. I do. I'll take it, but the rest of it, I have to do on my own. I'll keep them focused on me."

"Iphigenia."

"Mom."

"Your father won't understand."

"Please, Mom. This is how I can protect the family."

"No, I won't accept that. We'll say you're retracing the family ancestry. That's your new job. Will you accept that? We'll put everything in the castle. You can check the records and histories for scandals. That was already a project we needed to do. You'll lead it. That'll take you all over the world. We've been everywhere."

"Okay, Mom."

Her mother pointed at the ring on Genna hand. "Start with your great-grandmother's ring."

Ten

Genna studied cavaliers, cowboys, knights, mamluks, dragoons, and other forms of horse archery. She learned how to keep her seat and shoot straight at a gallop. The difference between short and longbows. How to hold and shoot arrows. Different saddles. Different techniques. Different climates.

Humanity had been fighting on a horse since the Iron Age. There were plenty of historical societies excited to share knowledge in exchange for funding.

As a child Genna's mother had instructors come to the castle to teach everything from dressage to the history of Black cowboys. Her mother always took the horses with the family on the trips. There was no use in learning how to ride other people's horses. Which also meant the dogs had to come and the staff with them. Genna maintained the same regime as she learned mounted combat.

She learned lance and fencing too but close-quarter combat was always a fight not to simply transform into a wolf and use her teeth and claws instead.

She left four animals at the castle to guard the property. Grim the grimhound. Toto the Carin terrier. Pirate the rooster. Schrodinger the cat. They had the largest amount of Miss Bootsie's magic.

Studying abroad was difficult. Homesickness was a full-bodied experience.

Genna did not believe the reports that everything was fine at the castle. Pristine and boring. The paramilitary security, gardening, kennel, and stable staff sent her a log of the animals' activities. It was more accurate. The four guardians always knew when the McBrides sent revenants and compromised people to the castle.

Genna spent three years studying abroad before things got out of hand.

The last straw was Sneakers. Genna named the baby horse 'Black Air Force Jordan' but even she called him Sneakers.

She was in Japan, learning female archery. Sneakers was barely a colt. He was wild-eyed and kicking and bucking in the practice arena. In the black dirt was a crumpled body wearing a black sweatshirt was nearly the same color as the dirt. The ribs stoved in. The legs were twisted. Sneakers kept trampling the corpse, whinnying and kicking.

The other girls ran around him. The veterans yelling. They had rope. They had Bibi who fought, but Sneakers was hysterical. He jumped and twisted, all knobby knees and enormous hooves. His high bugle of challenge. His hooves punched the air.

There was a strange mist drifting around him. It was Katie fucking McBride. She had learned a new trick.

"Sneakers!" Genna shouted.

Then Genna did something very foolish. She ran straight to the horse. She timed it so that when Sneakers slammed his hooves back down on the mangled body, his head down, mane flying, she could jump, swing up onto his back. He hopped sideways. Genna held on.

And all the rage she felt, the need to turn and kick and bite and kill, made sense.

Fire swept over her and the colt. They attacked the mist. He bellowed. Gouts of flame burned the mist out of his throat and nostrils. His ears pressed back.

Katie screeched. She drifted against the wind. She tried to jump into another body, but the flames corralled her.

Sneakers chased her up into the air. Flames under his hooves. Lightning in his mane and tail. Genna rode hard. She slashed her hand like it was a sword.

"Get away from him, you fucking bitch!"

The air tore with thunder. The clouds opened up into a storm, lightning in the sky. Katie was slammed down into the mud again, this time in vampire form. Sneakers' hooves stove in her chest. Katie, hair and scales singed, lunged at his chest, teeth out, and was kicked in her face. Anyone else would be dead but Katie wiggled free, slithering away fast as a snake into the brush. Sneakers chased, but there was nothing but leaves and bracken.

Genna howled her hatred. Would there never be any peace?

The rain pushed her back into herself. It doused the fire. Sneakers was too damn young for her to be on his back. She slid off. Soothing him. Petting him as he shivered and stamped.

"It's okay. She's gone. You're okay."

Bibi plodded over. She nickered and rubbed Sneakers along his flank. He exhaled gustily. Head low. Nostrils flared. Long eyelashes catching water. Bedraggled. Too big for this place. Genna rubbed his jaw. He nudged her and asked plaintively if they could leave this place. It was the first time he had spoken so clearly and directly to Genna.

"Yeah, let's get out of here," Genna said. "This isn't working."

She hooked their halters with two fingers. She walked over to the cluster of women and men. She did not recognize who Sneakers had killed but guessed she had been bitten by Katie. They shouted at her in an angry mixture of English and Japanese.

"What was that thing?" a girl sobbed. "It came from the air."

"You saw her too?" Genna said.

"Of course we saw it!" a man bellowed.

Hope. "That was a vampire. She killed my horses. Only these

two survived. She's chasing me. I thought I had run far enough away."

"You brought that evil thing here?"

"I thought Japan was far enough away. Usually oceans work. Maybe there is a difference between the Atlantic and the Pacific."

The founder of the women's riding club had taken her coat off and spread it over the dead girl. She stood up slowly, halting the growing argument by walking up to Genna.

"You want to learn *yabusame* to kill that monster." She spoke in icy English.

"Yes."

"If you leave, then it will follow you."

Genna flinched at her tired brown eyes. "Yes. I'm sorry."

GENNA PACKED. NO ONE SPOKE. THEY HELPED. THE wrenching sound of tape. The slam and shunt of suitcases and boxes. Genna's possessions were shoved into cars. They followed her to the airfield. They watched the Falcon and the horse plane take off as if their stares were brooms sweeping Genna and her horses up into the air and far away. Genna sat in the back of the horse plane, feeding hay to Sneakers, who *loathed* tight spaces.

She needed to find someplace remote. She picked Mongolia, fighting her own homesickness. The isolated equestrian training camp was a lot more rugged. The windswept scrub and ground were hard. It was the kind of cold that was a constant slap in the face.

Genna saw them shoot wild dogs. She was careful never to Turn. She wore the fur cloak to keep warm and dampen the need to Turn. Like Miss Bootsie said, the cloak helped her know where her skin was.

The remoteness of Mongolia eased the fire out of her eyes. She could focus on the day to day problems of living.

Katie did not show. That did not mean she wouldn't. Or that Genna had simply not detected her presence.

Genna found calm and clarity in those frigid mountains and wind swept plains. But barely a month later her translator looked her in the eye and said, "It's time you went home."

And she was right.

The Sweetwater was where she belonged. Sadly, the castle made sense in a way the world did not. She could run in the forest. She could be herself.

Genna went home.

Eleven

Genna put her headphones on. She trotted on Bibi along the trail that circled the entire castle property. Past the houses she had turned into apartments for people in the medical community. Past the lake. The orchards. The beehives. The gardens, herb, vegetable and floral. The pastures of drowsy horses grazing.

Sneakers watched but went back to hanging out with other horses. Sneakers was now a powerful three year old colt. Mongolia had been a good training ground. His muscles moved smooth. His coat had a black shine. Genna and Sneakers were still getting to know each other. He was not quite old enough to put a saddle on. He was still learning to be a part of the herd without his mother. Bibi enjoyed status as the lead mare.

Genna fit the archery ring on her finger as she entered the indoor practice arena. She squeezed Bibi with her thighs and whistled. Bibi charged for the obstacle course. The bales of hay. The targets. The point wasn't speed. The point was accuracy. How well she maintained a gallop. How many targets she hit. Bibi took a corner tight, a hoof clipping the blue barrel. Genna arched and shot through the wooden target. Bibi could corner better. All their practice paying off.

Genna sought to recreate that moment of complete harmony that day in Japan when she and Sneakers became flaming fury. Or when she and Bibi rescued Miss Bootsie. She could never quite hit that moment again with Bibi. The curious adrenaline flow. Fury and fire and vengeance. Maybe they had to be in dire need.

Practice. Patience. Persistence.

Yet in her heart Genna knew it was because Sneakers was her horse. Bibi was her mother's. For all their adventures together, the mare was getting tired of her antics. Still game, but Genna had to be careful of her bones and joints. Bibi was happy to be at the castle. Or maybe that was Genna projecting. Her mother always called to ask how Bibi was and scolded her for putting the horse at risk. Bibi was precious.

Bibi cantered into the forest. Genna pulled the bow, muscles twanging across her back, and shot through several trees. Missed the target. Hit a tree. *Damn.*

Bibi twisted and dodged through the roots of the uneven path, leaping up the slope. She added a little ebullient kick. Genna laughed at Bibi's antics. She pushed herself and Bibi harder. She shot another target. She turned Bibi back to the pasture. That was a good warm-up. Now to get serious.

Except her concentration wasn't much better than the first round. She shot. Rode. She circled the area, letting Bibi stretch her legs.

Genna forced herself to look at Miss Bootsie's apartment by the stable. Now a sublet like the other buildings. No one stayed for long.

On a whim, she turned down the trail mouth. This time, she headed for the cottage. This required a slower pace. The path was more treacherous. Bibi moved eagerly. Excited for an adventure.

The fur cloak flapped around Genna's shoulders.

The red cloak looked wonderful since she had it professionally worked on. There was something weird about that furrier in Belarus. The political unrest couldn't stop them from restoring the many coats she had gathered from the family. The Mongolian equestrians had approved of the cloak. They wanted her to add embellishments but she adamantly refused. Instead she sewed a helmet and saddle and bridle for both horses.

Genna graduated college. The family had a party at the mansion on Martha's Vineyard island instead of the castle. The McBrides did not show up.

"It's the Atlantic Ocean and this being our oldest ancestral home," Genna said to her father. "The other oceans don't have the same effect."

"I heard you got your marksman license," her father said.

"It's not a big deal," Genna said, minimizing her obsession with shooting things while on horseback. She wanted to kill the McBrides but could not figure out how. It was as if she were biting hard air. Her teeth scraped and snapped on nothing. The vampires smirked and fed on her rage.

Her family loathed that Genna had a hunting license and knew how to handle a rifle, shotgun, handgun, and even an elephant gun.

The last had been unwilling knowledge. A snotty twenty-something trying to impress Genna and other women at his party showed off his enormous rifle. He talked about his grand-father shooting down an elephant and pointed to the grotesque photograph. A White man with his hand on a great tusk and boot on the ankle of the dead animal. Genna had learned how to shoot imagining the braggart and his family tied to the gun range.

"You need to stop being so brittle," her father said. "What happened was tragic but you have to move on."

"You'll never get a man if you aren't gentle," her mother said.

"Then I don't want a man," Genna said. "I don't want anyone."

Her mother had not recovered from the stable incident either. She stopped buying black horses. She allowed her hair to go silver. It was a lovely gunmetal and black that required an entire new wardrobe change.

Genna stopped talking about what she was doing. She did not stop her cavalry lessons.

Genna slowed Bibi as they reached the forest clearing.

The cottage was quiet. The grass was wild and green but still in a neat circle as though freshly mowed. Bibi picked her way carefully into the clearing. Genna looked around. Nothing but mulberry trees, the silkworms crawling along the broad green leaves. She wondered why Miss Bootsie focused on the little cotton patch behind the cottage instead of harvesting the worms for their silk.

She slid off her horse. Her knees complained at the distance from the ground, but her time in Mongolia had taught her how to land. She did not bother to tie Bibi to anything. She fed Bibi a broken piece of carrot from her shoulder bag. Then an apple when Bibi nudged her. She carried the bow and quiver with her out of habit. She knocked on the door. Also habit. No one was home.

The door wasn't locked. She stepped inside.

The smells were the same but stale. The old TV. The pullout couch. The kitchen to the left. The bathroom to the right. It seemed so small. Or she was too big. She regretted coming in. Tarnishing memory with reality. Her fingers traced the rows of VHS tapes.

There was a Bible on top of the TV. The cover was puckered and sticky with age and neglect. The leather was scuffed and scratched. The pages were yellow and thin. Instead of printed, the Bible verses were carefully handwritten. The Bible was hand bound.

This was a different Bible from the one Miss Bootsie took with her to church in a special fabric bag. Genna's father had taken the familiar Bible as memento mori. Inside, there was a gold chain; on it hung a single mustard seed inside the pendant. Her mother had worn the necklace. Then changed her mind and buried it with Miss Bootsie. It was Miss Bootsie's in life. It needed to be hers in death. Yet here the necklace was.

Genna wanted to pick it up, put it on, but some things needed to stay. It was not for her. Perhaps it was for Naomi. Waiting with the same hope.

Genna opened the Bible without moving it. She read the passage marked in thin lead pencil lines.

Romans 12:20-21: *If your enemies are hungry, feed them. If they are thirsty, give them something to drink. In doing this, you will heap burning coals of shame on their heads. Don't let evil conquer you, but conquer evil by doing good.*

The writing was loping cursive but unfamiliar. Genna realized that this was Sable's Bible. Miss Bootsie had made Genna and Katie transcribe the entire Bible on lined paper to perfect their handwriting too.

Genna could hear Miss Bootsie. See her. Feel the room, warmed by afternoon sunshine. The light was golden in her silver hair. They sat together. She darned one of Genna's dad's black socks while Genna struggled to crotchet a hat. She always pulled the yarn too tight. The memory faded.

Genna took out the VHS tape of Whitney Houston's *Cinderella* off the built-in shelf of movies and played it to break the silence. The metallic churn and smell of plastic. The merry slightly tinny music made Genna swallow hard. Longing and grief wrenched tears from her eyes. Her nostrils flared.

Genna missed the boo hag with her whole heart.

The loss had changed her. The horses screams still echoed in every whinny. The ratchet of gunfire. Her mother hugging Bibi. Sekhmet's tears. Shadows. The buzz of horseflies. The stench of death.

Genna had bathed in hatred. She drank venom and combed it through her hair. The weapons were heavy on her shoulders and hips. The bow was light in her fingers. She felt so far from this sunshiny room. From everything gentle and good. She was trapped in vicious cycles of violence and revenge.

"Two wolves. Hate and love. Which one have you been feeding?" A voice said through the TV. Miss Bootsie did not

sound like herself. She sounded like Whoopi Goldberg. Genna rushed around to stare at the screen of Miss Bootsie's favorite actress resplendent as a queen.

"Miss Bootsie?" Genna said, hardly daring to hope.

"*Two wolves, Iphigenia*," Whoopi said.

Genna swallowed hard against the need to babble sentimentality. "It doesn't matter. They're both wolves. I can't allow them to eat my horses. I'll do whatever needs to be done."

Whoopi smiled at her, in her diamond tiara and dark blue gown. "You go, girl."

The music and movie returned to normal. Genna stood. She squeezed the bow. She should have said more. She should have told her she loved her. She should have been a better person.

She turned off the TV. She left the movie in the player. Bibi grazed on the edge of the clearing. She went to the horse, stowing the bow and quiver. Bibi stilled. Poised, ready. Ears up. Body forward.

"I miss her too," Katie said on the opposite side of the clearing. "Remember all the movies we watched? We saw *Cinderella* like a thousand times."

Genna attacked. Transforming into a wolf. No control. Only rage, hurt, and the need to tear.

Bibi reared and bolted, tail high like a flag as she thundered into the woods.

Genna let the grief and the rage consume her. She howled. The transformation was a jubilant pleasure so acute it was its own kind of pain. Her black fur rippled. Katie's yellow scales were hard as they collided. They slashed and bit each other. Genna smashed Katie's face into the ground several times.

Blood dappled the green grass. The last clear thought was to drag Katie into the cottage.

Katie kicked and squirmed. She spat venom into Genna's eyes but Genna was stronger.

Starving.

Genna hated herself. She hated what she was doing. But not enough to stop.

Genna bit Katie's wrists, breaking the bones. She ripped the tendons, and knotted the mangled meat together. She twisted the vampire like a pretzel to tie her ankles and wrists together with the shredded remains of her own clothes. She smashed Katie against the floor until her spine broke and her head lolled sideways. She punched her claws into Katie's belly at an angle. She yanked down to the thighs in a rough vivisection. Katie's intestines fell out with a wet splatter. Loops of purple tubes and red veins. Genna kept tearing. Kept digging out her guts. She wrenched and bit.

The last couple of months had been a fight to go another day without eating someone. To stay on the path when she had no idea where she was going. The need, the terrible need, that was taking over her life. She had made it three years without eating anyone. Three years without eating Katie. She made bargains with herself. One more day. All she needed was one more day. She did not need to play that doomed game of Prometheus and the Eagle.

Now it rushed back.

The cottage fed on the excess blood. It righted any toppled furniture. The TV stand moved itself out of harm's way.

Miss Bootsie was wrong. Genna was not human. There was no distinction between Genna and the wolf skin. She was a monster. She needed to eat living flesh. Going cold turkey had tested her self-control. The hunger never went away. She never cracked. Not once but the strain of pretending to be human had changed her as much as the rage and grief.

Katie's screeches wheezed as Genna chewed through her lungs. Up to her heart. The slippery goodness of a liver that grew back nearly as fast as she ate it. Genna loved liver. The taste of it. The purity slick on her tongue. Meanwhile, Katie's lungs inflated. The heart renewed. The stomach, kidneys, pancreas, and appendix were fine, but the liver was glorious.

"Every fucking time." Katie pushed and squirmed.

Genna ripped her jaw off. Bit her flapping tongue out of the savaged remains. Wrenched her fangs out of her mouth. Katie screamed and flailed.

Genna went back to eating. She ate the back meat from the inside out. Then moved to the thighs. The biceps. The shoulders. Spitting the scales out.

Then she tossed Katie down. She stood up, drooling blood and slivers of fascia. She paced in circles around the cottage to burn off the bloodlust.

Katie hugged herself as her legs turned into a yellow snake tail. Her hair solidified into a full cobra hood. She swayed in the middle of the living room, turning to always keep Genna in her line of sight.

Genna's snarls quieted. Her muzzle smoothed. The fur became skin. Her claws receded. She became a woman. Naked except for the red fur cloak that draped down to her calves. Her black curls were a wild frizzy mane. She rubbed her face. Remembered herself. Patted the skin to confirm no fire burned. She stuck her head under the faucet, guzzling the iron flavored tapwater. Cooling herself off.

"That hurt," Katie said.

"Good," Genna said between gulps.

"Do you want to kill me, Iffy?"

Would a world Katie didn't exist in be simple? Or fair? Or different?

A snake ain't nothing but a snake. I put her in my pocket. I knew better.

Miss Bootsie hadn't blamed Katie. She blamed herself.

But Katie was also the only person left who knew Genna. This was her life. Every bite of it. They weren't friends. They weren't enemies either. A pair of monsters in the forest who had no idea what to do with this empty cottage.

Genna slumped down on the couch. She yanked the red hood up and over her head so only her trembling lips were visible among her black curls and the shadows inside the hood. She tucked her legs up. Curled into the corner of the couch, hugging herself. Katie picked up a denim quilt with shaking hands. She wrapped it around her shoulders as she slunk over to the other side of the couch. She cried in the shadows.

Katie used her tail to pull the TV back to its usual position. She tapped the VHS player to turn the *Cinderella* movie back on.

The music blared. Neither spoke until Brandy was dancing with her handsome prince. Whitney Houston singing in sparkling gold.

"I can't stay this mad at you. It's not rational," Genna said.

Katie rubbed her arms over the denim quilt. "I didn't want to bite her, you know. I was mad at you. I knew you'd feel her pain. We were punishing her but she could take it. You were supposed to run into the forest and take her place but you always do too much. You think that's the first time Pipsy's burned her cloak? She wouldn't have died if you hadn't severed her connection to the forest."

"I know that now." Genna took a deep unsteady breath. "I shouldn't have jumped into that circle. That wasn't my business. I'm sorry."

"She asked me to bite her," Katie said. "I went to see her because the woods needed a guardian. It couldn't be you."

"So that's you now?"

"Everywhere but the cottage. That's tied to the cloak. Miss Bootsie died with her secrets. Pipsy's mad at me. Now I have to fill the pool and protect the forest. I can't do that. You know I'm a shit hunter."

They sat and watched the movie some more.

"How many people does it take to fill a swimming pool?" Genna said.

"A lot. And she doesn't want me padding it with animals or people from Sweetwater."

"If she's not picky about blood type then you have a lot of options. Why not expand upon the Happy Meal cipher we made? The world is full of serial rapists and child molesters. The pool will never be empty."

"You're the one with the cipher. I just showed up." Katie cocked her head, assuming a sly pleading expression. "Since you're back and you forgive me, we can start hunting together again, right?"

"I don't forgive you."

"Oh please, yes you do. You're being all sulky but you missed me. I missed you too. This bullshit has gone on long enough." Katie flounced confidently into Genna's personal space.

Genna tackled her, transformed halfway into a wolf, and roared so loud the cottage windows rattled. Then she picked Katie up and threw her out of the cottage. She slammed the door. Locked it. Sat back down on the couch.

"Okay, you're still mad. I'll give you some time to cool off," Katie said on the other side of the door. "But I'm glad you're back. It's no fun without you. Thanks for the cipher idea. I'll work on that. Next time, I'll bring the kills to you."

Genna turned the volume up to the highest setting.

Twelve

Seven Years Later...

There was a baby-faced trans-gendered kid with wispy facial hair hiding in the hayloft. The kid wouldn't tell Genna their name. Only that they were trans. *Needing* Genna to know. Adolescent defiance covered a deep trauma. Their mouth gaped open wide like a starving baby bird. "I'm not a girl. I'm not a girl!"

"Okay," Genna said, "now, will you come down out of my hayloft so I can fix those cuts?"

The kid swayed, hugging Schrodinger the cat until he wiggled free. He flicked the kid with his bushy tail and scuttled away. Genna retreated back down the ladder. She waited for the kid to creep down with her hands in her pockets. Toto panted at her feet. Grim leaned his big, curly head against her hip.

"You're a witch," the kid said as Genna helped them into the veterinary clinic.

"I'm not a witch. I live next door to monsters." Genna patched up what she could but she was not a doctor. She did have a drawer of morning-after pills. The kid spat in her face, cussed her out, then took the pill.

"Why, you rude little shit." Genna dabbed her face, clamped on to her temper. The saliva had gone right into her eye. Fire sizzled in her thoughts. Grim growled, filling the sterilized room with thunder. Teeth bright among the curls. The kid shivered and hunched. Their defiance shattered.

"I'm sorry." The kid started to cry. All snot and blubbery lips. They hunched on the stool, too consumed by their own misery.

Toto licked their face, whimpering and wiggling until they calmed down. Grim leaned against their hip, his big, soulful eyes watching.

Genna wanted to start cussing. The town used the forest as a place to let the monsters run wild. Every fox hunt needed a fox. Usually, the hunt wasn't near Genna's castle, but desperation could make someone run all the way up the mountain into the Heights to the only place the monsters could not tread.

She poured honey into a spoon from a jar on the shelf. "I want you to think of honey that's been sitting out in the sun. It's spilling onto your hands. Your fingers are sticky with it. You lick it off. Some has dripped down your wrist. You lick up because you don't want to get any on your pants."

The kid flinched. "What's in that?"

"Honey. From my garden." Genna waited.

Technically the kid was right to be afraid. It was rhododendron and mountain laurel honey. It was toxic to humans. The difference between poison and medicine was dosage. Genna had many types of honey from her apiary. This one was from Miss Bootsie's hive. It worked better on magical people. The kid was definitely magic if Schrodinger was involved in their rescue.

The kid leaned forward and ate the whole spoonful, sucking on the metal spoon hard. Teeth grating.

The kid wanted tap water in a cup that Genna had filled instead of bottled water. They sniffed the sprigs of peppermint, lavender, and sage from the hydroponic garden floating in it.

Then gulped it down. The kid panicked when she offered them an apple.

"No, I'm good!" They nearly dropped Toto in their haste to get off the stool. "I'm ready to go home now!"

"Okay," Genna said. She reached into her back pocket for her phone and called her security team.

The kid paused at the door of the black Range Rover. Toto jumped into the car. She sat on the backseat. The kid looked back at Genna, who petted Grim. "Your dog is in here."

"Toto likes car rides," Genna said. "It's her job to make sure people get off the property safely."

"There was a huge cat," the kid said.

"That's Schrodinger. He lives in the woods."

The kid opened their phone and held it out to show the infamous photo of young Genna and Katie fighting. *SLAY QUEEN SLAY* was written in white all caps.

"That's you, right?" the kid said.

"Yes? What about it?" Genna did not understand the significant looks.

Another picture. "This too?"

The second picture was Genna's debutant portrait. Genna wore a hand-embroidered white dress. She looked like a doll with her black ringlet curls. Her tiara was designed after the *Miss America* crown that Vanessa Williams wore.

The picture failed to show how everyone thought Genna was a joke. Katie had spread the rumor she was a lesbian to make it easier to come out herself. Genna's presentation ball to Black elite fell flat. It didn't matter that she was the best dressed, most elegant, and wealthiest by an order of magnitude. Any interested boys or parents suddenly had a complicated road ahead of them. Black excellence was about procreation, not sexuality.

"Yes, that's me."

The third inevitable picture was from the engagement. Genna the evil queen in black and glaring at the top of the stairs. Katie on the ground, tangled in her own wedding veil like a white moth in a spiderweb. Genna was vilified for declaring her independence.

That was seven years ago. Sometimes, it felt like yesterday. Funny how her life could be reduced to three pictures. All of them in a dress surrounded by opulence. All of them related to Katie. All seven years apart.

"Is there a point to this?" Genna said.

The kid stared some more. "No disrespect, but you're really pretty and super freaking scary."

"Katie's scary. I'm not scary."

The kid shook their head. "Different kind of scary. All the black animals. It's spooky."

"People dump animals on my property. No one adopts them. I take care of them. Normal. Nothing spooky about melanated animals."

"How is getting *that* normal?" The kid jabbed a finger at the fortress looming over the circular driveway.

"My parents gave me a castle for my birthday when I was seven. See? Normal. Don't you live in a mansion?"

"I'm not from the Heights. I'm not rich. I'm not even supposed to be here. I was going to a party. Then—then—" The kid's face crumpled like wet tissues again. "I thought they were my friend."

"You made it out of the woods. Congratulations. That's what matters."

"How are you so calm? Don't you know what's in the woods?"

"Yes."

"Then how do you sleep at night? Why haven't you run?"

"Why do people live next to the ocean when they know it's full of sharks? Or a bayou that's full of alligators?"

"It's not the same and you know it!"

Genna sighed. "You won't remember in the morning. That's part of it."

"You roofied me?" The kid recoiled.

"No, it's part of the fairy tale. You went into the deep, dark woods. You got out. You wake up in the morning. The sun is shining. It was all just a dream."

"Fairy tales aren't real."

"They're real enough to eat you if you don't run and you don't listen. Whatever happened in there, you did it. You faced it. You were brave. You were strong. You were good. You made it out."

Toto yipped from inside the car. Genna nodded. "You should go now. You need to get home. You need to get to bed. You will feel better in the morning."

The kid got in the car. "I'll remember you."

The security guard drove them home. Genna watched the red taillights disappear down the hill. "No, you won't. That's part of it too."

The kid hadn't thanked her, either.

Genna saw the kid two weeks later at the country club. They ignored her. Stiff. Ready to run. Their friends whispering and glaring at her.

That was the thing. No one talked to Genna unless it was an emergency. She wasn't a witch. She lived next to vampires that no one else could remember were vampires.

A certain kind of person made it to her pastures. It was the loners. The ones who had no one but themselves. The token brown or Black kid. The nerdy girl. The closeted boy. The divorced mom who hadn't had a good lawyer. The grandmother with dementia, looking for her dog or her husband or her long-dead son. The lost souls washed up onto the pasture's green shores. People who needed kindness. People who needed a mouthful of honey and a cool drink of water to soothe throats raw from screaming and dehydrated from weeping.

Whenever she left for work, the town demanded she come back.

Hysterical text messages, angrily demanding why she wasn't home. Hadn't she heard about the kid who OD'd in Katie's driveway? Or the girl who threw herself down Katie's spiraled stair-case? Or the old womanizer who ran the yacht club who got drunk and fell off his boat at Katie's party?

Katie's favorite meal was powerful white men. She had gotten a taste for them after eating her father. Katie's dad looked a lot like Donald Trump in the eighties. Something about the death of arrogant self-proclaimed masters of the universe. The ones who had pinched her cheek or bottom. The ones who locked the door. The ones who undid their pants and leered at her like a naked, flaccid penis was the best gift they could give. Those men never made it to Genna's property. Cruel women did not either. Katie hated her mother. Anyone who reminded her of her parents got all the vitality sucked out of their bodies.

Genna's hunting cipher helped Katie get away with murder.

Still, no one hurt black cats or dogs in town. Not on Halloween. Not ever. They belonged to the dark forest.

Thirteen

G‍ENNA GOT UP EARLY M‍ONDAY MORNING AND FLEW IN her Falcon to the South Carolina coast to her horseshoe crab farm. She was already annoyed by the reports by the time she finished her first cup of coffee. Reaching the factory gave her a rage headache.

Genna strode through the work floor with her assistants and the greeting staff giving her information she already knew. Since the Pandemic, the need for horseshoe crab's unique blue blood was at an all-time high. It was important for medical testing.

At a minimum of sixty thousand dollars a gallon of crab blood, the maintenance, security, and upkeep of the crabs was vital. Except not everyone cared about the crabs. Only how much blood and how quickly they could they get it. These men who ran the factory did not believe in the Covi-19, but by God, did they love making money from medical testing.

None of the crabs in her farm ever made it back to water. Even though she had specifically paid contractors to make an easy route to shuttle them from large holding tanks and back to the ocean.

It was difficult to see rows upon rows of crabs with their tails chopped off. Spigots were planted in the cavity. The froth of blue blood filled clear plastic containers. Their legs feebly kicked at the air until finally curling in death.

"Stop all production right now!" Her shout was answered by blank stares. The working staff wore white onesies, smocks, blue gloves, hoodies, and goggles.

Genna glared at the mousy man nervously clutching his tablet. "Where are the needles that I bought for proper exsanguination? Why aren't we doing any of the new regulations?"

"You'll have to talk to the senior floor manager." Not even a respectful 'ma'am' or 'miss' to show he was listening. Her glossy hair and healthy skin enticed the sallow-faced manager closer. He was too busy gaping at her cleavage to see the warning in her eyes. It didn't matter that she owned the company. She was too curvy and too beautiful to take seriously.

The senior floor manager was already on her shit list but Genna had time to chew through another scolding asshole first. Men whined if they couldn't win head on. They scolded if whining didn't work. They rallied together though Genna doubted the senior manager even knew this mouse's name.

The wolf was closer to the surface. She noticed the veins along his jugular. The butterfly beat of his pulse would be so easy to rip out. He would taste like cheap aftershave and Pert Plus all-in-one shampoo. He had taken his wedding ring off. She could see the indent on his finger. As if she would ever consider him as anything but a disappointing meal.

Genna prowled into his personal space. "You are the shift manager directly responsible for the crabs, aren't you? Or am I wasting my time asking you questions when I should be talking to someone who won't waste my time?"

"I'm the shift manager." He straightened to his unimpressive height. He raised his tablet like a shield. His scent was a mixture of fear, arousal, and annoyance.

Her fingers slid down the tablet's glass face. Her sneer revealing sharp and white teeth. "Then you are going to change the policy. Today."

He licked his lips. "You see, the thing is—"

"You seem to be under the impression that this is a request. It's not. The senior manager does not matter. I matter. You will do what I say. You will do it now. Say yes."

"Yes, ma'am," the mouse squeaked.

"Good boy." A growl feathered her words.

Genna spotted an exceptionally large horseshoe crab strapped to a sling. This crab was nearly four times the size of the other crabs. The crab was female and very old to be that big. Her shell was metallic blue, different from the others that were algae-green and barnacle-brown. Scrapes down the back ridges to indicate that she had mated many times. Males always left divots in the females they mounted. She barely fit into the sling they used to hold her tail-side down.

Genna snatched the manager's tablet and clattered down to the first floor, power play forgotten. She stopped the lab tech from chopping off the crab's tail by smacking the lopper with the tablet.

"Change the policy by the time I'm done returning this crab to its natural habitat," she told the manager, handing him back his tablet. He had followed her down the stairs. "You will put all the drained crabs back. Alive. Is that understood?"

"Yes, ma'am," he said, shoulders rounded inside his tweed blazer. Obedient. Beaten and a little dazed.

Genna picked the behemoth crab up. She felt her magic. Old. Timeless like the Atlantic Ocean. The crab was surprisingly heavy. The weird shape focused all of the pressure to her fingers. The briny stink of it. The wiggle of her ten legs. The heavy thunk of her tail against her thighs. The crab dribbled stinking seawater down her Valentino suit. Genna awkwardly carried her to through the narrow channel between crabs, the blue bottles of their blood, the carts, and equipment. Past the holding tanks. Over the enormous dumping ground whose stench was practically solid. She sidled through doorways held open by staring staff.

No one stopped her. No one helped her, either. Though a few did film her with their phones.

"Yes, I'm saving the crabs." She could not think of anything wittier to say.

She lost a shoe when she stepped onto the sandy shore.

The crab flipped on her back when Genna half-dropped, half-set her in shallow water. Genna wrestled her right-side up, yelling, "Don't die on me, you big bitch. You're gonna live, goddammit. Lay eggs. You have to repopulate the whole goddamn species. Come on!"

She dragged the damn monster crab into shoulder-deep water. Saltwater went up her nose. Wave after wave pushed her back to shore. She slipped on sea algae and rocks. Her hairstyle destroyed. Her Valentino suit was destroyed. Her second Manolo heel clung to her foot by suction alone.

Finally, the crab started swimming. Genna floundered her way back to shore. Exhausted, pissed off, and exhilarated. Her hair hung like black seaweed to her face and dripped down her clothes. The silk blouse was now see-through. The men holding the factory door for her openly stared at her black La Perla bra and waist cincher. Angrily, she buttoned her blazer. There was seaweed tangled in her Buccellati silver ruby necklace. She pretended not to feel the water seeped out of her Bvlgari triple-row steel-chain and black-leather watch. One of her stud ruby earrings was missing.

The adrenaline was short-lived as she looked at the dumping ground again. How many dead shells were stacked on top of each other? The sheer waste of it.

She was hellfire mad by the time she stomped barefoot and shivering into the CEO's office. She ignored the wittering administrative assistant.

The senior floor manager would not stop looking at her breasts. He was one of those big guys who liked to crowd women's space and pinch any available skin. He thought lewd comments were part of doing business. He was a big man and used to getting his way. His ponderous size, nearly as wide as he was tall, was usually all of the intimidation he needed.

Genna loathed the senior floor manager. It was nice to finally have an excuse to break him.

"I read your email," she snarled as she backed the manager up against the wall of the CEO's office. "I decided to stop by for a little visit."

She imagined carving a path through the swell of his belly, wrenching out his purple intestines, digging through the fat to get under his rib cage, and clawing out his lungs. Not his heart. No. She wanted to watch him suffocate on his own self-importance. He would stare down at her with bulged eyes. His thick double chin would wobbled as it mottled from red to purple. His lips would turn blue. The slobbering gasps of his punctured lungs would sound like wet balloons.

The only reason she hadn't eaten him alive was that he was on her payroll.

CEO huddled in his chair trying not attract her attention.

Genna did not shout, because ladies did not shout. Ladies let their voices get cold and hard, and sleeted disappointment down on them. Now was the hailstorm of her discontent. The executive wing all had hypothermia.

"I told you not to drain all of the blood from the crabs. I told you that twenty to thirty percent was all we needed to reach our quota from the FDA. You keep draining them dry, at this rate, there won't *be* any more crabs left. That's why I moved the farm. That's why I bought the shoreline and got it federally protected. The crabs need a spawning ground but also enough crabs to spawn with. Why didn't you listen?"

Staring silence. Genna dripped on the carpet. She pivoted. The CEO flinched as she pointed at the wall behind him. "I'm taking the bowling ball."

It was not actually a bowling ball. It was an enormous blue boulder opal with a fossilized horseshoe crab inside of it. The faceted blue stone made the crab seem to float inside a blue bubble.

"Now, wait a minute," the CEO said, galvanized by indignation. "You can't do that."

"This is my company. I can do whatever I want." Genna prowled over to his side of the desk. It smelled like cum and aftershave. She leaned into his personal space. Her lip curled in a frosty sneer. "Your incompetence disgusts me. Do better. Or I will come back and do much worse."

He stared up at her, swallowing hard enough that his necktie bounced.

Genna picked the boulder opal up and walked out.

The floor manager was still against the wall. Genna was proud she had not kneed him in his sagging balls.

Later, she would wonder how she managed to carry the incredibly dense opal. At the time, it felt barely heavier than a watermelon.

That was the thing about rage. Sometimes she could move mountains, or stuff one-of-a-kind fossils into her Hermès Birkin bag. It barely fit, but the handles of the bag did not tear off.

Fourteen

GENNA STOOD IN A FIELD OF SUNFLOWERS. SHE watched a black and yellow finch pick seeds from the dried center of a wilted flower. The bird blended in so well that its movements were a shock. As if another flower had gone rogue and started eating the others on the stalk.

According to her research, this sunflower field was where her great-grandmother's mansion had been. Genna could not find any stone markers of a foundation. All had been ripped up. Genna had paid a few contractors to find records to cross reference the starting point of the wild fires.

Genna was good at tracing her family histories. It was nice to be good at something. She had worried that she was basically useless outside of the castle grounds.

Out in the real world, she picked fights with boardrooms and CEOs. She did not have the temperament for politics. The wolf would get close to the surface. Instilling raw animal fear in her employees was not a good motivator. Katie liked to show up and disappear anyone who pissed her off. It was better to stay among the archives.

The family enjoyed Genna's yearly red leather-bound tome with some part of their history, complete with pictures. She revitalized jewelry. Restored art. Reupholstered furniture. Refurbished fur coats. Everyone wanted professionally framed and illuminated pictures to proudly display in their Good Rooms. They wanted to know their history. They were eager to ask what other interesting goodies she found.

It took a while to parse through the respectability politics in the family archives. Her great-grandmother's story was always about the tragedy of her death, never about her life.

Great-Grandmother had been the weird one. Ferociously independent. But Genna found herself sympathetic.

It was 1620 the first time the gold dried up. Genna's ancestors told their backers in Europe that it was witchcraft. They tried four local root women and one man as witches. The gold came back. In abundance.

Genna found evidence that the witch trials never stopped. It became a way to systematically kill off anyone who might organize against the gold mine and destabilize local politics. Desperation, turmoil, changing politics, declining fortunes, nepotism, and two centuries of festering corruption turned the area into a powder keg. Those that stayed at the gold mine were caught in the country's revolution.

Great-Grandmother was born when the gold mine officially dried up in the late 1880s. The gold nuggets she had were part of her rock collection as a child.

The family fled to North America and to Europe. Since the Great Chicago Fire in 1871 had destroyed their successful horse-and-buggy business and several smaller incidents had failed, the family moved to their coal mine in Bonanza, Arkansas. Great-Grandmother was twenty-four when the family was embroiled in the race-war of 1904 and fled from Bonanza as well. She lost her first husband, and both children. She was the only survivor.

During her escape she was stopped by a storm that flooded the rivers and the roads. She stayed at the Arkansas diamond mine that her family owned. She sold her shares to get enough money to bribe her way through the Underground Railroad.

Great-Grandmother found a large forty-two carat pure diamond laying on the surface of the mine, pushed up by the rainfall. It looked like an ordinary rock. She knew better. According to the records, 'diamonds littered the muddy fields like flowers waiting to be plucked.' She gathered diamonds in her purse.

She kept them for security in case she was stopped on her travels again. She painted the rocks a brick red so no one thought they were anything but rubble.

Her uncle, a buffalo solider known for his ability to ride, helped the family get safely North via the Underground Railroad.

She made it to Martha's Vineyard where she met and married a local man the family did not approve of. His family owned a laundromat in Oak Bluff by the Inkwell, the beach where Black people still frequented. Great-Grandmother scandalized the family by leaving them to go back South, which everyone believed was a death sentence. She and her husband started a logging company in North Carolina to supply wood for boats after a gold mine they bought turned out to be exhausted. They had more success in logging than in the silver mining. They reestablished old ties to the European elite she had known as a child. Everyone needed wood to build boats.

The rest of the family moved North or West. They went to New York City, where they were avid collectors and patrons of the Arts during the Harlem Renaissance. They bought silver and gold mines. They were horse wranglers. They owned railroads, trains, and steel plants. They went to Tulsa, sinking a lot of money in Black Wallstreet. They knew mines, and there were plenty of coal mines in the Appalachian mountains.

The family chose businesses that were isolated enough to not be picky about skin color as long as they had money. They were light skinned and often mistaken as White. They stayed away from the South, cotton, and gemstones.

Great-Grandmother kept the gold nuggets and uncut diamonds in her purse everywhere she went. That purse was used as a bludgeon more than once. Some of the diamonds went to purchasing the logging company and other deals.

Finally, to celebrate when her first grandchild, Genna's mother, was born, she turned the remaining gold and stones into a ring.

Her diamond was so big, that it looked fake. It had a yellow-brown metallic sheen which was common among the diamonds from the Arkansas mine. It was called a champagne diamond. Also it was a type two, incredibly rare stone.

But Great-Grandmother made a mistake in trusting a local jeweler to make her ring.

Genna rubbed her sternum as she walked through the rows of sunflowers. She frowned at the photocopy of a found letter written from the jeweler's wife to her sister who lived on Roanoke Island. It was the primary resource Genna used to triangulate the correct location of Great-Grandmother's mansion but it was painful to read.

According to the letter, the jeweler's wife embellished Great-Grandmother's already extravagant design because she planned on wearing the ring herself. She was so confident that she used a selection of her own favorite diamonds to form a halo around the big yellow centerpiece.

The jeweler's wife bragged that the gold band was so thick that her husband had room to add little flourishes and motifs. There was so much pure gold to work with that there was no need to mix it with other alloys. How wonderful that she and Great-Grandmother were the same ring size. She told her husband to agree to everything Great-Grandmother wanted and prioritize its creation over his other work. With a diamond like this, the wife was certain that the mansion had a cellar full of treasure.

She invited her sister and her whole family to join the picnic. There was the date and time and directions. Uppity folk needed to learn a hard lesson in respect and their place in this world.

In the middle of a hot October day, roughly a month after the letter was written, a posse came to the mansion with torches and glass bottles full of moonshine. It had been a long summer full of drought that stretched into a dry autumn. All of the windows and doors in the mansion were open, hoping to catch a nonexistent breeze. The sunflowers were no longer a field of sunshine yellow, only desiccated brown stalks.

Great-Grandmother stood in the large picture window as her enemies crested the hill. According to the family diaries, there had already been rumors. Side comments in town indicated a dangerous sea change in the ambient currents of micro-aggressions and everyday racism. The family argued about where to run. How much to pack. Who to trust.

Great-Grandmother could have run. She had lost her second husband to tuberculosis that previous winter. He was buried in the sunflowers. Her children were alive and married with their own children to worry about. She had plenty to live for. She knew how to run better than anyone. Instead she took off her new ring and gave it to her firstborn daughter.

"Never forget," she said.

The first thrown bottle broke the glass of the picture window and hit her in the chest.

Everyone in her family made it down to the river. They set fire to the boats as they escaped. The drought-dry fields burned fast. The wildfire swept across the logging business.

Only her family survived because of her sacrifice. Not the people with their bottles of moonshine. Not the jeweler or his wife. Not the businessman who wanted the logging business for himself or paid bullyboys and firemen who knew where to throw a molotov cocktail to burn a house the most efficiently. Not the town, neighboring towns, or the hundreds of hectares of farmland and forest. The fire reached all the way to Roanoke Island.

In those days, all that could be done was get to the nearest body of water and pray for rain.

No rain came. Only a warm breeze to push the fire farther along.

The family sailed one of their own boats all the way up to Oak

Bluffs, Martha's Vineyard. The family stayed. Rebuilt. Made connections with the Black elite of the Mid-Atlantic and Northeast. They kept moving. They embedded themselves in the Harlem Renaissance.

In 1924, the Uncle Sam diamond was found in the same Arkansas mine. It was the largest and chemically purest diamond ever to be found in North America. The Uncle Sam diamond was two carats smaller than the family stone but they stayed quiet. They did not forget.

This forgotten field and the surrounding area had never been redeveloped. Every time someone tried, it inevitably burnt down or had a landslide. Nothing grew but wild sunflowers.

Other branches of the family had also run into difficulty.

The family that went West lost their fortunes in Black Wallstreet due to the Tulsa Massacre. The silver mines collapsed and ran dry. Their railroads had rebellions. Their banks were robbed. Great-Grandmother's now elderly cowboy uncle died getting the survivors through the Underground Railroad. Tragedy, strife, illness, and racism plagued every ancestor.

Genna folded the letter back into the portfolio. She trudged towards her waiting car. She tried not to glare at her White assistants and the local historians. Her anger felt like heartburn. There was nothing to do but remember.

The smell of desiccated growth lingered in her nostrils even after she climbed into the SUV and drove away. She passed the scratchy stalks of dead sunflowers. It was easy to imagine the field awash in orange flames and white-gray smoke.

She traced the ring with her thumb, staring at it. The ring was a nexus of so much death. Genna had always wondered why the big ring was never cut down to a more conventional size. The ring was at odds with its message. Now she understood why. The ring fit Genna's great-grandmother's defiantly ostentatious personality. She never backed down. She never changed herself to fit in with other people's standards.

Genna shuffled through her portfolio to a stack of page sized portraits. Teenaged Genna in her white debutant ballgown wearing the ring. The photographer had taken many pictures to catch the ring's sparkle. She had been so proud to wear it. Afraid to lose it. Afraid to wear it. Her mother was photographed in her debutant gown. Her grandmother in hers. All wore the same ring on their gloved finger.

She flipped to the last picture. Great-Grandmother was a regal woman who did not smile in her portraits, instead she glared at the viewer. Her presence burned through, undaunted by age, an abundance of lace, and an ugly floral hat squashed on top of her piled hair. Genna could absolutely believe she had been burned alive. She was a woman who apologized for nothing. She wore the same ring over her lace gloves that sat on Genna's finger now.

She was born a princess. She became a queen. America's narrow view of her ethnicity could not break her self-worth.

Genna was eager to get back on her Falcon and get away from the sunflower field. To watch the land dwindle under its wings. She was scheduled to go to Diamond State Park in Arkansas. It had once been the diamond mine. She went but skipped the tour. She merely stood, her ring turned so the stone was hidden inside her palm as she slid her fingers into the ground like the other tourists industriously digging in the dirt. Everyone hoped to find a diamond.

It was surreal to know that once upon a time, her family had owned this place. Little was left of the gold, silver, and coal mines but ruins and holes in the ground.

What was strength? What was freedom?

There were a lot of uncomfortable similarities between Genna and the family accounts of her great-grandmother. What kind of person stood firm when the enemy charged her home? Was Genna the kind of person who would die protecting her castle?

No, she was the type who ran away.

Genna found a diamond at the Arkansas mine. It turned out to be twenty carats. She had to bribe the authenticator to shut up about it. She took it to her own jeweler to have it cut.

"Do you want it set into a ring?" The jeweler asked.

"A stud earring," Genna said, spontaneously.

"That's one big earring."

She nodded but did not change her mind, trusting her instincts.

She flew back to the castle.

That night Genna dreamed of a regal Black lady on fire and screaming.

The lady fought to stay standing, her back was unbowed, and her posture was perfect even while her floral hat and the pomade in her hair turned the top of her head into a terrible orange crown. Her dress was smoke and flames. The lace decorations was a lattice of lightning around her neck, breasts, waist, and wrists.

She did not break eye contact with Genna even as she screamed. Her eyes boiled in their sockets. Lightning for her eyelashes, eyebrows, and sparking from her nostrils. Her lips peeled away from her teeth. The grease of her makeup bubbled flesh off of her jaw.

Genna tried to call her name but the smoke filled her throat. She reached out to take her hand, to heal, to do something other than watch, to bear witness. Genna wanted her to live. She loved her. She wanted her to be free from the flames. Genna wept but the lady had no time for tears. She boiled them off of Genna's skin.

Their fingers threaded together. The fire leapt eagerly into Genna. It hurt which was a shock. Fire usually recognized her skin. She and the lady did not look away from each other. Pressure built in Genna's chest. The same burn. The same fury. The flames were her flames. The fury was her fury. Magma was in Genna's veins. It pushed at her skin, erupting out of her pores while smoke clouded her vision. Lightning was in her hair as Genna howled her rage and sorrow. She ran, as fast as wildfire. Her wrath spread across a field of sunflowers, devouring the land, sucking it dry of everything. Devouring their enemies.

The lady did not become ash. Instead she became pure orange flame. Unrecognizable. Simply flame. Then gone.

Genna ran on. Carrying the fire through a tinder dry sunflowers. Howling. Roaring. Flaming. Wild with grief and rage.

Genna jerked awake. She looked around her bedroom. The ordinary pre-dawn gloom slopped the cold sludge of reality over the dream. There was no fire. Only cold stone. The only odd thing was being in wolf form. Her body was slick with sweat. Her sheets were kicked off.

She got up. She shook herself off to break the tension. She transformed into a human. She lay back in bed, staring at the ceiling, rubbing the diamond face of her great-grandmother's ring.

Fifteen

Genna knew there was trouble as soon as she walked into the Grand Concourse private dining room. Not even a carafe of water was on the round table. Only her parents and a brown skinned woman with pressed hair and a gray no-name-brand suit. They wore silk face masks. An empty beige padded chair was strategically set between her parents and the stranger.

"What is this?" Genna said.

"Please sit down," her mother said with a tone that was pleasantly sunny with a forecast of a thunderstorm if Genna did not mind her manners.

Genna had used her Glamazon team to dress nicely for a lunch with her parents as one might wrap their hands before putting on boxing gloves. The good diamonds. The perfect turquoise and white linen Gucci suit. The lack of food told her the preparation had not been enough. She had brought a knife to a gun fight.

Genna sat down. The unfamiliar woman's tar black eyes watched from inside a mask of pleasant professionalism. She was dangerous. What had her parents gotten into now?

"We have decided to employ a matchmaker," her mother said. "For you."

"Why?" Genna said.

"We only want what's best for you, Iphigenia," her father said.

"As long as that includes marriage and children."

"You've had plenty of time to sow wild oats," her mother said. "It's time to settle down. You're not getting any younger."

"Yes, I'm the doddering age of thirty. It's amazing that I still have any teeth." Genna seethed. "I have work to do."

"Your siblings are all married," her father said. "Your sister has two children. Your brother is waiting until after he and his wife both graduate from medical school. Didn't you catch the bouquet at all their weddings?"

"They threw them at me." Genna had batted the last bouquet at her baby brother's reception so hard that it exploded in a fountain of pink rose petals. "I have companies to run."

"Your companies run better without your interference." her mother said.

"That is not true!"

"Unilaterally." The gloves were off. The claws out.

"I'm sorry, honey, but you don't have a head for business or medicine," her father said.

"You told me that I didn't need to be a doctor."

"Yes, your brother is doing very well," her mother said.

Much depended on birth order. And gender. There was nothing like being compared to her younger brother. The first-born son. The third born child. Genna despised how he got things she didn't even know were options. She wasn't bitter. Not at all. Fighting to be taken seriously honed her to a sharp edge.

Worse they had done this in front of an audience, appealing to the matchmaker for help.

"You see? She's got a good heart," her father said. "She means well but she keeps telling people the truth."

"Why are you talking to her and not me?" Genna said.

"We've had this conversation a dozen times," her mother said. "You can't bully the executive team of your own company and expect them to perform."

"If I was a man—"

"You're not," her mother said. "You're a lady. Ladies do not swim in the ocean fully clothed, storm into offices, knee the CEO in the balls, and steal rare gemstones like a pirate."

"I wasn't swimming. I was reintroducing a horseshoe crab back into the water. It wasn't the CEO. I didn't knee anyone."

"Iphigenia!" Her mother said.

Outrage. Humiliation. "They were killing the crabs," she said sulkily.

"You can't be a social justice warrior and run a good business at the same time," her father said. "This is why you have your fundraisers and crab farms."

"Yeah, but it's like raising cows for slaughter, not actually changing anything."

"The Pandemic has required that we all make allowances," her mother said.

"Allowances? Horseshoe crabs have been around for 450 million years, but the second we figure out that their blood is good for medical testing, we're headed straight towards extinction. At the rate that we're draining crabs there won't be any of them left in fifty years. That's how I got the funding and the federally protected spawning ground in the first place."

"The crab farm is still your most successful business. Besides the prisons." Her father wrinkled his nose. "I can't believe my daughter owns prisons."

"I needed money because you said yes to the wrong people. I've had to work twice as hard to bring real change to make sure the right people are incarcerated."

"You've used your prisons to arrest people you find personally offensive," her father said dryly.

"Like the medical team that was sterilizing Black and Brown women in our hospitals?" Genna said sarcastically. "You know, the ones I found, told you about, and nothing happened?"

"We were dealing with it," her father said. "A hospital and its staff is a delicate ecosystem. With the dropout rate we needed all hands on deck."

"You're allowing evil to exist."

"You're taking things too far," her mother said. "That free hospital you've made on castle property is questionable at best and illegal at worst."

"It's not a free hospital. It's a safe space."

"You should've told me what you were doing," her father said.

"It's not a hospital, Dad. They're doctors and nurses who burned out during the Pandemic. It's more of a shelter for traumatized professionals who couldn't handle all the death. I asked them to ride my horses, walk my dogs, and socialize my cats. That turned into working the bee hives, the gardens, and the lake. They pay their rent on time. They go to work. Come back. Everybody's happy and my pets aren't neglected. It's profitable."

The speech was broadly true. The free not-a-hospital had been Miss Bootsie's idea.

Not every renter was a doctor with a medical degree. A lot of them had some form of magic that made it hard to exist anywhere but in Sweetwater. Sometimes a person who made it to the pasture had nowhere to go back to. Genna gave them a place to stay. There was plenty of space.

Miss Bootsie had smiled. "That's real nice of you to let them stay, honey child."

Then there were other renters. They were people were a part of Miss Bootsie's social network. Some called themselves witches, or prayer warriors, or ignored any question that required identification.

They were a part of the forest. They did not interact with Genna. Even after Miss Bootsie's death. They paid their rent on time. The nine mansions kept their dramas to themselves. The plants grew well. Most of Genna's diet was grown right on the property.

Then in the bad early COVID days, Genna had been desperate to do something, anything, good. She was surrounded by an ocean of the dying. The political upheaval. All of it was too much. She focused on achievable goals.

Who could she help in Sweetwater?

To give back to the community. All she did was expand her safe haven. She focused on the healthcare and service industry professionals who were on forced isolation. It expanded to people who lost their jobs. Single mothers. Women and children escaping untenable situations. Older folk too spry and rightly terrified of nursing homes but with no family either. The stunned newly orphaned or widowed or childless. Helping those people got her out of bed. Caring for the horses. The animals. The people who needed her.

Sweetwater's magic did not make people immune to hatred. The medical staff had plenty of people who needed care who couldn't afford to pay. There was seemingly no end to the need.

"You still should've told me," her father said, "I know a few people who need a place like this."

"Send them my way."

Genna had a few other safe havens. She had quietly taken over a few towns. Poured money into the community. Invested in properties. But only people with magic lived and worked in the castle grounds. Otherwise the woods ate them or changed them into something.

"Ehem," the matchmaker cleared her throat.

"No one's talking to you," Genna said, sneering at the woman. "You're not wanted and not needed."

"Iphigenia, you will apologize to Miss Tituba right now!"

Genna raised her eyebrows, incredulous. "Tituba? As in *Tituba, the first person to be tried as a witch in the Salem Witch Trials?*"

"Oh, you have heard of me," Tituba said, taking off her face mask. "Good. That makes this easier."

Power, heavy and old, hit Genna between the eyes and across the back of her neck like a slap. The air was ponderously heavy. Genna choked on the stench of old blood, a leather tanning factory, and rusty metal. It felt like sitting under a mountain range made of dead bodies. She sat back, inhaling.

Genna's parents went still. Their skin was waxen. Their bodies listed slightly back. Their glassy gaze focused on the ceiling.

Genna glared at Tituba. "What'd you do to them?"

"As far as they're concerned, we're getting to know each other in a civilized fashion."

Genna did not believe a word of this, but the power was real. She was so damn tired of her parents being enchanted. "Release my parents."

"No harm will come to them as long as you give me the respect that I am owed as your elder."

"It takes respect to get respect."

Power tried to slap her again. This time, it glanced off, reflecting back at Tituba.

The ancient witch inclined her head. The barest flex of an eyebrow. A slight firming of the lip. "I can see that Miss Bootsie taught you well. You wear her cloak lightly but with respect. She was part of my circle. She is missed."

"Prove it."

"You saw me the night she was attacked. I was the black bear."

"That doesn't prove anything. Tell me the truth. Why are you here?"

"My circle and I sponsor young ladies and gentleman to the Talented Tenth. We facilitate matches with other young Black elite, preserving their family legacy and magical power. Given your abilities and your failure to blend in with human society as a whole, you need our skill set for your preservation."

"You're matchmakers for the Talented Tenth."

"That is what we call those among us Night Skins who have magic and refinement."

"The Talented Tenth is an exploitative myth created by W. E. B. Dubois and Booker T. Washington to further stratify the Black community."

"That doesn't make it any less real. Or necessary for the preservation and advancement of Colored people."

"It's a skewed lens. What about the Guiding Hundredth? That was more inclusive."

Tituba clicked her tongue against the roof of her mouth dismissively. "The Black community needs leaders."

"The Talented Tenth is a bad thing!"

"What do you know of bad? You, who were born with a silver spoon in your mouth?"

"I know plenty and I will not apologize for who and what I am. Keep that elitist gaslighting garbage to yourself. I don't owe you or anyone anything."

"Of course you do. It's a waste of your time and talent and the money spent making you what you are if you don't pass on your gifts."

"Then I'm a waste of time," Genna said, the wolf slipping into her smile. "Find someone else to be your brood mare. It's not going to be me."

"Can't you see that's exactly what makes you a diamond of the first water?"

"Tell me something I don't know."

"You're going to die alone, badly, and soon if you keep this up." Tituba nodded at Genna's right hand. "Exactly as your great-grandmother did."

Genna raised her chin. "At least I'll die free and true to myself."

Tituba threaded her fingers together. "Ordinarily, this is the part where I get up and walk away. However, you have been fighting the McBrides and Pipsy Montgomery your whole life. I believed that Miss Bootsie did the majority of the work. I can see that was incorrect. She could not protect you. She could not teach you, either. I thought that you were Miss Bootsie's champion in the absence of her child Sable and granddaughter Naomi. She was trying to keep you from burning up her forest."

Genna pressed her lips together. There was no point denying it but she refused to agree either. She owed Tituba nothing.

"Your fight with the vampires is entirely separate. That began here." Tituba set three photos down side by side like cards in a tarot deck. Genna's birthday party. Her debutante ball. Her engagement party. "It has not changed since Miss Bootsie's death. Neither you nor Katie McBride are bound to the cottage. Yet you both protect it. Usually, vampires and werewolves don't get along so well."

It was not lost on Genna that the trans kid had shown her the exact same pictures. The forest had warned her and she missed it. Damn.

"I don't get along with Katie at all. If I had a mortal enemy, it'd be her."

"You haven't killed her yet."

"I have chosen not to."

Genna had realized that killing Katie would only breed more problems. Mimi was doable, but Genna had no idea how to kill an elder vampire. Now she was confronted with someone twice as old and a whole lot worse than Pipsy Montgomery.

Miss Bootsie had not been powerful. Not like Tituba. She was a hearth fire compared to a supernova. Tituba was a good witch determined to protect Black women. Miss Bootsie was a nice witch, willing to humor the whims of a lonely magical girl and a baby vampire. Good and nice were not the same.

Privately Genna wondered if she would be so different after four centuries of hardship and sacrifice. That only added to her unease.

"If you want to be free of the vampires, then you have to give them something they want," Tituba said.

"No, it doesn't work that way. They're like sharks. They fixate on their prey to the exclusion of everything else."

"And if you're wrong, Iphigenia? If you're the stand-in for a different talented Black American princess?"

Tituba set a fourth photograph down. A young, curvy

woman laying on her side, wearing kitten ears, a bell, fake paws and a smile. "This is Naomi York. Pipsy and Miss Bootsie's granddaughter. The heir to both legacies. How noble of you to protect Naomi, but it will not change her fate or yours. She is supposed to be in the woods. You cannot be free as long as you stand in her place. You are a coywolf, a hybrid. The independent spirit of a coyote. The love of family like a wolf. Give Naomi her cloak. It is her birthright. Then you will no longer be tied to the castle. Find love. Move on. Or do you like being hounded?"

"Abandon everything and join the Talented Tenth?"

"Your parents are desperate and scared for your safety. They believe that once you're married to someone else, you will be safe. The McBrides have not stopped targeting them. You need to be committed to someone else. You believe vampires can't change their minds, because you have been the object of Katie's desire these long years. Your narrow perspective is a byproduct of your isolation."

Tituba sounded like members of the Black community. The same ones that were impatient with self-exploration and loathed interracial marriage. They wanted pretty Black babies as if their race were on the brink of extinction. They told women trapped in abusive relationships to 'make it work' for the good of the family. Respectability politics. Blackness defined by someone else. Impossible standards Genna still tried to meet. Much as Genna loved Miss Bootsie, she had been one of those people. It was discouraging to know that long life had only reinforced the belief.

"The Talented Tenth is a cage," Genna said.

Tituba gave Genna a look. "How do you know when you've never met another Night Skin or anyone in the Talented Tenth?"

"A cage is still a cage."

"You are not a child. You know that you are a big fish in a little pond. You dream of the ocean and long to swim in its depths. You believe you are protecting people with your isolation. You are not."

Genna leaned forward, goaded. "And what happens to

everyone who isn't Black enough to fit into your ideals? What if they don't want to marry inside their race or opposite gender or get married at all? Or is everyone in your safe haven true believers happily wed and bed? Do you own their children? Their wealth? Do they get to leave? Or do you show up again when their progeny is of age to have similar conversations?"

"You know that you are special yet you scorn those who acknowledge your talents. You should be among your peers. Share your skills instead of being selfish."

"Selfish," Genna repeated flatly. Here it was. The demand to accept without questioning.

Tituba tented her fingers. She contemplated Genna. Quiet for a moment as though slotting her words into place. Or trying to hold onto her temper like Genna. "You have an abundance of virginal and sapphic power that only strengthens the longer you fight other women. Your name, Iphigenia, already channels bridal sacrifice. Your purity for another."

"Purity?" Genna wanted to spit but wasn't sure what an ancient witch could do with her saliva or how she would react to obvious disrespect. Her parents were hostages. She needed to be careful.

"When was the last time you had sex, Iphigenia?"

"None of your business," Genna said, abandoning caution.

Tituba smiled thinly. Her face had been a mask that simulated expressions without saying anything. Now she took off that illusion.

Genna saw an ocean of black tar next to a limitless field of fluffy white cotton. There were Black women in boats trawling through the tar. They lifted nets filled with human bodies. They carried their haul to the plantation. Other women took those bodies, cleaned off the tar, then lay the bodies in neat rows. They planted a cotton seed in the chest cavity. Green tendrils grew out of bodies, stretching upwards. Leaves unfurled. The white puffy cotton inside popped out.

Women dressed in starched white picked the cotton from the

plants. They stepped delicately over legs and arms. Other women took the satchels of cotton. Hand spun it then loomed it into white fabrics. They sewed the fabric into dresses. They embroidered delicate patterns and wove lace. They tailored the dresses to fit smiling young Black women.

The young women in their white dresses danced and twirled on a wide square dance floor. They waved white feather and lace fans. There were diamonds and pearls and cowrie shells braided into their black curls. They danced with young smiling Black men in synchronized unison. They switched partners again and again. Then one Black man would get down on one knee, put a ring on a young woman's finger, they would kiss.

The young woman's dress transformed into a wedding gown. Her tiara grew a veil that covered her black hair and face. The newly weds walked sedately off the dance floor.

The image dissolved.

Genna remembered. "You made my debutant dress."

"Yes, I did," Tituba said. "I made your mother and grandmother's dresses too. They met successful matches."

Tituba set a fifth picture down. This one of Katie. She tapped on Katie's face. "The vampire keeps you preoccupied with hate so you can't fall in love, therefore becoming immune to her sway. Two wolves live in your heart, Iphigenia. You've starved love. You're consumed by hate. You attack anyone who even mentions marriage, because Katie has trained you to spurn the advances of anyone, thus giving her time to erode your defenses. Your every thought is about her, even when she's not there. Your hate is so strong that it is a kind of love. She is the only person in your life. The only person you have sex with, and when you do, it's hateful, toxic, and wild. You both tear into each other with all of your might. It's pure and it's vicious."

Genna wanted to throw up. "No. I haven't done that."

Tituba's thin eyebrows raised insultingly high. Not in disbelief but respect. Which was somehow worse. Genna did not want to impress the witch. "Ah, then you have better control than most. What about when you were young? Before the engagement. You were each other's first sexual partners."

"That was a long time ago. It doesn't matter."

"Ah, but it does. You are her ruler by which all others are measured. You are exceptional in all things. That is your nature. Black excellence is your life. Your own libido you view as a thing to be controlled, managed, and maintained. You deprive yourself of true passion. The delight of sex magic. It is a revolutionary magic. It can save you, but you have to allow yourself to be touched. You must let love in."

Genna stared down at the pictures. She had a rage headache. Tituba wasn't right. Except it made sense. Damning sense.

Years of fighting, working, shooting things on horseback. Bibi and Sneakers were chiseled warhorses. The castle was a fortress. The renovations included very archaic and lethal booby traps for all the glamoured and paid people who came in to rattle her cage. She was constantly on edge. Brittle. Unable to think of any real human connections with anyone. Battling alone. Locked inside her fortress. Never feeling safe. Waiting for the next fight. The next crisis. Unable to relax.

"I am not your enemy," Tituba said. "Neither are your parents. They want you to be happy. They worry that you've put all of this responsibility on yourself to protect the family. Who protects you?"

"They were compromised by the McBrides. I've done what I had to do to get us out. They'll always be weak to their influence. I have to triple-check to make sure things are fine."

"Is that what you believe?" Genna's father said. "That we're weak?"

Too late Genna saw the enchantment had eased. How long had that been? She stared at her parents. Their raw hurt. She tried to think of the right thing to say. "That's not what I meant."

Genna's mother got up, the chair screeching on the polished marble floor. She walked away quickly.

"We knew you were angry with us," her father said. "Family forgives."

Genna glared at her father. "Then why are you constantly trying to take my power away? I can't run a business? You have to get me married off to someone, anyone, and sit around being pregnant? Like that's all I'm worth to you? Why is it so hard to imagine that I don't want that? Why is that my only option or I'm a total disappointment? I'm not broken. I'm not besmirching the family honor. Why can't you leave me alone?"

He nodded gravely. "Very well, Iphigenia. We'll leave you alone. We love you very much. We're proud of you. We forgive you."

"I love you too, Dad. I don't love what you're doing."

He stood up. He nodded at Tituba as he buttoned his dinner jacket. "You are right. She is worthy of love and so much more. Please help my daughter."

Tituba nodded. "I will do what I can."

He walked out after his wife.

Genna squeezed her hands under the table. She was fine.

Tituba remained at the table. Genna tried to stay cool instead of glare. "I feel like there's something you're waiting to tell me."

"You are correct."

"Well, no time like the present."

"Your family's gold mine was where my home once was. Your people are why I was enslaved, sold, and taken away to what you call Massachusetts. You destroyed my culture with witch trials. Your people blamed the root women and men for the gold drying up. Those of us left cursed the gold. We cursed the men who destroyed our mothers and fathers and families. We wanted everyone to die, crushed under the weight of that gold. After Salem, I ran for a long time. I tried to disappear. I tried to go home, but all of the magic had been carved out of the land and my people. I am all that is left. You are the recipient of an imperialist tradition. All of your arrogance comes at the expense of more lives than you can count. Miss Bootsie has never lost her home.

She could forgive what you are. I do not. You will pay for what your people have done."

Tituba stood and smoothed the wrinkles of her suit as she looked down on Genna. "I wanted to see that ring. I wanted to see those deaths you carry. The weight of gold. As you traced the steps of your ancestors, so you woke their memories in your blood. It is good to see the fire never burned out. It is strange that it has become your strength."

"Then why are you my matchmaker?"

"Who but me understands a monster like you?"

She walked out.

Genna sat for a long time. Mind blank.

Sixteen

GENNA WALKED TO THE EDGE OF THE GRAND Concourse deck. *Stormy Weather* sung by Lena Horne played from the speakers in the ceiling. Humans sat at tables, stylish and conservatively dressed. They were focused on their business deals or unwinding from a long day of work with their favorite alcoholic beverage.

Yellow leaves were swept up into the air from the tree lined waterfront. They spun and danced along the Monongahela River. Past the bridges.

She could go home. Nothing to stop her but she was not ready to leave the Grand Concourse. It was easier to think about Tituba than confront the damage she had done to her family.

She felt scalded by her close encounter with the witch. Bigger and also smaller. Until now, she thought Pipsy was the worst monster. Genna had thought of herself as the hero in the story. Not the villain or the oppressive tyrant.

Was Tituba right? If so, what could be done about it? She needed to do a deep dive into her family history. This time from a different perspective.

Her thoughts drifted like mist over the river.

You have more control than most.

Did she? Self-control was the greatest challenge in human or wolf form. Genna did not think she had done anything special. Only kept herself alive and safe. She worked hard not to get caught.

Genna pushed away from the deck. The Grand Concourse had a great menu of seafood but she needed meatier game. She needed to hear something squeal. She needed to feel blood between her teeth.

Her Lamborghini Urus and the driver were waiting for her by the time she reached the front door. She leaned her head against the padded black leather seat, watching the city of Pittsburgh pass by through the tinted car window. She wished she had driven the Mustang. She needed something to occupy her thoughts. Now all she could do was sit and think for the long drive back to the castle.

She thought about sex. She thought about Katie. Genna was disgusted by her own hubris. This whole time she thought she was clever.

You are the ruler she measures all experiences against.

In Sweetwater, sex was everywhere in all of its forms. Adolescence was one giant obstacle course of navigating disaffected parents, downright predatory adults, other horny adolescents, and one's own hormones.

The death of innocence. Not everyone lost it at once. Some innocence drained away. Some bled out in little cuts until they learned to grow callouses. Some stayed protected. Others were kept in a state of immaturity by their parents or willful ignorance.

Mimi loved to devour the innocent. Katie's puberty was an open declaration of war. Mimi actively tried to eat her daughter and reclaim her youth. Sweetwater was their battleground. The McBride mansion parties reached a fevered pitch.

Genna's parents took her to the hospital to learn in excruciating detail the biological mechanics of procreation. They did not talk about pleasure. Only consequences.

Katie lost her virginity when her vaginal teeth came in. The McBrides' predatory approach to sex was a direct result of the way they fed. The teeth in their mouths were the secondary set. Draining prey through their sex organs during coitus was a fuller feeding.

Genna never went to the McBride parties. Terrible things happened to proud unpopular loners who went to parties without backup or loyal buddies. She did not have to go. The battle always spilled into the forest. Her classmates might ignore her at school but on clear full moon nights they ran for the castle which shone like a bone-white crown over the dark green forest. Survivors made it to her pasture.

Genna and her siblings stayed home. Katie had been warned not to touch her sister or brothers with a brutality even she respected.

Genna went to events with other Black elite kids sanctioned by their parents. She did not do anything there either. Too often the first thing a boy would tell her was how good of a father he would be.

Miss Bootsie was not helpful. "Practice abstinence. You are a princess. None are worthy. It is vital that you control yourself."

Glumly, Genna obeyed. Her parents said the same thing. Genna had everything to lose. Sweetwater had everything to gain.

"You can't always be good, you know," Katie said. "Aren't you hungry?"

Genna was hungry. Adolescence was hard. Hormones did not care about looks. No matter how much she hated Katie, she envied the vampire's ability to be as monstrous as she wanted to be. For Katie, consequences happened to other people. There was nothing Katie could do that the McBrides had not done worse, with more people, and with more malicious glee.

The hunger. As a child it had been manageable but now the need to eat and fuck and dominate were tangled together. People had changed into prey.

Genna got quieter and quieter, all of her focus was on keeping the wolf locked tight in her skin. She gained weight, over-eating to fill the void in her stomach. Her butt and thighs got big. Her boobs got heavy. Other well-endowed girls hunched. Genna's posture stayed straight. Her back and shoulders did not hurt. Her bones and joints stronger. It also meant that her generous abundance jutted forward. Boys looked. Everyone looked. Genna hated wearing clothes that were tight across her butt or exposed her sternum. Her mother taught her the value of tailoring.

"You are beautiful," her mother said. "It is a weapon. Don't hide it. Use it. Master it."

Genna got her own glam team for Christmas that year.

Genna spent more time at Miss Bootsie's cottage and the woods. She killed a lot of wild pigs and deer. Sometimes to eat. Sometimes to slack the bloodlust. Katie was there, killing and eating next to her. Often times it was the two of them alone. Miss Bootsie was at the stable taking care of Genna's younger siblings. They paid for Genna's eccentricities.

Genna and Katie sat on the pullout couch and watched Disney movies. They did their homework. They didn't talk about school. Or their home life. Katie needed a place her parents couldn't reach. Genna needed a place she could turn into a coywolf.

Miss Bootsie had enchanted Genna's skin so her family could not see her Turn or remember any strange magical incidents that happened. It was for their safety. Ignorance was bliss. Except for Genna it was lonely. The world already thought she was weird. The obligations and stress of finishing high school. The terror and excitement of going to college. How was she supposed to be a werewolf on campus?

Sex was easy. Choosing the right partner was hard. Genna might loathe being a good girl but she did not want to lose her virginity to some random and unworthy person. Also, she had a very real fear of eating her sex partner like Katie had. Abstinence was her only option. No matter how boring and difficult.

The hunger was not so easy to ignore.

Then Genna and Katie started to play a game. It began with a painting. They were studying Greek mythology. The story of

Prometheus and the Eagle held a particular fascination. Genna studied every version.

Her favorite was *The Torture of Prometheus* by Jean Louis Cesar Lair. The eagle crouched, eyes tracing the muscled contours of the titan's naked torso. The shackled arms and legs. The eagle had not struck. Not yet. Genna identified with the eagle's hunger. That frozen moment of anticipation. The hunger battling self-control. Willpower winning. Moment to moment.

She thought she was clever. Then Katie painted a full sized reproduction. Only instead of Prometheus, a naked version of herself was chained down.

Katie had an obsessive eye for detail about herself in suggestive but artistic forms. She loved to paint herself into classic arts. *Narcissus* by Carravagio. Herself as the woman with the octopus in the *Dream of a Fisherman's Wife* print by Katsushika Hokusai. Or drapery that implied nudity like the woman in *Flaming June* by Sir Frederic Leighton.

The mansion had many paintings, sketches, and drawings of Katie. Mimi attacked them, stabbing and clawing them, slacking her hatred. Donnie sold them or hung them in his office. Kyle masturbated to them. Pipsy critiqued them. She had no time for modern art. She tried to assassinate Andy Warhol. Those she deemed the best were allowed to be hung in the pool room. As of yet, none had made it past the foyer because Mimi happened to them.

Katie kept painting. Attention, good or bad, was attention. Katie had no intention or need to get a job. She had plenty of time to devote to art. Oil, acrylic, watercolor, charcoal, and other mediums. She tried everything. Loving the shape of her body. Every scale. Every strand of hair.

Katie had a permeant exhibition at the Sweetwater Art Gallery. The exhibition was received with a mixture of praise and discomfort since they were pornographic versions of her teenage self. Yet there was no refuting her genuine talent.

Genna went to the gallery because everyone did. She walked

among the paintings she had seen as sketches. The illumination and public exposure made it more real than at the mansion.

She stopped at Katie's reproduction of the *Torture of Prometheus*. She stared at the eagle, blushing with embarrassment.

Katie walked over, pretending to look at the painting. "I'll heal. You can't hurt me."

Genna stared at her. Until that moment she had been battling the smells of humanity and the noise. There were a thousand reasons to say no. They were both on their period. The copper tang of blood had been in Genna's nose all week. The ache of cramps was like a rusty saw slowly drawn across her bellybutton. The brittleness of her temper. The urge to hurt someone was closer to the surface and harder to ignore.

"We'll do it at the pole," Genna said.

"My thoughts exactly," Katie said.

There was pole in the forest where the shadows were always quieter and nothing grew but thin weeds. The pole stood slightly off kilter. It was thick and a little green from the mold growing in the woodgrain. A rusted ring on the top. It was easy to overlook. The pole had been where slaves, wives, husbands, and children were punished. Under the weeds were bones.

Miss Bootsie would never go near the glenn. She wouldn't talk about it or speak to Genna if she went there. But the silent treatment was not enough for Genna to stop going. She needed that quiet hateful place to pile her kills.

The part of her that always watched the world instead of participating whispered that this glenn was hers. She could do what she wanted here in the dark green shadows of the forest's heart. It was her place. And Katie's. If anyone did find it, Genna could eat them too. This place was for hunger. The forest fed on the excess blood and magic. Genna could howl and it never left the glenn.

This evil place fed on every toxic emotion steaming from her pores. Old ghosts woke and suckled on the perfume of arousal and violence. This was wrong. She knew it. She was bad. There was nothing funny or sexy about the blood soaked into the pole. The wood could be the sacrificial altar of some ancient god of war. It had fed on the pain in Black bodies. The innocent sent screaming into death. Those sent to the pole never walked out of the glenn again.

The ghosts recognized Katie. Her ancestors had been the ones holding the whip. They lapped at her blood like it was a rare and delicious vintage. Genna was happy to feed the ghosts.

Here she could allow herself to feel all the hatred she usually suppressed. To stop going high when everyone else happily went low. She made things worse when she tried to help her siblings survive the septic waters of private school.

She couldn't slaughter everyone in Sweetwater. She couldn't maul the girls with their nasty little comments. Or the boys who asked if she liked doing it doggy style. She couldn't make the wives treat her talented mother better. Or the men stop treating her brilliant father like tolerated staff. Her legacy and wealth was not a gift bestowed upon the Bellwethers by some benevolent White slave owner bequeathing the family plantation to his favorite bed wench. She could devour the people who thought that they were superior because they lacked melanin. The stupidity and arrogance of new money. The liars who got their wealth from narcotics or guns or war. They weren't worthy to even speak to her and yet they dared mock her family to her face.

She was better than them. A thousand times. No, a million times over. Yet still she had to let them laugh. To squeeze the family ring until her hand shook. To never forget.

The pole was Genna's chance to scrape the festering puss of hatred out of her heart. To cleanse herself with blood.

In a real way, Katie *was* Sweetwater. The McBrides had built the town. There wasn't a part of it immune to their influence. Katie was healed by Sweetwater.

The first time they played the game, Genna attacked without preamble. Katie screamed as Genna slashed open her belly and stuck her whole head into her chest cavity. Genna bit and ripped and ate. Katie tasted like the sweetest poison. Her meat was better than anything human or animal. Genna needed more, had to eat more. Gulping and slurping. Her fur slick with so much blood that it seeped into her ears. Her hand on Katie's throat. Her thumb and index-finger claws ripped open skin.

Genna ate until she was full. Then staggered into human shape and slumped panting on the tree stump by the pole. Her hands shook. Her front soaked. She watched Katie heal. The verdant green grass perfectly framed the swollen purple and oozing red meat. The pale peach-gold skin smoothed.

Genna blinked, drunk. She leaned her elbows on her knees. She licked the gore off her claws. She tried to reconcile with the calm that had settled into her body. Had she ever felt full before?

Katie stretched lethargically. "Mmhmmm, that was amazing. I knew you'd say yes. This is the best. You're the best. I love us. I love the way you make me feel. You have no idea how long I've wanted to ask. I've dreamed of this for so long."

Genna tried to form words beyond a growling, "Why?"

"I wanted to see you smile. I wanted to hear you laugh. I've never heard you laugh before."

Genna had laughed. A wild berserker cackle. She giggled as she flayed the meat off Katie's back, sucking on her fingers while her cheeks were distended. She chuckled as she snapped bones, lapped marrow, and belched blood. She howled with hateful jubilation.

Katie was her willing scratching post. Her chewtoy. Slashing Katie apart kept up the illusion that things were fine and helped Genna keep her mind clear.

"Aren't you worried that I'll eat you?"

"Then you'll have me in your heart forever. Sometimes I swear you're already a vampire. That's what we do to our brides." Katie smiled, a hand sliding between Genna's thighs to rub her crotch.

Genna grabbed her by the throat. She pinned her down with casual strength, growling. She was already halfway into the transformation. Katie grasped her wrist with both hands. Her blue eyes were luminous. Her mouth stretched into a lusty smile.

Genna stared down at Katie. Flames licked along her back and turned her eyes to orange coals. Smoke roiled in her fur.

Katie bit her lip. She wiggled suggestively under Genna. "This is a good look. I'm ready for round two. I could do this *forever*."

Genna squeezed as hard as she could. She fought temptation. The freedom to be a monster. To never have to think. Never smile. Never be a good girl. Only a wild hungry beast with no thought beyond the next meal. The ecstasy of violence.

There were consequences. Indulging Katie's whims always did but this time she provided an effective solution to a very real problem.

"I say, Prometheus, you come running," Genna said. "This is between us. No one else. Don't talk about it. Not to Pipsy or Mimi or anyone."

Katie lifted her hand. "Pinkie swear."

They locked pinkie fingers. A grim head nod. An unbreakable promise made. Playground rules.

They never got caught.

Miss Bootsie repaired their blood stained and ragged clothing. "Make sure you do a Clothed Turn *before* you go to the glen."

The Lamborghini bumped on a pothole. Genna blinked out of her reverie. The car purred its way out of the forest, past the security gate, and up to the castle. Genna got out. She thanked the driver. She walked into the castle to change into casual black on black t-shirt, leggings, and laced up her knee-high turquoise snakeskin Doc Marten boots. She washed her face. She tied her hair back and put on a black felt hat. A padded vest. A houndstooth scarf.

The pictures Tituba had given her and her business card were in Genna's purse. She put them in her vest pocket then walked through the garden, down the path, and entered the trail mouth. It was a long way to the glenn but she needed time to think.

Even though it made her cringe, she thought about the first

time she had sex with Katie. Right now it was the rainy beginning of autumn but the first time had been early summer. Genna had worn the same boots that day.

They had just graduated high school. Genna had worn her debutant dress and tiara to the graduation ceremony. The other girls in their filmy white summer dresses looked as if they had walked out on stage in their slips. The boys in their slicked hair, blue blazers, khaki slacks, and red ties were an equally forgettable background.

Genna glided like a queen across the stage. She was triumphant in her glory. She had dyed crimson highlights in her hair and pretended that it was the blood of her conquered enemies. She took her diploma then paused at the center of the stage to execute a flawless curtsy of the highest refinement to declare her independence from Sweetwater. Her sneer of disdain was replaced by beatific calm. Sweetwater had tried its best but could not break her. Only polish her to a diamond hard shine.

That photograph was Genna's favorite picture of herself. It was in her office. A reminder of victory. And also the last picture before she crossed a line.

Two weeks later, Genna had decided she wanted to lose her virginity before college. She wanted to be prepared. The temptation to turn the Prometheus game into full-blown monster sex was always there but now she was motivated.

Katie had taken her clothes off and hooked herself to the ring on the pole in that quiet glenn. She smiled at Genna over her shoulder, streamers of sunlight through her pink hair. The green of the forest around them. Birdsong. Rustling leaves. The breeze tickling the fine hair along Genna's forearms. The squelch of mud under the soles of her boots.

Genna put her backpack down on the tree stump. The heavy thump of tools inside.

Genna was hungry. Genna wanted to hurt Katie. A lot. All the time. But the need had moved down her belly. Her crotch throbbed. She could not remember why she was not having sex.

Katie was right here. Constantly hinting or outright demanding they have sex. To not be afraid of her own arousal.

"You've gone quiet," Katie said.

Genna's eyes traveled up the curve of Katie's calves. They were long and muscled from advanced point ballet. Usually she simply pounced but this time she paced forward. Her fingers traced skin. Katie stiffened and shivered. Every movement was confident and easy. As if Genna had touched someone with desire a thousand times before.

"Iffy?" Katie said, her voice tight.

"This is a dangerous game we're playing, Katie."

A pink flush slid along Katie's neck and down her back like spilled cherry koolaid. Her legs shifting from side to side. Her eagerness mixed with something else. Fear.

"I know," Katie said.

A handful of hair turned into a tight fist. Genna slowly pulled Katie's head backwards. She could be gentle now. Soon she wouldn't have to be. "You want to do it anyway. You think it's funny? All that pain and torture. You can hear them, can't you?"

Katie's blush pooled across her sternum. Along her ribcage. "I want this. I want to feel it. Take me, Iffy. I'm your slave."

The whine of mosquitos. The heavy green heat of summer. Cicadas in the trees and the brush. The rest of the world far away. Her heartbeat chugged slow. The wind like a hot breath along her biceps, her stomach, her belly, and lower. Her teeth changed shape and strained her gums. She snuffled the creases of Katie's sex, her buttocks, the back of her knees.

Katie tugged on the metal rung. "Iffy."

She stilled as Genna shushed her and kissed her naked hip. Genna had not kissed her. Ever.

Instead of rushing Genna slowed her movements. She pressed against Katie, fully clothed against her nakedness. She growled, soft and velvety. Katie inhaled sharply.

"I'm going to bite your skin open," Genna said, her lips soft against the crest of her ear. "I'm going to make you bleed. I'm going to make you scream. I'm going to fuck you and eat you and rip you and tear you. Tell me no. Tell me to stop. Tell me you don't want this."

Katie moaned. Her eyes fluttering.

"Tell me, Katie. Tell me you don't want this. Tell me to stop. I'll go back to our regular game. What would your mother say if she knew I was fucking you?"

Genna massaged Katie's hips. Her buttocks pert and round. Not big like Genna's, but handfuls to squeeze and spread. The diamond in her bellybutton ring was big enough to pluck and tug. Her skin soft and surprisingly dense with muscle. Katie pressed her butt into Genna's crotch.

Genna's claws extended and traced the pillowy flesh of Katie's breasts. A different shape and weight than her own. She pinched nipples that were long and pink-brown eraser points. "Is this what you want? I could rip them off."

Katie gasped and shivered. Venomous drool slopped along her chin. The warm patter on the back of Genna's wrist. A brief pinch on a nipple, traveling up the sternum, the throat, and settling on the base of the jaw. Katie bowed back, her hair a bounty of pink cotton candy, soft and filling Genna's gaze.

"Answer me," Genna commanded. "Is this what you want? A vampire and a werewolf. They'll be able to smell it. We're breaking the rules."

Katie rubbed her head against Genna's shoulder, licked her neck. She tried to bite but Genna moved fast, wrenched her neck back. Katie's teeth were bright white in the sunlight. Her lusty moan at the strength of Genna's grip on her hair.

"Or do you tell them that we've been having sex this whole time? Lying to them."

"Yes," Katie hissed.

"Are you seducing me, Katie?"

"Trying but it's hard. So hard."

Genna slid her hand along Katie's smooth waxed vulva, no barrier of nether curls to hide her pink labia and protruding clitoris. Genna licked her fingers and rubbed. Her claws cut and pinched. The wet of blood mixed with saliva. Knowing it hurt. Wanting it to hurt. Knowing Katie wanted that edge of pain too.

Katie hummed and sighed, "Yes, Iffy, yes."

Katie liked pain. Processing it. Not fighting against it. Riding it. Focused entirely on her body. Leaning into every sensation.

Genna felt the edge of teeth scrape along her fingertips.

"Don't bite me," Genna whispered in Katie's ear. "You keep that vagina dentata to yourself or I'll stop. I'm not one of your bitches."

"Iffy, don't stop." Katie wiggled and moaned as Genna pulled her hand out.

"I'm not going to play with you if you don't listen," Genna said, tracing her wet claws along Katie's lips. "Control yourself. Keep your vag teeth sheathed. Be good."

"I'll be good." Katie's voice was reedy with need.

"Be good."

"Please. Please. Please." Katie's breath hitched, her shoulders strained. The metal rung clanged as she pulled on it.

Genna stepped closer. Slid her thumb into Katie's mouth. She traced the claw along her tongue. Scraped the edge of her gum. Watched Katie suck it, head bobbing like it was a penis. Tongue sliding. Increased suction. "Don't bite me."

The other hand on Katie's throat spread down her belly. Tweaked her clitoris and slid inside more firmly.

"Don't bite me."

Katie squirmed. Panted wetly as Genna yanked her thumb out. Her fingers moved to Katie's throat, squeezing tighter. Her claws sinking into the arteries. Her teeth clamped into Katie's shoulder. Genna closed her eyes, letting touch rule. Her tongue lapped at the blood spilling warm into her mouth. She growled and slurped and gulped. The smell of Katie, of blood, and old creaking wood. Genna's hand pumping harder, slapping her clitoris. Her hips thrusting, shoving Katie into the pole. The wood creaked. The metal clanged.

Then Genna wrenched away. Katie whimpered, twisting. "Iffy, no!"

Then gasped as Genna reached into her backpack. Katie's eyes rounded at the long metal dildo. "I want to fuck you, Katie. And eat you. Both. Maybe at the same time."

Genna buckled the leather strap-on harness across her thighs and her belly. She cinched them tight. Enjoying the constriction under her butt cheeks. The pressure and weight of the long metal dildo as she fit it into its holster. Its metal was bright silver like a polished sword. Genna squirted lube on the dildo. Rubbed it and smirked. She allowed herself a small piratical smile of smoldering dominance. Thrust into her own hand.

"Say no and I won't. You can tell me no."

"I want to touch you too," Katie said, nostrils flared. Eyes dilated.

"No, I don't want that. You have to suffer." So what if Katie smelled her desire? It wasn't about her. She had said yes.

"I'm going to do what I want to you. Say yes."

"Yes, Iffy. Anything you want." Katie whimpered. Her thighs rubbed together. Masturbating against the pole. "Fuck me."

Genna prowled forward. Growling. Katie spread her legs. Whimpering. Genna pushed the dildo's wide head past Katie's swollen pink-brown labia. She watched in fascination as Katie's body spread to accept the dildo's girth. Finding the right angle. Going slowly to find a sustainable position to push it in up to the hilt.

Katie moaned. "You're inside me. Filling me up."

Mechanical words. Straight from a bad porno. But Genna growled with delight. "I made this for you."

"You did?"

"It's slightly curved and longer than the average vagina can accommodate. I want to hit your cervix and g-spot. I wanted the pain and pleasure to be intertwined. Tell me when I do."

"You are. You are! You made this for me! Iffy, love you!"

Genna changed the position. Clenched her fist. Pumped her

hips. Gained confidence. Their breaths harsher, faster, goading each other on. Katie's head arched back against Genna's shoulder. Her gasps became higher pitched, edged in a pleading whine. She lifted her leg up, hooking Genna's hip, standing balanced on tiptoe, offering more access to her crotch, more flexibility. Katie gasped as Genna bit with punishing strength, jaw trembling with the effort, as she bit harder, slobbering on herself, jerking her hand. Katie moaned louder. Genna thrust harder. Katie slammed herself down on the dildo.

Genna bit down, ripping her shoulder off. Katie screamed.

A laugh bubbled up from the dark well in Genna's chest. Rising higher. A deep belly laugh of pure hateful joy. Katie whimpered and shrieked as Genna clawed up her sides, slamming into her while she devoured her neck and shoulder. The warm spill of blood into her fur. Her tail fluffed and high. The strap-on harness strained against her thickened muscles. Genna was lost in a surfeit of bloodlust. She was focused on filling all that pristine skin with rubies. Unable to control her laughter. This was the best!

Katie screeched and bucked. Genna bit her on the shoulder again for balance. She pumped her hips harder. Genna snarled, and growled, and called Katie terrible things. Mocked her for pleading. Dared her to say she wanted to stop because she wouldn't.

Katie's face was covered in snot, tears, and little rivulets of blood from scrapes on the pole. She moaned Genna's name. "Iffeee."

Genna gloried in the sensations. The rough frenzy. Pounding. Grunting. Claws digging troughs into muddy weeds. Metal clanging as Katie's body shredded under the onslaught. Katie bit Genna's arm and clung by her ankles to Genna's thick thighs. Hair swaying.

Their bludgeoning orgasms. Genna's howl. A deafening bugle of dominance and ecstasy. The forest tolled like a bell. The Old Night filled her with power. Maturity. Sex magic fill them, spurred them, and deepened every thrust. Faster. Harder. Sloppier. More more more!

Until finally, Genna was finished. Sweat clung to her fur. Her long tongue dangled from her mouth as aftershocks eased.

Katie hung limp. What was not bloody was purple with contusions. Her toes dragged the ground. Knees sagged. Shoulders swollen from strain. Her hair slick against her head, strands clinging to her back, and curtaining her face.

Genna pulled the metal dildo out. Sure enough, it was warped and marked with all the teeth inside Katie's vagina. Genna slowly turned the dildo. Marveled at the strength of Katie's vaginal teeth. The dildo was solid metal. Katie had bitten it into chunks. Genna licked the blood and pleasure off its warped contours. She took off the strap-on. Stashed it and the mangled dildo into her backpack. When she got back to the castle she would make a mold. Then she would have a rough map of a female McBride's primary set of teeth.

The sunlight dappled Katie's broken body. Haloed her in light. Hunks of epidermis ragged from teeth pulling what had already been split by claws. It would be easy to finish what she started. Bite her throat and listen to the bubbling wheeze against her ear. Bury Katie here with the other bodies. Plant goldenrod over the gravesite. Think about Katie and this moment whenever she visited the glenn.

Then the contusions healed. Genna licked along Katie's body. Katie roused to whimper as Genna turned into a wolf and started to eat in earnest. "What kind of aftercare is this?"

"I'm hungry," Genna said, "I worked up an appetite. I told you that I was going to fuck and eat you. Why are you so surprised? Or would you like me to bite your crotch open and eat you from the inside out?"

"Yes, please," Katie said. "I like the dildo but I like your teeth more."

Genna pounced. Happy to oblige.

More than ten years later and Genna wanted to smack herself

for allowing the game to keep going. Tituba was wrong. Genna knew plenty about sex magic but it was from a monster and human perspective. Not as a Night Skin. Even Katie had her limits. The pervasive edge of dissatisfaction a part of every interaction. Katie was a vampire but she did not have magic. Not like Genna. She couldn't turn into anything but a snake. Genna took what she could. Tried to be satisfied.

Of course Katie had been training her like a goddamn dog. Exclusively eating vampire flesh. There had to be some kind of addictive enzyme in her blood. A defensive mechanism. The same kind of venom they used to make revenants. Those dreams of devouring Pipsy were like fantasies of eating the world's biggest funnel cake. Nothing good would come from it. Genna had lasted three years without Katie's blood. She spent the next seven proving her independence. She believed she was grooming Katie. Winning the battle by compromising the enemy.

Hubris. Damning hubris.

Genna walked past the cottage. Her hubris had killed Miss Bootsie too. When was she going to learn from her mistakes?

Katie waited in the glen. Naked. On her knees in front of the stump. Her hair draped artfully over one shoulder. Nipples hard. Skin flushed from masturbation.

She frowned, sniffing as Genna walked out of the trees. "You smell funny."

"I met Tituba the witch." Genna sat down on the stump. She held up the business card. "She says she's a matchmaker but she's also found where Naomi is. Pipsy doesn't want us to marry anymore."

"What!"

"That's why she's put Naomi on the table. Tituba is an intermediary. I'm supposed to give Naomi back her cloak. Get married. Have babies. Let the McBrides and Yorks go back to fighting over Sweetwater. Mind my own business." Genna tilted her head thoughtfully. "I guess Pipsy thinks you're lazy because you haven't had to compete for the title."

"This isn't possible." Katie pointed a finger at Genna. "It's that witch at the Grand Concourse. She gave you a taste that's spoiled your appetite."

Genna smirked in recalled admiration. "Not going to lie, Tituba has some serious power. Compared to her, Pipsy's just a snake in the grass. You're that bland chicken salad they have at the country club."

"Bland? You think I'm bland?"

"And now you're crying. Katie, this isn't about us. It's about the Bellwethers and McBrides. They want heirs producing heirs. We're not producing. We need to focus on our legacies before we get erased. That means I have to meet whoever the hell they arrange and take it seriously. And you have to fight your half-sister to become a Montgomery. An ocean of tears won't change the tide." Privately Genna wished it could.

"You're lying. This is some kind of game."

Genna offered Katie the photos. "Tituba had these. There was a large envelope full of handwritten and wax-sealed invitations waiting for me at my office. This is happening."

Katie picked up the one of herself. "This is me at your debutant ball."

Genna had not known she was there. She passed Katie the picture of Naomi. "Look at little Miss Sunshine."

Katie's face crunched into an ugly scowl. "She's not prettier than me."

"And if she is? Killing her won't change that."

Katie glared at her. "Shut up, Iffy."

"You sound like Mimi. Are you going to be a dumb bitch like her or are you going to be smart? We don't know anything about Naomi but this picture. Go home. Learn what you can. Don't throw a temper tantrum. You're not the favorite anymore. Which means your position is a lot more precarious. Pipsy could eat you because you're annoying." Genna snapped her fingers.

Katie hissed. "Don't do that. I'm special."

"This is a test. For both of us. The old tricks won't work.

We've got to adapt. They've made their move. Now we make ours." Genna gestured at the glenn. "We have to be careful. Things have changed."

"What about Prometheus?"

Genna gathered the pictures and the card. Stood up. "I don't know, Katie. If you had no idea about this either then we may be fucked without lube."

The next day Genna called her parents to apologize. She endured another lecture about fear, motherhood, and responsibility as penance. She knew it was not enough. She could hear the wounds in her family tree as though she had hacked it with an ax. She was not alone but she was separate. That was okay. It was safer for all of them.

Seventeen

Genna started digging into the gold mine's history. The impact it had on the indigenous people and the African slaves. How the land was destroyed. Everything stripped and burned and sold.

She went through the castle. Instead of putting everything in storage, Genna had used all of the old furniture, art, and so on to furnish rooms. She collated not with new eyes but better understanding. A morass of facts changed into a skillful tap-dance across centuries.

Tituba's hostility was inspiring. Grounding, like a pin in the center of the map which everything else connected to. Genna's family *were* monsters. Old dragons on a mountainous hoard of gold and skeletons. Genna was not a good person from good people. Her family had already achieved and maintained a level of dominance that monsters like Pipsy Montgomery had only tasted. She was wasting her time with Katie McBride. Genna's family was older than the United States itself.

Yet in that was also the contradiction. Genna's family had always been Black. Carefully curating their bloodline. Wealthy Black people marrying Black people. Wealth could not protect against prejudice. She stroked her gold ring. *Never forget.*

There was a cycle to the family's success. At the pinnacle of every financial triumph came a sacrifice by fire.

The fire followed Genna's maternal side all the way back to that original gold mine. The Great London Fire in 1666 happened after the initial witch trials. Everyone and their properties in that branch of the family were burned except for those who owned the shipping company. They were on a boat on their way back to the mine, having delivered the lie that it was witchcraft that caused the gold to dry up.

The great Chicago fire took out the family's horse-and-carriage empire.

They made millions in Black Wall Street. Then the family burned in their own house in the Tulsa massacre.

The coal bonanza in Arkansas. Driven out of town by fire and death.

The coal mine explosions in Mather, Pennsylvania.

A silver mine explosion. Unreported because it was from internal sabotage. Nepotism killing both feuding limbs of that particular branch.

They were in Nagasaki, Japan, taking advantage of war tensions to do business, and got caught in the fires from the dropped A-bomb.

Fires in hotels. Fires in circus tents. Fire fire fire.

Yet fiery death inspired them to rise like phoenixes from the ashes. Those the cursed gold failed to kill became galvanized into action.

Genna's maternal grandparents survived the Nagasaki fires. Her grandfather, a military OBGYN, returned home and built inner-city hospitals to bring good medical care to Black American communities who had been largely ignored or used for medical testing. Her grandmother focused on dentistry.

When the World Trade Center destroyed a large swath of businesses and tanked the stock market, Genna's father pointed to the television and the smoke rising from the collapsed twin towers. *"All that smoke is in everyone's lungs."*

The family pivoted to drill down on medical enterprises. More hospitals, clinics, pharmaceuticals, and medical computer technology.

The most unsettling part of the timeline was the lightning strike that burn down Genna's home when her mother was pregnant. Her mother had bought the nine properties of Sweetwater in a frenzy of celebration and nesting. Both of her parents excited about their first child. On the map it looked like a Mrs. Pac-Man with the lake as a hair bow. She had just become a squillionare due to her investments in video games, like Mrs Pac-Man, Madden, and Mario Brothers. She liked the plantation home because of the view, not realizing it was haunted.

A lot of old bad things had happened in the plantation home. The stable had always had horses but the kennels had been slave quarters. Mimi had been pregnant with Katie. Genna would be her first meal.

The lightning strike was the same day Genna was born.

Miss Bootsie had helped Genna's parents into her cottage. Genna was born right there in the bathtub while fire swept through Sweetwater.

Genna rubbed the diamond face of the gold ring. Fire was the family magic.

She finished writing in her personal journal. The handwritten one the family would not see. The parts with magic in it. She jotted an update to her field guide for surviving the McBrides.

Genna unfolded the map she kept stashed inside the journal's back pocket. Grimaced at the atlas.

She went to the map room. She walked in a slow circle. The walls were covered with a painted corkboard reproduction of the planet. Easier to pin things too than paper. The map marked major activity hubs in her ancestral timeline. Copies of events. Rolling filing cabinets and tablets with compiled information were along the base of the walls. Genna had two family history books. It wasn't cooking the facts to keep some things out of the book she gave everyone for Christmas each year. History was messy.

She could draw a straight line from Accra, Ghana to the gold mine.

Her company historians had explained it delicately. Genna had all the current timeline catalogued. Now she needed to go back. To the other side of the TransAtlantic Slave Trade. There was no way around it. She had traveled to every part of the family tree except one specific place. Out of fear.

On the historical manifests and archives she found her ancestors.

Who the hell wanted to know that their ancestors funded and directly profited off the Middle Passage?

Her ancestors owned the boats, the shipping companies that employed felons from Britain sent down to Ghana for a life sentence. They were privateers who worked directly for or were members of the Spanish, French, British, and Portuguese aristocracy. There were only diffuse records of regions where the kidnapped Africans came from. No direct way of knowing besides generalizations. *Possibly Angola, Ghana, and Mali* was hardly an accurate statement. One of her family members willfully liked to claim they descended from Mansa Musa, the wealthiest person of all time, but that did not factually hold water.

Genna had avoided this particular part of the family tree until she met Tituba. Initially, she was shocked to be confronted by so much hatred that it felt like standing in a lava waterfall. Why would Tituba want to help Genna? Was it to purposefully destroy her? Then why introduce herself at all? Genna couldn't help but feel there was more to it all. Maybe she was stupid and arrogant to do what she was told but perhaps ego could get her through when she had no answers.

It was time to visit the Cape Coast Castle.

KATIE TOOK SELFIES ON THE RAMPARTS OF THE CAPE Coast Castle slave fortress. The other members of Genna's tour squinted into the sun, smiling and twisting themselves into angles that made them look younger, carefree, and excited. The turquoise ocean, azure sky, yellow sand, and whitewashed stone were a perfect background.

Genna stayed on the other side of the parade ground, exhausted from weeping. Her body angled as if she held a bow and arrow. Or for Katie, an elephant gun with pure silver bullets.

"You pestilential, tone-deaf harpies," she seethed quietly, so angry she wanted to burst into flames.

Katie glanced her way, preening. "I'm *so* glad we took this vacation together, Iffy."

There was no plausible way Genna could push her over the ramparts.

The Cape Coast Castle was responsible for ninety-five percent of the kidnapped Africans transported across the Atlantic Ocean to North America. Katie glowed like a lightning bug, absorbing the abundance of negative energy. She had already bought a bag of souvenirs from the gift shop. Fans, baskets, and fabric that had been marinating in old nightmares. She walked into the large white church, stomping her foot. "It really is soundproof."

Genna went down into the men's dungeon directly under the church with the rest of the tour to get away. Katie stayed above in the light while Genna walked into the ghosts of abject despair.

The shadows had been screaming for so long, they were nothing but pain. There was no hope there. No future. Only the depravity of humanity distilled to its cruelest essence. After walking through the punishment room next to the women's dungeon, Genna never wanted to have sex with anyone again.

Genna was not fine. Genna was also never going to admit weakness to anyone here. Especially not her all rich and all-white tour group from Canada and the States. They spent a lot of time telling her how *their* ancestors had *nothing* to do with slavery.

Let's all sing Negro spiritual songs to truly flog this awful place of every ounce of racial trauma.

The wolf was far away. Every shadowed hallway was a throat. There was no refuge here. Only forward. Onward. Get through. Get out. Stay out. Never come back. Never forget.

The ring felt heavy as iron shackles. It dragged her down to the floor.

There was a Dutch woman on the tour with her worried husband. Her glazed eyes met Genna's. They exchanged a look so vividly clear, the words hung in the air between them. The weary salute of two soldiers stuck in the same foxhole in the middle of a war zone. Barbed-wire fences. Warm mud stinking of death. Screams all around them. Death and more death. If they thought about their feet, they had to admit they were standing on four hundred years of dead Black bodies. Packed so tight, they were part of the stone. Their endless screams a soundless echo. The pressure felt nonetheless. A vast and terrible silence of a tomb. Their ancestors had survived this terrible place but they had been there.

Genna walked through the narrow doorway hauntingly named 'The Door of No Return' and called her driver. Ten minutes later, she was in a car. Two hours later, she was flying over the Atlantic. She cried in the Falcon. Cried in the car. Cried in relief at the sight of her castle rising above the green forest. Then cried at the tasteful architecture because it reminded her of the fortress she had left.

Annoyed messages from Katie that Genna had once again slipped through her long, manicured fingers. Genna hoped Katie ate the tour group during one of their endless tone-deaf Christian singalongs.

Tears failed to wash away the guilt. Her inability to change anything.

"Calm yourself, Iphigenia, you're being hysterical," her mother said when she called looking for reassurance.

Genna went back to bed at noon, giving up on the day.

She ignored her phone and tablet and computer for a whole second day. Then she got bored and went riding. This time practicing archery.

Sneakers was eager to move. She pushed her own endurance. To not change horses. To do as she had been taught in Mongolia. The twang and sting of muscles. The accomplishment of an arrow reaching a target while on horseback. Genna spent hours riding and shooting hay bales and archery targets. Then she took a trail ride through the forest.

The sky was an empty sapphire blue. The leaves heavy brown under Sneakers' great hooves. A beautiful summer day full of sunshine she could not enjoy. Grim and Toto ran in circles around Sneakers and through the trees, scaring off any wild game. The sun warmed through her black t-shirt and jeans.

Guilt settled into resolute sadness. She went to her office in a storm of good intentions.

She would make sure her employees of all her companies were being properly compensated. She would help the environment. Save animals. Clean up the oceans, the rivers, the forests. Plant trees. Fund reputable animal preserves. Help the disenfranchised. Feed the poor. Shoe the children. Help those stuck in foster care, immigration, and unable to pay for complex surgery. She would do good as much as she could, wherever she could.

Genna's staff had a list of non-profits waiting open mouthed like shrieking baby birds. Most of her assistants were social justice warriors. She was fairly sure she did good. Mostly. Hopefully.

Cynically, Genna acknowledged her wrath of finding corruption in her nonprofits was worse than her expectations for her other companies. She was the money. She wasn't supposed to have an opinion of where it was spent. She was supposed to trust. Which was absurd. It was her damn money.

Her parents were right. Genna wasn't great at business.

"Africa was that bad, huh?" an assistant said with the ingratiating smile of a kiss-ass determined to shunt today's windfall towards her bevy of prison reform organizations.

"No, Africa was beautiful. There's so much to explore. I loved it. The people were kind. The dancing and music was fun. The clothing. I need to update my wardrobe. It was just the fortress. It was a real-life haunted house."

Genna regretted her poorly planned trip. She was scheduled to travel to twelve different countries in the continent. She only made it to Ghana, Rwanda, and Tanzania. Her enjoyment mitigated. The whole trip was an endurance competition. A surreal hellscape of being trapped in an old school bus that resembled a mission trip built to reinforce every donor's White-Savior complex. Genna mistaken as White because of her light skin. She thought she was better than them. She wasn't.

Then Katie showed up in Zanzibar with her minions while Genna was buying local tanzanite jewelry and everything got worse.

Genna paused to focus on the assistant. "You know what the shittiest part was?"

"All of it?" The assistant said, not prepared to receive Genna's undivided and angry attention. Even when her eyes weren't glowing she had a glare like a blowtorch.

"The rest of the tour didn't care. About anything. Like it didn't matter. There were people taking selfies on the ramparts because they liked the view!"

The assistant clicked her teeth in disgust. "Some people will take selfies in Auschwitz."

"Exactly!"

Genna stormed out of the office. The assistant sagged, fanning herself with her folders. Genna noticed and felt bad. She was angry with herself. Angry with her family too. She had just received a polite but firm request that she not send anyone a history book for Christmas this year.

"We don't descend from slaves." Funny how her family said the same thing as the one-percenters on the tour. They were desperate to divorce themselves from the murky past. Ironically telling the truth.

Genna tried to find balance. She ran through the forest filled with restless energy. She was gently but firmly told not to ride the horses so arduously. No one wanted Sneakers or Bibi to get lame due to overexercise. She wasn't supposed to do combat training with the dogs. Or anything else that disrupted the usual schedule of the castle. She ran. She weeded. She picked apples. She gathered honey and wax. Until someone offered to do the job she paid them to do and get her to stop.

Finally she went to the cottage and binge watched Disney movies. She cried and hugged the cloak. She flossed her teeth because she hated meat stuck in her gums. The wild boar had put up a good fight.

Her phone was full of pictures Katie sent of herself enjoying Genna's tour. *Wish you were here.*

Finally, desperate to feel normal again, Genna walked to the roof of her castle to ask for help. It was night. No moon, either. Last night had been a sharp sliver of a crescent. The darkness was old and still. The trees whispered to each other. The animals quiet in their burrows. Other things walked among the bracken. Things so old they had no name, only a description, a smell, and a growl.

Humans unconsciously increased the volume of their televisions, music, phones, and computers. They turned on the exhaust fan over the stove or put extra ice in the blender. The washer and the dryer chugged. They checked to make sure that the curtains were drawn. Parents and children already in bed woke up, staring at the darkness. They pulled the covers over their heads, snuggled close to their loved ones, and tried to fall asleep, genuinely worried the sun would not come up soon enough. The animals inside the house watched the darkness, ears up and eyes wide as the Old Night padded through Sweetwater.

Genna spread her arms as wide as they would go. She arched back. Taking one deep breath. Two. Three. On the fourth, Genna howled. The night became her fur. The moon was a black pearl earring. Stars scattered across the velvety darkness of her engagement dress that she kept because she loved it. Her hair became a soft cloud of curls.

Miss Bootsie had called her a Night Skin. Genna had dismissed it as another way to highlight the melanin of her skin. It was better than other names. Now she understood what the boo hag meant.

Genna was a monster. That was who she was. *Why* she was. It explained so many things that had seemed incomprehensible until now.

The truth was a relief. Finally, she was free.

She embraced the night and it filled her skin. Remote and cruel and terrible. Welcoming.

Eighteen

Genna wanted to throw Tituba out of the castle. Her plan to meet at the country club was overruled. The witch was given full access to inspect the castle grounds. Even a perfunctory tour was too much exposure but her parents were done talking.

Now Tituba in her stupid gray suit sat in the Good Room with the flared nostrils of someone resisting the temptation to slide her finger along the mantle to check for dust. She was prune-faced with disapproval.

Genna dreaded a marathon of suitors. Instead, there was only one.

"His name is Quincy Snodgrass," Tituba said, tapping a fingernail on a gold-leaf framed headshot. "He is a witchfinder. The Snodgrasses have approved of the meeting with their son. He has all of the pleasing qualities your parents specified for your husband-to-be."

"I thought you of all people would hate witchfinders." Genna said instead of *go fuck yourself.*

"Times have changed. Those with magic must make allies with old enemies against the prayer warriors to survive."

They gave each other a matched look of loathing.

"You need the help," Tituba said, "You also need to get off the witch finder registry of unaffiliated magical people. I didn't need to have magic to be accused of witchcraft. Simply existing was enough. I saved myself. Now I do what it takes to preserve other Black women who have been blessed with magic. You know exactly how important it is to preserve and protect what would be forgotten. You know safe havens for Black people are needed because no one will save us but us, *princess.*" She added with a sneer.

Genna clamped down on her temper. Princess was her title. She had the tiara to prove it. "Aren't witchfinders part of the church?"

"This is the age of logic and silence. Magic in any form is taboo. Even those who kill monsters and protect humanity from magic are hunted as ferociously as their enemies. Dragons are not supposed to exist. Therefore, dragon slayers cannot either." Tituba leaned forward with an unpleasant smirk and pushed a printed itinerary across the table. "You will spend the weekend with Quincy. He lives with three roommates in Chicago. A man and two women. Each have elemental magic."

"Three roommates?" Genna said, unenthusiastically reviewing the prescribed itinerary. "Are they polyamorous?"

"Naomi York is one of his roommates. Their relationship is immaterial."

Genna put the itinerary down. "Naomi York? That's a coincidence. If I'm going to be Pipsy's errand girl then I want to be paid."

Tituba gave her a look that she ignored. "It is not a coincidence. It is your opportunity to return what was never yours."

Thus Genna flew to Chicago with her glam squad. She stayed in the Four Seasons hotel where she was told to stay. A selection of clothing and jewelry waited on her bed. Genna wore her own clothes and gems instead. There was a limit to her compliance.

Her Dior gown was as purple as twilight. The long slit up the hip was emphasized by a diamond brooch flower. A lot of her brown skin was bare. The built-in corsetry buoyed her bust. The open back invited the dress to be peeled off her bare shoulders. Her hair draped down one shoulder in a waterfall of curls and held in place by diamond encrusted combs. She wore a silver threaded pashmina cloak as modesty cover that draped like a floor length cape.

She wore her favorite gold Jada Dubai high heels. The diamonds sparkled. More importantly, her feet were comfortable.

Her parents were in the hotel foyer when she came down. She ignored their approving compliments. She knew she looked good. "I'm informing you now that while I'm willing to meet this possible suitor, I will burn everything down if you've signed any papers."

Their tempers flashed like lightning but both nodded.

"We're aware of your extreme reactions, Iphigenia," her mother said stiffly. "There's no need to be dramatic."

"Don't you trust us?" Her father said.

The awful silence that followed frosted all three with ice until the Snodgrasses walked into the hotel lobby.

Her first thought when she saw Quincy Snodgrass was *Wow*.

Quincy was the most beautiful Black man Genna had ever encountered. His picture failed to do him justice. He was a boulder of muscle wrapped in a tailored, if unimaginative, Gucci suit. His long black dreadlocks were tied neatly back by a black silk Gucci scarf. His goatee and eyebrows were manscaped. His prominent cheekbones and pouting full lips gave the impression that he was sucking on the inside of his cheeks. Best of all, his long black eyelashes framed an intelligent black stare.

She wanted to rip the suit off of him the moment he walked into the warm chandelier light. Expect his parents, Camille and Reginald, were here. They greeted Genna with paternal and unearned sincerity. As far as they were concerned, this meeting was a mere formality.

Camille and Reginald Snodgrass were the standard mixture of pleasant and ambitious well-to-do members of the Black elite.

Their clothes were standard Armani and Versace. Their jewelry were simple gold and diamond crosses, Rolex watches, and solid gold cufflinks.

Camille Snodgrass was a regal Black woman who wore large prescription glasses. Her hair was pressed into a soft bob to show off the real sparkle of her diamond earrings. Her clothes were perfectly pressed but not tailored, comfortably loose. While her physique was indoorsy, she had a coiled presence. She was dangerous. A steely early sixties. According to Tituba's file, Camille was a witchfinder who specialized in wrangling spellbooks and undoing curses in grimoires.

Reginald Snodgrass loomed while sitting. His hair was a tight salt and pepper fade thinning in the back. His beard and eyebrows were scrupulously trimmed. He moved slowly, unhurried and self-contained. His glasses were too small for his face. He took them off so often that Genna suspected that these were recent and reluctant necessities. His bad knees might slow him down but Tituba warned her not to bet against the prayer warrior.

Quincy got his size from his father and his features from his mother. His long dreadlocks were an obvious act of rebellion. Camille's fingers twitched like she wanted to arrange them. There was genuine affection between the Snodgrasses but the covetous way they looked at Genna made her seethe with resentment.

That was the hazard of the Black elite. They saw her and got ideas. They believed that Black American princesses existed for the honor of bearing their children and furthering the legacy of Black Excellence. They had already planned where they would summer. Which HBCU their children would attend. The hardest decision to make was where they would host Thanksgiving, Christmas, Kwanzaa, Juneteenth, and the 4th of July. They knew where the wedding would be. How she would look in her couture wedding gown. Their many children would want for nothing.

The parents smiled too damn much during the introductions. Genna and Quincy stood like trained show dogs during a championship inspection. Both were used to being seen and silent.

Genna focused on modulating her voice to stay perfectly pleasant. She endured the mortification of her bisexuality being discussed as a long-term problem for finding suitable matches. Not for the Snodgrasses. Their son was not only an out-and-proud bisexual but had recently ended a long term relationship with a man. They were delighted that the Bellwethers had a similarly difficult daughter.

Quincy was an earnest twenty-seven. Genna was the old maid of thirty. No children. No diseases. No debt. No problems.

Genna glanced at Quincy whose eyes had emptied. Were the Snodgrasses trying to find their son a match that fit their standards when he already had partner? Or did they secretly not approve of his sexuality? Was Genna supposed to be his beard? She hoped not.

Finally, the parents let their children get into a waiting limo and drive to dinner.

"You kids have fun," Reginald called after them. Her parents and the Snodgrasses were so damn excited, already heading to their own waiting Range Rover.

Genna slid into the limo and scooted down the cabin to get out of the way. Quincy awkwardly folded himself down to squeeze through the door. Why hadn't they taken an Escalade or a stretch Hummer?

Neither spoke as the limo joined Chicago traffic. This was like an awkward prom date.

Instead of a restaurant, Quincy had booked the entire Driehaus Museum. Genna adored the lavish Art Deco interior design. She strode around the rooms, taking photos and notes on what she could do to her castle. There was carved wood, marble, onyx, and originals of her favorite stained-glass artist, Lewis Comfort Tiffany. She inspected the floor. It was not painted but six different colors of wood joined together in geometric floral patterns.

Reluctantly, she sat in the dining room that was set with a white table cloth woven with gold kente-cloth patterns that matched the bone china setting and gold flatware. Delicate white roses painted with gold were the centerpiece.

She tucked her phone away. The Snodgrasses had obviously made an effort. She needed to try and get to know him.

The food promised to be good, but they began with hot chocolate in a gold and white bone china cups.

"This is from my family's cacao plantation." His skin was the same color as the dark chocolate he sprinkled red pepper into. He delicately stirred the spice in with a tiny gold spoon, and then served her. Every movement was careful and polished. "We also make shea butter from shea trees."

Genna thanked him and sipped the truly delicious cup of hot chocolate. His long fingers moved around the table setting, straightening what he had already placed in perfect alignment. She watched him and thought about other uses for those big capable hands.

He talked about the production of making this particular cup of hot chocolate. How his family had success in coffee. That he and his parents preferred focusing on their passion for forensic history. Researching criminal organizations. Finding their connections. Investigations and record preservation. As someone with a PhD in esoterica and African-American studies, he was interested in Genna's deep dive into her family ancestry.

She let him talk because it was interesting and her active listening made him nervous.

She felt his eyes track her movements as she arranged the stacked emerald and opal bracelets on her wrist. The gemstones in her rings caught the chandelier light.

Genna could have put him at ease. She could have asked if he found being a grown man set up on dates by his parents as annoying as she did. Except she had met his parents.

She sighed. She had nothing to complain about but damn it was depressing that she couldn't find love on her own.

Quincy trailed off into silence. He poured himself another cup of hot chocolate. He looked at Genna as he sipped. She flattened him with an arched glance as she flicked her long soft black curls over her shoulder.

"I'm talking too much, aren't I?" Quincy said, with a small smoldering smile. His teeth were bright white.

She could wake up next to a smile like that. Lean against his chest. Feel as much as hear the sleepy rumble. Feel safe. Trace the tattoos he hid under his suit. He did not wear socks with his loafers. Their closets would have to be on opposite sides of the bedroom because there was no way she was dealing with the funk of sweaty shoes.

He looked like John Henry with dreadlocks. However, the most intriguing thing about Quincy was that he was a Night Skin. He was different. His parents were scary but they were human. Quincy had magic. They did not.

Under all that delicious flesh was a dragon. Black moss had settled on scales long enough that it had grown into a swampy forest. Mangroves caged his thick claws. The mud was warm and the silt was as dark as chocolate. There were also dead people, a lot of dead. Thousands of bodies in that mud. Drowned and tangled in nets. The dragon had eaten well.

He was different from the McBrides snakes. Quincy watched, restful. Mouth on autopilot while the rest of him studied Genna.

She was careful. That mud was suffocating. Thick with obligations and expectations. His worth might not have the same monetary value as her own but he knew he was a Black American prince.

Quincy was here to find a wife. He watched her, clearly expecting her to cave to family pressure as he had. To be the good girl. To sacrifice her wants. To not make waves. Which made him an enemy to be summarily destroyed.

Genna clamped down on that thought. No, that was the fear talking.

The meal was good but Genna did not concentrate on the food. There was only so many ways steak and potatoes could be creatively cooked. She had so many questions. Where to start?

This was a date. A formal handshake. She needed to change her attitude. To see him as an opportunity, not an opponent. She was not buying the story that he had broken up with his boyfriend. Quincy had the hallmarks of a confirmed bachelor dragged to the marriage bed by parents who wanted grandkids while they were still young enough to chase a giggling toddler.

Two wolves, honey child. Miss Bootsie whispered in her ear.

Quincy was a stepping-stone. He might be, with a little coaxing, fun. If she could get him to relax and not see her as the enemy, too.

"It's interesting that we know the same people," Quincy said, "Where did you meet Naomi York? I'm guessing at one of her fashion shows?"

"I haven't met her. I know her grandmothers."

A look she could not interpret calcified his expression. He spread his napkin across his lap. "Naomi is a good friend. She's practically family."

Quincy postured like an older brother. According to Tituba's files, Naomi was thirty-seven. Quincy was twenty-seven. No mention of how they were connected. Or where this protective hostility came from.

"Where did you two meet?"

"Hurricane Katrina." His tone was a brick wall. Genna had said the wrong thing. She tried to fathom why but decided to change the subject.

"When did you know you were a Night Skin?"

A muscle jumped in his jaw. "I prefer the term *magi*."

"What's the difference?"

"More education. Less archaic hedge craft. Root work has its place. You know this as a healer, yourself, but you have to be careful not to dive too deep into animism."

"Is that why you caged your dragon?"

His fingers turned the cup handle in a different direction. "I don't know what you're talking about."

Genna stood up smoothly. She let her pashmina cloak slide off her shoulders and onto her chair. Quincy stayed where he sat. She liked the way he watched. The hunger. The interest. He was mildly hostile because her presence unnerved him. She could smell it in the air. His anxiety was sweeter than gourmet hot chocolate.

Her gown whispered against the patterned wood floor as she circled the table to his side. She traced her hand along the muscled edge of his bicep. He turned her way. He knew he was beautiful. He liked her attention. Her fingers traced up the buttons of his shirt. Then slid up his tie. She distracted him with her other hand wandering along the swell of his shoulder. His hand stayed on his lap but he shifted his leg. She stepped into the channel between his leg and the table's edge. His wrist turned sideways so his cool palm cupped her bare thigh in that seam of her dress.

His nostrils flared. His eyes hooded. She tracked the micro-movements. She stayed above the belt, though she allowed the intimacy of his hand on her leg. Intriguing danger. The alligator's mouth wide.

She bent down slightly. Enough to give him a view of her breasts, round and inviting. Easy to lift free from her bodice and feel their weight.

Quincy's hands stayed still. His face tilted up to focus on her eyes and not her breasts. Too polite. Refusing to be taken in so easily.

Genna inhaled, drinking him in. The difference. The male power. The contrast in their size. For all his denial, the dragon was strong. The cage was there, thick and overgrown from habit. She could swim inside, but it would be more fun to watch him fight. To come to her.

Genna's hands firmed on his jaw and tugged his tie. Once, sharp. She straightened up, looked down the cliff of her substantial cleavage. "I don't care who you are, what kind of husband you'll be, or your procreation abilities. I want cunnilingus. The question is, will it be from you? Or will I find someone else?"

He leaned into her grip. "I'm a savant at licking pussy."

A savant? A warning bell. Was he actually good or did he think he was good?

"I'll be the judge of that."

He blinked. It was subtle but her cold dismissal had him more focused. Not angry. Chin raised to the challenge. More excited.

"Do you have a problem with female domination?" She said.

"Hell, no," he said.

"I will decide if we have penetrative sex. Whether it will be you or me. What kind. And when. Do you have a problem with that?"

"None whatsoever." He licked his lips. His nostrils flared. His breathing fast.

Genna leaned close. He stretched up, expecting a kiss. She slid her cheek past, held his jaw. Then she *growled.*

The pitch sent a deep subsonic ripple through the mud and frothed the silt. It shivered along his scales and seeped into his bloodstream. Her teeth closed on his scaled neck. She dragged him straight up out of the mud. His tail was unable to flip him back under the water. His feet dug at the air. She let him go. He sank back down with a splash into the churned mud and swaying mangroves.

She stepped smoothly back into the physical world and her skin. A piratical grin flitted across her lips. "No hiding."

Quincy's eyes rounded. His hand firmed on her thigh. "My penthouse is in the Gold Coast."

"Why not here? Right under the Tiffany-stained glass dome."

"I knew you liked the museum." A pleased little smirk. "The mansion was originally—"

"Quincy, now is the time, so say you're not interested. I'm a grown woman. I can handle rejection."

"I'm interested. Emphatically. However, we need to relocate. When I cut loose, things can get a little swampy."

That was sufficiently intriguing. She climbed into a behemoth Lincoln Navigator. A much better fit than the limo. It smelled like Quincy. Clean and pristine. This was his car.

Quincy's house was also from the Gilded Age. Sadly, only the exterior had the same complex architecture. The inside was stone and modern.

"I know you're disappointed with the architecture and interior design," he said self-consciously as she walked to the double staircase. "They'd already done a full-gut remodel. There's very little left besides the facade. They don't make things like they used to."

Genna smirked. "I think you'd like my castle."

"I've read the architectural journals. I know I would." He closed the distance between them. "Genna, I know we both have a lot of pressure to make this work but I'm genuinely interested in you."

Genna pulled him down to kiss him because she wanted to and to shut him up. He smirked. "Okay. I'll stop talking. You make me nervous."

"I know. I like it."

He took her into an interior greenhouse. While Genna's greenhouse was closer to a butterfly garden, this was a solarium. The plants green and heavy with moisture. A pool in the middle. Stone waterfall. Rounded edges. There were white leather cushions on wrought iron furniture.

He unbuttoned his shirt and jacket without prompting. He spread his shirt and vest wider, his chest puffed and stomach clenched, angled to show off. With a soft lustful sigh, she spread her hands across his sternum, the curve of his pectorals, down his belly and up the strong cords of his neck. His skin was a network of scars, puckered and pitted skin under the ink. Those scars were sometimes hidden and other times decorated. He inhaled as she grazed his skin with her nails.

She wanted him. It was dangerous to want things, especially other people. They were unprepared for what seethed inside her fortress of little rules, habits, and ritualized affectations that she kept between herself and the world. Good girls did not rip, tear, yank, possess, and demand. They definitely did not bite hard enough to leave bruises in the shape of their dentition. But he knew she had magic. Surely he saw her fire wolf as she saw his swamp dragon.

Genna growled as he kissed her. Quincy inhaled. A deep, sonorous roar rattled the glass in the distant skylight. The jungle plants. Red macaws screeched out of the trees.

She felt drunk and utterly sober. Her skin was sensitized by his touch, as if all the layers between them were gone and they were flesh against flesh, sweaty and hot. She traced a long divot in his scalp behind his ear. She tugged harder on his tie, his belt, all command.

It was a test to see what he would do. Would he flinch, get mad, shake his head free and retaliate, or would he, as she hoped, like the demand?

The strength of his hands on her butt cheeks firmed. He liked it.

She wanted more. The desire sweeping clean the panic about danger. He kissed her with those big pillowy lips. Mouth against mouth. Tongue against tongue.

Yet he slowed the movements. Deep, steadying breaths. His hands bunched tight, biceps flexed, as though stopping himself from ripping her dress apart. She liked feeling his struggle. The tension along his neck. To be surrounded by leashed strength. His mastery of his own self was fascinating. The taste of his sweat. She nipped his nipples. Light kisses and sharp pain.

He swept Genna up into his arms and off her feet so fast, it left her breathless. His mouth on hers. Their tongues sliding together. Teeth biting soft flesh. Urgent gasps and grunts exchanged instead of words. She clawed his back. His arms were tight around her torso. She held on to his neck, careful of his dreadlocks. The ground was far away from her toes. Sizzling arousal flared into pure need.

He walked over to one of the white couches. He held Genna almost over his shoulder. His grip on her butt slipped under her skirt. A hot callused hand explored the thin satin of her panties.

She loved his strength and the way he mastered his space. He set her down on the couch. Then knelt between her legs. Quick kisses on her breasts. His focus on her legs. He gripped her ankles, right above the straps of her heels. His hand slid up her calf, asking permission with his hesitation. No hostility. Only frank admiration. She lifted the edge of her skirts.

"Tell me what you want me to do to you," he said while kissing the inside of her ankle. He looked up at her, body curved around her foot.

She lifted her foot and placed the toes lightly on his chest. "I want you to use your beautiful lips, your clever tongue, and those long fingers to pleasure me until I stay stop."

"Yes, ma'am."

Quincy dove between her legs. He slid her panties off. The naughtiness of exposure. The strange pressure of his nose against her nether curls, smelling her. The tickle of his goatee. His primal moan of delight she felt more than heard. The first contact of his tongue against her labia, searching and then finding her clitoris. The pressured suction of his lips.

He was as good as he said he was.

Genna writhed on the couch. She felt as tall as a mountain. Divinely feminine. Aware of every curve of her body. The tight constriction of her corset. She tugged her neglected nipples. Kneaded her breasts. The noise, the heat of the solarium pooled on her skin.

She felt amazing, shiny, and invincible. All the gloom that had settled on the evening burned away in raw lust. He paused. Raised his eyebrows.

"How am I doing?"

"Fantastic. Continue."

His deep rumble of a chuckle made her smile. He yanked her farther down the couch, spread her wider. Genna clawed at the white leather upholstery for balance, her thighs clamped on his broad shoulders. His tongue circled her labia. She tapped him to turn the darting quick licks into long strokes. He nibbled and tugged and teased her by leaving her throbbing to suckle on the back of her knee, a location that was as startling as it was erogenous. Genna held on, moaning with abandon.

He slid one finger into her hot, moist interior. He curled his finger, stroking and pumping. Gradually adding a second digit. Then three fingers. She bucked her hips and slammed her crotch into his mouth, needing more, demanding more, commanding he stop stymying his strength and give her everything. He complied, eagerly suckling, slurping down her pleasure, the sharp edge of his teeth making her jump and wiggle. She curled over him, barely on the couch anymore. All of her focus was on the building pressure.

"This right! Just like that. Just like that! More more more!"

She screamed for him, and again, and again. Swept up in a tsunami of sensations, rolling her over, pounding her flat, scouring thought beyond the need for more.

He sucked and teased her. Genna stopped counting orgasms and instead categorized them by the colors she saw.

One climax was chrysanthemum flowers blooming on a midnight lake. Another was a golden dragon tangled in roses made of lightning. Wolves made of fire. Tigers made of storm clouds. Golden bears loping across a purple glacier. Briar roses covering a mound of human skulls. Red krakens fought black orcas in a purple ocean.

She screamed for him, as each image was overshadowed by the next. She clawed at his back. Lightning in her veins. Glorious pleasure. Only his strength kept her from toppling off of the couch. Sweat dappled her dress and stung her eyes. His fingers clamped firmly on her ass. Slurping eagerly and encouraging more.

She grabbed the condom she had stashed between her breasts. Cellophane scratched flesh. She yanked her dress back.

"Sex. Now," she panted. "With you."

"Yes, ma'am." Quincy smirked, facial hair glistening with her pleasure, very pleased with himself. Her hair was in frizzed disarray. Her makeup sweated off.

She leaned down and held the condom close. Unsmiling. Glaring with need. "I said *now*."

"Yes, ma'am." His belt jingled, slacks unzipping as he stood up. He stripped fast. His breath caught as she grabbed his erection. He was big and broad. He had a little bottle of lube in his pocket. Also a condom.

"No offense, but I like to use my own condoms," he said. "You're welcome to check it if you want. No holes."

As she wrestled free of her dress she took a moment for appreciation. He was sculpted. Glistening and brown. Surrounded by emerald green and pale white and brown stones. Elemental. As though he were made of the earth and water. The faintest hint of scales under his skin. His dreadlocks were like ropes of black moss.

He tried to ram in but she kept a tight grip on his erection so only the meat of her hand hit her mounds.

"Slow down," she commanded. "I want this as much as you do."

He bucked and twitched but obeyed. She squeezed his shaft firmly to control his movements. He groaned. She wrapped her legs around his hips, scooting forward to get the angle right. Her other hand was firm on the back of his neck for balance. Slowly, she slid his blunt head past her swollen labia and into her hot interior.

He was long, so long. And wide, so wide. Her fist was a necessity to keep him from bludgeoning her cervix. He listened as she whispered directions. She let go and he sank up to the hilt with a gusty groan. Slow, long strokes in and out. Their bodies singing with tension, backs quivering. The furniture creaked. She held on to him. She stopped holding back as she adjusted the depth of penetration. But the angle wasn't right.

She pushed him onto his back. He landed heavily on the ground, which flexed around him, as though the stone had the tensile strength of a bog.

Fire licked her skin. Steam filled the air. Mist glittered like diamonds. Lightning curled her hair. He shuddered as it leapt along his skin.

Genna slid down, slowly, carefully. Controlling the pace. He inhaled. Steam rose from his skin in thickening coils. Until she was like a hot iron pressing on wet fabric. She shivered at the fullness. She fought her own hunger. She wanted to bite and yank but she needed to concentrate. These were not Katie's scales. She did not need to rip his belly open and eat his liver.

She lifted up again. Slid down.

The fog surrounded them. Moisture dripped off the trees. What pattered on her skin steamed. The hot air was thick enough to swipe away. Quincy was a dark, hazy figure.

He orgasmed in a rumbling crescendo with another bass alligator bellow. He arched back, his hands clamped on her hips as he thrust and thrust, jackhammering. She rode him.

The water of the pool sloshed upwards and swept her off Quincy.

Genna spun. Shocked into choking. Spun in bubbles. She changed into a wolf. Dog-paddling. Still drowning. The heat flared.

A burst of fire that knocked the muddy wave apart.

She landed on the stone edge then slipped on the edge. She fell into the pool. The bottom of the pool was mud. She floundered her way to the side. She coughed and spat as she heaved herself up the rocks. The waterfall washed some of the mud away. But not all.

Quincy lay on the ground, panting. He rolled to his side. He pushed his dreadlocks across his face. The water on the ground seeped up into his skin. "Marry me."

"No," Genna said, squeegeeing mud out of her hair. She was pissed off and trying hard to hide it.

She was *caked* in mud. As if she had just finished a mud bath at a spa. Her pores felt suffocated. The mud rapidly hardened into clay. She needed a hundred showers.

He pulled the condom off. Knotted it. Set it down. He slid

into the pool with an exhausted sigh. He paddled over. "That was amazing. You're amazing."

Genna searched for her dress. It had washed up along the trees. The purple was now a sloppy rag. Her lingerie was twisted and ripped. Mud dribbled onto her feet. Her heels were long gone. Her jewelry was warped wreckage. She yanked them off. She could buy new ones.

"Want to cuddle?" Quincy smiled at her in a glazed afterglow. "Do you want to go back to the Driehaus for dessert or eat here?"

"After I shower." She rapped her knuckles on the hardened shell.

"Oh, you're like Troy. He's a fire type too. He's lightning. You're more volcanic. You can use his shower."

"He's your boyfriend?"

"My partner," he said firmly.

"It's okay if he is."

Quincy wrinkled his nose at her, searching her expression. "You really don't want to get married, do you?"

"You would be correct. Though I wouldn't mind having sex with you again."

His skin darkened in a pleased blush. He reached for her but she stepped back from the pool's edge. "Which way is the shower?"

Nineteen

"Ow!" Genna cussed as the clay shard stripped off another hunk of skin. Her hair was a matted mass sloppily braided away from her face. The dull patter of shower water on the top layer of her scalp sounded like rain on an adobe roof.

The water failed to erode the encrusted brown mud. She had already caked three washcloths and a gray loofa. Muddy footprints marred the gray bathmat. Mud clotted on the edge of the white sink. The toilet looked like something unspeakable had happened to it. She made the mess worse when she tried to wipe the mud off.

"You're in my shower."

A tattooed White man stood in the bathroom doorway, poised like a surprised tiger. He wore a sweaty black tank top, sweatpants, and boxers boots. His dyed black hair was loose around his flushed face. There was a corona of ambient frizz to his curls.

He looked like a Viking. Tall, big, and dangerous. The same muscular size as Quincy but differently proportioned. Sleeker. He smelled like lightning. Even with the mud his scent was over-whelming.

"Do I have to fight you?" Genna growled crankily.

"Do you want to?"

No, she wanted to do other things. Lots of things. Quincy had impeccable taste in men. If only she didn't feel like the Swamp Thing.

"Sorry. I thought the mud would wash right off but it turned into this shell." She snarled and went back to clawing at the mud. "Give me a minute. I'll clean things up."

"Mud is a pain in the ass," he said, a hint of amusement.

She tried not to snarl. The mud had hardened again. Now in runnels of her fingernails. She cussed more pointedly. "Fuck this mud!"

"There's a trick to it. You need to increase and randomize your fire into lightning. Right now, your ambient heat is baking the mud hard. It's a common mistake. Water and earth types do it to smother our flame. They dunk us like a churro in chocolate then we seal ourselves up and snuff our own fire out. It's a defensive technique but it also happens during sex. Quincy must like you a lot. He's into fire types."

Genna thought about Quincy's eggshell thin cup of hot chocolate. She scrubbed harder. "That sounds very *Avatar: The Last Airbender*. Don't be Zuko. Be Azula."

"It's better than being called demons and hellspawn. Fire types don't have the best reputation."

"Why not go by Night Skins and be done with it?"

He pushed off the doorway. "You called him a Night Skin?"

"It seems it's the wrong word." Genna picked at a clump of mud and winced as it pulled skin. She tried to use her magic but it only thickened the clay shell.

He stepped closer. "Here. Like this."

Blue lightning spread from his eyes. It arced from his outstretched hand to her body. It tickled along the clay. It sparked as it hit the water.

She extended an arm. She tried not to feel self-conscious at his proximity. She did need help. She was being smothered. His hand passed a foot above her forearm. The clay disintegrated but turned into mud again with the water.

Genna concentrated, watching the pattern of lightning like it was choreography in a dance. She loosed her fire.

She exploded. The clay disintegrated.

The bathroom bowed and then flexed back into shape. It wobbled like it was made of rubber then it solidified. The shower head retracted into the stone wall like a startled moray eel. The ambient magic braided itself back together. The bathroom restored itself to pristine clinical white and stone gray again. Genna remembered how the pool room floor had moved under Quincy. She would have to learn how they installed these regenerative spells into the building.

His clothes were on fire, peeling away from his skin. His hair was blown into disarray. She expected him to scowl but his smirk had not changed.

"Oops," she said.

"Oops." He grinned harder. He took off the charred remnants of his clothes. He was comfortable naked. His suntanned torso was densely covered in tattoos. They were a shifting green and opalescent rainbow from the shell of his ears to the tip of his dick.

The shower head extended itself out of the wall again. Water poured down. Now on bare skin. Her breasts, her nipples, and her nether curls. She scrubbed her hair with a sigh of relief.

"I'll wash your back if you wash mine." He put his hand on the wall by the sink. He opened a cabinet door that seemed invisible until he pushed it. He picked up two pumice stones and a jar. "Salt scrub."

She locked her knees against the urge to retreat. "I'm not sucking your dick."

"Fair enough."

He walked closer. He stepped sideways into the shower area. She felt ticklish. Lightning kept arcing between them. She wiggled. "Stop that."

"You're the oldest fire Night Skin I've ever met. I'm excited." He gestured at himself and his semi-erection.

She stepped closer, nostrils flaring. Her hands already out. Wanting to touch.

His tattoos gleamed like a ball python under black light. Images artfully layered on top of each other. A cluster of chrysanthemums on braided ivy latticed across snake scales and waves and geometric patterns. No one particular theme or style. All woven together with the intricacy of camouflage. His body was painted in colors, shadows playing with light. His muscles were sculpted, hard as if from warm marble.

His big hand gently trapped hers against his chest.

She belatedly realized she had touched him without asking. Flustered and horrified by her imposition, she tried to reestablish some semblance of decorum. "Oh, I'm sorry. I should've asked your permission. Your tattoos are magnificent. May I keep touching them?"

"Yeah, you can," he said. "May I touch you?"

"In a minute. I need to concentrate. You're the first fire type I've ever met. I want to see you."

He released her hand and stepped forward. Her thumb flicked a nipple as she traced his pectorals and along the muscled ridges of his torso. Slight smile lines around his eyes. His smoldering presence was hypnotic.

He was made of lightning. Shifting and woven together. A violent rainbow in constant movement. She felt hot. The anger that exploded was quickly replaced. That fire was perfectly controlled inside of his skin. She learned as she explored.

She traced the scars hidden among the tattoos. She spread her hands wider. Her heartbeat chugged in her ears. His scent was compelling, like smoked copal wood, cloves, and something spicy.

His eyes hooded, shards of opals in shadow. Her body throbbed, watching the shift of muscles. Her hand cupped his jaw. He was so tall. Her other hand drifted across his waist but hesitated. It was more difficult to touch him the second time. Intentional instead of imposition.

He cupped her cheek; his fingers stroked the shape of her jaw. She jerked in surprise. She looked up at him, startled. His fingers curled away.

She was conscious of every breath. Of the shower water along her hairline, down her back, the shape of her body. Her tender and soft flesh while he was so close. So naked. She had just had sex, but this felt more intimate. She was hyper-aware of how she licked her lips. The air between them vibrated. All he did was stand there.

There were edges in his lightning. He wasn't just dangerous. He was lethal. A killer. He did not try to hide his nature or apologize. He simply was. Genna found him an intoxicating relief. She always had to rebrand her fire. To filter it. To make her wildfire pretty and safe when she never was.

"May I touch you now?" His quiet plea was not impatient. Excited but contained.

"I don't know what your lightning will do to me." She resisted the temptation to relax. The door to the shower was open. There was space enough to run.

"I won't hurt you. I won't betray you. I just want to touch you back."

She shook her head. Never trust a man who says *Trust me*. "I don't know you."

"I won't do anything. I swear it in my blood." He bit down and opened his mouth, a well of blood puddled in the lee of his tongue. His teeth where white and sharp. His breath was fresh, like ginger and mint.

She sniffed the blood. Already on her tiptoes. Her mouth open. Hunger and lust pushed past caution. She pressed her lips against his as her tongue darted into his mouth to scrape the wound. Blood filled her mouth. It sparkled and foamed as she swallowed. Little fireworks down her throat and into her stomach.

He leaned down and kissed her, cupping her face, giving her a chance to retreat. Instincts shrieked, but she kissed him harder. Their tongues ground together. Their fronts rubbed. She wished she were taller. Both were too slippery to manage climbing up his torso. His pleased rumble as her fingernails sank into the meat of his butt. Yummy handfuls.

"Tell me your name," she whispered.

The stubble on his jaw brushed her wet curls, his voice deep and soft. "I'm Troy."

"I'm Genna."

He smiled for her. "Hey, Genna."

Her name in his mouth felt like butter melting in the sun. Like fresh honey sliding over fingers. Like coming home. Like a warm bed and welcoming snuggles.

She kissed him again.

The rest of the world felt far away. As if they were in a little bubble of their own. The bass pulse of her heartbeat. The sizzle of lightning. The roar of fire as their magic blended together for the first time.

Her tongue rubbed against the edge of his canines. The wet slide of their thighs. Her muscles clenched, lower heat coiling with need as his dick brushed her front. His deep rumble she felt as much as heard. Their breaths had synced. He curved around her, protective and welcoming. His jaw brushed her hair again, closer, the soft press of his lips against the side of her head. His hands along her shoulders, her waist, her hips. His fervent want matched her own.

He was lightning. She was fire. They discovered each as they touched more. A wondrous need. A joyous relief. Tears flowed like lava. She pushed him away. Hands fisted. He kissed her forehead. She petted him and took steadying breaths. To slow down. To rein in the wild jubilation.

His hands were on the swell of her butt cheeks, lifting them up. He squeezed. Not hard. Savoring. Not rushing her. Simple touch. Comforting as it was arousing.

There was a particular knot of flesh diagonal across his chest that was perfect for her teeth to gently sink into. He stilled as she leaned forward. Her tongue followed the blue lightning-bolt patterns along his left pectoral. She felt the soft groan against her tongue. His hands fluttered around her shoulders, squeezed and encouraged. His nipple hardened at the puff of her breath and the tease of her tongue. Her hands pressed his ribs as she kissed and sucked. His broad hand upon the back of her neck as he arched, sensual and enticing.

She looked up his body and met his slitted eyes. She delighted in the glazed lust that she had put there. "Too much?"

"Harder."

"Even if I draw blood?"

His fingers cupped her jaw. "Promise?"

Genna's nostrils flared. A soft growl curled from her lips.

She licked the corded scar and opened her mouth wider to bite harder. His small, delicious shudder trembled through them both. He added a little more strength in the grip on her shoulders. She increased the power of her bite until she tasted blood. She held him, suckling like she was a short vampire. He ground his crotch against her front.

Genna hugged him tighter, gripped by howling possessiveness, as she sucked his blood. He curled forward. The thump of his fists against the wall behind her. The hiss of the shower. He undulated against her mouth, widening his stance to lower more of himself into biting range.

Her blood sizzled. The little-good-girl voice that warned about Quincy, commitments, and breaking rules burned to ash.

She wasn't a freak. She had merely never met anyone who was like her. She could not stop touching him. The rightness. The wonderful, glorious heat. She was burning with it.

He arched, belly exposed. His legs wide and hips thrust forward. His forehead against his curled fist, his gasps ragged, lost in sensation. His lips soft. Mouth wide. Closed eyes fluttering. Giving himself to her until he stopped her with small urgent pressure on her back.

Reluctantly, she disengaged. Her mouth was swollen and jaw wet with her own saliva. His deep, rumbling breaths in time with his squeezes. She delighted in the way he fought his own shivers, pulling himself from the brink. She lightened her touch.

She did not see a wolf in him. Only sharply ended lightning. Her teeth felt too big for her mouth. She licked him, her tongue lengthening. Her fingernails turning into claws. Her height lengthening. Smoky fur slick from the shower. His eyes opened, watched. He did not scream or flinch.

She could back off. Shoved herself into her human skin. Funnel the storm into something socially acceptable like fellatio. If it were Katie, she would have attacked. Ripped and chewed.

Genna was swept into a vortex of hunger and fire but finally it was okay. She could not burn Troy any more than he could burn her.

She slid against him, breast to crotch. On her hind legs, she was the same height. Her muzzle against his jaw. She focused on teasing him with her fur, her claws, her teeth, and the friction of her long long tongue. No need to rush. Better to feast on the heady sensations of having so much muscle and man quivering at her touch. He was gloriously uninhibited. Sensual and free with his interest.

She shifted her weight, undulating. Fur against flesh. She felt his erection rise at the friction. Her tail flicked for balance. Her claws clicked against the tile.

She slid her hands up his biceps, her claws leaving red trails along his skin. She crossed and then pinned his wrists against the wall behind him. Her eyes were orange embers. There was purple lightning in her eyelashes.

"Are you going to bite me?" he whispered.

"Ask me and I will." Her soft velvety growl against his ear.

His fists thumped against the wall behind him. "You could make a man give up his vows."

She traced the tattoo along his muscled neck with her tongue. He shifted and shivered under her claws as they danced down the edge of his ribs and back. His lips parted, his lips were soft. A blush like spilled wine. His ears magenta.

There was a slight vulnerability as his lightning sizzled faster, contracting tighter. She could read the colors as if it were a mood ring. She knew what that this furious opalescent rainbow meant. Lust. Excitement. Vulnerability. Loneliness. Surprise. Recklessness. Need.

She cupped his face, holding his against hers. She licked his cheek. She was calm with purpose. A deep pulse in her chest. She felt an impact, like an invisible bomb had detonated in that small space between them. It was not pain. It was a change that sizzled through her enflamed skin and fluffed her fur. An acknowledgment that this was only the beginning of something. There was a world before now. There was a future and Troy was in it.

She was keeping him. Whatever it took. However much it cost. If she had to marry Quincy. Only have threesomes. Whatever.

She exhaled and back up. *No.*

Troy was wrong. The scars, calluses, and tattoos told a story. She recognized the symbols even if she wanted to ignore them. He was a killer of magical things like her. A monster hunter.

He looked like every boy she was never allowed to date. His hair was golden under the black dye. The face of the enemy. The charismatic smile and shark eyes. The frat boy who won MVP during lacrosse tournaments. The best golfer. The captain of the army. The Ivy League legacy. He never questioned his own authority. He was casual with his money. He was tan from his boat. His wealth was understated but present. He looked like a hero. The guy on the white horse. The gunslinger. The pirate king. The man with the sensual mouth and smoldering gaze. His long fingers and husky voice. His thick grabbable hair. His long-torsoed masculine beauty that made other men insecure and women desperate.

He was the quintessential bad boy. He probably had a Harley, a big black truck, something rugged like a Bronco. The tattooed blond rich guy.

She needed a weapon, a harpoon gun to kill all the great white sharks that circled her life. Troy was standing right here like a perfectly balanced sword in an armory. What could she do with him in her hand?

Her instincts screamed at her for asking anyone for help, especially this guy. What was she doing? Coward. Traitor. *Bed wench.*

Quincy was downstairs. This was his mansion. She was letting some pretty random guy flirt and impose. She was not that person. She did not have random sex with random strangers. It didn't matter how much of a connection she felt.

This could not be. She was not here to feel this much for anyone. It wasn't safe.

He swayed. His hands flashed out. He grabbed her, looping her close. She did not claw him. She looked at him as she sank back into her human skin. "Release me immediately."

His hands slid off her body but she felt the strain. Lightning licked her, tugged her forward. Their lips were close. His forehead pressed against hers. Their blunt teeth bared. They were breathing hard like they had raced a marathon. Water steamed off their skin. Her hair curled into a frizzy cloud.

She stepped out of the shower. She grabbed a towel. She never took her eyes off of him. The heat in his chest flared, reaching toward her, wanting more. Plaintive. Confused. Longing.

She shook her head.

His burnt-honey hair dripped water into his eyes. He slicked it out of his face in frustration that also displayed his muscled beauty. He was wet and willing. She fought the urge to pounce. To take him. This was not the way.

His dark brown eyebrows pressed together. His full lips were in a dangerous frown. Shadows darkened as his magic burned into the physical world. "What the hell are you doing, Genna?"

"You know me but I don't know you. I am done with people looking at me *exactly* like you are right now. At least Quincy was respectful with his sanctimonious suit. He wooed me. You walked into the shower, expecting me to spread for you because you've got some extra sizzle in your sausage."

He squeezed the edge of the shower door. She could hear the whine of straining stone. Ceramic cracking. "You want me. Take me."

She raised her chin. "I am a luxury than you cannot afford. Not some casual bitch you fuck."

"I don't know who fucked you over, but it ain't me, lady."

She kept walking. Needing distance. The long straight hallway had only one connecting corridor and a stairwell. She was already lost but each step was against the current pulling her right back into his arms. Her body was already dry as she tucked the towel tight around her chest.

<h1 style="text-align:center">Twenty</h1>

Genna glanced back as she turned the corner. The bathroom door was still open. Troy's head was bowed. One hand was flat against the wall. The other hand jerked his erection. Water boiled off his head and back. She watched, her view perfect. The fluctuations. The flex of his butt cheeks. The slither of his tattoos. Color rose in her skin.

She was disgusted with herself for being aroused. His head canted back. Teeth bared. Hunger. Anger. She could not stop watching him masturbate.

"I can feel you watching me," he growled. "Come back."

"No."

He groaned a snarl. "Come back. I'll respect the shit out of you."

"What about Quincy?"

"You want a threesome. I'm fine with that. I know he is too. Anything you want."

Footsteps. Quincy was at the bottom of the stairs. He carried a neon yellow Blue Ivy tracksuit, a small Coach bag of makeup, and a pair of white Air Jordan high-tops. He knew her sizes.

"Everything okay?"

They both had magic. Water. Earth. Fire. Genna was having a

hard time thinking. Her thoughts were slow. The hunger raw and real. She should have eaten before the date. Now real hunger and arousal mixed together.

Troy shoved away from the shower. Pissed off. Predatory. The pulse of lightning like a star. "Genna, come back."

He was a monster. She could feel it in those blue lightning eyes that were brown in real life without magic to light them. He was a monster with blood between his teeth and fire in his heart. Just like her. She felt exposed. The howl of the Old Night called.

Quincy moved slowly up the stairs. He moved wide of Genna. She glared at him too. He had Troy and he was still looking around?

Lightning filled every hair follicle. Her body quivered like a tuning fork.

Quincy stepped into the hallway. He looked between them. "Troy, be nice."

"I can be very nice." Troy was close. His tongue licked the air. She jerked as if he had laved her clit.

Think. She had to think. She went on attack. She glared at Troy, backing towards the stairwell. "You're a monster hunter. I know what those tattoos mean."

"I'm part of the Luparii and other organizations," Troy said. "We've been hunting wolves since before Charlemagne."

"I'm a wolf."

"I won't hurt you. I gave you my blood and my word."

"You did?" Quincy said, shocked.

In the clean white light of the hallway she could see Quincy's tattoos more clearly. Tituba had told her and yet Genna hadn't thought he was a threat until now. "You kill witches. You're a witchfinder."

"It's more complicated than that," Quincy said.

"Not really. I've outed myself to both of you. I've betrayed my own ignorance. You haven't killed me but you will." She had been on her guard before but Troy had opened her up. She couldn't form a consistent defense against them both.

"I gave you my word," Troy repeated.

"I let you into my inner sanctum," Quincy said. Then glanced at Troy, a hand up. "She's new. She doesn't understand. Don't push."

"No, she's fire. Stop trying to smother her flame." Troy rumbled like thunder.

The hallway shrank down. Troy and Quincy's power pressed against her skin. Lightning eroded her meager defenses. The ground was soft under her feet. She pressed against the wall. Hyperventilating.

"Genna, you're okay. We mean it." Quincy's lips pressed tight.

Genna was suffocating. Her opponents were composed. They frowned at her like she was a feral cat hissing and spitting. Quincy's magic spread like an oversized towel ready to wrap her up. Troy was determined to keep crowding her space. He showed his sincerity through magic.

She was angry with herself. She was only wearing a towel. Naked in a way she had never been before. They could do anything. She was alone. She trusted. She ignored her instincts because she wanted sex.

Why was she sure this would work? She was stupider than stupid. Hubris. Again. Goddammit.

How to get out? Where to run? Nothing but white hallways and white stairs. Like Katie's mansion but worse. Every exit closed.

"I know about Katie McBride," Quincy said.

Genna stared at him. What was his angle? "That's not hard. Look me up and she's there."

"I know that you've refused to be a vampire bride. We're sorry if we've triggered you."

"Is that why I smell vampires?" Troy rumbled.

"Troy, you're scaring her," Quincy said, scales formed along his cheekbones in aggravation.

"You're scaring her! She hates the mud, Quincy. Put it away!"

Quincy shoved him. Lightning spat. For a moment, both men

were focused on each other instead of her. Genna fled down the stairs, snatching the clothes and shoes as she passed Quincy. Both men followed. She tried to find a bathroom. Some place to close a door.

The hallways were eggshell-white walls and exposed cement with gray rugs down the center. The framed pictures between the white doors were uninspired mass-produced Jackson Pollock-equese blotches of color. The recessed lighting emphasized the stark decor. She was in a maze of hallways with less personality than a hotel.

Genna rounded a corner. She hopped into her pants. Stuffed her feet into the sneakers. Now her head was tangled in her borrowed hoodie as she charged through the mansion chased by Troy and Quincy's shouts. The tug of their magic braided into a lasso. She ducked, unwilling to be dragged back the way she came.

She yanked the hood off of her face just in time to slam into a soft wall. Muscled arms wrapped around her, smashing her into great pillowy breasts. Thick thighs and sturdy hips barely rocked on impact as the woman absorbed all of her momentum.

Genna's chaotic focus ricocheted out of her body and into magic. She was trapped in the eye of a hurricane whose vast wings churned the air. A great tail stirred ocean water, silt, and sand up into a solid column of deadly force. Lighting danced through scales and teeth. The power was older and harder than Quincy's. A crocodile instead of alligator.

A female dragon.

Many things lived in the forest. Genna had seen dragons but none were like her. She had the beautiful destructive power of a category five hurricane contained inside of a large curvy woman. Genna liked to think she had some 'cushion for the pushin' but the dragon woman was more. Everything more. Genna had been wrong to call Quincy and Troy a Night Skin. This woman was a Night Skin. Elemental and ancient power.

She also had Genna clamped in a headlock. Genna was back

in the real world, in the hallway, in a hard forearm squeezing the air out of her neck. Troy and Quincy were close, strides away.

Genna burned free of her clothes in a burst of flash fire. She bit the dragon woman on the breast, knocked out her knee and hip in a judo strike, wrenched free of the chokehold, spun her upside down, bounced her on her head, and slammed her flat on her back with a knee in her sternum. The dragon woman's head bounced hard against the stone floor. The woman flopped, knocked unconscious.

Genna pinned her wrist with one hand. She slid her free hand along the back of the woman's head, through the thick afro of curls to check for a concussion. Her knees kept the woman's legs spread wide. Her breasts brushed against the woman's magnificent cleavage.

The dragon woman opened her eyes at Genna's pulse of magic to heal any internal damage.

"You have gorgeous cheekbones," was what Genna meant to say. Instead Genna roared fire into her face. All of her sexual frustration, the need to prove her dominance, her fear about hunters, finders, that this was a trap coalesced into a solid column of flame.

Genna's initial bite had broken through the dragon woman's thick scales and into her core. The dragon woman bellowed as magical and physical wildfire speared through the opening and burned up everything inside. Her scales glowed a bright dangerous turquoise gilded in lapis and gold. Her spiraled blast of wind, water, and supercharged mud turned to steam and dust.

Then Genna was wrenched away by her hair. She fought and bit as she was yanked upwards. Her mouth was wrenched open. The pressure of air shoved inside her throat.

A different woman coalesced out of the wind. There were rainbows in her hair and a sunrise in her skin. Her muscular body was fluid. Wind and dust swirled like layers of a voluminous skirts and sleeves. She danced as she spun out of Genna's reach. Her long thin braids slapped her eyes like a flair as she twirled. She was beautiful. Delicate brown toes planted on air as if gravity were a suggestion. Her scream twisted into a tornado roar. Her vampire teeth extended.

Genna's fire was sucked away. She couldn't breathe. She flailed. Desperate. Invisible claws scraped the inside of her lungs. Magic reversed the flow of blood. Squeezed her heart. Twisted her guts. Agony eclipsed thought as she was juiced like a lemon. Only instead of blood it was air being wrenched out of her body.

Quincy and the dragon woman grabbed Genna by her ankles, hauling her downward. The hurricane was back and stronger. Two swamp dragons smothered her. There was no air. Only mud. So much mud. Genna couldn't see. Mud in her skin. Mud dragged her under. She fought them. She tried to scream as she was ripped apart but she was dying.

Then a bolt of blue lightning from above blasted the dragons off of her and knocked the tornado woman up into the ceiling. Troy tackled Genna. The mud exploded away.

"Get away from her!" Troy roared.

He turned his bladed magic on the others, driving them back, slashing and snarling with possessive fury. The others fell away, surprised. The tornado woman shrieked as she was pierced. She landed hard, cocooned by ropes of lightning. Quincy and the dragon woman jerked and thrashed. Also pinned to the floor by lightning.

Troy held Genna's limp body, wiping her nose and mouth clear. The other three bellowed in agony as their skin blistered and their magic focused on fighting his lightning instead of on Genna.

The room cracked. The glass ceiling melted as it fell. The walls caved in. The pool dried up. The floor broke. The embedded magic burning up as lightning filled every electric wire. Water burst every pipe. Stone disintegrated into mud.

Troy held Genna inside a floating vortex of lightning. He lifted her lolling head. Her skin gray cement. Eyes strained to open against the weight. Her breath the thinnest wheeze. Mud inside her mouth. Her nostrils.

Troy smashed his lips onto Genna's sagged mouth. He

wrapped around her. He filled her with lightning. Instead of sharp pain he filled her with love, scared and defensive. He put his hand in the deepest core of her magic. A searing ocean of healing scoured her clean. He gave her everything. Calling her name. Telling her to wake up.

She already had swallowed his blood. Now it ignited. It was too much. Too good.

Genna exploded like a volcano. She swept the others up into a cascade of lava. Billowing gouts of black smoke. Lightning and fire incinerated every other magic.

Twenty-One

GENNA HUNCHED IN A SCRATCHY WOOL BLANKET. SHE was dressed in loose scrubs but felt as vulnerable as a freshly shucked oyster. Cracked open and waiting for teeth and forks to bite and stab.

Every breeze, every movement was a new pain. As if the skin of her soul had been peeled off, leaving raw nerves and tender flesh. She touched her face to remind herself that she was still sitting on the edge of an ambulance.

There was a crater in the middle of the Gold Coast. Like someone had tried to smoke a stick of dynamite and taken half of their mouth out.

At the epicenter, Quincy's mansion looked like a science-fair project that had gone terribly awry. Charred sludge and warped steel clung to the melted stone. The rubble had knocked in the sides of the neighboring mansions. The cold breeze from Lake Michigan swept most of the smoke away.

Whirling blue and red lights painted the shadows. Fire trucks, ambulances, police, and gawking people filled the street. Many people had been hurt when the building exploded. Genna's Glamazons and PR team had kept her safely away from the humans. Her parents were not happy either.

Genna tried to feel guilty. She felt nothing. Not happy. Not scared. Not angry. Empty.

Too much magic. Way too much intimacy. Too much exposure. Too many emotions. She did not know if she would ever be ready to talk about what had happened.

Troy and Naomi were thirty feet away. Quincy had not stopped yelling and gesticulating.

It was Naomi York who had sucked the air out of Genna's body. Naomi looked like Miss Bootsie. The same face. Same eyes though hers were a stormy gray. The same smooth brown skin. Gorgeous. Taller. Thinner as if her curves had been stretched.

Naomi was also a vampire. The same gaunt hungry expression Katie had. Her hair were in thin micro-braids that shifted like restless snakes. Genna understood why Miss Bootsie had been afraid. All her boo hag power combined with vampiric selfishness made a beautiful and deadly combination. Genna had been powerless as every cell in her body, magical and physical, had turned against her. Helpless. Dying. Confused inevitability.

Then Troy saved her. She wasn't sure how to feel about that.

The dragon woman walked over. She gave Genna a neutral but friendly smile. "Hi Iphigenia, I'm Cleopatra. May I sit down?"

Cleopatra had wrapped her hair up into multiple colorful scarves, a few curls peeking from the top. Somehow her clothes had survived the explosion. The others had too. Only Genna needed to borrow scrubs from the EMTs.

Genna flexed shoulder. "Call me Genna."

"Don't call me Cleo. It's either Cleopatra or nothing." Cleopatra sat. She handed Genna her Jada Dubai high heels.

Genna stared at her shoes. "They're okay?"

"I fixed them."

"Thanks." Genna put her shoes on. She felt a pulse of a tracking spell in the leather and the diamonds. Two stomps was all it took to burn them away.

Cleopatra raised an eyebrow. "You bounce back fast."

"I try."

Genna remembered pinning her down. The feel of her body against her own. Genna wanted to lick all that fine brown skin. To taste her sweat. To snuffle the little black curls escaping the scarf at the nape of her neck. To feel the weight of her heavy breasts. To lick the under-curve of her butt cheeks. To kiss her toes. To fuck her until she forgot everything.

Genna cleared her throat and shifted on the ambulance's cold metal bumper. She was embarrassed that the first thing to come back online was her libido. Meanwhile the rest of her felt loosely tethered to her skin.

There was a bandage under Cleopatra's shirt. Right where her breast met her sternum.

"Hey, I'm sorry I bit you," Genna said. "I don't react well when people go for my throat."

"I'll heal."

Genna looked down at her hands. "Sorry I blew up your house."

"It wasn't the first time. It won't be the last."

"You're a dragon. That's cool."

"Technically yes. In the real world I look like a crocodile. I live in the pyramid in Memphis, Tennessee."

"Isn't that a Bass Pro Shop?"

"Hey, don't knock it. The pyramid used to be a weird basketball stadium. Sticking the Bass Pro franchise in the building made it perfectly reasonable for a few gators to lounge in the shadows and water. Until you showed up, I was having the time of my life, being Cleopatra with my very own Julius Caesar and Marc Antony. Naomi had her anchors and her firestarter. Now look at what you've done."

"Sorry." Genna stared at the crater. "I'll pay for the medical expenses of everyone hurt in the fires. I'll pay for everything. The remolds. If anyone wants to sell, I'll buy. All of it."

"It's the Gold Coast. There won't be a lack of buyers." Cleopatra glared at the growing crowd.

"I'll make sure things are built according to the original design. I'd like to keep it historically accurate. No modern garbage."

Cleopatra tilted her head. "I'll keep that in mind. Quincy said you liked the Driehaus."

"I loved it." The Driehaus felt like a lifetime ago instead of twelve hours.

They sat in silence for a while. Genna tried not to watch the wrinkles on Cleopatra's hip and side. Dear God, this woman was beautiful. Like an avatar for a fertility and death goddess. A shield maiden. A valkyrie. Sensuality smoldered off of her pores. If Genna encountered her standing hip-deep in a body of water, wearing nothing but a wet dress, she would have walked right in. No questions asked.

Troy. Quincy. Now Cleopatra. After a sexual desert, Genna was in surrounded by epically beautiful people. No wonder she had short-circuited.

Genna darted another look at Naomi. She was pretty too but painfully. Like Katie but wrong. All Genna had were questions.

"Quite a splash you've made." Cleopatra said in the awkward silence.

"Sorry."

"You're very calm."

"I'm not." The urge to cry pressed hard against her self-control.

"Naomi snuffed you out. Troy attacked her. Kaboom. You're not dead, either. That's what's freaking everyone out. Quincy said you were smothered in some heavy mojo. Naomi thinks you're here to kill her. That's why she attacked. And Troy is Troy."

"Sounds about right." Genna had a feeling that Troy had broken trust in protecting her and attacking his roommates but she wasn't willing to think about his motivations too hard. She wanted to go home.

"You and Quincy were very involved in the pool room."

Genna imagined Cleopatra watching among the potted

plants, protective and ready. Genna exhaled in frustration. "Matchmakers. I don't get why he's even in the dating pool when he's got you three."

"Quincy's a lover, not a fighter. It happens with us border types."

"Border type?"

"A shore or a swamp isn't water or earth. It's both. When our powers combine we recreate the storm that woke our magic."

"What storm was that?"

"Hurricane Katrina."

Genna pulled the blanket tighter around herself. "That's one hell of a superpower."

"Superpower." Cleopatra pursed her lips. "I was trapped in a car. Dad didn't think the water was deep. The engine got flooded when he drove through it. I was strapped in. The floodwater swept the car off the road before I could get out. I remember people clinging to trees. Watching as my car floated past. I broke the window to get out. I swam and swam. They said it was a miracle. I didn't know I was magic. Swimming through all those drowned and bloated bodies fucked me up. I ate them. Disgusting, right?"

"You're a Night Skin. Your power came when you needed it. From what I've seen, magic translates itself to fit the circumstances. How it manifests into our world depends upon the person it uses as a filter. You've got a personal connection to ancient Egypt, it makes sense that your magic manifests as a Nile crocodile instead of a Louisiana gator. The dragon makes sense too. A vessel to hold all the elements. Leviathans were credited as forces of nature. Like you."

"Yes, well, everyone has power around here." Cleopatra waved her hand at the air, clearly uncomfortable. "Naomi and Sable got sucked into the hurricane. They ran and ran. They didn't know they were flying until they were above the clouds. The air was thin. They were freezing. They kept running to get away from the storm. They didn't know that they were a tornado."

Cleopatra nodded at Troy and Quincy. "Their dads were best friends and hunting partners. They were in New Orleans, helping people evacuate to Texas. There's a lot of old magical artifacts and spellbooks that needed to be safely extracted. Galveston was the nearest magical stronghold. Pacos Bill, that's Troy's dad, died teaching Quincy how to swim through the storm. He got tangled in a net. He told Quincy to find Troy. Quincy did. The boys found the Waffle House their moms had turned into a safe haven. I found it too. So did Sable and Naomi."

"Troy's dad was Pacos Bill? That explains the lightning rope and how he could grab Naomi."

Cleopatra wrinkled her nose and raised an eyebrow. "Most people don't make that connection so quickly but yes, Troy is a direct descendent of Pacos Bill, the man who roped a twister. His mom's side are monster hunters who's line goes all the way back to Greek mythology."

"That's quite a pedigree."

Cleopatra gave her another look. "We're not the only ones with old names. Naomi's name is Old Testament. Quincy's name is Quintus, which is Roman. Troy's real name is Achilles."

All the muscles locked in Genna's body. "That's interesting."

In the *Iliad*, her namesake, Iphigenia, was supposed to marry the warrior king Achilles but was sacrificed on a pyre instead. She chose to die so her husband-to-be could become a great warrior. Her death pleased the gods into showing the way to the city of Troy. Helen's abduction by Paris was 'the face that launched a thousand ships' but Iphigenia was the first innocent victim of the Trojan War. She died for the love of a man she had just met.

There was no such thing as a spooky coincidence when a pissed-off witch nursing a four-hundred-year-old grudge was involved.

Cleopatra gestured in a circle, unaware of Genna's internal turmoil. "We survived Katrina because of what we are. Maybe our names are part of the power that got us through the storm. It's been us since Katrina. You probably think it's weird. We're not even the same kind of magic."

"I don't think it's weird. I figured you neutralize each other's power. That's how you keep things stable and can live your lives."

Cleopatra wrinkled her nose and raised an eyebrow. "Were you there?"

"At Hurricane Katrina?" Genna tried to think of where she was in August 2005. She was ten. Her family had donated a lot to the relief effort, medical teams, supplies, and rehoming projects. "No, I was at my castle fighting vampires." Genna grimaced at the crater again. "I've always been wildfire but I've never exploded before. That's not something I want to repeat."

Cleopatra rubbed a thumb over her breast. She looked at her roommates with a slight frown.

"Did I hurt you?" Genna said again.

"I'll live." Neutral. Another wall.

Genna fidgeted. Unhappy. Self-conscious. The bite was a mark of dominance. Ownership. The need to prove her power had pushed Genna to a level of desperate violence she only let Katie see. That wasn't okay. "Cleopatra, I need you to tell me if I hurt you. I need to know. There's no excuse for my behavior. I'm sorry."

Cleopatra gave her a long look. Slowly she reached down the collar of her shirt. Genna swallowed hard. She watched tape pull against skin. The flex of Cleopatra's muscles. The pulse of her throat. Cleopatra tugged her collar lower to give Genna an unobstructed view. Genna swallowed hard as drool filled in her mouth. She was self-conscious of how she leaned close. Her nostrils flared to savor Cleopatra's scent.

A perfect imprint of Genna's dentition set inside of a large purple and red bruise lay upon Cleopatra's breast like a rose. As Genna watched the contusions faded. The imprint healed. Scales grew over it then smoothed.

"See? I healed. I've a very tough marshmallow. You can't hurt me." Her voice stuttered as Genna lightly traced a finger over that fine skin.

Genna ignored the whisper of disappointment. It was better that she healed. She looked up at Cleopatra. She paused at her full lips. Then concentrated on her dark brown eyes. She saw the crocodile look. Cleopatra made no move to stop Genna's touch. There was no hint of enjoyment either. Weaponized beauty luring her close to bite.

Genna sat back and squeezed her fingers in her lap. "Sorry, I should've asked first."

"What do you want with Naomi?"

"I'm not here to kill Naomi," Genna said, earnest and formal.

"Others have tried," Cleopatra said, the same neutral inviting tone.

"The matchmaker told me that Quincy would introduce us. I know Naomi's grandmothers, her bitch-ass stepsister, and stepmother. They live on the other side of the woods from my castle. I was the stand-in for Naomi, the sunshine girl."

It hurt to say. Old pain and inadequacy.

"The McBrides are vampires," Genna continued. "Naomi's a threat to the current heir. Her whole family sucks. The boo hag side is dead except for Naomi and Sable. Is Sable still alive?"

"Sable is around. You're looking for both of them?"

"I thought I could fulfill a promise I'd made. Miss Bootsie wanted them to stay far away from the forest."

"Naomi thinks you seduced Quincy and Troy to betray us."

"I'm not here to kill Naomi. Or seduce anyone. The matchmaker set me up."

"But Troy did save you from us."

Genna sighed with frustration. "Fucking Tituba. I should've known better than to go along with her meddling."

Cleopatra straightened up. "You know Tituba the witch?"

"My parents hired her as a matchmaker. You know her? Have you used her services?"

Cleopatra slid carefully off of the bumper. Genna glanced at her, distantly surprised. Until this moment, Cleopatra's chutzpah seemed to fill the world. Now she was small, like prey. "Tituba's *your* witch."

"I wouldn't put a possessive on anything. It's complicated."

"Complicated how?"

"She hates me for what my ancestors did to her and her family." Genna waggled her right hand so the diamond sparkled. If Cleopatra could be honest then so could she. "It turns out that my people tortured and enslaved hers then accused them of witchcraft when our gold mine went dry. We're the reason that she ended up in Massachusetts during the Salem Witch Trials. She wants revenge. We didn't know that until I started researching my ancestry. I guess you could say I woke up a generational wealth curse?"

"Troy!" Cleopatra's full crocodile bellow momentarily eclipsed all sound, rattling the windows of the ambulance. Genna nearly toppled from her perch.

Cleopatra stormed over to her roommates who had stopped arguing. She grabbed Troy and Naomi by the arms and pointed them toward Genna.

"You did this." Cleopatra snarled at Troy, whose expression had not changed much. "Tituba's gold is right on her finger."

The four looked at Genna. The stance was now hostilely appraising. Genna wanted to cover her ring.

Cleopatra shoved Quincy in the chest, rocking him back on his heels. "We're going. Now."

"Cleopatra, stop," Quincy said, batting her away.

She trapped his hands and shoved him again. "Shut up and come on, dumbass. We need to go. We need to go now. Tituba sent her. Iphigenia's people owned the gold mine."

"We just found out," Quincy said, offering Cleopatra his phone like it was a tiny shield. "Tituba set us up. Our folks are meeting with her right now. She wants us all to move in with Genna. She has a stable location. A castle."

"You want to move into her castle." Cleopatra looked like someone trying not to turn into a dragon and rip his face off.

Quincy shrugged, ingratiatingly apologetic. "I'm surprised too."

"Not that surprised," Cleopatra said archly.

"She's like us," Troy said.

Cleopatra gave him a look, pointing a finger like the nose of a gun at his chest. "You've done enough."

Troy raised his chin. "We're meeting the family for Sunday brunch to iron out the details."

"Since when do you do brunch?" Cleopatra snapped.

"It's not a big deal," Naomi soothingly. Her light touch along Cleopatra's shoulder spoke volumes.

"How isn't it a big deal? Look at our house!" Cleopatra said, aggravated enough to shrug off Naomi's placating hand. "That's what you've been planning while I'm putting myself into her teeth?"

"You're the only one who hadn't gotten a chance to know her," Naomi said.

"Only because you were spying on her the whole time!"

Genna blinked. It had been a long time since anyone had so skillfully mined Genna for information. Even in human form Cleopatra was a force of nature. The other three had waited for her to work her magic instead of trying to interrupt. They were a team. She was heavy artillery.

Genna glumly wondered if she should have lied or simply kept her mouth shut. She liked them. It was sudden and volatile, but these four were real. They were magic. They understood. She wanted to join their circle, not destroy it. What would it have been like to have friends, real friends, instead of Katie? But they were not her friends.

The trick was to stay calm. To think. What was the move here? All Genna could do was wait for more information. She had to trust her parents.

Genna retreated into a waiting car and went straight to the Falcon. Her PR cancelled her stay in Chicago. Katie sat in the Falcon's main cabin. Her hair was stuffed under a floppy beige hat. She wore oversized Chanel sunglasses. She hunched inside of her beige Burberry trench coat. Her pointed heels were already off. She sat down in the padded chair disguised as a rich WASPy bitch.

"That was intense," Katie said as Genna sat down across from her. She took her sunglasses off. Her skin looked like it had undergone a chemical peel.

For once, Genna did not care that Katie was in her personal space. She used the time to study the vampire's micro-movements and compare them to Naomi. "You were in the house?"

"Close enough." Katie waggled her penciled-in eyebrows. "How was sexy fun time?"

"It was fun right up until Naomi snuffed me out like a goddamn candle."

"She couldn't kill you."

"I got lucky." The absurdity of being saved by a guy she had only just met and refused to have shower sex with at war with her vulnerability and terror. Without Troy, she would be dead. She fiddled with her ring, fuming. "We need to deal with Naomi. Sable too."

"Bitch, please, we need the deal with all of them. They're from Roanoke and Galveston, the most well funded monster hunter and witch finder strongholds in the country."

"I believe it." Genna's phone pinged. She stared at the message with growing incredulity. "My parents just invited the hunters to live at my castle."

Katie straightened up. "You're shitting me. Why would they?"

"It's gotta be Tituba," Genna shook her head. "She's got them wrapped around her fingers. It was never about Chicago. She wants them in Sweetwater."

"You think they're after Pipsy?"

"Bitch, they're after all of us. Hell, they might try to chop down the forest. Who knows what her end game looks like."

Katie took Genna's compact mirror out of her purse and reapplied her pink lipgloss. "But you've got a plan, right?"

Genna exhaled slowly. The numbness had faded. "Our number one problem is Naomi. Her air magic made my blood flow backwards."

"I know. She bit me too," Katie seethed. "I'm going to get her back."

"I have an idea but I need your blood. You're tied to the forest so it'll hurt worse than anything I've ever done to you but it'll work. We can't bite air but we can damn sure contain it in a wind catcher."

Katie closed the compact with a snap and simpered, flipping her hair over her shoulder. "Oh Iffy, you say the sweetest things."

By the time the Falcon's wheels touched tarmac Genna had hired several kinetic wind catcher artists and paid them at four times their usual rate to get an accelerated timeline. Genna even allowed Katie to use glamour to grease the wheels. There was no room for mistakes.

Genna and Katie invoked a spell in the forest while Genna's family took over the castle in preparation for Sunday brunch. They met at the pole.

Genna hefted the bowling ball opal out of a Tumi backpack. She rubbed a hand along the edge of the opal. "If Miss Bootsie can sever their connections then we can make new ones but in a way that neutralizes their ability to hurt us." She presented the opal to Katie. "I need you to swallow this."

"Easy enough." Katie expanded into an enormous yellow snake. She had gotten longer, more muscled, and was taller than the pole. Her head was narrower than Pipsy's because she only had a single pair of fangs instead of four sets. Her cobra's hood was thick.

Genna stepped away from the stump. She angled her body like a pitcher on a mound. "Ready?"

Katie uncoiled, speeding like a train, her jaw wide enough to swallow Genna in one long gulp. Her long, muscled body unwinding. Her clothes were forgotten rags below her scales. Genna spun in a circle and hurled the boulder opal straight into Katie's mouth. The force hit Katie like a cannonball. It knocked out all of her forward momentum and her fangs. She gulped as she fell sideways. She landed, coiling and uncoiling as she rolled over the weeds. Her body shriveled into its human shape. Her belly was now swollen. Her legs and arms were spindly. Blue veins crawled along her neck. Her eyes bulged as she choked.

Katie stared at Genna as she clutched her belly. "You impregnated me."

"Did you forget that you swallowed an opal?" Genna said, staring down at the vampire. Her skin prickled with dread.

"I'm all yours now, Iffy," Katie said. "I never told you pregnancy was our weakness. How did you figure it out? You're so smart."

"Focus!"

"Yes, Iffy." Katie gargled and coughed. She bent forward.

Brackish water seeped from her pores. Her scales coated in algae slime. Her hair changed into water reeds. Then fell out entirely. With great effort, Katie vomited up the opal again. It rolled across the weeds. Genna dropped the fur cloak on it. Then she yanked it out of the water. She swept the cloak in a wide circle, the rippling edge flaring, the fur fluffed. The clasp now a small blue opal at its center, the size of a marble.

Meanwhile, Katie's body kept transforming. It widened and hardened. She had ten limbs. Her tail was long and hard. She shrank down into a giant blue horseshoe crab.

Genna picked up the backpack. She walked over to the crab scuttling along the sodden grass. She lifted her up. Katie the crab was too big to fit into the bag. Her legs wiggled. Her gills flapped. Genna carried the crab back to the cottage. She set Katie into the sink upside-down. Katie kicked and wiggled, her long tail scraping against the counter edge. Her layers of gills struggled for air.

Genna added several pine logs to the fireplace. She glared at them, gathering her feelings, then blew out a steady stream of fire. The hearth warmed as the logs burned. Smoke streamed up the chimney flue.

"I'm making wind catchers for your sunshine girl," Genna announced to the cottage. "Help me."

The furniture began to move. Wood screeched and scraped as a spinning wheel, loom, and other less familiar equipment trooped themselves out of the closet.

Genna opened a drawer. The kitchen knife was long polished metal with a curved point at the end. The wood handle was old and worn shiny. The knife had lived in that drawer in its little wooden stand since the cottage was first built. It was polished and honed. The wood replaced itself when it rotted. It was not a sword, but sometimes, when it needed to be, it was a weapon.

Genna cut herself on the edge of her bicep with the kitchen knife. Then she used the bloody knife to chop Katie's tail off. She set the tail and knife on the counter. She put a mason jar under the stream of blue blood. Katie had no voice to scream as her blood frothed while filling the jar. Genna drank thirstily. She filled the jar three times before she was satisfied. Then she filled a few pitchers and buckets she found in the cabinets with blue blood. Then she turned on the faucet. The blue blood mixed with the tap water, pouring down the drain into the hungry mouth of the cottage plumbing.

All the death. All the pain. All the magic Katie had ingested went into the cottage and then into the forest.

Genna opened the pullout couch. She spread the cloak across it, the red side up. She set all of the items in the backpack across the cloak. Dozens of gold, silver, copper, wood, shell, and clay hoop earrings. Some empty circles. Other were woven, beaded, enameled, and other forms of decoration.

She set buckets of water and Katie's blood on the floor. Baskets and bags of cotton and silk cocoons arranged themselves across the couch. Genna added jars of peanut butter, beeswax, honey, and herbs from the garden to the formation. Apples from the orchard. Freshly brew coffee. Freshly popped kettle corn. Strands of hair from Bibi and Sneakers' manes and tails. Tufts of fur from Toto, Grim, and Schrodinger. Pirate's shed tail feathers. She fiddled with their layout while the sink hissed.

Genna left the cottage and walked along the perimeter of the castle grounds as a wolf. She stayed inside the tree line. She marked strategic places.

"I will not be snuffed out," Genna said to herself as she fed the spell but she looked at the crab still bleeding out into the sink. She was unnerved by Katie's confession.

It made a horrible sense. Power dynamics defined Katie and Genna's relationship. To make a vampire into a bride instead of being her bride. Mimi always complained that Katie ate all of her power. If that wasn't euphemistic but a statement of fact. Genna had made a mistake.

It took three days and three nights to drain Katie. Genna's power drifted through the forest like warm mist. The trees budded. Ferns unfurled from the mud. The rain lightened. New channels of creeks formed. Tree roots clung tight to rocks. The forest strengthened and reinforced its hold on the Heights. It spread down Backbone into Sweetwater. It added neutral trees and decorative landscaping to the forest's domain. Things slaughtered and maimed. Blood turned the dirt into mud. Water flowed fast and sweet.

Finally, Genna turned off the tap. She hoisted the crab out of the sink and wrapped a muslin cloth the tail to tie it back on. Then she doused the crab with honey. Katie transformed back into her human body. She was as pale as a fish belly. Genna stroked her face.

"Thank you," Katie whispered. "I didn't think you'd undo the transformation." She tried to kiss Genna. "I love you."

"Yeah, well, you're welcome," Genna said gruffly dodging the hug.

Genna had followed her to the edge of the woods. Mimi and Pipsy stood waiting, as worried as she had ever seen them. Genna retreated back to the cottage. She could hear them as she hung the larger wind catchers and wind chimes along the porch's edge. She arranged the metal tubes in pleasing harmony and listened.

"You stupid child, you gave her everything. I should throw you back in the woods," Pipsy said.

Katie batted her hands away. She stood up, smiling proudly as she shook her head. "Do you like my new earrings?"

The earrings were a pair of wind catchers. Gemstones glittered at the juncture of every knot. Beads hung along the end like bells.

"She bled you dry," Mimi said. "Look at your face."

There was a small divot on the side of Katie's face. Between her eye and her ear. Most of it was hidden by hair. There was a perfect ring of dentition where Genna had bitten her. Faint seams of skin from where she ripped part of Katie's face off.

Katie rolled her eyes. "It's a love bite, Mother. She's finally marked me as hers. Stop being boring."

Pipsy traced a fingernail along the mark and then contours of the earring. Katie stepped out of her reach. "You can't have it, Pipsy."

Pipsy's lips thinned. "Can't I?"

Katie fidgeted nervously. "She made them for me. She's never made me *anything*."

This was not true. Genna had made Katie a pink diamond tennis bracelet that matched Katie's hair. But that did not have magic in it.

Pipsy grabbed Katie's wrist, shaking her hard. "I am checking for traps, you ungrateful child. Give me the earrings now!"

Katie sniffled and unhappily took the earrings off. She offered them to Pipsy with open palms.

Pipsy inspected the earrings. She felt the humming power and seething rage. Yet the spells were not directed at Katie. Instead, protections were smelted into metal. Pipsy smiled at her grand-daughter. "Iphigenia is protecting you from the hunters. Your obedience training is going well."

Katie simpered, delighted by the compliment. She took the

earrings back with undisguised relief. She put them in her ears and fluffed her hair.

"You look like a hippie," Mimi muttered.

"I look amazing," Katie preened.

"You do, my darling," Pipsy said. "A love bite. A worthy trophy indeed. You finally have leashed that obstinate wolf."

The bite on Katie's face had healed but would never be invisible. Had Genna accidentally leashed herself to Katie? Perhaps to a vampire, any connection counted as control. Genna might think she was the top but really she was the bottom. That was depressing.

Genna had her own set of earrings. They were chandeliers style. Tiny tear drops of peridot, amethyst, sapphire, diamond, and citrine gemstones hung from the mixed metal struts. Strands of silk were woven in between the gemstones in each section. They did not match Katie's. They were build with different specifications. They could change shape to fit her outfit. All Genna had to do was feed them whatever earrings she planned on wearing. Their weight and magic were comforting.

She petted the cloak, upset with herself. She was sick with chagrin but she could not worry about the McBrides. There were monster hunters and witch finders coming to Sunday brunch.

Twenty-Three

THE COUNTRY CLUB WAS ABNORMALLY FULL. THE valet and wait staff were exceptionally attentive. Delighted gossip about this new infusion to Sweetwater's elite and exclusive community echoed off the frescos and chandeliers.

Sweetwater was abuzz. Everyone wanted to see. To be there. To smell the inner lining of Troy's coat and ask what Quincy's inseam was. To stare in unabashed amazement at Cleopatra's cleavage. To greet Naomi like a long lost relative.

Genna thought Sweetwater Forest would greet Sable and Naomi's return like an excited dog. Instead it was neutral. Cautious. It treated them like McBrides instead of Miss Bootsie's progeny. Troy and Quincy's family were greeted with bristling growls. Cleopatra was the one greeted ebulliently. Genna could feel it, the buzzing under her heels. Along her skin. The quiet call of the forest.

Something had changed since Chicago. Tituba had mentioned the power of sex magic. Genna felt bigger. She was more aware of herself and the world around her. She felt the nuances in the forest and the inflections in the Old Night. The country club was too loud and too bright but she endured it.

Genna got credit for bringing monster hunters and witch

finders to the country club. Anywhere else, Genna challenging despotic vampires might be met with gratefulness but even the humans of Sweetwater viewed their own species as meat to eat and skin to wear. The town worshipped the McBrides. Their fury came with the respect of an acknowledged enemy making moves that upped the ante and forced them to respond in kind or risk being wiped out. They adapted. The weak left town on a sudden vacation or hid in the forest's shadows. The powerful sat in the dining room demanding the same menu the Bellwethers had at their banquet table and daring anyone to say anything.

Genna's family flaunted their triumph like whales dancing in the waves. The country club bent to their delight that finally, their troublesome daughter had acceptable friends. Genna's castle was talked about like it was a wonderful staycation. The explosion in Chicago was a happy accident. The suitcases had already arrived at the castle. The staff was excited that Genna had guests. All of the horses were given a thorough brushing. The property was land-scaped to perfection. Everything was polished and decorated with Halloween themes.

Despite Genna taking great pains to emphasize not inviting her siblings, they had brought their spouses to the table. Their children were safely sequestered at the castle. Their parents did not want them near Mimi, Katie, and Kyle.

Katie wore a frilly pink Dior dress that matched her hair. Katie's gross brother Kyle managed to look sticky and possibly contagious in his beige brown Armani suit.

Her mother's seating arrangements were a perfect act of sabotage. On the surface, it appeared to be an ebullient Sunday brunch. It did not look like peace negotiations. They were united in collective hatred of vampires. Naomi and Sable were given a pass.

Pipsy stayed home. Without her, the McBrides could not effectively undermine the moment.

Genna had the distinct impression that her siblings' spouses had been deployed by her parents to pump everyone at the table for information. Thus leaving her sister and brothers free to take turns skewering and slow-roasting Katie. None of the humans had forgotten that the McBrides were vampires. They had been spoiling for a fight since the engagement party. Troy was happy to add fuel to the fire. Without the insulation of her glamours, Katie was as red as a steamed lobster.

Mimi was not faring any better. She was hard-pressed to find her footing. Her plan to curry favor with Olympia Billson, Troy's mother, led straight into the teeth of five irate mothers. Genna's father focused on cementing friendship with the other fathers. Though he occasionally stomped Mimi into the ground with a decisive comment.

Cleopatra was resplendent in an off-the-shoulder Dior gown. The orange organza and metallic black trim emphasized the contrast between her wide hips and the abundance of her curves. Her onyx-and-diamond necklace disappeared into her cleavage, which threatened to bubble out of her dress. She had gold woven into her braids. Orange glitter was on her full lips. Gold dusted her cheeks. The seam of her dress scandalously went all the way up to her hipbone. Genna ate and tried not to spend too much time looking at how much of Cleopatra's thigh was on display.

Genna wore a conservative black dress. Her glam team had done their usual best. They piled her hair up into a chignon and pinned it with pearl combs. She sat at the far end of the banquet table, marooned in a pocket of silence. She had the disconcerting honor of sitting at the foot of the table. Cleopatra to her left. The empty seat to her right. Naomi flitted around the table, basking in the attention. Genna was the least interesting person at the table.

Cleopatra's parents were those uncomfortable kind of Black people who believed in Black Excellence so much, that it was its own kind of racism. Her father, Kwami, took pains to emphasize that he was not mixed-race. That his red hair, pale skin, and freckles did not capture his Blackness.

Cleopatra's mother, Zenobia, clacked and clanked with gold encrusted cowrie shells, seed beads, amber, and red coral. Her earlobes were dragged down by the weight of her earrings. She made up for the lack of a name brand with tacky gold. Her headwrap and kaftan were threaded with gold. The shoulder pads under her jacket was covered with gold sequins. Gold was on her nails and on her eyelashes.

Kwami stared at Genna and her parents with hungry admiration. Zenobia was downright hostile. Genna's parents did not notice. They were focused on Genna. They smiled, genuinely happy to host the brunch, eager to make the acquaintance of these young people and their families.

Camille and Reginald Snodgrass were greeted like old friends. Genna's brothers engulfed Quincy with enthusiastic back-slapping hugs.

Sable, Naomi's parent, was welcomed with delight. Genna's family admired Naomi's wonderful clothes.

Troy wore a black-on-black tailored suit with a silver brocade vest, silver tie, silver cufflinks, and silver lapel clips. His polished black gator boots had pointed silver toes. His mother Olympia, stepmother Shelly, and three stepbrothers Hector, Ajax, and Paris were greeted with such refined politeness that Genna internally winced. Her parents placed Troy next to Katie. The two were locked in a heated but thankfully quiet battle of wills at the far end of the table. They looked like a cute couple from far away if you did not know either of them.

Troy's stepbrothers were big slabs of meat in Easter egg–colored polo shirts who kept walking off to watch the football game by the bar. One look from Olympia had them sitting back down.

Mimi kibitzed with Zenobia, the best of friends. Their laughter was brittle and sharp as broken mirror glass.

Genna avoided looking at Sable while her heart clenched at their voice. Genna focused on her food. Recognition bashed her ears. Her heart twisted into her stomach.

Miss Bootsie had told Genna the story of Sable a thousand times. It failed to explain seeing the damage to Sable's skin.

Magical seams like keloids connected a frayed patchwork tissue to the original skin. Sable was beautiful like a broken vase glued back together with gold paste. Old healed cuts like stress fractures in porcelain. Not entirely healed. Some parts glued back together. Others were still seeping. Worse yet, Miss Bootsie had used her own body like it was a mold to make Sable's new skin. Genna had forgotten that soft, curled texture. The fine eyebrows. She could see all the magic that had been absent in Miss Bootsie humming in Sable and Naomi's bodies.

Mimi made the mistake of watching Sable like someone with a hammer staring at an armoire full of bone china. Perhaps old habit. A long time foe. Sable had grown up in Sweetwater.

The whole table went on attack. Mimi was desperate enough to look at Katie for help. Only to find her daughter equally destroyed. Kyle was a floppy punching bag for Troy's brothers and Cleopatra's brother Ramses. Genna's brothers were focused on Katie.

Mimi looked at Shelly in outrage, as if expecting the mousy woman to speak up against Olympia. That was unsettlingly familiar. Mimi had an instinct for transforming forgettable women into bitter turncoats. Olympia looked ready to leap across the table and stab out Mimi's eye with a fish fork.

"Is it okay that we're moving in?" Cleopatra said, while their place settings were cleared for another course.

Genna blinked. She had been so immersed in the verbal warfare that she forgot others might be watching. "I think it's too late for that."

"I didn't think it would get this far or this fast," Cleopatra said. "There's been so much confusion. If you haven't noticed, our parents are all up in our business same as yours. They're like a wolf pack guarding their young. Usually we're too much. Being welcomed with open arms is new."

Genna stared at Cleopatra. She felt exposed.

Cleopatra smiled faintly at the rest of the table. "I'm the only dragon in my family too. They tried hard to hide it but we were all relieved when I moved in with Naomi, Troy, and Quincy. I don't know if I could've survived on my own like you have."

Genna shrugged. "I did what I had to."

Cleopatra chuckled. "Don't we all?"

The soup was cleared away. The next course was crab cake puffs. The white wine was a perfect blend. Cleopatra drank daintily but drained the crystal glass. Genna ate and waited as Cleopatra gathered her courage.

After the crab cake puffs was a salad course of field greens, roasted candied almonds, goat cheese, and raspberries. Then they were served a delicately flavorful filet of Scottish salmon on a bed of pureed mashed potatoes and sautéed broccolini.

"Your castle has an actual enchanted forest," Cleopatra said. "I thought that was something that only happened in a Disney movie."

"I'll have to show you my Disney collection. It got me through a lot of tough situations. Fairytales are the only things that make sense in the forest." Genna rubbed the edge of her fork. She decided to barrel forward. "Miss Bootsie knew the old stories. She's the one who made them into fairytales. Logic, no matter how absurd, helps build a path. Whether it's a yellow brick road or bread crumbs or following a black cat. But sometimes the only thing you can do is stay out of the woods. I'm happy to show Naomi all of that."

Sable and Naomi both stiffened. They glanced at Genna. She focused on eating her salmon.

Cleopatra stroked the edge of Genna's hand. "I should warn you, air types can hear everything that's said in a room. There's no such thing as a private conversation. Naomi doesn't have fond memories of her grandmother like you do."

Genna chewed on the salmon's soft pink flesh instead of picking up Cleopatra's fingers and nibbling on the soft skin of her wrist. She thought hard about that nugget of information.

"That doesn't mean stop talking," Cleopatra said with an anxious smile.

"I appreciate the openness," Genna said.

She did. She liked Cleopatra. More than she could explain without betraying her own intentions. Cleopatra was solid but Genna could not ignore her wings. Or her hurricane power. Air types were even more dangerous than she thought. Sable only looked as fragile as a soap bubble. Naomi had already tried to kill her once.

"The boys don't like being spied on either," Cleopatra said. "Naomi says it's not intentional. She says that it's harder to focus in on one conversation. She'd rather flit around like a butterfly instead of stay tied down."

"It sounds like you and Naomi are together."

"Yes. Also no. I'm also engaged to Quincy. But here they both are."

"I'm sorry. That's a lot of ambiguity."

"It is what it is." Cleopatra shook her head. "I'm pansexual but I always end up with a woman. Quincy trots me out whenever someone gets too serious. Or he did. Now, there's you. They're both serious about you."

"I see." Quincy kept trying to catch Genna's eye but thus far stayed where he had been seated.

"May I ask you how long you've been magic?" Cleopatra said, bluntly. "I'm curious if it's the woods, like you mentioned, or something else?"

"I'm not sure," Genna deflected, "What about you?"

"Our parents. Galveston and Roanoke have a pretty extensive academic selection but honestly, I learned more from them." She nodded at the table. "We have a unique situation."

The plates were cleared away. The next main dish was set down. A plate of perfectly roasted lamb chops. Genna was lost in the flavor. Cleopatra picked the bones clean. They both noticed each other's monsters were closer to the surface at the near unison of dull cracks as their teeth broke bone. They giggled self-consciously.

"I love lamb," Genna said, dabbing grease from her lips.

"Me too," Cleopatra said gustily.

"It's that one perfect meal where I'm in total alignment with myself." Genna licked and sucked the marrow out of her lamb.

Cleopatra snapped her fingers in enthusiastic agreement. "I don't even need the other courses. Just give me a tray of these and I'm good."

"Genna, do you want my lamb?" Troy said, standing next to her with a plate. He had moved so quietly that she had mistaken him for a server.

Genna looked up at him. His blue eyes vibrated. Her skin prickled. Wrath surrounded him like a haunting perfume. She was shocked by his lack of decorum and the fact that she had not seen him leave his seat. He urbanely slid his plate next to hers. He sat down in Naomi's empty seat.

"Don't stab anyone," Cleopatra said.

"Why do you think I'm down here?" Troy grumbled.

"Because she's smiling at me and not you."

Troy harrumphed. Genna blushed. Flattered. Embarrassed. She took the plate even though it was uncouth. Lamb was lamb. Also Cleopatra eyed the plate. The dragon's hunger was so obvious that it was amazing that her skin had not sprouted scales.

Genna swallowed a hostile snarl. Her fingers curled around the edge of the plate. Troy smirked. Cleopatra blinked. She sat back and huffed. Troy passed her Naomi's plate of lamb. "Better?"

"You should've lead with that," Cleopatra said.

"I wanted to see if she's into sharing type," Troy said.

"Not with lamb," Genna said.

"What about me? Don't I get any lamb?" Naomi said, flouncing over.

"You snooze you lose," Cleopatra said.

Naomi smiled winsomely at Genna, eyeing the last lamb chop on her plate. Genna went very still as vampiric persuasion tried to pressure her into compliance. She maintained direct eye contact. No blinking. No breathing. Her eyes did not glow but the ambient temperature went up a few degrees. Her hand gripped the steak knife's smooth handle. The chandelier light glinted dangerously off the serrated metal.

"That's a good way to lose a hand, Naomi," Troy said.

"Go ask with her brothers. They might share," Cleopatra said.

Naomi flipped her hair over her shoulder. The pressure evaporated. She swept down the crowded side of the table.

Genna chewed slowly. Her hand relaxed on the knife.

Troy put his elbows on the table, smirking fondly. He clearly found Genna's hostility hilarious. She sneered and raised an eyebrow, unimpressed by his table manners. His smile stiffened. He straightened up to full sitting height. His shoulders squared. His arms slipped off the edge. His hands folded themselves neatly. She nodded minutely and focused back on eating, satisfied.

Cleopatra watched them both as she daintily devoured her lamb. No one spoke but the silence was loud. Genna felt warm from Troy's side and cold from Cleopatra. It was confusingly contradictory but not unpleasant.

"Troy, can you come here a second?" Olympia boomed in a tone that was a thinly veiled command.

Troy glanced at Genna. "If you'll excuse me."

He got up, took his time pushing the chair back into place, and went down to his mother. Genna admired the view. Troy was resplendent in his tailored dinner jacket and suit. It brought out his suntanned skin and the breadth of his shoulders and his tapered waist. The black luster of his hair had a hint of gold underneath. His boots added a nice tightness to his butt.

"Girl, you got it bad," Cleopatra said. "You're going to get us both in trouble."

Genna glanced at her. "I find you very attractive."

"Damn, it's like that?"

Genna did not have to answer since the servers were back, clearing the table.

The lamb course was replaced by small personal plates of duck pate, a selection of artisanal cheeses, baguette slices with an olive oil mix, and thin apple slivers arranged in the shape of a rose. This was paired with another wine. Genna had been too focused on the lamb to drink the last glass. Now she had two.

"You're only into women?" Cleopatra prompted.

"No, that's not what I meant." Genna stabbed the apple apart. Eating quickly. "I'm interested. I'm just a little gun-shy."

Cleopatra pursed her lips. "I get that."

They finished their plates in thoughtful silence.

"It's okay if you like him." Cleopatra deconstructed her apple rose. "He's a good guy. He's got a good heart."

Genna spread the last of the duck pate on a baguette. "Is it really okay?"

Cleopatra gestured a long, manicured finger in a circle, encompassing Sweetwater. "This is like his personal heaven. You're his dream girl. His fairytale warrior princess made real. Quincy has finally found his queen."

Genna stabbed an almond and ate it to shut herself up. Why had she thought Cleopatra meant Troy?

Cleopatra was so easy to talk to because she was once again pumping her for information. She was a master at active listening. Her beauty was distracting. Genna was already raw from nostalgia. It had been so long since she had brunch with her family when they were happy to see her. She needed to stay on her guard. Cleopatra was not her friend.

Olympia's blue eyes focused on Genna as if feeling the pressure of her gaze. Lightning sizzled into the shape of a dragon. Wings flared. She was big and tough and covered in scars. Her chest puffed with hostility.

Genna raised an eyebrow. If mama dragon wanted to test her patience then she was happy to play the dozens.

Olympia turned away. She focused on Genna's mother. They started talking about horses.

"She's protective," Cleopatra said. "She's like that with everybody."

"So am I," Genna said, battling her own home training not to growl.

"Troy's her pride and joy. Their whole family are hunters. Both sides. For generations. All the way back to Greece and Norway. A lot of women throw themselves at Troy."

"I remember. You told me."

"What do you think of his brothers?"

Genna ate a slice of cheese. She did not like Troy's brothers. In terms of power, they were obese tabby cats compared to a sleek wild Siberian tiger. They fit in with Sweetwater's spoiled dude-bro demographic. Neurotic. Entitled. Unimaginative. They revered their brother. She could see it in the way they told stories and looked at him for approval. Troy ignored them with crushing impatience and flared nostrils as if the smell of them was offensive.

Cleopatra took a thoughtful mouthful of wine. Set the glass down. "Okay, cards on the table. I know that we're staying in the castle but if you fuck with my family there won't be enough of you left to bury."

"Don't fuck with me and I won't," Genna said, tired of pretending to be nice too.

"You blew up our house." Cleopatra gave her a look that Genna returned with heat.

"And suddenly I have complete strangers who've already tried to kill me once living in my home. This is not my idea either."

"You want to marry us," Cleopatra said.

"That is bullshit. Genna is marrying no one but me!" Katie shouted, jumping up and slapping her hands on the table.

Conversation stopped across the entire banquet hall. Genna gritted her teeth, hating the feel of eyes on her skin.

"Katie, be quiet." Genna's command crackled with lightning. "Mimi, Katie is very tired. You should take her and Kyle home. It's been a long day."

The vampires swayed like bowling pins whiffed by a bowling ball. They wobbled out of the banquet hall. They forgot their purses, their jackets, and phones. The wait staff opened the doors for them all the way to the parking lot.

Genna's brother turned to her with an admiring grin. "You've got to teach me that trick!"

Half the table watched her with penetrating stares. The other half was her family puffing with aggressive glee. Champagne was demanded.

Genna glared at Cleopatra, ready for more, but the crocodile was either satisfied or had decided to wait to interrogate her later.

Genna's father stood up. He raised his champagne flute. "A toast to new friends and beginnings."

The banquet hall toasted. Glasses clinked. Servers hastily poured refills.

Genna drank her champagne. She had not seen her father smile at her so proudly since her debutant ball. After so long, it was surreal and uncomfortable to be bathed in approval.

She wondered what the hell she had done to the McBrides. Or *how* she had done it. Or if she could do it again but this time on purpose.

Dessert was more champagne and a generous slice of hazelnut chocolate torte cake with a chilled bowl of raspberries, strawberries, and blueberries and a dollop of clotted cream on top.

Twenty-Four

Despite Genna's fears, the 'light repast' of a twelve-course banquet passed without further incident.

After the meal, the table guests separated into conversations, which turned into eighteen rounds of golf. Then they took a party bus back to the castle to change their clothes. Then a guided tour of the castle. Her family was impressed by Genna's collection of restored art, furniture, and said so. Then the stable. Then an evening of live music on the grounds. Those who wanted to finally had a chance to watch the football game from the comfort of the sports room with a bartender supplying them with beer and cocktails.

Then there was karaoke. Genna did not want to sing. Troy and Quincy both sang love power ballads. Her brothers tried to do a rap battle only to be destroyed by Cleopatra. The parents had their favorites songs.

Soon enough it was time for another meal. This one heavy on desserts. The castle dining room was resplendently appointed.

Genna had lights woven among the flower gardens and the greenhouse to make it easy to walk outside.

Her greatest concern was when the parents retired to the

Good Room. Instead of wanting to listen, she headed for the stable.

"Genna, hey," Troy said.

Genna stopped him with a look. He backed off. She felt mean. Troy had been polite and charming but if she did not get some quiet alone time, she was going to shatter a well-executed day with a misplaced word.

She quickly changed into blue jeans, riding boots, a t-shirt, and black leather jacket. Her aching feet were grateful to be in supportive flats instead of heels. She did not pay attention to coordination but still looked put together. She finished unpinning her hair and got out of the castle.

Cleopatra and her parents were huddled in tight circle over Sekhmet's mounting block.

"That is Sekhmet's head!" Zenobia said.

"Mom, we can't move it," Cleopatra said. "It's tied to the land."

"It's supposed to be in Egypt," Kwami said.

"It's more complicated than that, Dad."

"You marry that girl or you get that stone back to the pyramid," Zenobia said.

"No, I'm not going to do that," Cleopatra said. "There's some serious mojo tying the stone to this land. It'll eat me if I try to move it."

"Then don't bother coming home," Zenobia said.

"Fine! I'd rather stay here than another minute in that stupid tomb. Don't touch it!" Cleopatra pushed her brother away from the mounting block when he bent down to trace the lion's face. "All of you, go. Stop being embarrassing. You'll miss your flight."

They argued as she herded them up the path.

Genna watched them go. Then walked into the stable. Halted.

"Mom?" Genna said, startled.

Her mother was in the stable feeding Bibi apple slices. She still wore her dinner finery. Except for the rubber boots on her feet.

"I like what you've done with the renovation." Her mother

nodded in the direction of Miss Bootsie's apartment. "I showed Sable where their mother lived. We knew a very different woman." She combed Bibi's mane with her fingernails. "It was difficult to express how important Miss Bootsie was to us, knowing that she raised you and your siblings instead of her own child and granddaughter. Sable would not go near the forest either."

Genna joined her mother. "Donnie McBride was Naomi's father. It wasn't consensual. That's why Sable left town and hasn't been back until now."

Her mother sighed with weary aggravation. "I wish you'd told me but I understand why you didn't."

"Are you worried about the mounting block?"

Her mother shrugged, focused on Bibi. "The mounting block is just one of many heirlooms. You need a partner who understands the weight of responsibility. Someone who isn't closely tied to anyone else. Even their families or past. You have four different suitors. Use this time to observe them seriously."

Genna rubbed her hands against her pants. "I don't know if I want to get married. This is a lot. What happened in Chicago spiraled out of control so quickly. I'm sorry."

"I appreciate you making an effort, Iphigenia." The kindness was worse than disappointment.

Sneakers kicked his stall, demanding Genna stop ignoring him and give him treats. Genna complied, mock-scolding him for being a greedy-guts after he gobbled all of the apple pieces she had.

"You've done a good job with him, too," her mother said. "He looks so much like the Shire, it takes my breath away."

Even though there had been many Shire and Shire mixes in the stable, Genna knew which one. They had never talked about the stable or any of the horses from that time. Genna picked up a curry brush and started brushing Sneakers' neck, unsure of where this was going. "He did get big. I can't believe I once carried him across my shoulders."

Genna focused on grooming Sneakers. Her mother wasn't going to tell her the truth.

A third set of footsteps. Genna expected it to be Naomi or Sable. Instead, it was Olympia. She had changed into simple motorcycle boots, jeans, white t-shirt, and a green canvas jacket. Her hair was pulled back in a high ponytail. Olympia looked around at the drowsy horses in their stalls. She lit a joint between her lips, took a puff, then passed it to Genna's mother. "I haven't been to a stable since my husband died."

Genna's mother took a pull and passed the joint back to Olympia. "How long has it been?"

"Since Katrina." Olympia passed the joint to Genna. "Troy told me about the castle and stable. I didn't believe a word of it, but he was right."

Genna wondered what the little head nod meant. Was it approval? Was it a warning? Or was she talking to herself?

She took a tiny puff and passed the joint back, not entirely comfortable smoking in front of her mother. Or seeing her mother smoke.

"I've seen the way you look at my son," Olympia said. "He's not a stick of dynamite you can use to blow up your life."

Genna inhaled, caught between with embarrassment and fury. She fumbled for a comeback but started coughing. She missed the moment.

"I've seen the way your son looks at my daughter," Genna's mother said, the edge of steel like a half-drawn sword. "I believe he is the escaping his obligations."

"We're just passing through, Dr. Bellwether," Olympia said. "Just passing through."

Genna wanted to fade into the background. To let the mothers square off. But she was a grown ass woman. She could not back down. "Mom, did you know that their ancestors used to work for us in the gold mine? They were the witchfinders."

"No, Iphigenia, I was not aware. That is an interesting bit of information."

Olympia smoked, the faintest hint of blue lightning behind her heavy bangs. "I guess you're not a powder puff after all."

"I guess not."

"You be careful now. Dr. Bellwether. It was a pleasure."

"Likewise, Olympia."

Genna and her mother watch Olympia swagger out of the stable and down into the mouth of the forest. Her boot kicked the storage container where Genna kept her spare clothes. She glanced at Genna, the still smoking joint hanging from her lips, and kept walking.

Genna's mother waited until Olympia was out of sight. "She is right, Iphigenia; her son is not for you. I would not have put it so bluntly, but he is not suitable. He's a stableboy. You're the princess in the tower. Don't allow jealousy to block you from your blessings."

"Jealousy?"

"He and Katie are a wonderful match. Don't interfere."

Genna couldn't help it. She giggled. Her mother frowned severely. "Iphigenia."

"Mom, Katie and Troy together is like putting a snake and mongoose in the same cage and expecting them not to attack. It's hilarious that you set them next to each other."

"Mimi and Donnie were the same."

That was upsetting. "You think he's like Donnie?"

"Iphigenia, he's not for you. That's what matters. Especially when you and Cleopatra clearly have a connection."

"Cleopatra?"

Her mother raised an eyebrow. "You think I don't have eyes in my head?"

"We just met. I'm hoping we'll be friends not anything else." Which was its own thing to treasure. She had not had another Black American Princess as a friend. She refused to ruin the budding trust with sex. Besides, they were not compatible. Cleopatra was justifiably afraid of Genna.

"Don't take yourself out of the running so quickly, young

lady. You have to fight for what you want. Naomi is interested in you too."

"Mom, it's not like that."

"It could be. If you allow it to happen."

Her mother walked over, her eyes slightly glassy. She kissed Genna on the cheek. "Good night, my darling girl. Thank you for inviting us. Today was lovely."

She walked to the golf cart she had driven to the stable. She got in, settled her skirts so nothing dragged outside of the cart, and drove back up to the castle.

Genna focused on brushing Sneakers, who sighed but leaned into the scratches. The stallion pressed close, his long mane draping Genna. His chin against her back pressing her against his chest. The equine equivalent of a hug. Genna hugged him, glad that he was here.

If Pipsy had even a pinkie toe of a hold on Naomi, she could hook everyone else in the process. Troy and Quincy were too used to winning. Over-confident. Not guarding in the right ways.

"A stick of dynamite," Genna mused.

GENNA ENTERED THE CASTLE FROM A SIDE DOOR. SHE ran through the wall passages and back stairs to reach her turret. Troy was in her office. He sat on the padded window ledge, absently flipping a butterfly knife. His jacket was open, button-down shirt rolled to the elbows, his nice cowboy boots exchanged for scuffed boots.

She stared at the patterns on the hand loomed rug. Her falcon statue collection on the shelves. The framed paintings. The frescos painted on the ceiling of flying dragons and Pegasus. As a child, this had been her playroom. Now it was her business office. The frescos were the only holdover. The lower part of the room was painted white. She exhaled and inhaled, counting breaths as emotions rushed through her at the invasion of privacy. First the bathroom. Now her home office. She was angry, wasn't she?

"Are you looking through my stuff?"

He stood up quickly. "I've been waiting for you." He gestured at the room. "It feels like you in here. More than the rest of the castle." He rubbed the back of his neck as his ears pinked. "Christ, it looks like I was snooping, doesn't it? I mean, I was, but I wasn't reading anything. I was just looking for you."

"Why?"

"I wanted to finish what we started in Chicago."

"So you can kill me? Get your mother to stab me?"

"I won't let her. I want this."

"Why Troy? Tell me now."

He inhaled, chest expanding. Muscles shifting. "I'm not what she wants me to be. I'm this. I want you. I don't care about the rest. I want you."

"You're a hunter. You could use this against me. Betray me."

"I promised. I won't. I'll never."

"What about your family? Galveston? Roanoke?"

"They kill what they don't understand. I want to protect it. I'm yours. Take me."

The Old Night whispered truths. Troy had changed in Chicago. The whole group recognized that Genna had a real connection to the Old Night but he wanted to be a part of it instead of kill it.

Genna remembered what Tituba said. *Dragons can't be real. Dragon slayers can't be either.*

Troy had reached a tipping point.

Olympia's hostility had been one of fear. She knew Troy was tired. He wanted to shed his skin. His mother was here to save him but he did not want to be saved. He wanted Genna, just as he said.

Everyone at that table loved their magical children and siblings. They knew they had reached the limits of their ability to protect them from the world. The four had reached adulthood.

They tried to be human. Tried to be good. Tried to be something other than the monsters they were. They had done everything right and were cracking under the pressure.

How many explosions had they covered up? How many deaths had they explained? How many houses and cities had they moved to?

Mimi's motives were hardly pure but Katie needed friends and enemies besides Genna. Naomi was her half-sister.

Sweetwater was a safe haven. The castle a sanctuary. The forest somewhere they could thrive instead survive. Weirdly, having powerful vampires to fight only made Sweetwater the place to be. Genna's parents wanted her to be with her own kind.

Yet it wasn't Quincy or Cleopatra looking at her with burning desire. It was Troy. This wasn't a trick. Or momentary insanity. It was real. His scent was unfiltered desire. She liked the anxious grip of his belt and the flush along his neck as he endured her silent inspection. His earnest little smile and head bob broke the last of her recalcitrance.

She tackled him but swayed back at the last minute. His arms caught her retreat, pulled her close. He kissed her quick. She looked up at him, her hands on his chest. They kissed deeply. Arms tangled. Mouths unable to kiss fast enough. She needed him and he needed her. Lightning sparked on their tongues but the embers faded before they could burn the curtains or the rugs. He lifted her up as she tried to scale his body.

The castle walls hummed as it closed in around them, answering her wish for privacy. He glanced at the magic then added his own. When she growled, his hands tightened and he growled harder. His mouth was hot. His hand was on her crotch. Lightning on her clit, her labia, filling her as his fingers and tongue slid inside. Genna screamed. They braided together in lightning. Then coalesced back into their physical bodies. The air smoked around them. The carpet was burnt.

"Holy shit," Genna panted as the ashes of her clothes floated down to the floor.

"Hot damn," Troy said. His suit was rumpled but immaculate. Only a few rouge strands of hair had fallen across his forehead.

She hugged him, too overwhelmed to cry. He rested his chin on the top of her head for a moment. Genna sniffled, fighting tears. Troy's cheeks were salty too. She could not hide her open confusion. "What is wrong with me? Why am I crying? We had sex. What's happening?"

"I thought it was just me," Troy sniffled, wiping his face clear. "When I'm lightning I feel everything all at once."

"It's like a system overload."

"Exactly."

Slowly they loosened their hold. Yet they held on to each other as though expecting outside forces to rip them apart. She looked out of the window but the evening sky was empty of anything but a few stars. "There aren't any storm clouds outside. Where'd the lightning come from?"

"Me. I'm a bolt from the blue. I can hide it everywhere but my eyes. Contacts always melt."

"How are your clothes fine?"

"Naomi makes them. She's got a gift." Troy traced her bare hip.

Genna shifted. Self-conscious. Naked in her own office. Disliking any mention of Naomi.

"Sorry about your clothes," Troy said sincerely.

He took his jacket off. She slid it on, wiggled to feel his warmth and scent around her. He coaxed her over to the bay window. She perched on his lap. She patted his thighs, all loose limbs and flushed cheeks. She giggled and climbed onto him. She snuggled close. His long sleeves bunched so only her fingertip traced the contours of his neck. They leaned against the stone. Magic pulsed like two heartbeats.

He hugged her tight. It was intense. His breath in her ear. She wantonly straddled his thighs. Her mouth on his throat. She pressed her forehead against his.

She threaded her hands with his. "I'm sorry I panicked in Chicago."

"I came on too strong. I've never felt a rush of connection like that. Most of us burn out so fast, I try not to know any other fire types. When Naomi grabbed you, it scared the shit out of me. I didn't want to lose you. I've never moved that fast in my life. Now that I know it's the gold, I can think."

"What gold?" Genna wanted to hear him say it. To compare what she found.

"My ancestors go all the way back to that gold mine too. Our gold is in the watch," he pulled his sleeve back to show her the watch. He was left-handed and wore his watch on his right hand. A gold Patek Philippe Sky Moon Tourbillon. "The gold is in our hair." He waved at his pompadour. "I keep it dyed black so you can't see that it's pure gold. We cry diamonds. It hurts like a sonuvabitch. The doctor says that it's from a build up of calcium deposits from behind my eyes but Dad said it's part of the gold curse. He cried little white rocks. My magic turns them into diamonds."

She rubbed against his erection. "I've made my intentions known. Now you tell me. Why are you here? Why did you come? To kill me?"

He groaned as he pushed his forehead against hers. "You smell like fire and growing things and wolves and Deep Magic."

"Tell me," she said, rocking back and forth. "Tell me. Tell me. Tell me."

He bucked and thrashed. "Genna, I can't think with you doing—" His breath caught as she grabbed his erection through his pants.

"This is what you want? This is why you came? Quincy told you that I like cunnilingus; that's why you went straight for the clit." He shuddered, snorting and straining as she stroked him harder, stretched and massaged his balls. "You doing the same things. Hoping for the same result."

"Yes."

"Then you're going to kill me? That's what you do, right? Kill wolves? Is that a fetish? Track the wolf down, fuck them, then kill them." She squeezed him harder, getting excited again. Stoking her own flames as she teased him. "Tell me why you're here. To fuck me, right? That's all you want. Then you'll leave."

His hips thrust in her hands. Her fingernails ripped into his clothes, tearing up the inseams, and burning up its defensive magic. Drool filled her mouth. She hastily moved her things off of her desk. She grabbed him by his tie. "Come here."

He moved eagerly. He sank down to his knees and spread her butt-cheeks wide. She held on to the desk. The lightning on his tongue tickled her labia. She swallowed her sighs and moans as he suckled and teased. The crinkle of cellophane as he opened a condom. She watched him over her shoulder. She lifted her butt up to get a better angle. She hissed as he slid inside.

The desk was old and sturdy and filled with magic. It did not buckle or strain to take their weight. She yanked on his tie like it was a leash. He slammed into her. He bent down. Lifted her up. Hugged her as he rammed in from a new angle. She held on. Fingers fisted in his hair. The orgasm made of lightning. A sharp flash.

He sagged. Her hands slapped the desk. Her legs trembled from the aftershocks. He pushed back. Peeling the filled condom away, knotting it, and putting it in the trash. She rolled on her side. Impatient. The magic hummed in her skin. She was hungry. She wanted more. The need was deeper. Darker. Illicit.

The wolf killing tattoos on his skin mocked her. She wanted to rip them off. Bite deep. Tear. Feast. Wrench. Punish. Devour. But not here in the castle.

The shadowy glenn pressed against her thoughts. All she had to do was push him against that pole. Tie his hands.

Then they were standing in the forest glenn. Troy looked around at the pole, the stump, and the weeds. Nostrils flared. Smelling the blood and magic. She stayed perfectly still.

Then Troy did something that surprised her. That shocked her. That aroused her.

He crouched down and pressed his fingers into the thin weeds and the mud below. He turned his head to the side. He stroked his hand across his neck and down his shoulder, a sensual slow gesture that drew her eye to his throat while his clothes disintegrated. His tattoos peeled away. The beautiful colors slid like sentient silk down his body and into the weeds. Then there was nothing but bare scarred skin.

He backed up to stand against the pole. His hands up to cling to the rung. His head tilted sideways. His blue eyes glowed. Lightning in his skin. All the delicious scent and power ripe and tender. He glanced at her through his eyelashes. Blushing. His erection bobbed.

"Prometheus," Genna said, barely louder than a whisper.

"You can call me anything you want." He bit his plump bottom lip. He writhed against the pole. "You need it. So do I."

"Need what?"

"I remember what you said in the shower. That I had to ask. I dream of your teeth. Your claws. Your fire as you burned me. I was jealous when you pounced on Cleopatra. You gave her everything. It should've been me. I'm not here to kill you. I want you to make me into a wolf. To bite me. Rip me. Devour me. Take me. Swallow me whole."

Genna stepped forward. The shadows were soft. Her eyes were a steady glow. The quiet of the forest settled on her thoughts. The Old Night was here. All she had to do was be still. Everything that felt so immediate was put into perspective. It was okay. She did not have to do anything or talk to anyone or ask for permission. She could take what she wanted. She would deal with the consequences later.

Cleopatra had warned her. Olympia and her mother too. Troy was wrong, all wrong.

But she had made her decision. He was here. Whispering to

himself. Undulating against the pole. Flushed and wanton. "Please, Genna. Please please please."

She had already half-turned. Her teeth bulged from her gums. She sniffed hard, dragged her nose from his shoulder to the top of his head as if there was a line of cocaine up his neck. He shuddered.

"Don't let her shoot me," she whispered.

"I won't." His hands drifted down from the pole. She tensed but let his fingers to pet the fur over her breasts. She had never allowed Katie to touch her. The vibrating sensation as her fur became lightning. Answering Troy's sizzling skin.

She growled against his throat. "Do you want this?"

"Yes, Genna, yes. Please, Genna, please."

Refusing to bite Troy changed nothing. He was supposed to be hers.

Genna yanked his head back and bit him on the thick tendons of his neck. She dumped wild magic into his body. Troy became pure lightning as she ripped out his throat.

Genna forgot what Katie tasted like. Here was gourmet power. She devoured him. Stripped his skin. Troy's screams were orgasmic.

POWER FILLED THE FOREST AND GROUNDED ITSELF IN the castle's foundation. It spread out through the property. Genna could hear everyone as if she sat in the same room.

Genna's family adroitly kept the non-magical members locked inside the castle. They cheered at the football game with beer-soaked delight. They sang karaoke too loudly.

Quincy sat in the Good Room listening his parents and Genna's parents talk. His hands clenched. He excused himself. He walked into the hallway. Camille followed.

"You knew this day would come, Quincy," Camille said. "Focus on your future."

"That werewolf and vampire princess are best friends," Quincy said. "There's more going on here than they're saying."

"Of course there is," Camille said. "Naomi is a vampire princess too."

"What about her other grandmother? The boo hag who lives in the woods?"

"She's dead. Sable finally can come home."

"They're both witches. We can't leave the forest. We're still inside the fairytale. The enchantments are thick. I'm Prince Charming. Cleopatra's the dragon princess. Troy's the knight in shining armor or the huntsmen or something." Quincy rubbed his forehead between his eyebrows as though smoothing away a headache. "There's so much wild magic that it's hard to think."

"Yes, you *are* Prince Charming, Quincy."

Quincy stared at his mother. "Mom? Did you hear what I said?"

"I'm so proud of you. This is your moment." The iridescent light of enchantment in her eyes reflected the chandelier above them. "Marry Genna. Become the king. This is what you were meant to be. This castle is everything we dreamed for you. Come talk to your future in-laws. They want to know all about you. Have you seen the art gallery?"

She patted his arm. Bemused, he followed her back into the Good Room. He glanced behind him as though he had forgotten something important until her insistent tug propelled him back into a padded chair.

Meanwhile, Cleopatra had already bundled her family into a car and was personally driven them through the forest to the airfield. The racket of their argument was too loud to hear Troy's howl. Her magic kept the road straight and clear.

Sable wept in the cottage living room, holding on to the denim quilt. Genna saw, as if through a window. Naomi stood on the porch glaring at Katie. "Fuck off, bitch."

"Oh whatever," Katie said, fluffing her hair. "My daddy loved Sable. Miss Bootsie got in the way. Sable wanted to be a vampire and Miss Bootsie burned you in the fireplace as punishment. That's the real story. Who cares about a mangy old cloak?"

"Get away from me," Naomi hissed.

Olympia was on the edge of the forest that faced the McBride mansion. Mimi and Shelly were on either side of her. Pipsy stood in front of her in the same ruffled dress and hat she wore to Genna's engagement party. She swayed like a snake. Her blue eyes focused on Olympia. "Do you hear him howling like a wild bitch in heat? An ungrateful child is crueler than a serpent's tooth."

Olympia shoved away. "Fuck you."

Shelly's protest was stopped by Mimi's smile. "Come here little mouse. Tell me everything. I'm sure being with a strong women is so annoying."

"It's just so hard," Shelly said with a sniffle. Mimi patted her shoulder as she led her to the mansion. Pipsy slithered after Olympia.

TROY WAS A WOLF WITH FUR AS RED AS OLD BLOOD. HIS undercoat was gunmetal gray. Scars were across his muzzle and chest. His eyes were the same phosphorus blue. Lightning sparked along his sides.

He pounced on Genna. She arched, transforming into a wolf of smoke and fire. She was slimmer than Troy. Her body flexed. Tail fluffed. Her claws and teeth out. They slashed and bit and fought. He kept trying to pin her, but she wiggled free.

She ran through the forest and he chased. She was fleet and she knew the land, but he was big and each leap swallowed the distance between them. He shoved her. He tried to crowd her into a tree. To back her into a corner. She bounced off the trunk, spun over him, kicked him, landed, and sprinted off in the opposite direction.

Her breath was fast. The forest was a green blur. The deep, grunting pant of him right behind her, closing in. He bumped her and she snarled, running faster. He caught up. Then they were running and together while everything else was green shadows. Stride for stride. Breath for breath. Nose to tail. Their heartbeats were in sync.

They ran for hours. They ran through the forest, the mountains, out of the Heights, down to the bottom of the ravine next to Backbone Road. Through the golf green. Along the narrow channel of trash-lined trees between the public high school and the grocery store. Past the library. Under the narrow waterway by the water treatment plant. Behind the community center by the highway. Through the trees along the railroad tracks and the river. They stopped to drink at a creek. Then kept running.

They left Sweetwater behind. They kept running. Playing games to tag. Darting through the underbrush. Up hills. Over fences. They ran through apple orchards and pastures. Horses and donkeys brayed in warning. On they ran.

Past old steel mills and abandoned factories. The socioeconomic bracket decreased as they followed the Ohio River Boulevard. They skirted little towns. The trees and bracken were a constant coverage. The slate and shale under their feet firmed. The towns became sparse. The mountains grew greener and more wild.

Full night set in. It was easier to run with less traffic. Coyotes and stray dogs panicked at their scent and fled as they loped along the forest.

Finally they headed back the Heights. She led him through the forest to the back of the castle property. She avoided the cottage.

Toto, Pirate, Grim, Bibi, and Sneakers were in the pasture when Genna and Troy padded out of the tree line. Schrodinger was in the brush, watching. Genna did not stop. Troy did. He chuffed in question. Genna licked his muzzle, but if he wanted to get past the guardians, it was on their terms.

She trotted past Grim, who was particularly unhappy about the big red wolf. He lunged at Troy with a bark of declaration.

Toto and Pirate were game. Sneakers and Bibi pranced in circles, wanting to join in, corralling the fight while providing defensive backup. The rest of the herd joined in, stomping and whinnying.

Genna wiggled under the pasture fence. She stayed out of the fight. The animals let go of Troy. He jumped over the fence. He ran up to her. He changed into a human at a run, clothed and tattooed again. He swept her up into his arms to kiss her soundly. "Thank you!"

Then he let her go, transformed again, and sprinted into the forest before she could reply. Lightning sparked off his fur. He became a thick bolt of blue lightning. He arced up into the sky, racing through the clouds. His laughing howl was like thunder.

Genna stared up at the sky. She traced her own lips with a finger. She walked up to her castle. The animals trotted around her with insistent nudges and barks to pay attention to them. Absently she petted them. "Well done."

Genna felt Olympia stalking through the woods, drunk and swaying. A gun out in one hand. A sword in the other. She slashed at the trees. She hacked at the ferns. The forest shunted her to the outskirts of Sweetwater, refusing to let her attack Genna or the castle.. She tripped on asphalt. She spun around. Gun out. But there was nothing but solid cliff of slate and shale. She screamed in frustration. She began to climb the mountain. It would lead her back to the McBride mansion. She would not find the castle.

Troy landed at the base of the cliff as a man not a wolf. He sighed. Looked up as Olympia. "Mom, chill out. I'm okay."

Olympia shoved off the cliff. She jumped into the air, spun like a high diver, then landed, sword out. Magic flared. Olympia attacked with a battle cry. Troy blocked. They stepped into magic as they battled. Two titans. Equally matched. They fought and argued in a language she did not know.

Genna retracted her awareness.

She walked to the rose garden. It was designed like the three circuit labyrinth. The same pattern image had been carved into cave walls for four thousand years. The roses had grown tall. Their thorns and bushes were braided together by clever landscapers to be self-supporting. Smooth white stones had been laid in patterns on the ground. It was easy to follow in the lush gloom. Genna focused on her steps. She let the tears flow. She fed her emotions to the roses as she tried to think.

At the center of the labyrinth was a small grove of black oak trees. Their branches stretched liked hands clasped together in group prayer. Benches were built into the trunks. The trees had grown into a shelter. Genna sat down on a stone bench. She stared up at the castle. All the lights were on. The castle was full of life and noise and people. It would be easy and expected to rejoin the party but she needed this solitude.

Had she done the right thing?

Twenty-Five

Genna walked through the McBride mansion. She searched for answers. She found death and cruelty.

"Iffee!" Katie shouted from beyond the porch. She jumped excitedly over the banister. Ran up to Genna. "You came to see me!"

"Where's the art gallery?"

Katie stopped wiggling. "You want to see my art?"

"It's been a while."

Katie smiled. She wrapped her arm around Genna's elbow. They walked down the hallway. Genna listened to her feet instead of her eyes. The magic flowed around her in a sinuous maze.

The walls had seven foot oil paintings of Katie. Then they changed. Genna stared at herself. She was painted over and over again in various states of undress in excruciating detail. She was in frescoes, mosaics, paintings, sculptures, and tapestries. Her face warped into expressions that she would never wear. It was hard to decide if the explicit pictures of herself intertwined with Katie were worse or better than the depictions of Katie devouring Genna. Katie as a snake wrapped around Genna. Or an eagle picking out her liver. Or burning at the stake. Or Genna trapped in a web in a bondage style cocoon.

Katie rubbed her fingers anxiously. Her hair curtained her face. Not entirely hiding her eager expression.

A snake ain't nothing but a snake.

The whisper could have been Genna's own imagination. She clung to it. The cloak was as warm as a maternal hug. Was Miss Bootsie right? Was Tituba?

"What do you think?" Katie said. "I'm actually a big deal, you know."

"You doctored them," Genna said.

Katie tucked her hair behind her ears. She grimaced. "Pipsy and Mimi didn't like the other ones."

Genna's sympathy was nonexistent. She waved a hand. A whisper of magic. The paintings transformed themselves. The original pictures that Katie had painted over to please her mother and grandmother returned.

A thousand and one beautiful depictions of Genna torturing Katie. The emphasis on Katie's face was always twisted in ecstatic agony. Genna's expression were disturbing. Joyful. Caught mid-laughter. Grinning like she had heard a good joke. Amusement that added depth to the depravity. Even the uncomfortable monstrous hunger. Blood dripped through smile lines.

The paintings were grotesquely violent and sexual. A tour through Katie's feverish obsession. As good as the revisions were, the originals were better. The brush stroke freer. The color choice as bold as the imagery. The raw beauty chilled Genna. This was the exact reason why she never went into the mansion. But the castle's visitors had goaded Genna to tread deep into its fetid heart. To confront her own monster before it was used against her.

"There, you see? This is the real deal." Genna said, voice strained. "You think I don't know what your art looks like? The other stuff has no soul."

"Pipsy doesn't like the originals," Katie said. "I'm supposed to be Dracula. Not Renfield."

"You never wanted to be Dracula. That requires thinking. You just want to be. If you did any of this garbage to me then the game would end. That's what you want, isn't it? To be the death of me? You think that's control but it's not."

"I'd find someone else."

"Would you?" Genna looked away from the paintings to focus on Katie. "Or would you recreate me in other people? I think you'd play Prometheus and the Eagle again and again. You'd tortured whoever. Maybe they looked like me. Or remind you of me. You'd warp them into shape always knowing that they would never be me. Even when you broke them. Even when they said the right words it wouldn't be enough. It would underscore that you'd made a mistake in killing me. My absence would be the punishment for your lack of self-control. No one to tell you when you're full of shit. Until you devoured yourself because you couldn't handle a world that I'm not in. You'd be nothing but a miserable snake desperately hoping to find me in the shadows you put me in. All this is bullshit, Katie."

Katie stared at her, tears flowing freely. Genna waited for an answer to her challenge. Instead Katie ran down the hallway, covering her mouth as she sobbed.

Genna followed her to the pool room. The doors were closed. Mimi stood in front.

"Run along, bitch." Mimi said nastily.

Genna lunged forward in a blur of fur and aggression. Her claws slashed muscle and broke bone. Mimi shrieked as she rolled in the twin spurting puddles of blood from the force that had Genna wrenched her arms off.

"Next time, I'll rip your fangs out," Genna growled. She held Mimi's arms, the ends ragged and dribbling on the floor. She watched Mimi writhe, kick, and stomp, losing a shoe.

Kyle watched from the corner of the hallway. Genna threw Mimi's arms at him. His big frog mouth opened. A nearly perfect circle of teeth. His tongue wrapped around the arms like they were a pair of oblong flies.

"Kyle!" Mimi screeched.

He bustled down the corridor, cheeks bulging as he chewed.

"This is why I can't stay mad at you," Katie said, giggling from behind Genna.

Hissing curses, Mimi turned into a snake and arthritically wiggled up the banister to the second floor.

"Iphigenia," Pipsy's hiss filled the hallway.

Katie stiffened. Genna fought the pull but still went into the pool room.

"You go to my head, and you linger like a haunting refrain." Billie Holiday sang from the built in speakers in the ceiling. The acoustics of the pool room were perfect.

The plastic plants crowding the veiny green marble walls and floor created the illusion of a lush jungle in a geometric cavern. Dried blood droplets dappled synthetic leaves and fabric petals. Pots of oiled perfume sat along the air vents, piping in the cloying sweet scent of roses, peonies, and jasmine.

The pool room bustled with revenants. None were remarkable enough to have names. They were drained of personality. Their purpose was to keep the swimming pool full of blood. It was a constant chore. Blood coagulated easily.

Genna stayed by the door while Katie stripped and dove into the pool. Mimi staggered past Genna and fell in with her bloody clothes still on.

Several glamoured humans bathed like mermaids on the pool steps. Katie swam over and took a pumice stone from one of the humans. She scrubbed her arms and chest, shedding scales onto the water.

Mimi attacked one of the naked women. She dragged her under, fed, then surfaced with newly regrown arms. She stretched, humming to herself. Her pert breasts rose high out of the blood. She glared at Genna then pretended that she was not there.

"You go to my head, and you linger like a haunting refrain." Billie Holiday sang from the built in speakers in the ceiling. The acoustics of the pool room were perfect. The rhythmic squelch of

pumps and the metallic churn of meat grinders next door were background noise.

The fresh corpse floated to the surface. A werewolf attendant dragged it out of the water with a pool net. Then carried it next door to dump it into the intake chute of the pool's enormous plumbing system.

The corpse landed in an empty metal cage next to trapped humans. The humans gargled their last moments as the werewolf cranked on the machine that Genna called the Juicer.

The Juicer's primary mechanism was repurposed from a junkyard. It was originally designed to crush cars into cubes. The impact of the stone slab fitted to the bottom of the Juicer burst skin, splattered blood, and pulped meat. The remains were compacted again through a second and third Juicer to wring out residual liquid. Then funneled through a series of meat grinders. Blood was separated through holes in the bottom and shunted into smaller chutes. Sieves caught finer hair and teeth shards. Filtered water from an underground river was mix in. Another set of sieves kept sand and silt out. Then the liquid was pushed down the pipes. The vampire equivalent of lemonade trickled into the pool. The rest slopped into plastic rolling buckets like rank applesauce.

Werewolves and revenant vampires cranked the Juicer's levers like organ grinders. They trudged up and down the complex pipes and handmade machinery, keeping the water to blood ratio liquid enough for a constant flow. They scooped out viscera into buckets with ladles. Werewolves wearing plumber utility belts took apart any clogged pipes and washed them out with wire brushes to catch the hair and bone clots. Revenants hand-sorted the blood from bone, teeth, hair, and skin into smaller buckets or carried the pulped leftovers out of the processing room and down to the kitchen. Emptied buckets were washed out and slotted under the Juicer's bottom-most funnel to await more slurry.

The processing line had the humdrum chaos of a factory.

All of the kitchen staff were werewolves. It required more mental sophistication than a nameless revenant had to cook food. Humans and wild game were chopped and prepared for the dining halls. Revenants ate bloody burgers, chili, and spaghetti with meat sauce. The werewolves ate offal out of slop toughs. Leftovers were shipped in supply trucks to local packs in large plastic drums. Everyone needed to eat.

Genna had tried and failed to talk to other werewolves many times. They worked for Pipsy. Genna was nothing but an enemy disrupting the status quo. She never felt more helpless than in the pool room with its smells, the sounds, and the Juicer's unvarnished reality.

Pipsy preyed predominately on Black folk. Especially lost girls and lonely women. The homeless. The addicts. The teenage streetwalkers desperate enough to be collateral in a cop game. The criminals running from the law and their own guilt. The confused elderly with dementia and arthritis. The bitter runaways. The exhausted overachievers. The destitute divorcees. The beaten wives. The heartbroken widows. The hopeless romantics. The jaded gangsters. The scheming pimps. The hustlers, the gamblers, the makers, and the takers.

Many revenants were the descendants of the plantations and factories Pipsy still owned. She did not need to hunt them down. They came to her, looking for answers to questions that had whispered in the back of their minds. She laid traps that always netted the poor unfortunate souls who slipped through the cracks of society.

One and all were catfished right into the swimming pool after a large meal and a night in a warm bed.

Pipsy loved to drain them right after rekindling their will to live. Their blood filled the swimming pool. Their moans and whimpered prayers filtered in from the Juicer. *The darker the berry, the sweeter the juice* had a whole different meaning in the pool room.

And Genna couldn't save them.

She had plenty of fundraisers and companies to help but still the pool stayed full. She could not stop Pipsy. This was no place for a hero.

Pipsy watched Mimi and Katie with predatory disinterest. She sat in an overstuffed chaise lounge that looked exactly like the one Genna had reupholstered. Expect Pipsy's chaise still had the tiger skin and was stuffed with curly black human hair. She smoked a cigarette through a long ivory holder, doing her best impression of Audrey Hepburn in *Breakfast at Tiffany's*. The thin yellow snakes in her hair were bundled into an upswept chignon. She wore a black velvet dress. Three strands of white pearls and large clip-on pearl earrings. Her oversized sunglasses were propped up on her tiara.

Two men sat at her feet on the damp stone. She sipped from an IV that connected to their carotid arteries. They were gray from exsanguination. A few twitches and wheezing groans were the only indication that they were still alive.

"Iphigenia," Pipsy said, her unblinking stare felt like a blow-torch. "Come here."

Resisting the elder vampire queen was like swimming in the undertow of a tsunami. Yet Genna could think. She could move. She surfed the crushing wave of power instead of drowned. "I wanted to inform you that I have guests staying at my castle."

"I was curious why you brought them until you compromised a highly trained monster hunter right under their noses. Achilles Billson is an excellent specimen in wolf and man form. His magic is unique. Killing him would be a waste. Well done. You have made yourself more valuable to me. My granddaughter has exquisite taste. I have fed well."

Katie flipped her hair. "Thanks, Pipsy!"

"You will continue to undermine the witch finders and monster hunters, Iphigenia." Pipsy took another pull from the IV. "I look forward to what other games you have in planned for your guests."

Genna wasn't sure what she expected but it wasn't compliments. "Okay, well I'm going to go."

"No, you will stay. You will watch. You will do nothing." Magic clamped down hard. Genna was forced into the plastic floral garden to sit on another tiger skin chaise lounge. She sat down hard enough to make the wood creak.

A nameless female revenant came in and bowed her head as she knelt. "Camille Snodgrass, Olympia Billson, and Shelly Billson request an audience."

Pipsy dragged a long nail down the revenant's neck. She sniffed it to confirm that there were no enchantments or grenades. She tugged on the woman's hair, revealing a wig, wig cap, and cornrows underneath. "Go get them."

"Yes, ma'am." The wane-faced revenant swayed upright, blinking with the droopy eyes of someone half-asleep. She did not try to adjust her wig as she minced towards the door.

"Not through the front door, you stupid by-blow!" Pipsy said, sharp like the crack of a bullwhip. "The servants entrance."

"Yes, ma'am." The revenant turned around and toddled out of the same hallway where the buckets of viscera were carried.

"Revenants have no respect," Mimi said, obsequiously. When Pipsy ignored her, Mimi dove back under the blood to grab another woman and devour her in a thrash of bubbles.

The revenant led Camille, Olympia, and Shelly into the pool room. Hector, Paris, and Ajax Billson trooped behind them. They were dressed in full hunter regalia from their matte black body armor to their combat boots but their sheathes and holsters were empty. Except for Shelly Billson, who wore fluffy Chanel, panty hose, and low slung kitten heels. She fidgeted with her pearls, a doughy civilian who looked out of place between Camille and Olympia.

"Pipsy Montgomery," Olympia began, standing wide-legged like a gunslinger. "We are here for our sons."

Genna blinked. The illusion lifted. The two men by Pipsy's

chaise lounge were Troy and Quincy. Her heart clenched in dismay but she could not move.

"You have an abundance of sons, Olympia," Pipsy said. "I told you what would happen if your sons interfered with my granddaughter. You assured me that it was a mistake of a hunt. Yet here we are again."

"Genna Bellwether *Turned* my son into a werewolf!" Olympia's disgust vibrated the air.

"Of course she did." Pipsy purred while Mimi and Katie tittered.

"Pipsy, we didn't know that Iphigenia Bellwether was one of yours," Camille said.

"Really? Has Roanoke's information network failed to do a simple google search?" Katie said. "Everyone who is anyone knows that Iffy is my bride."

"Looks like Galveston dropped the ball," Mimi added and they both snickered.

"We made amends for that offense," Camille said.

"But you won't leave," Pipsy said, "You want Quincy to be the king of the castle. He is a good boy. He understands the importance of family."

"Quincy's good at a lot of things." Mimi licked her lips lasciviously.

Camille's shoulders squared. If her glare was a laser beam then Mimi would have fried where she floated. "We request that you release our sons."

"Troy, on the other hand, believes his actions have no consequences." Pipsy continued, ignoring Camille. "He allowed himself to be Turned. He ignored my warnings. Not only did he refuse the advances of my granddaughter but he tried to kill her several times."

"What do you expect? He's a hunter," Olympia did not hide her proud smirk.

"He's an asshole," Katie hissed.

"He wouldn't sleep with me," Mimi pouted.

"Your kind have forgotten that to interfere with my family is an insult neither forgiven nor forgotten." The pool room echoed with thunder. Pipsy circled the air with her fingernails. "Bring your brood mare forward, Olympia."

Katie and Mimi climbed out of the pool with sinuous grace. Katie's hair flared like a cobra hood. Mimi's hair pressed against her sharp jaw. Their smiles were too big. Their fangs extended. Their nipples hardened.

Shelly tried to hide behind Olympia who shifted in her stance. "Pipsy, this isn't necessary. Neither Roanoke nor Galveston want to renegotiate our amnesty. You have taken the blood of our sons as punishment and payment. That should be enough."

"No, I am far from satisfied," Pipsy smiled coldly. She beckoned with a long finger.

Ajax, Hector, and Paris broke rank and woodenly strode past their mother. Shelly tried to grab them.

"Not my sons," Shelly said. "Anything. Take me. I'll do anything!"

"Shelly!" Camille and Olympia said in harsh unison. They tried to stop her but Shelly flung herself at Pipsy.

"Please, they're all I have!" Shelly's messy sobs echoed off the ceiling.

The Billson brothers watched blood slide along the vampires' smooth pale breasts, down their narrow hips, and over their shaved mounds. Mimi raunchily stroked herself. The wet squelch of her fingers and thrust of her hips drew Hector away from his brothers. Katie prowled in a wide arc away from Mimi, predatory and indifferent. Ajax followed her, taking off his armor and tossing his gear over his shoulders.

"Hector. Ajax. Stop!" Shelly said. "Paris, what are you doing? Wake up!"

Paris knelt on the other side of Pipsy's chaise from Troy and Quincy. He took off his armored clothes, sliding them down to catch on his elbows. His muscled chest was exposed. His neck arched towards Pipsy. He rested his chin in her outstretched hand with a happy sigh. His face was blissfully empty as he looked up at her with glamour glazed eyes. "Lady, you're fucking gorgeous."

"I know," Pipsy said, preening.

Shelly flung herself at him. "Paris, no! Not my baby. You can't have my baby. Olympia, help me!"

She scrambled and slipped on her heels, rolling her ankle. Her stockings tore as her feet dug at the stone floor. Her necklaces broke at the force of her fall. Pearls clattered around the floor, rolling towards the drain. She tried to strike Pipsy but her hand bounced against an invisible barrier. The triple wet snap of a broken wrist, elbow, and shoulder echoed off the ceiling. She fell backwards, shrieking and holding her destroyed arm.

"Shelly has a secret, don't you, Shelly?" Pipsy said. "I know you didn't tell them."

Shelly cradled her arm but she was focused on her sons. "Hector, what are you doing? That's disgusting. She's a vampire!"

Hector was on his knees, suckling at Mimi's breasts, his red erection projected out of his reinforced black cargo pants. Mimi played with her hair and let his big hands touch her all over. He yanked her down onto the ground. She arched as Hector thrust inside with a rough grunt. She hissed and cooed, sliding along a puddle of blood as he pumped fast and hard, butt-cheeks flexing. Her thin hair drank the blood under them like a yellow mop.

Ajax ripped his clothes off. His blue eyes were set deep inside a low sloped forehead. Veins rose along blocky muscles and a shaved head as he flexed his bodybuilder bulk. His steroid swollen arms shunted muscles into sharp relief while tendons on his tree trunk neck stood out. He had tattoos like Troy without the magical glow. Only green with age against tanning-bed brown skin. He grabbed his dick in his hand, jerking on it with rough intensity. His pants were around his boots. The muscles of his thighs flexed.

"You like what you see, bitch?" Ajax leered at Katie, ugly with desire. Violence simmered in the way he fucked his own fist.

"Yes!" Katie went from a prowl to a leap. He caught her, spread her legs wide, and slammed her down onto his crotch. Her pale body was bright against his tanned bulk. Her feet flopped. He grunted as he thrust. She gripped his bald pate while she bit down on his neck.

"No! No! Stop it! Stop it!" Shelly wailed. "Help me. Somebody! Anybody! Olympia. Camille. Olympia. Please. Olympia."

Olympia stepped forward. Camille grabbed her elbow and yanked her back, muttering a quiet warning. "She broke the code."

"Don't sacrifice yourself for this ungrateful sow, Olympia." Pipsy said at the same time. "Shelly betrayed you, didn't you, Shelly?"

"Shut up!" Shelly shrieked. "She lies!"

"Shelly was more than willing to work with me after she used up your money. Ignore those pretty fake tears. She thinks she's better than you, Olympia. She stole your husband. She stole Galveston and turned Roanoke against you, Camille. You thought there was a mole. You were right. Here she is. She has no respect for the amnesty written in blood on the flesh of your people. She's just a greedy human. She even gave me the original contracts. She didn't care what happened as long as her sons got everything."

Olympia and Camille pursed their lips. They were not surprised. This was grim confirmation of their own suspicions. Olympia took a large step back away from Shelly who crawled towards them.

"Help me! Someone! Help me! Olympia, you can't do this!" Shelly's teased blonde hair was wild from her throwing her weight into dragging Paris away from Pipsy's hand. Yet he seemed carved from stone. Pipsy knocked her on her back with a flick of a finger. Shelly kicked the air like an overturned cockroach. Pipsy watched Paris suckle on her fingers.

"Olympia and Camille, your sons will retract their claim on

Iphigenia Bellwether. Is that understood? No more king of the castle. You get nothing."

"Yeah, sure, whatever," Camille said. "I want Troy and Quincy made whole."

"Yes, yes, of course," Olympia said. "What about the contracts?"

"I burned them." Pipsy waved a hand.

Troy and Quincy groaned out of their stupor. They shifted and pushed themselves to a swaying stand. They yanked out the IVs and slapped their bleeding necks. They looked around wildly. Their mothers rushed to the lounge chair. Camille heaved Quincy away from the fornicating Billson brothers. Olympia grabbed Troy by the ear, choosing pain as she dragged him stumbling away from Pipsy.

"Come on, dumbass!"

"Mom, ow!" Troy slapped at her hand feebly.

"You never listen!"

Shelly was still on her knees, wrestling Paris. "You can't do this. You can't do this. You have to help me!"

"Did you sell us out to Pipsy?" Camille demanded. "After everything we did for you? After Katrina?"

Shelly clung to Paris, covering his mouth so he licked the inside of her hand instead of Pipsy's fingers. "We needed the money. Hunting doesn't pay."

"Hunting pays plenty," Olympia's hand was planted firmly on Troy's chest.

"You know the code. You gave Pipsy the original contract. You're dead to us." Camille stopped Quincy with her hand gripped his wrist tight. "No, stay right here."

Olympia's fingers tightened against Troy's chest. She put more strength in her hand and stood squarely in front of him. "Don't you fucking move, dumbass."

Camille never wavered. Quincy and Troy tensed but stayed with closed expressions of rage and sorrow. Shelly's wails clawed at them but they did not disobey their mothers' command.

The four watched. It was all they could do.

Hector rutted hard and harder. His pale hairy butt checks flexed. Mimi fastened against his throat. Blood dribbled on her breasts.

Ajax toppled backwards and did not try to catch his own fall. The dull crack of his skull against stone was overshadowed by Katie's orgasmic laughter. The bottom half of her face was smeared with blood. Ajax's throat was an open savaged wound. Katie continued to ride him as his bulk started to shrivel. His blood was drawn inwards to his crotch. The skin tightened around his skull. His eyes shriveled like raisins. His lips pulled back from his teeth. His chest became concave. His fingers turned into wizen claws. His legs sank in on themselves.

Katie's pale skin flushed. Her hair turned as pink as a cranberry mimosa. She ripped his pectorals into shred, tearing them into bloodless jerky. She gripped his exposed clavicle and ribcage as she slammed down harder. Ajax was a brown mummy. His pelvis cracked off during a thrust. Katie rolled off of him, arching back, her legs wide as she writhed. A brief flex of her swollen labia revealed her sharp vaginal teeth.

Pipsy grabbed Paris by the neck, her claws sank into the tendons and arteries. He shriveled into a mummy then disintegrated into dust.

Shelly wailed and tried to catch his ashes. "My baby!"

Pipsy looked at Shelly, stroking a finger down her cheek. Shelly's screams stopped. Fear replaced by raw lust.

"You're beautiful," she whispered adoringly.

"I know," Pipsy said, "Strip, bitch."

Shelly took her clothes off. She unbuttoned her blouse, shrugged off her blazer. She fumbled her skirt with a broken hand. She struggled with the elastic of her beige shape wear. The heavy compression of her pantyhose. Her breasts swung pendulously against her belly rolls as she peeled off the velcro shape wear. Her pale body was bruised and striped with red seams from her undergarments. Her hair was lank and clotted with ash. Her arm was swollen from internal bleeding. Yet she stared worshipfully at Pipsy.

Pipsy lifted a leg, turning her dress into a tunnel. Shelly crawled under her skirts. Pipsy straddled Shelly, demurely smoothing the black velvet folds. She rocked back and forth. Her eyes were Olympia as her skin blushed with color. Her lips full. Her eight fangs extended and retracted. Her hand pressed against the back of Shelly's skull. Pipsy flexed. Under the skirts Shelly trembled and then sagged, collapsing into dust. The tinkle of metal from a hip joint and gold fillings bounced on the ground. Pipsy relaxed back against the chaise, brushing ash off her skirts. She flicked her spent cigarette into Shelly's ashes and fixed a new one to the holder.

Hector was still thrusting. He had aged. His liver spotted skin hung off his bones like wet paper bags. His bald head had a frizz of white hair. His dull eyes were rheumy and sunken. His bellows were now congested wheezes. Mimi had aged him as she drank. Then Hector jerked, twisted, losing his rhythm. He tried to clutch his chest as he fell over. Mimi clung to him like a tick. Her hips thrust forward. Her feet under her as she lifted her butt upwards to maintain the angle. Hector floundered then sagged. His feeble twitches of death, mouth gaped open. His tongue was a purple strip of leather flopped over his warped brown teeth.

Mimi tossed him sideways. He rolled.

"Finish," Pipsy said. "No by-blows, you sloppy cunt!"

Mimi cringed. She hurried over to the corpse and jabbed a thumb into his eye-socket. The body jerked stiff. Then disintegrated. She wiped her hands free of ash.

Katie prowled over to Troy, bloated on her last kill and her own arrogance. "Hey asshole, you've got the hots for Iffy, don't you?"

Troy, Quincy, Camille, and Olympia coiled like wolves.

Pipsy and Mimi tensed. There was fun and there was pushing too far. Olympia and Camille would kill Katie before she got a step closer to either of the boys.

"Katie," Pipsy said, "That's enough."

Katie flicked her hair over her shoulder. "Fine. It's not like I care."

She strutted to the pool and dove in. Mimi slunk back into the pool. She submerged herself up to the bridge of her nose. She and Katie watched like crocodiles, their hair spread out across the carnage-red water.

Pipsy flicked her hand at the door. "Is there anything else?"

"Troy and Quincy will be staying in the Bellwether castle," Camille said. "The Bellwethers commissioned Roanoke and Galveston to curate their historical archives they keep in the castle and surrounding buildings on the property. They want more extensive and exhaustive reports than Iphigenia unearthed. This contract has no connection to your arrangement."

"You won't find what you're looking for," Pipsy said indifferently then focused on Olympia. "But you should stay here."

"Why would I?" Olympia did not sound as dismissive as she should've been.

"Aren't you tired of being undermined? Look at yourself. Don't you hate what Shelly did to you? Don't you want power, real power? You deserve respect. "

"I don't know what you're talking about," Olympia said.

"Be mine, Olympia. Take Mimi as your bride. Throw away that old name. That old life. That gold curse can't touch you once I make you mine. There is no future for you as a hunter. Only more betrayal and disrespect. There is no honor for a warrior queen like yourself. No name. No legacy. You deserve so much more than what Galveston and Roanoke deign to give. I can make you powerful beyond your wildest dreams."

There were muffled sounds of fury from Mimi and Katie but they stayed in the pool. Troy, Quincy, and Camille did not move a muscle. They were ready to fight to the death.

Olympia drew herself up to her full height. "No deal. We're just passing through."

Pipsy smirked and lit another cigarette. "Welcome to the neighborhood. I'm sure we'll see plenty of each other."

A brigade of revenants surrounded the four hunters and escorted them out. The hard stomp of boots echoed down the hallways. The work of cleaning the pool resumed. Kyle peeked out from the backroom.

Genna waited for Pipsy's hold to relent but she was still trapped on the chaise. Pipsy's magic coiled around her like a python. It was heavy and cool to the touch. The shimmer of the glamour had kept her hidden this whole time. Impatiently she squirmed and strained.

Genna felt the human hair in the cushions underneath her. Rage rushed through her body. Purple lightning crackled along her skin. Pipsy recoiled with a hiss. Genna stood up, brushing herself off. "If you'll excuse me. I need to see to my guests."

Pipsy watched her exit without comment. Genna walked out of the mansion. Katie followed. They went into the forest side by side.

"Well, that was fun," Katie giggled. "I thought for sure that you'd try to save them."

"That wasn't any of my business." Genna rubbed her arms. Pipsy wanting an audience was not a new game but escaping her hold with Troy's electric eel technique would not work twice. She regretted using it so soon.

She considered the deer path that eventually ended at Miss Bootsie's house but instead chose to walk back to the castle. Katie tugged at her elbow. "Hey, aren't you hungry? It's been a while since our last Happy Meal."

"You're hungry already? You just ate a bodybuilder."

"He was nothing but empty calories. Not a single drop of magic."

Genna stopped walking. Katie glowed like a lightning bug in the forest's gloom. She smiled at Genna as if nothing was different. But Genna felt different. The light was wrong. The shadows were in the wrong place.

"She would've let them kill you," Genna said barely a whisper.

"No, she wouldn't've," Katie scoffed but there was a brittleness to her tone.

"I'd tell you to be careful but you're going to do what you want."

"Are you worried about me?"

Genna turned away. "Don't get the wrong idea."

Katie kissed her on the ear and ran off with happy giggles.

Twenty-Six

QUINCY WAS IN HER BED WHEN GENNA WALKED OUT IN a robe. He was naked. As if nothing had happened in the pool room. Maybe he didn't remember.

"Quincy, what the actual hell?" Her eyes itched as her glow burned the swampy moisture permeating her room away.

He patted the comforters of her own bed with a winning smile. "We can cuddle."

Genna's self-control started to fray. "I can also set the bed on fire. Getting a mattress this size up a spiral staircase is a logistical nightmare but I'm willing to do it again."

He stuck out his jaw. She thought about ripping it off. "I didn't think I'd catch feelings either. Your parents told me about how hard it's been to date with the vampires breathing down your neck. Don't worry."

He really didn't remember? She felt ill.

Suitors. Plural. Even Troy had passed her parents' the inspection. Tomorrow she could start the process of getting to know her suitors. Right now she wanted Quincy out of her bed.

Genna took a deep breath. She pinched her nose to stop smelling man flesh. All the naked oiled muscle looked like gourmet meat to bite. Her fingers curled into fists. In the morning, she would be genteel and complimentary and lock the gate and check the vault to make sure nothing had accidentally slipped into someone's pocket. But right now, she was done. More than done. Why was privacy suddenly so hard to achieve?

No, she was seeing this the wrong way round again. Quincy was hers to take. Same as Troy. They needed protection from Pipsy or they would keep going back to the pool room without knowing why until it was too late.

She needed to claim him.

Genna thought hard. No more Turning. Olympia was scary but Camille and Reginald were loving Black parents. That mattered. She needed another way. More traditional. A human way.

"I have something I want to give you." She walked into her jewelry room and found the box.

He was dressed and standing by the time she came into the bedroom again. "Genna, I'm sorry. I wasn't trying to make you feel unsafe. I didn't mean to overstep. I thought. No, I *think* we have a connection. I don't want to fight you."

"Me neither." Blood was difficult to remove from antique Persian silk rugs.

Genna opened a small velvet box. Inside was the twenty carat cushion cut diamond stud earring with a silver and gold backing that she had commissioned in Arkansas. It sparkled like a captured star.

"This is for you, Quincy." She lifted the earring towards him with an opened palm. "I won't force you. Put it on or don't. That's up to you. I won't sap your will or control your thoughts or make you do anything you don't want to do. However, you need to pick a side in Sweetwater. The woods are full of old and hungry magic. I can't control how your blood reacts to it. The best I can do is say you're mine. As long as you don't try to hurt me or the things I love or exploit my trust, you'll be okay. I can protect you. The earring will keep your eyes clear and your mind right."

Quincy swayed with indecision. "That's a nice cubic zirconia."

"It's a real diamond. I picked it myself. It's from Arkansas. No blood diamonds. There's a certificate of its authenticity and origin included in the box."

He raised both eyebrows. He picked up the box and unfolded the certificate. He frowned, squinting to read it in the gloom. "It's twenty carats."

"Yes."

"You got this a month before we met?"

"Yes, but I didn't know why I made it a stud earring. I was tracing the ancestry of my ring." She wiggled her right hand. "I found it myself at the same diamond mine this ring is from. Now I know it was for you."

Quincy tried to hide his shock with a brusque nod. Genna smiled at him hesitantly. "I like you too, Quincy. I know our parents are pushing for marriage but I think we'd be better allies. I've had so many people try to marry me that it's hard to see you as anything but an enemy. We're too similar. You're like everyone I've met at Jack & Jill. It'd be easier to trust you if I didn't have to keep up the performative bullshit."

He angled the earring back and forth. "I was at your debutant ball."

"You were?"

"I was a kid. They had us in the balcony. They didn't want us messing things up. But I remember how you shone like a diamond. Realer than real. I knew you were something special."

"Quincy, I don't know what to say."

"It's okay. You're right. I'd forgotten all about you until Mom showed me your cotillion picture. I keep trying to shove myself back into the dream that kid me had when my dad said I'm supposed to marry a girl like you."

"Supposed to."

"Yeah, supposed to."

They shared a mutual grimace. He lifted the earring to watch it sparkle then put it on.

"I have an idea." He was nervous. "If there's ever a point where you want kids. I'll be the father. No strings. We don't have to marry but I do think we'd make a good team. And if I wanted you to be the mom, would you consider it? You don't have the carry the child. We could get a surrogate. Like Cleopatra. She's a dragon. I've already talked to her about surrogacy for me and Troy. But I think I misstepped when I asked her. I gave her the wrong impression that marriage was involved. You get me. You get us."

Genna stared at him with horrified chagrin. "Oh Quincy, you need to talk to Cleopatra."

"I have." He brushed a long finger along the edge of her wrist. "Think about it, okay? It's okay if the answer is no. Troy said that it was too soon to ask you but I think you needed to know that I want to be a dad. I'd love for you to be the mom. Troy and I will raise the kid. You can be involved as much as you want. Our families will be happy. You don't have to change anything. I think you think that I'm trying to get in your way. Take the castle. I'm not. I want to live it in. With you. With Troy and Cleopatra and Naomi. All of us in a big happy family. Together. Here."

Quincy had been in the castle less than twelve hours. He'd been drained by Pipsy, had sex with Mimi, and who knew what else happened inside McBride Manor before she got there. Now he wanted kids? Had his mother also forgotten what happened or were they pretending that everything was fine because they wanted this union come hell or high water?

"It's too soon," she said, seeking refuge in the familiar.

"You've already made my dreams come true."

"How?" Her question was closer to an incredulous shout.

He gestured, curving his arms into a big circle. "The brunch was like a dream come true. Everyone sitting there. Talking. Laughing. Being themselves. You did that. I've tried but it's never worked. I thought I needed to be the head of the house. I don't. I want to be the glue that keeps us all together. I want to change diapers and drop kids off at school and make sure my dad gets cataract surgery."

"Um, okay, but that doesn't mean that I want kids."

"When you blew up my house in Chicago, I was pissed but I got over it. That place wasn't a home. It was just a place. This castle is a home." He took at step back to spread his hands. "You've built this castle. It's beautiful. I want to celebrate that. Honor that. I think you miss your big family. Shit happens and it's hard to fix. That's okay. You keep growing. You keep hoping. You can make your own family. Your way. With people who understand what you need and how you need it. Like me and Troy."

Quincy paused. Licked his lips. Grimaced. Shook his head ruefully. "I'm talking too much again. I didn't even say thank you." He tugged on his earlobe with the diamond. "This means something, Genna. More than you know. More than I've got words to say. I'll prove it. You won't regret this decision."

"I haven't made a decision about anything. I'm letting you stay in the castle. That's it."

He stopped talking but kept massaging his ear. His eyebrows knotted as he looked down at his feet. "Just think about it, okay? Before you say no?"

Genna cleared her throat. "Okay. I will."

There was a long awkward moment before Quincy realized that she had no intention of elaborating.

He nodded. "Yeah, sure, of course. See you tomorrow."

He strode out of her bedroom. Closed it. Genna walked over. She rubbed the door. She counted his steps as he retreated down the stairwell, rubbing his ear. She locked the bedroom door. She climbed into her bed. It smelled like him. She stared at the ceiling.

The Old Night's soft shadows and warmth surrounded her in a protective blanket. She tugged the black-out curtains closed. Paced around the room, needing to fill it with her scent and not

Quincy's. To calm down. To stop counting bodies. To remember that she was human. They were not enemies but invited guests.

Troy's blood was still in her belly. The slaughterhouse perfume from the pool room was still in her nose. Had she ever refused to play Prometheus with Katie before?

She thought about Quincy instead. What he was offering. What he asked of her. What he had done to Cleopatra bothered her. He easily set her aside the second he found a more pleasing woman that his parents liked. He thought that he was offering Genna the highest of compliments. She got to be the mother of his children. As if a child of a witch and witch finder wouldn't have an existential crisis their whole life.

Quincy had completely misinterpreted the earring. She wanted to walk into Cleopatra's room and ask her if she was okay. Knowing that there was nothing she could do to fix years of neglect. No wonder she tolerated Naomi's easy-breezy affection. It was better than being on Quincy's back burner.

What about Troy? Did he want kids? Or was that Quincy unwilling to let Troy go?

The worst part about Quincy's fantasy was how little of Genna was in that picture. She wasn't human. Humanity was the skin she wore to survive. Or maybe Quincy's fantasies didn't include anyone but himself.

Troy wanted Genna to be the monster in the woods. That was its own kind of dangerous exposure. He didn't care about the consequences. Meanwhile Genna waited for Olympia or someone else to shoot or stab her in the back.

She knew it was bad when Katie felt like the safest choice.

They were competing for her attention. She should be flattered. Instead she loathed the attention. The pressure of formulating an answer. If she ran, they would chase.

Genna buried herself under blankets. She turned into a wolf. She released her own scent from inside the habitual defensive scent-less shell to burn Quincy out of her room. Only then could she relax.

Genna curled around a pillow. She was confused, frustrated, and already sick of people.

She wanted to stand on the roof and howl. Staying silent was a strain. The sex magic had better be worth all of this damn drama.

Twenty-Seven

CLEOPATRA, NAOMI, QUINCY, AND TROY STOPPED clustering together like lost duckings. They started to bloom. They kept complimenting Genna on the castle's architecture as if amazed to see no cracks in the walls or burst pipes or black mold. The castle and the forest drank their magic like it was a delicious milkshake. The flowers were now perpetually in bloom. The vegetables in the garden and fruit trees in the orchards were always ripe, regardless of their normal growing schedule.

Genna remembered the strain of staying away from the castle after the horses died. That had been their lives until now.

The days settled into a comfortable rhythm. Naomi was focused on making costumes, usually holed up in Miss Bootsie's apartment, sewing. She slept among a forest of dresses and fabrics as often as she slept in Cleopatra's bedroom. Cleopatra lived by the pool and garden. Quincy lurked in the library. Troy had no particular spot. He was in constant motion. His whole business ran from a single laptop and phone he kept in a worn backpack.

The maintenance staff smiled at Genna more. They adored Naomi and Cleopatra; were mildly afraid of Troy; and annoyingly treated Quincy like her unofficial husband. Quincy basked in the attention.

Unfortunately, as Quincy got comfortable he got bossy. He reminded her of an obnoxious college dorm RA monitoring everyone's behavior. He expected Genna to accept his sovereignty. The earring was confirmation. Only he ran smack into a solid terse wall of icy politeness.

The difference between Quincy and Genna was that she had been running her own show for years. Her wealth wasn't from her parents. Yes, it started from theirs, but she was no longer hostage to their whims. She could say and had said no. No matter what he, his family, and her staff believed, the castle was hers and hers alone.

The irony was, if Quincy allowed it, she could help him, too. He defined himself by being the rock. Except he wasn't. Genna could see the strain he was under. Genna had heard of living inside of trauma. These four hunters had literally recreated Hurricane Katrina. Genna could see how the four had survived the hurricane by working together but they never relaxed.

The Waffle House was built inside of a perpetual storm as if they lived in the eye of Jupiter. The door seeped mud as the wind pushed it open, skirting cold around their ankles, and wind rippled waves down twinned channels into the flooded drains in the tiled floor. Lightning painted stark shadows. Thunder shook the fixtures. The spell kept the ponderous building standing while the walls groaned, the boarded windows rattled, and the ground trembled.

Once upon a time, this Waffle House had been a real place but now it existed entirely in magic. It was a memory frozen in time. It was also a sanctuary that they retreated into whenever they wanted a private conversation she could not overhear.

Quincy was the center of the spell. This had been his job for so long that he did not question why he was standing here. His pride came in never buckling. He did not care about the cost. He was intimately aware that there was a limit to his strength. Yet he never hesitated to push back the flood.

Every time Genna pressed her hand flat against Quincy's sternum, she could feel the hurricane in his chest. His heart beat painfully fast. His breathing was too rapid. The strain shuddered his limbs. He wheezed like Samson straining to pull the pillars of a temple down.

He never asked for help. His doomed hope that someday Troy would notice and control his power and that Naomi would gain self-awareness instead of stir the storm to a feverish pitch was written into his need for their attention. He expected Cleopatra to stay within reach because she was responsible and a good girl but he never paid her enough attention. That irked Genna. Cleopatra was no one's nanny.

Genna ignored Quincy which set him off kilter. There was no more mention of marriage. Possibly he was afraid that she would say yes. He liked being a bachelor. He was a lover. The matchmaking service was better than any dating app, because the women were specifically curated for his tastes. He was always impressive. Always beautiful. Always emotionally unavailable because he had three different people who loved him. If he was overbearing and controlling, it was for their own good. Genna still got pings from dating apps with his profile on it.

Now that the initial rush of attraction had ebbed, Genna realized how little dating experience she had. She had never become serious about anyone. She did not want to see Katie happen to them. She was still worried, but it was different.

Her feelings were not so complicated about Troy. She spent a lot of time tracking his movements as her reserved curiosity turned to frank fascination.

Genna would wake up to find him doing handstand pushups by the bed. Not to show off but because it was his routine. He was used to being alone. He drove an enormous black tank of a Bronco with oversized reinforced tires that looked capable of scaling a sheer cliff face. He strode into the forest and patrolled the castle grounds. He got to know every renter in the mansions. He knew the groundskeepers, the stable hands, and the security team by name, their family, and their opinion of Genna.

At first, it unnerved her but she saw it as his way of getting comfortable. He did not try to change anything. Only learn the ecosystem to better blend in.

Troy did not like to sit on chairs. He liked to sit on the floor and lean his back against the couch. Or sit in corners where he could see the whole space. She now knew every defensible position in every room of her castle. She made a note of this useful information and adjusted strategic elements of her home security system accordingly.

How did one flirt? What did they have in common besides fire magic?

The wolf.

Which brought her to peanut butter.

Genna perched on the couch, holding the plastic container steady. Troy pressed his face against the edge, eyes rolled back in his head, his face elongating into a muzzle. His long pink tongue traced the insides of the container. His weight pressed against Genna's legs. His hands gripped her calf and the side of the jar. His desperate licks. His little grunts of pleasure. Genna giggled as he crammed as much of his face as would fit past the rim.

He focused on her, trying to reclaim some dignity as he licked his muzzle clean. He settled back into his human form so naturally as if he were born a werewolf instead of newly Turned. "Oh, my god— This is— Oh, my god. *Peanut butter.*"

"I know, right?" Genna grinned, pleased with herself.

"Is this why you're growing peanuts? I thought it was about crop rotation. This is— Oh, my god."

"Salted and honey roasted. The honey is from my own apiary. Things taste different when you're a werewolf." She snuck a dollop of peanut butter off of the jar's lip. His mouth closed on her finger. His teeth were sharp but not breaking skin.

He looked up at her as the phosphorous blue hum of lightning traveled between them. His hands around her ankle firmed, sliding up her calf and under the hem of her Ankara maxi dress. Her breath slowed down as he lifted her skirt. She shivered at the wet friction of his tongue against the soft skin of her calf. The jar was loose in her hand. He took his time working his way up her legs, spreading her knees wide. The light nibble of his teeth on the inside of her thighs. Genna smiled. She allowed herself to relax. She clutched his head through her skirt, riding his face as his tongue laved her clitoris.

An hour of Sexy Funtime later, Troy checked his watch as they put their clothes back on. "Supper time."

He offered her his hand. The chandelier light caught the scars crisscrossed over his palm and down his wrist until they were hidden in a forest of tattoos on his forearm. She took his hand, charmed by his courtesy. She was a sucker for high protocol. She traced his palm, marveling at what she read. This was a weathered hand, marked by burns, knives, teeth, and bullets. Troy watched her but did not ask what she saw.

Hand in hand they walked through the castle, following the smell of roasted garlic and onion.

Dinner was always in the garage sports den. The group liked the garage better than the many banquet halls, dining rooms, and even the kitchen, which Genna found odd but accepted.

The den was filled with trophies and all the right things but ultimately created with performative disinterest. Genna was not into sports. Some earnest interior decorator with a hard-on for Pittsburgh teams was allowed to do anything they wanted in this so-called man cave. Given the dated pictures and memorabilia, this room was part of the original remodel organized by her parents.

Quincy and Troy had loved it instantly. They loved the cars in the garage which were well maintained but barely driven. They spent a lot of time building and repairing things in the metal shop. Carpentry in the wood room. There was a wonderland of things to make, tinker with, and simply drink beer on comfy couches while watching television that had been ignored until their arrival.

Genna's father and her brothers had their own mansions.

This place was for guests who found all the fairytale elements of the castle unsettling. It was a single anchored point between two worlds.

Genna had kept the fridge and bar stocked as a little sign of her affection. Both Troy and Quincy awkwardly thanked her in small ways. Genna had only offered them the same thing the medical personnel renting apartments in her mansions received. Yet it mattered. Their lives were full of hard truths. This garage was a refuge where they could shed the skin of obligation. Sit. Drink beer. Watch the game. Ride horses. Play with dogs. Weed the garden. Harvest honey. Hunt deer in the forest. Have barbecues. Make dinner for the women in their lives.

Cleopatra and Naomi were more aloof. They had many spots around the castle grounds to eat breakfast and lunch but ultimately wound up at the sports room for dinner.

It was strange to share a meal with other people. Their conversation and laughter were genuine instead of performative. Genna learned their movie preferences and political stances. She watched sports, listening to them argue about teams, stats, and players. They played video games which bored her but she still participated with moderate success. She ate food she had never tried. The chefs were happy to oblige, overcooking because finally they had more than one person to feed.

Genna finished her exquisitely tasty mapo tofu. Today Troy had made dinner. The whole den smelled like spices. She waited until after dinner to finally ask the question that had been on her mind.

"Hey, Troy, I'm sorry I turned you into a wolf," Genna said, ignoring his stare. "I'd never bitten anyone before. I don't know if I can undo it, but I can try."

"Undo it? It's permanent," Quincy frowned a little as he ate his food. Naomi drank her wine in a gulp. Cleopatra smiled a crocodile smile.

"Is that what you want?" Troy's growl rattled the chandelier.

"Are you kicking me out? You don't want me to be your wolf anymore?"

Genna fried under the laser of his stare. He was intense about everything. But she could not forget about the pool room. "No, Troy, that's not what I want. I'm happy you're all here but you're on a mission from Galveston and Roanoke. You're doing a threat assessment of myself and the McBrides. Also, everyone's got their animals caged and yours isn't. Your organizations can't be happy with your recent activities or your transformation. Your wolf is big and wild. He can run here, but most places shoot wolves and coyotes."

Troy's eyes flashed like blue lightning. "You've been shot?"

"A long time ago." She folded her hands neatly.

Quincy growled like a landslide. "Someone shot you?"

"I ate him," Genna said.

They looked at each other instead of her. Their disbelief annoyed her but she stayed surly and quiet. If they wouldn't be honest then she was done sharing too.

"Okay, changing the subject," Naomi said loudly. "It's getting a little heavy in here. I love that stable apartment, Genna. It's perfect for my sewing. You've turned this whole place into a magic kingdom."

"Queendom," Quincy corrected.

"Kiss-ass," Naomi muttered.

"No, we've got to be respectful," Quincy said.

"Both of you," Naomi snapped, fingers flicking between Troy and Quincy. "She's a lesbian."

"I'm bisexual," Genna said. "Nobody believes me."

"Yeah, I get that," Cleopatra said. "Folks think it's one or the other. They be like, ooh, but I saw you with a guy yesterday. It's a lie. Like really, dude? Can I live?"

Nods all around the table.

"I'm bisexual too," Quincy said.

"I'm demi," Cleopatra said.

"I'm pansexual," Naomi waggled her tongue, "Anybody can get it."

"I can't believe you've got a Bugatti Type 57 Atlantic," Troy said, who had clearly stopped listening the second his lycanthropy was not under threat.

"We know you like her, Troy!" Naomi snarled.

"This is a car museum," Quincy said, trying to head off an argument. "I've never seen some of these cars in the real world."

"I know," Troy said, lustily. "They're not even in a cryogenic chamber. Have you seen the mechanic spot? There's everything."

Cleopatra and Naomi gave him a look. He shrugged it off.

"I love your wardrobe, Genna," Cleopatra said, smiling at Genna. "You're so fashionable."

"Yeah, I'm into La Sapologie, but your closets are next level," Naomi said.

"I'm unfamiliar with that term," Genna said.

"It's Senegalese," Naomi said, "It's dressing to the nines. With panache. It's a type of social activism. I learned it when we lived in the Democratic Republic of the Congo. I'm part of La Sape, the Society of Tastemakers and Elegant People. I love how the fashion of European dandies were reimagined." She stroked the air towards Quincy and Troy. "They're lovely models. Especially Quincy."

"I needed suits," Quincy said. "Alpha Phi Alpha, the Shriners, and the Masons. There's always some function. Some soiree. It never ends."

"You know, half those people called me Ken or Kendall," Troy said, sulkily. "I'm not your Ken doll, Naomi."

"Oh, whatever, you look good, *Kendall*," Cleopatra said, making kissy faces. Troy raised both middle fingers.

Genna bit the inside of her cheek to keep from giggling. She liked their informality. They were comfortable with each other. They had money. They weren't soulless or boring. Maybe it was because their magic kept things interesting. The money was incidental. Naomi, Cleopatra, and Quincy took the edge off Troy.

They kept Quincy from being too serious. Cleopatra worked on Naomi's hair. Troy was allowed to help twist Quincy's dreadlocks with supervision from both women.

They treated her and her castle like a fairground. She was equally fascinated by their hunter lifestyle built on friendship and familial love. She had to get over her own isolation. The need to disappear into the forest for no other reason than the quiet. Katie would bother her but Genna was not in the mood for her comments.

But something was wrong. She could feel it and smell it in the air but could not pinpoint its source. She hoped that with time there would be trust but they showed no signs of opening up.

Cleopatra quietly took care of the others. She indulged Quincy's whims. She discussed strategy with Troy. She was Naomi's anchor if she drifted too far up into the clouds and pulled her back to land.

They finished dinner and went out onto the porch to smoke a joint.

"I like the wind art installation you built." Cleopatra smiled at Genna, gesturing at the wind catchers that spun like metal jellyfish along the ridge between the forest and the pasture.

"I like wind chimes and kinetic wind catchers," Genna said, embarrassed to be thanked. Her motivations were hardly altruistic.

Thus far, Genna could not tell if the wind catchers were working on Naomi. She decided to push a little. She took her coat off and it changed into a familiar fur cloak. She unclasped the bone-and-leather fastener and offered the cloak. "Here, this cloak is for you, Naomi."

Troy stepped in front as she approached. Protective. Emotions clamped tight. "What's that?"

Genna looked down at the cloak self-consciously. "It's Naomi's fur cloak. Miss Bootsie asked me to wear it until I saw her sunshine girl."

"I don't want it," Naomi said loudly.

Genna stared at her. Not upset. Incredulous. "How can you not want it? People died for this. Miss Bootsie died protecting it for you."

Troy reached for the cloak but Genna stepped back. "No, she has to take it. No one else. It's her heritage."

"I said I don't want it," Naomi said. "Everything you said is bullshit. I want nothing to do with you or any of that! Get that away from us, you cursed thing!"

The wind rustled. The wind catchers spun faster. The wind chimes jangled.

"It's not bullshit. It's your legacy. That's why I invited you to my castle," Genna hugged the cloak protectively from the angry breeze. "I saved your grandmother from Pipsy Montgomery but I couldn't save her from Katie McBride. You're the heir to both the York and Montgomery legacies, but I hope you choose Miss Bootsie. Donnie McBride forced himself on Sable because he and Pipsy wanted power. He tried to do the same to me because they wanted mine. Donnie is dead. Katie ate him. I'm supposed to be her bride but I refused. You have to beware of Katie McBride and Pipsy Montgomery. Wear this for protection. I'm trying to help you."

"All of it means *nothing* to me." Naomi snarled like a tiger. Quincy and Cleopatra formed a protective wall. "You're not trapping me in that skin. I'm free. I'm never coming back!"

The wind slapped Genna's face. Cold air like needles in her skin.

The cloak shivered. The lush soft fur disintegrated. Genna stayed quiet as the fine ash was sucked away by the wind. It spun around like a dust devil. The cloak did not entirely fade. It thinned. It became only coyote and wolf fur. The clasp changed into an onyx wolf with ruby eyes.

"Okay then it's mine now," Genna said, lifting the remains.

"Whatever," Naomi said, "Get it out of here."

Genna twirled the cloak, now crimson as fresh blood. The inside the same light-eating black as her fur. She settled it on her shoulders. The forest was quiet. The land hers. The Old Night was soft against her skin, smoothing the wrinkles off of her shoulders like a pair of old loving hands. Genna did not cry, but she smiled as she tucked her hair into the deep hood. It wasn't a large smile, a mere flex of the lips, but one of deep contentment. Naomi was free. Miss Bootsie's legacy would continue.

The forest was Genna's territory now. Her eyes glowed orange inside of the shadows. Her skin glowed purple as the heart of a candle. Her hair was purple lightning and black smoke. Cleopatra, Troy, Quincy, and Naomi stood in a row, protecting of each other. Ready to attack again. Beautiful and deadly. The power of Hurricane Katrina thrummed in their skins but Genna was not afraid of them, not here on her own turf.

"Why did you do that?" Naomi said angry and tearful. "We had a good thing going."

"I needed to know," Genna said, with heartfelt sincerity. "I think you did too."

Naomi turned into a breeze and flew away. Cleopatra glared at Genna. "That was rude and unnecessary."

"It had to be done. I'm not going to be accused of stealing her birthright again."

"Whatever." Cleopatra turned into a dragon and flew after Naomi.

"You didn't even ask about her side of the story," Quincy said. "You have no idea what she's been through. What Sable's been through after they left Sweetwater."

Genna raised her chin, disliking that he was right. She had not asked. She also genuinely did not care. McBrides used empathy as a trap but she was supposed to be acting nice. "You need to wake up and pay attention. The McBrides are dangerous vampires unlike any you've ever encountered. Naomi will get sucked into Pipsy's thrall if she's not careful."

"Naomi isn't a McBride, Genna," Quincy said. "You keep treating her like the enemy and she's not. She's trying but you're putting up a stone wall."

"There are better ways," Troy said. His glance of disappointment speared Genna through the chest.

"She shouldn't have done it at all!" Quincy slapped his hands together.

"It's done," Troy said, hands in his pockets. A shake of his head.

She gripped the inside of the cloak and did not let the apology slip past her gritted teeth. "Do you remember what happened in the pool room? Have you asked what happened to your stepmother and stepbrothers, Troy? If you go back there then it'll happen again. Only worse!"

Quincy and Troy walked into the forest. Shoulder to shoulder. Their backs to her. She stood in the pasture. "You can't trust the McBrides! Don't go into the pool room!"

Even she didn't believe her own words.

Twenty-Eight

CLEOPATRA AND NAOMI HAD NOT COME BACK TO THE castle yet. Troy and Quincy told Genna to give them space. The tension had also cooled off some of Troy's ardor. It was a mixed blessing. As an apology, Genna invited them on a trail ride. Troy grinned as he walked around the stalls.

"Look at all these warhorses! Hey buddy, aren't you a beauty." Sneakers tried to bite his fingers knowing damn well he was the red wolf. Troy laughed and stepped out of reach. "Easy now!"

Quincy was less distracted. He loomed in Genna's personal space as he scolded. "You don't know Naomi's side of the story."

"Look at the horses and shut the hell up, Quincy." Genna said, hefting her saddle.

Quincy shook his head but joined Troy instead of arguing.

Troy wanted to ride Bibi but she tried to kick him. Both Quincy and Troy had to go through the stable from stall to stall to get chosen by a horse. Most of the herd followed Bibi and Sneakers recalcitrance. A skittish dappled gray Appaloosa Shire mix chose Troy. Genna quietly loathed the gray horse from almost killing her mother when she bucked her off. She had not gotten around to selling her. Troy loved the gray.

"Hey, pretty girl," Troy murmured, petting her thick neck. She lipped his shirt.

Quincy was picked by a painted Clydesdale- Percheron mix. The draft horse was a recent purchase. Genna had bought him for a dollar from a slaughter house, realizing he was a pure bred with a misaligned back. A few months of chiropractic work and he was a prancing addition to her stable. He was easy to train but so big that no one wanted to ride him. He leaned against Quincy and nickered with affection.

"They're now yours," Genna said magnanimously. "Ready to go on a trail ride?"

The frost warmed out of their gazes. They grinned like school boys. Eager to brush and saddle their new horses.

For the first time, the enormous horses had men whose size and skill matched. They plodded after Sneakers. Content to be out of the stall and into the forest.

The forest displayed its autumnal best. The bright yellows, red, and oranges of the trees were so bright that the tree trunks looked black in contrast. The pine trees swayed. Grim, Toto, and a bunch of barn dogs ran through the forest with them. The dog handlers had let their Bouviers and Akitas out to show off to Troy and Quincy.

"I missed riding," Troy said, "After Dad passed I didn't have the heart to ask Mom not to sell his mustang farm."

"You can ride as much as you want," Genna said.

Troy lifted a harmonica to his lips. Quincy did too. They started playing some old-timey, bluesy, jazzy duet. The horses flicked their ears. Sneakers gave the weird noises a look but decided that they was okay. He stepped forward. The other horses followed.

Quincy pulled out a second harmonica and started alternating between the two. It was so absurd that a tired smile escaped her stoic expression. "That's nice."

"It's called the '*Orange Dude Blues*,'" Troy said, "My dad used to play it whenever we were coming back from a bad day and no one knew what to say."

Quincy solemnly offered her the second harmonica. "Follow my lead."

Genna took the harmonica with a raised eyebrow. She wiped it off, turning it over in her hands. Quincy and Troy started to play again. Genna hesitantly blew. But soon enough, she figured out the sounds.

The horses walked at their own pace through the forest. No vampiric laughter or malevolent pink hair bothered her all the way home. Mimi was by the shadows, scowling. "That *stupid* harmonica is giving me *such* a headache. I have to go lie down. Stop playing that wretched music!"

Genna glanced at Troy and Quincy, still playing. She went back to playing the harmonica badly, tuning out the vampire's angry shouts.

Not everything was easy as horseback riding. Somethings were downright uncomfortable.

"No shit. Your grandpappy was Ol' Swifty?" Troy pointed to the vintage picture of her buffalo solider ancestor.

"Great-great-uncle," Genna said. "Ol' Swifty?"

"My grandpappy had this story about Ol' Swifty. He was the fastest cowboy in the West. He could out run, out gun, out shoot anyone. He took out a whole posse that had been chasing him from the San Fernando Valley up to Chicago." Troy slapped his thigh and laughed. "He could shoot the eye out of a fly. He could ride like the wind. No one could catch him. He picked the best horses. He could make a two-dollar nag outrun a Kentucky champion. Pappy would be tickled pink to meet you."

"What was your grandfather's posse?"

"They were Texas Rangers. Ol' Swifty shot them." Troy didn't sound that upset about it either. He strode out of the

Good Room and down the hallway. "Quincy. Quincy! Where the hell did you go? Check this out. Genna's related to Ol' Swifty!"

Genna stared at her ancestor. She felt ill. The buffalo solider had been an active part of the Underground Railroad. He had fought his way through several incidents across the West. He negotiated horse trading for the Union and Confederate calvary. He had started a horse and buggy empire in Chicago. The story was that he had outrun the Chicago fires on the horse of a bounty hunter he had killed to keep from getting lynched.

She went to the red leather bound book and flipped through the pages. There it was. A photo of Texas Rangers. There wasn't a posse. Only one man and a couple of local boys with guns who had joined in on the fun. Genna's ancestor had killed Troy's. She crossed checked the timeline and yes, it was at the same time period when he saved Genna's great-grandmother.

She carefully closed the book. She slid it gently onto the shelf. She walked out of the Good Room after Troy but paused to stare at the old photos and artwork. This could not be coincidence. Troy's family were hunters of animals, of people, and of artifacts. His ancestors were the ones hired to torture those accused of witchcraft at the gold mine. They were employees of the Cape Coast Castle where they hunted Africans, specialized in killing lions and big game. They were bullyboys and catchers. They massacred buffalo to starve out Native Americans. If there was a wrong side of a fight to be on, his people were the mercenaries that terrified their bosses.

Genna tried to sort through her feelings but only ended up turning in circles. What was the right move?

Quincy was in the library. He slid along the rolling ladder. Troy chased him. His face awash in wonder. "Quincy. Quincy, look! Her uncle was Ol' Swifty. Remember that story I told you about the Black cowboy they couldn't catch? It's him. Her people. That's why she can ride. It's in her blood."

"I can ride because I practice." Genna frowned.

Quincy ignored him. He spotted Genna. He jumped off of

the ladder. He waved a leather bound book at her, bellowing. "How many editions of *The Count of Monte Cristo* do you have?"

"We have several first editions. Alexandre Dumas was a friend. We have an extensive collection of all his works."

"A friend?" Quincy parroted. "The author of the *Three Musketeers* was a friend?"

Genna walked back to the Good Room's wall of historical archives and thumbed through to the right section. She handed it to Quincy. "Here are copies of the letters they exchanged. They helped him with a little funding. A few private salon concerts. A word or two in the right place with the right people so he could get the right kind of patronage."

Quincy stared at her, as though remembering who he was talking to then got flustered. "So your family has been rich and Black for a long time."

"Yes, I was pretty surprised myself."

Quincy stared at her, read the page, and stared at her again. "This is incredible." Then he spotted a painting on the wall. He charged over. "Wait a minute. Is that a genuine Romare Bearden?"

"Yes."

"On the wall. Just hanging there. Not a lithograph. The genuine thing."

"Yes."

"Do you have any idea how much that is worth?"

"Yes, my grandfather bought it from Romare Bearden when he lived in Harlem."

"Your grandfather was in Harlem during the Harlem Renaissance?"

"We have an extensive collection of art, literary works, and a few statues from the Harlem Renaissance. The collection's part of a mobile museum. It's in South Carolina right now or maybe France. I can't remember."

Quincy shook his head. "This is incredible. It's like a museum."

He was distracted by another piece of artwork and ran off again. Genna enjoyed listening to him geek out about a painting or a tapestry or book. After all the work she spent curating the collection, it was nice to be appreciated.

It was easier to deal with Troy and Quincy without Cleopatra and Naomi. They wanted to be here.

"Where'd you get that big blue fossil?" Troy asked, pointing at the shelves.

"I took it from a CEO." Genna frowned. She had meant to put the opal back in her office. She had left it in the Good Room after making wind catchers with Katie and forgotten about it. Another thing she had stolen because she wanted it. She was no better than her ancestors who took Sekhmet's head from Egypt.

She stood in a room full of stolen treasure. These were things she would not return and rationalized that they lasted this long because they were safer here than their homeland. She had told no one about using Sekhmet to make anti-venom. In that moment, she needed that ancient power. It had been right there. Without the mounting block there would be no Sneakers or Bibi.

She stared up at Great-Grandmother's enlarged portrait, looking for guidance. Great-Grandmother would not be impressed by Genna's angst. Yes, the world was not fair and full of degradation, move on. Live. Stop whining. Never forget. Her family had the wealth and inclination to preserve their history because so many died in fires.

Genna pivoted and walked out of the Good Room. Troy easily matched her stride. They walked together through the hallways of artwork. Quincy occasionally shouted some other remark about a statue or painting but for the moment, it was just the two of them in the hallway.

"It's pretty cool that you know where you come from." He took a moment to gently trace the contours of her fingers with such care that she blushed.

"How do you reconcile with your ancestors?" Genna said.

"There's a lot of stuff that I couldn't frame on the wall, if you know what I mean."

Troy inhaled and let it out slowly through his nostrils. "I try not to be an asshole like them."

She chuckled bleakly. She dared to reach out and touch the back of his hand, selfishly needing comfort. One monster to another. He cradled her hand as if she were a sacred artifact that he was not supposed to touch.

~

NAOMI AND CLEOPATRA CAME BACK THAT NIGHT. Genna suspected that Quincy had called them. Naomi pretended that nothing had happened and Genna was fine with the lack of confrontation. Cleopatra was brittle. She had a mission. And that was Sekhmet.

One of the disadvantages of having strong spacial awareness was overhearing arguments. Genna could hear Quincy and Cleopatra arguing from where she stood in the castle. The two stood close to the mounting block, arguing, hands on hips, scowling severely at each other.

"You were talking to your parents again, weren't you?" Quincy muttered, shoulders tense. "They don't understand magic. You're always like this. Just cut them off."

"I can't believe Sekhmet is a mounting block surrounded by horse shit," Cleopatra said, "It's disrespectful to the goddess."

"Her horses are prized possessions," Quincy said. "This is the nicest stable I've ever seen. It's the crown on the castle. Sekhmet is like a diamond in the crown. That's what you told me when we got here."

"She's using it as a stepping stone."

"This place is full of magical items. They're woven together. Their magic is fed and maintained. That's one of the best preserved heads of Sekhmet I've ever seen."

"It's not supposed to be here."

"It's a keystone, Cleopatra. You can't yank it out. That'll disrupt the whole ecosystem."

"It's not right."

"Says who? Where should it be? Your pyramid? To sit and collect dust in some storage closet? Feel the stone. It's humming with power. Sekhmet has been connected to this family for centuries with sacrifices and everything. You can't judge her for this."

"Like hell I can't. That castle is filled with stolen magical items."

"That she's been returning. I've seen the records. She's walking the walk trying to make things right. She puts them back where they belong and some of them belong right here."

"Not everything." Cleopatra shook her head scornfully. "They stole Sekhmet from her people."

Quincy crossed his arms, biceps flexing. "And if Sekhmet is the reason this land is protected and taking it destroys that? What then?"

"Fuck you. We shouldn't be here. You dragged us after Troy. He's fine. He's always fine."

"She turned him into a wolf. He's smitten."

"In every sense of the word. Olympia told us. Troy told us. They're all or nothing types. He's all in. Are you really so petty you can't let him move on? You're sleeping with everything that moves, why can't he find somebody else?"

"You're putting on an act," Quincy said with the edge of a snarl. "You don't give a shit about Sekhmet or the dragon hoard or Troy. You're worried about what your parents think. What did they say this time? Some bullshit about how they're Blacker than the Bellwethers? That's bullshit. That pyramid is just a pyramid. They can't buy magic. They won't ever understand you, Cleopatra."

Cleopatra planted her hands on her hips. Her chin jutted. "Fuck you."

Quincy got closer. "No, fuck you. Stop rocking the boat.

Everything is fine. Leave Sekhmet where she is, okay? You can see the curses as well as I can. You know better."

Cleopatra glared down at the mounting block. "Fuck you, Quincy. The only reason you give a shit is that you want a threesome with her and Troy."

It was Quincy's turn to recoil. "You're the one who's too chickenshit to do anything! I've seen the way you're slobbering over her."

Naomi stomped out of the stable apartment. "Okay, both of you shut up and come inside. Help me with the fittings, or fuck off, or find somewhere else to be annoying. We're guests in someone else's house. You don't get to complain about the family heirlooms. We've seen a lot worse. So both of you shut up and get in here." She snapped her fingers and pointed at Miss Bootsie's apartment. "We have a mission. Don't fuck it up."

Quincy and Cleopatra scowled at each other but obediently trooped after Naomi. Genna retreated her awareness back into her body. She went back into the Good Room. She stared up at her Great-Grandmother's portrait. Her hand covered the ring, squeezing it.

There was no good way to have that conversation. No leg to stand on. Cleopatra was right. The castle was full of stolen things that she used on a daily basis. She tried to be respectful. Maybe it would never be enough.

Was that what Tituba wanted her to know?

She cared what Cleopatra thought of her. She needed to work on that.

Twenty-Nine

GENNA WENT DOWN TO HER POOL ROOM. SHE STRIPPED off her plum silk power suit and tossed it at the laundry basket. She hastily wiped her makeup off. She bundled her hair up. She had just driven in from a long series of meetings and phone calls at her office in Pittsburgh. She wanted to swim until the rage leaked out of her body.

She stopped in the doorway.

Cleopatra floated in the pool in a beam of sunlight. She wore only the thinnest of gold bathing suits. Her long brown limbs glittered slightly from her body lotion. Her gold and black mermaid braids were piled high on her head. The diamond in her belly-button was a constant temptation.

"Hey girl, nice to see you. I love your pool. And the sauna." Cleopatra's smile was slightly glassy. Genna guessed it was from the jar of weed-infused gummy bears that was three fourths empty on the table by the lounge chairs.

"Hey," Genna said. She dove into the deep ended and swam a few laps of the pool, back and forth, until finally coming over to Cleopatra. She rose from the water slowly. "Hey," she said again, "Sorry. Long day. Even when you own the company, work sucks."

"I know what you mean." Cleopatra closed the distance between them. "I could help you relax."

She kissed her way along Genna's shoulder. Genna stayed still, intrigued and aroused. Cleopatra's gold nails slid along Genna's hip, coaxing her to stop floating. Their limbs slid against each other. The saltwater from the pool flavored their sleepy, exploratory kisses. Their hands massaged breasts, buttocks, and hips. Genna bent down to push aside Cleopatra's bikini. She suckled on a firm nipple, enjoying the full weight of the breasts filling her hands. She pulled and tugged the nipple with her teeth and tongue. Cleopatra shuddered and clasped Genna's wet curls that spread along the top of the water like a black cape.

They walked up the shallow slope and onto the pool's stone edge. Genna was still in the water. Cleopatra spread her legs. Her feet arched and pressed against the stone, Genna's shoulders, and splashed the edge as she lay back. Genna moved slowly, reading the ebb and flow of every sigh. She followed the tremble as she traced the purple edges of Cleopatra's labia, suckling on each swollen iris petals. By her ecstatic moans, Cleopatra loved it when Genna slowly sank her teeth down and sucked hard.

"Ooh, girl, you're about to suck my soul right of out my pussy," Cleopatra said, squeezing and playing with her own breasts.

"Want me to stop?"

Cleopatra's powerful thighs locked around her shoulders. "Hell, no!"

Genna chuckled as she pressed her face more firmly into Cleopatra's mounds. Her tongue circled her clitoris. Cleopatra liked long, darting strokes. It made her jump and wiggle. Her magnificently full butt cheeks trembled. Genna slid her fingers inside. Then her hand. Then her whole fist pumped harder and harder. Cleopatra moaned and gasped.

Genna and Cleopatra rolled and frolicked, but there was a limit to it. Both finally stopped. They smiled awkwardly as Genna slid her hand out and swam back into the pool.

"Sorry," Genna said, flustered. She was better at this. What was wrong with her?

Cleopatra pushed her braids out of her face. "No, I'm sorry, I'm a little gun-shy myself. You're a beautiful woman. Of course I'm interested. You're good at fisting. I haven't had an orgasm like that in a while."

Genna kissed her gently. "It's okay."

Cleopatra smirked as if she did not quite believe her.

Genna swam over to the stairs. She took a maroon towel waiting across the back of a chair. She quickly dried off. "I can always watch. You're gorgeous. I like to think we'd be friends if things weren't like this. The kind that can have fun together. No strings."

Cleopatra looked around as though worried about ears. Maybe Naomi could hear every conversation. That was certainly a skill for spying. "I'd rather be friends."

"Me too."

Cleopatra walked over to a small bag to get a waterproof dildo and some lube. She smiled at Genna as she stretched on the couch. Cleopatra flexed and moaned. The vibrator hummed. Her hips swayed. She spread her thighs wider, sinking down and riding the dildo. Its vibration were softened by the towel it was wrapped in. Also obscuring Genna's view. Genna walked over and flipped the towel over Cleopatra's thigh. That got a sultry chuckle. She waggled her tongue, putting on a show. Exaggerated moans. Humping the lounge chair, the metal legs screeching with each jerking motion.

Genna grinned with hungry affection. Cleopatra knew how to have fun. She wondered how much love was between Cleopatra and Naomi. In a real way, Naomi's vampiric nature informed her witchiness. No one loved Naomi more than Naomi.

Cleopatra shuddered and relaxed. Genna sat on the lounge chair next to her. Marveling. "You are exquisite."

Cleopatra simpered. "That's nice of you to say."

"Not compared to me," Naomi said.

Cleopatra looked down. She tucked the towel around herself. She folded her long legs under herself. Genna wondered how she could put wind catchers in every room. Naomi's strategic entrance was so similar to Katie's that Genna nearly threw a towel at her.

"We should fuck," Naomi said. "I've made a fireproof dress."

Genna studied Naomi, a hand tucked under her chin. The harmonics were familiar.

Genna had learned about the power of self-control from the BDSM community and applied it to her lycanthropy. She recognized Naomi's sexual aggression. She liked the attention, any attention. She gloried in the pain, the rage, and the power of forcing someone to lose their shit against their will. Sex was a game to Naomi. She wanted to win. Even if it was a meaningless victory. She wanted to be the prettiest. The smartest. From moment to moment straining to be on top. Not for any particular reason other than winning. Her vampiric nature warped her further.

In short, Naomi was a brat.

Genna loathed brats. Their particular flavor of disrespect had goaded her into eating a few.

Genna had seen a brat just like Naomi once smack an emotionally violent Sadistic Dominant at a kinky house party without warning just to get his attention. Genna had climbed through a kitchen window to get away from that fight.

Once a Sweetwater brat had swung a riding crop at her. "Where's your fur? Show me your teeth. I bet you're not even really a werewolf. You're a liar."

Genna had eaten that bitch alive.

Brats also made her feel helpless. They welcomed her wrath with nihilistic glee, throwing themselves into her teeth. There was no winning. She ignored them. She hoped that they would lose interest and go away to find someone else to annoy. Someone who couldn't rip their spine out.

Worse yet, Naomi stank of grave dirt. She had gone to Miss

Bootsie's mausoleum and taken the skin. She wore it and covered the maggot holes with lace and makeup. That was what she had been crafting in Miss Bootsie's apartment, using the stable as a cover. Genna could see Katie, Mimi, and Pipsy sitting in Naomi's eyes. They walked through the castle grounds. Cleopatra, Troy, and Quincy hadn't noticed. But Genna knew her stronghold was compromised.

The spiteful brat wanted her to get mad and retaliate.

It was impossible to relax. Her muscles were tense, ready to launch straight up out of the water. To bite. Snap. Tear. But there was no winning if she did. Naomi was safely insulated and protected from retribution. Genna had to play along with this stupid game and be the loser.

"Cleopatra *is* exquisite." Genna repeated. "Brat."

Naomi gasped. Tears in her eyes. "You're so mean. Why don't you like me?"

"Try your negging on someone else. I'm not the one."

Cleopatra frowned at Genna. "That's my girlfriend."

"Yes, and she's a brat."

Naomi sniffled dramatically. "It's fine. I know when I'm not wanted."

"You could apologize for trying to kill her, Naomi," Cleopatra said. Then glanced at Genna. "That's what this is really about isn't it? That's why you tried to ground Naomi to that old fur coat because you're still mad about Chicago?"

"I apologized!" Naomi exclaimed.

"Actually, you haven't." Genna said.

"I thought we were cool." The pouting was theatrical.

"Naomi, if you want me to fuck you then be pleasing instead of obnoxious. This petty shit isn't cute. I eat brats. I don't play with them."

"Who do you think you are?"

"I'm the head bitch in charge." The shadows became darker as steam rose from Genna's skin. Her voice feathered with a growl. The wolf was close to her skin. "I'm the top dog. The alpha. The queen of the castle. The only head wearing a crown on this land. I don't share my power. You obey. Or you get the fuck out."

"That's why sex would be fun," Naomi said, unrepentant. She played with her breasts, so they jiggled like bags of tapioca pudding. "Put me in my place. Show me who's boss."

Genna growled with disgust. A bratty McBride. She wanted to *kill* this bitch and be done with it.

Cleopatra slid off her chair. She knelt at Genna's feet. She pressed her hands on Genna's toes. "Don't be mad at her. Please. She isn't trying to offend you. She's flirting. She's calling your fire with her hot air. She wants you to devour her as fire eats air."

Genna was breathing hard. Trying to focus. She hated being manipulated. She hated it. "Not interested."

"Naomi, go," Cleopatra said. "You're sending the wrong signals."

Naomi's nose wrinkled. "What did I do wrong?" She gestured at herself. "I'm fucking gorgeous!"

"Just go. Please?"

Naomi flounced out of the pool room through the door that led outside. The door slammed itself hard enough Genna wanted to check for cracked glass.

Cleopatra stroked Genna's feet, massaging the muscles and tendons. "Come swim with me?"

Genna silently followed her into the pool. They swam back and forth. Racing. Cleopatra was fast in the water like a mermaid. Genna focused on the elegance of her free-style. The silken flow of bubbles. Slowly her rage ebbed. She felt stupid.

Why did everything have to be so damn awkward with Cleopatra? As if forces were pushing them apart. She was right here. An arms length away but it never right. Not just bad timing but incompatible.

"Why'd you grab my feet?" Genna said as they slowed down their swim and returned to the shallow end.

"To keep you grounded. Troy taught me that."

"Is that why he sits on the floor?"

"You burn enough butt prints into the couch, you'll avoid furniture too." Cleopatra rubbed Genna's hips. "I think it's amazing that you've managed to do this on your own. The four of us need each other to maintain balance."

"I had to learn quickly. The McBrides eat anything and everything."

Cleopatra sank deeper into the water. She twisted through the water with ease. She blended in with the mosaic mermaids, as if she had leapt from the tile. "Can you try to see Naomi and not who she comes from? It's not fair to be judged on things you can't control."

"She snuffed me out." Here they were again, talking about Naomi. Cleopatra kept deflecting away from herself.

"That was your first time being snuffed out? My first time was Katrina. But it's not fair to compare. We'll slow down. We can work on trust together. It's tough to feel so exposed. Like a snail without its shell. All gooey and vulnerable."

"Something like that," Genna said, not committing to anything.

Genna flipped on her back. Cleopatra swam away from her and climbed out of the pool. Genna wanted to be the water soaking up her bathing suit. She wanted to lick the edges of her sides. To trace the knobs of her spine. She contented herself to watch the heavy jiggle and swing of Cleopatra's butt, hips, and thighs.

Naomi was a slight haze pretending to be steam from the sauna. Genna could see Naomi's magic now that Cleopatra wasn't hiding it.

Another McBride Genna couldn't kill. She was forced to rely upon the earrings that had she made to slowly net and nullify Naomi's hostile magic. Genna used the same lightning lasso Troy roped Naomi up with in Chicago. He had shown her the lasso several times. Only Genna's strands were gossamer thin.

The water started to steam and bubble. Genna went back to swimming laps.

Thirty

Genna and Troy rolled in the bed. They had knocked the sheets off of the mattress and onto the floor. She counted down to Quincy walking through the door. *Five, four, three, two...*

"Hey, you two." Quincy was a large shadow in the doorway. His clothes were on but his feet were bare. His hands were in his pockets. His head was low. His dreadlocks were loose, swaying around his face like heavy cords of black moss.

"Come join us," Genna said, keeping Troy's head firmly between her thighs.

Quincy shrugged. "Maybe later."

"That wasn't a request." Genna reached out a hand. "Come here. Your queen commands it."

Quincy knelt next to Troy. He put one fist on his heart. The other on the ground. "By my life or my death, I'm yours, my queen."

Genna took a deep breath. She cupped Quincy's face. Kissed him on his big pillowy lips. She reached over to Troy. Kissed him too. "My sword. My shield."

Both men smiled in her touch. Shy and vulnerable. Happiness

was as fragile as a soap bubble. This was a kinky dynamic they all enjoyed.

Her bed had more than enough space for the three of them. Their bodies were slick with sweat and warm. Genna was now thoroughly and delightfully warmed up. Quincy's tongue tickled her anus. His broad hands squeezed her haunches, spreading them wide.

Troy, on his back, cupped Quincy's balls, tugging and massaging them. His cheeks flexed as he sucked on Quincy's growing erection. Genna lay on Troy, sucking on the back of his knee because it was all she could reach. Troy bucked and shuddered, moaning around a full mouth, his hips flexing. Genna grinned in surprised delight at finding an unexpected erogenous zone.

Quincy replaced his tongue with a lubed finger. Genna exhaled and shuddered. "Slow down."

He complied. Also swayed. "Troy, I'm not going to last if you keep that up."

The smack of lips. A throaty chuckle. Quincy shuddered. Cleared his throat which deepened into a soft moan.

Genna twisted. She grabbed Troy's semi-erection. She began to suck on it.

The broad blunt head of Quincy's cock slid into her wet swollen pussy. His finger continued to stroke the tender sensitive flesh inside her anus. She forgot what she was doing. She shuddered and moaned, holding onto Troy's thighs.

Troy wiggled around her, trying to find the right angle. He shuffled into a new position. Quincy and Troy knelt with Genna in the middle. Troy slathered on more lube then slid into her anus. Quincy was still inside her vagina. She hung onto Quincy's neck, lifting herself up and sliding down. Full, so gloriously full. Every tiny clench of her body shuddered through them all.

Troy and Quincy kissed, sucking hard on each other's tongues. The growling grunts. Her higher, breathier moans. Their muscles flexed. Hands in each other's hair, scratching and stroking down backs. Quincy lay back, thrusting harder and faster. Genna hung on. Her hair tangled under his shoulder. Troy's feral growl against in her ear as he bit her on the shoulder.

Genna arched, shrieking her way through an orgasm.

Her vision was striated by colors. Outside, it thundered. A storm churning. The lightning felt like it was in her veins. The thunder rolled along her skin. Quincy was like an ocean's roar.

She was transported somewhere else. A beach where the waves clawed chunks out of the sand. The wind slapped her, gnawed her, snatched her up into the air. She was the lightning. Troy was too. They collided. They tied themselves into knots and tore free. They buried themselves inside of Quincy and filled him with light.

She needed more. Not just another magic ride. She wanted physical pleasure. She grabbed both men by the hair. Her teeth bared. Her snarl was braided with lightning as she yanked them back into the real world. "More. Give me more. Give me everything. Stop holding back!"

She clamped down. They pounded into her harder. Their movements no longer rhythmic. She refused to let them climax. Not yet. Spurring them on. Driving them harder. Their bellows mixed with her own and the thunder. Their bodies slapped together, frantic now, desperate to reach the crest. Blind to anything but sensation. Harder. Their real strength slammed into her. They moaned her name like the rough prayers of the drowning.

She did not care. She wanted more. She was going to get more. Slashing and biting and slamming. Hot breath. Spittle against the skin. Head wrenched back. Fists in hair. Bloody skin.

Her orgasm rose like magma in a dormant volcano, rock shoved aside and melted in haste, the smoke billowed up, filled with projectile stone, purple lightning and orange molten flaming rock arcing around the blast.

Genna roared until her throat tore from the pressure. Quincy thrashed. Troy arched. Thrusting and thrusting and thrusting.

Outside, the clouds burst open. Rain poured down, flattening the grass. Genna slumped sideways, tinier orgasms shivering through her body as Quincy slid out of her and rolled sideways. Troy pulled Genna the opposite way in his arms. Lifting her free. Hugging her and kissing her throat. Genna was limp. Her hair stuck to her face.

Both men quickly knotted and discarded the filled condoms into trash cans underneath the matching nightstands. Their synchronized movements from habit. This was not their first threesome.

Quincy got up and went into the bathroom. The fluorescent light was bright, garish. She whimpered, not ready for the light that stabbed her pupils. Troy curled around her protectively. He tugged the sheet from the floor and pulled it over them both. He piled the pillows around her, creating a nest. She smirked at his fussing.

Genna yawned, boneless and relaxed. He snuggled close. He kissed her deeply, cupped her face. "Rest, my lady. No more dragons to slay. You're safe."

She had a rebuttal, something about no dragon-killing but she was too cum-drunk to be articulate. Their fingers threaded together.

She ached but it was a good ache. Her body hummed like a tuning fork. Quincy rejoined them. A moment of cold air and damp skin as he slid under the blankets, snuggling up from behind Troy. The long sleepy kisses along the side of her face. Quincy cupped Troy's jaw and kissed him deeply. Troy leaned into the lingering touch. The heavy weight of two sets of muscular arms and legs spooning with hers. Genna cupped Quincy's hand against her cheek. She kissed his wrist. He stilled and stroked her hair, then arm, then rested a firm, possessive hand against her hip.

Outside, the storm eased into simple rain.

In the twilight gloom she took a quick bathroom break without the lights on. She came back to the bed, pausing to watch

Troy and Quincy sleep, their faces gentled by slumber. She liked the way they curled together. Back to back. One hand under the pillow even when there wasn't a weapon underneath. Even in sleep they guarded the other.

It was easy to join them again. She wanted snuggles. She wanted to stay.

They both woke up when she entered the bed. Quincy slid his hand over her hip. A kiss on the forehead. Then he climbed out of the bed. Gathered his things. Strode out.

She frowned, disliking the empty space. Troy cinched her arm around his waist. Kissed her hand as he pulled her deeper into the bedding. "He needs a moment."

Genna nodded. "Turn over. I want to be big spoon."

Troy's eyes glowed in the darkness. Another flex of power bathed over her. They wiggled in bed to get comfortable in their new positions. She hugged him closer, pressing his back against her front. She kissed his shoulder blade. Then put her nose into the back of his hair. Breathing his scent in. They fell asleep.

Magic shimmered. Two wolves curled in a nest of sheets. At peace.

Thirty-One

GENNA TAPPED HERSELF IN THE FOREHEAD. POWER rang through her. The gong was a deep and sonorous warning. The castle was full of little curses and burrs. Scratches and frayed edges. Things scuttled and slithered away. She marked them as intruders and enemies.

Pirate the rooster attacked them, pecking and clawing. Toto chased and savaged. Sneakers stomped. Bibi gathered the herd. Schrodinger hid. Grim stayed quiet. Genna scratched his ears as she made a notation of the location, frequency, and kinds of attacks. Grim ignored her and went back to watching. The grimhound only moved when it was an emergency.

Genna had increased her patrols since Naomi came back to the castle. She stepped out of magic and back into the physical world. She picked the office because the eight paneled bay windows had the best view of the wind catchers. Then recoiled with a snarled curse.

Troy stood in her office. He leaned in the window sill. He smirked. Genna strode over and flicked him in the forehead. He caught her wrist before she could make contact but all she needed to do was touch him. She flicked him in between the eyebrows. He flinched. The wolf lunged forward. She snarled at him to back the fuck down or she would rip his throat out for being a dumbass. He rocked back. Let go of her hand. Shifting back into his human shape, astonished by her dominance and chastised.

To be safe she also flicked Naomi, Quincy, and Cleopatra. She heard their startled bellows as she rang them like bells.

"Ow! Goddammit!" Quincy and Cleopatra slapped their foreheads and reeled back.

"What was that for?" Naomi hissed, her fangs extending and retracting.

"You're in the deep dark woods. I'm cleansing out the unwanted visitors," Genna said, irritated. "It's an anchor as much as a protection. Otherwise, Pipsy's sitting between your ears."

Naomi, Quincy, and Cleopatra grumbled as they settled back down. Pipsy's presence was not purged from the castle grounds.

"No offense, but you're scary as hell," Troy said, rubbing his forehead. "I was wondering how you'd get Naomi back."

Genna raised her chin. "Are you going to stop me?"

"I know better than to get into women's business. Especially Black women business. I like to think I'm pretty damn good at my job but I know when I'm wrong. Naomi shouldn't have attacked you in Chicago. She fucks with my lightning too. It took me years to do what you've done on the second try."

"Katie's stronger." Genna did not add how Pipsy compared. There was no point.

Troy lifted her journal. "You have beautiful handwriting."

"I'm pissed that you're reading my journals without permission."

"Are you? Or are you curious about what I think? Hunter to hunter."

She glared at him but he was right. She had written the journal pretending it was a conversation with some unknown but equally knowledgeable person. "Well?"

He grinned with affection and closed the journal. He walked over to the opal. She had returned it to the office for safe keeping yet still it attracted Troy's attention. "You missed something."

"The opal?" Genna looked over the opal with dismay. She thought she had cleaned up after her spell.

"Here, it's pretty cool." Troy put her hand on the boulder opal.

Genna stood on a shoreline. She was naked but that was okay. A peach-pink sunset filled the sky. A purple mist drifted along the water. The gentle lap of waves flowed against a shoreline that reached out to the horizon in both directions. It could be now. It could be millennia ago.

The water was so warm that it felt like soup. The air was thick with salt. Desiccated seaweed carpeted the sand. There were horseshoe crabs spawning across the shore. Millions of them climbed on top of each other. The surf foamed around their shells. The horseshoe crabs spawned as they always had. Creatures in the water left bioluminescent trails.

Genna stayed still, wanting to scream as things crawled over her feet. She spotted the enormous horseshoe crab lumbering through the spawning ground. A much smaller male was on her back.

Troy stood behind her. He was also naked. "My family calls places that don't exist anywhere else but right here a porch."

"That seems profoundly mundane."

He smirked. "It's a place of transitions between worlds. A porch isn't a house or the outside. A yard isn't a house or the woods. A farm is land worked by human hands, but if the humans aren't around, the woods will take it back. A pool isn't the ocean or lake. When it's a saltwater pool like yours, it's connected to the ocean. That's why we're at the beach."

Genna looked around at the sand dunes and prehistoric plant life. "Troy, unless I'm gravely mistaken, we're standing in a memory of a fossilized horseshoe crab when Pittsburgh was a sandy beach of an inland sea. There's so much cadmium in the air that we should be writhing on the ground, clutching our throats."

"We haven't gone back in time. It's a collective memory. The salt water in your pool. You. Me. The crabs you saved. We've all been at a beach at sunset, when the water is warm and the waves are tranquil. We all made this place. We are welcome to stay. Did you tell the crabs something? Because they recognize you."

"I yelled at the female crab when she tried to die on me. I told her to repopulate the species."

"Seems like she listened. You have a way of speaking and knowing secret hearts." He sighed and hugged her. "I've stopped trying to categorize you."

"Is that a good thing or a bad thing?"

"It's the third category. You're an entity all of your own. When names are a cage. We call those people a *Nunya* and leave it at that."

"Nunya?"

"Short for 'None of your business'. If you know, you know. But many asshole newbies take that as a challenge. They think they can walk in anywhere because they want to. They want to kill a dragon before they know why it's here."

"Not you?"

"I've been a hunter since I born. Most don't make it past their thirties."

"You don't seem like the average hunter."

"I'm not. That doesn't mean I have a right to walk into the forest without your permission." Troy's eyes were shards of blue opals. The fluorescent tattoos on his skin moved lazily like a nest of sleepy snakes. His expression was soft. "You know your business. This is your castle. Your world. I'm just passing through."

"It's not mine alone. I was taught."

"That doesn't guarantee understanding. Especially in the Deep Magic you've been swimming in. My mom trained my stepbrothers and they're a trio of corrupt trigger-happy dumbasses." Lightning crackled in his tone. "Or they were."

"I'm the oldest of four too. Younger siblings are hard."

"They bring shame to the game. They think they can buy magic. Or they did."

"You remember the pool room?"

"You were there?"

"I didn't have a choice. I'm sorry for your loss."

Troy grimaced. "I'm not. It was always going to happen. Now Mom's free and I'm here. I don't have to keep cleaning up their mess."

Genna struggled not to impose her own feelings about her siblings on what was clearly a loveless and complicated relationship.

He stepped closer, barely lifting his feet to keep from stepping on crabs. His touch along her hips was slow, waiting to get smacked away. When he had sloshed close enough, she leaned back against him. She let herself be held. Let the waves coat her ankles with sand while the crabs crawled past.

He hugged her tighter. His face against her scalp like he wanted to hide in her curls. "I don't know what to say to you, Genna. I don't know the right words. I can see how you do it but I can't follow it. I introduce you to a new environment. Instead of jumping around, going 'Oh my god, where are we? How'd we get here? How can we get back? Who am I?' You're simply here. Letting yourself be a part of this moment. Most hunters don't make it this far."

"I've done what I can to survive."

"Have you ever considered how dangerous that makes you?"

Genna thought about the woods and Katie. "There's a logical explanation. Logic, even fairytale logic, has a rhyme and reason." She pointed at the enormous female. "I rescued a crab that turned out to be magical. She's hard to forget. I'm guessing this is a magic fish situation. Maybe a genie in the lamp, too, because of the opal."

"Logic is denying the existence of a thing. Acceptance isn't usually the first response. It's a good camouflage."

Genna tilted her head but he swayed, keeping his face in her hair. "Camouflage?"

"I know seeing the wolf tattoos upsets you but you've got the same mindset as a Luparii hunter. Sweetwater is your territory.

You know the monsters, the layout of the land, and you've done it alone with limited resources. Money doesn't equal much if you don't know how to use it. Fairytale logic, as you call it. I respect that. This forest is old and wild. But you're not worried about it. You're worried about them. The McBrides."

"I have good reason. And you should be too."

"Let them underestimate you. You're clever. You're ruthless. You've got good aim. Let them get close then you strike. You don't hesitate. Why be a wolf when you can be a coyote?"

Genna raised her eyebrows. "You don't like wolves? You are one now."

A small sad shake of his head. "Mom is pissed."

"Yeah, I noticed."

"Wolves are dumb. They're battling extinction. They can't handle being alone. They're desperate to keep the peace and social norms. Except what is normal is defined by the pack's beliefs. Mob rule. Petty infighting. Coyotes are cooler. It's rare for any species to adapt so well to humanity that we don't even know how many exist. I hoped I'd Turn into a clever coyote like you but I'm a big, dumb wolf."

His hand slipped down her waist and brushed her clitoris. She tried to think of some kind of protest. Like sand in uncomfortable places. He hugged her tighter. "That place with the pole. I gave it my tattoos but they grew back. I don't have anything to give that I don't need. I need your permission. I need a talisman. Some kind of protection. Something that marks me as yours. Like a collar."

"A collar?" Genna was always sensitive about necklaces and dog collars. The ones with prongs. Shock collars. Leashes and locks.

Troy knelt. The crabs had vacated their part of the beach. It was just them and the waves. She watched the sunset but Troy looked up at her, waiting.

"I'll think about it." She lifted one leg and draped it over Troy's shoulder. "Right now I want to watch the sunset while you pleasure me."

He immediately began to suckle her labia and clit. When she was ready for more she sucked on him too. She did her best to make sure that there was no wayward sand then sank down onto his erection. They rocked together, as gentle as the waves.

It was late in the evening when they returned to the physical world. The others were asleep. They showered. He tried to leave but she gently but instantly tugged his wrist.

"Come to bed."

He watched her, his blue eyes at a banked glow. She felt more naked than naked. Her damp bare skin was sensitive to every fluctuation in his magic. It was a vulnerable experience. No one but Genna had ever slept in this bed but now she was used to Troy's presence. She did not want to sleep alone anymore.

He stroked along the curve of her hip. It was strange and wonderful to be held. To feel the lightning lick along her skin. To be genuinely okay. She didn't have to be gentle or nice or hide her fire. She couldn't hurt him. He couldn't hurt her. Yes, the sheets sometimes smoked around them but they were okay.

"What are you thinking about?" Troy said.

"What you asked for. A talisman." She stopped his touch.

"Kneel," she said, opening the curtain enough that moonlight could paint her curves.

He hopped out of the bed. She knew he loved it when she commanded him by the blush on his neck. He knelt, one knee on the ground. The other up. His back straight. His hands were at rest on his knee.

Genna stood in front of him. The fantasy of a knight blending with hers of being queen until there was nothing but the truth. For Quincy, it was a sexy game. For Troy, he was her warrior. This was what he needed to be. The vulnerability of his unasked question on the beach underscored that knowledge. It was in the way he looked at her. How he was always there, right where she needed him. Not overbearing. Watchful.

It was important to show him that she understood that unasked question. For herself. And for him.

She stroked his cheek. "I think a talisman has to mean something. It can't be a random trinket. It's more than a backstage pass to a concert. You'll be representing me. You're not going to exploit my trust. You're promising not to embarrass me. I'm also declaring that you're important to me. That I trust you and you trust me."

She reached into the shadows. She knew exactly what she was looking for and where its box sat in her vault. She placed a simple but sturdily made necklace around his neck. In the moonlight, it looked made of mercury and freshly poured silver. Her fingers traced the braided silver chain. It was heavy and old. A wolf's head was the toggle clasp. "This was handmade by a silversmith. I found it in the collection while cataloguing jewelry made from the family silver mine. I want you to wear it."

She leaned down to whisper as she fastened the clasp. "I've decided to keep you. Today I offer you this collar and my love. Do you accept my love?"

His hand slid up his chest, to trace the weave. His gaze shone. He took off his watch. He gently placed it on her wrist. It was heavy and warm with power. She felt a resonance of the gold ring and the watch. Troy kissed her knuckles. "By my life or my death, I'm yours."

"I'll take your life."

"Yes, my queen." He smiled. She kissed him.

Troy reached under the bed. He pulled out a medium sized matte black case. Inside was Genna's leather and vinyl strap on harness. It was freshly oiled and gleamed in the dark. Troy fixed his favorite of her dildo selection to the ring.

"Ask me. Be specific," Genna said, knowing demanding him to voice his desires was exquisite torture.

Troy ducked his head and raised the strap-on and dildo in the flat of his hands. "Will you please put your sword in my sheath?"

"To the hilt."

"Thank you, my queen."

Genna fastened the straps to her thighs while he attentively folded the bedding out of the way. He spread a towel across the sheets. Then he lay upon it on his back, his body relaxed in pure supplication.

She took the jute rope she used for Shibari from its drawstring cloth bag. She crawled on top of him. He kissed the underside of her breasts as she leaned over him and tied his wrists to the headboard, expertly looping it around his forearms. She checked the constriction, making sure that there was enough space between the rope and his skin to allow circulation.

She traced his muscles with her fingernails. Troy responded more dramatically to the softest touch. His deep inhale expanded and contracted his chest in shivering excitement. She massaged his nipples. Then dragged her nails along the soft skin of his ribs, his sides, to the sensitive area around his hip bones. She used his breathy gasps as a guide. He shivered as her hands feathered the air above his enflamed skin. His erection was semi-hard from excitement. She teased him, tugging and kneading his scrotum. Then put a latex glove on. His eyes flashed like lighting at the rubbery snap. She watched him while she drizzled lube onto her fingers.

He stilled as she traced the circumference of his anus. She slowly slid her index finger in, giving him time to adjust. He was warm and already trembling. He took deep gulping breaths as she gently pumped her hand, seeking and finding his prostate. She stroked him, preparing him while her other hand massaged lube onto the dildo. A pulse of magic made it feel like her clitoris had expanded. She exhaled slowly to keep focused.

She pushed his legs wider apart. He arched as she moved the dildo's head down his perineum and centered it on the bud of his anus.

"Breathe," she commanded as she slid inside.

She used her fist to guide the angle. To go slow. No need to rush. To spend a little time with only the tip inside as he adjusted. Then she pushed in deeper and deeper. She felt the resonance as her magic penetrated him. He moaned, knowing she liked to hear his gasps and exhalations. She pushed her non-gloved hand into his mouth, letting him suck on her fingers while she gripped his jaw for balance. Slowly she increased the tempo, leaning in as she added strength to each thrust. Until the bed was shaking. His eyes fluttered shut. Lost in the sensations.

His erection bobbed. He jerked as she massaged his shaft. Her grip on his dick was a helpful barometer to gauge how close he was to climax. She kept her rhythm steady, not allowing herself to rush. Just as he was starting to climax, she let go and pulled out.

"How are you doing?" She purred.

"Fuck," he gasped, "Don't stop!"

Genna stepped back. "Turn over, slut."

He stilled and then immediately complied, struggling with his bound hands. Genna was sparing with the name calling. She didn't like it but Troy loved being called a slut.

He knelt on the bed. His ass up. His dick hard. His muscular haunches spread wide. Her finger was already in his ass again, teasing him while she added more lube. She pushed inside, slow and steady in one long thrust. Her free hand on his back, admiring the way moonlight painted his tattoos.

She put her magic into the dildo. He gasped and bucked when she thrust into his core, physically and magically.

"Breathe!"

Troy exhaled gustily, blushing and sweating. "Yes, my queen!"

She grabbed his hips and started a fast pace, yanking him backwards. Strong and steady. She changed the angle. He arched like a cat and lightning spat from his skin when she hit his prostrate. His rising moan grew louder and louder until he spent himself onto the towel, rutting into it as she fucked him from behind. She rode him while pleasure rippled through her body. Her own lightning braided with his until the bedroom flashed bright white. Thunder shuddered through the stones and rattled the windows in their mooring.

He slumped on the bed, breathing hard. She hugged him as she pulled out. She quickly cleaned the glove away and into the trash. She pulled the towel out from under him. A tug on the knot undid the whole bondage tie. She coiled the rope back into its bag. She went to the bathroom to damp a washcloth. She cleaned him quickly then put a blanket over him. She tossed the towel in the shower to wash later. She washed the dildo and the harness. She got a cup of water and roused him to drink it.

He watched her fuss over him through slitted eyes, his lips soft and a blush in his skin.

Once she was satisfied, she joined him on the bed. He snuggled against her, vulnerable and relaxed. She combed her fingers through his hair then pushed him downward. He wiggled under the bedding. His mouth eagerly lapped at her pulsing pussy. She moaned and writhed as he suckled and slurped. His fingers slipped inside of her. She gripped his hair and orgasmed again and again.

Finally she shouted, "Enough!"

He kissed her apex. Then kissed her lips. She tasted herself as their tongued danced. Her fingers tingled as their bodies and magic thrummed in harmony. She hugged him tight. He pressed his face into the crook of her neck.

She loved him. Acutely. No one had ever matched her so deeply. It was excruciating.

She fell asleep in a surfeit of contentment.

Troy was still awake. He lay in her arms, listening to her heartbeat and her snore while his chin brushed her breast. He wiped a tear that had slipped free before it could touch her skin. His fingers traced the silver collar. His tender smile bloomed like a fragile flower.

He was careful not to wake her when he left the bed to shower off but Genna roused at the sounds of running water.

He was almost finished with his ablutions when she walked into the shower.

"Hey," she smirked, "This is familiar."

Troy opened his soapy arms wide.

Thirty-Two

THE MASSAGE AND SAUNA ROOMS WERE NEXT TO THE pool. Candles warmed oils and illuminated the wooden slats on the walls. Sweat beaded on Quincy and Cleopatra's brown naked bodies. Genna stared at them and drooled on herself, incoherently.

"This is the best staycation," Cleopatra said, stretched out on her side of the sauna.

"I can't remember when I had one," Quincy said from the opposite side.

Genna mumbled an affirmation while Troy massaged her muscles on the padded table. He dribbled melted soy candle wax on her back and used lightning to hit the deeper spots. His big capable hands reduced her tension into putty. His silver collar rested on his reddened skin. Sweat dripped from his hair.

After the massage Genna changed into a loose t-shirt dress and trudged up the spiral staircase to her office. Her body felt heavy and resented excessive movement. She wanted to lay in the sauna but she had work to do. The others understood.

Genna sat at her desk, computer on, emails open, phone crowded with unread text messages and voicemails, yet she stared out of the window at her land. The world seemed to end at the edge of Sweetwater.

Genna was happy. She kept waiting to get punished for it. Then fought to ignore it. Sex with Troy got easier. Less soul destroying. She learned how to play. How to have fun as she modulated the frequencies in her lightning and magic.

It wasn't only the sex that required an adjustment. It was the emotional and physical intimacy of sharing her life. She learned how to accept Quincy's sunshine smiles and sleepy morning snuggles as genuine instead of scheming. Troy's admiring compliments when he came into her office and wanted kisses in exchange for freshly made coffee weren't a trick.

Troy's belief that she was a Luparii hunter was reinforced by Quincy and Cleopatra. They shared their version of magic and their perspective as hunters and witch finders. Finally she had the honesty she craved. The tension eased from their expressions.

Troy made exquisite jewelry for fun. Genna had bags and bags of it on her dresser. He cuddled her every chance he had.

He transformed into a wolf whenever they were alone in bed. He never changed in front of the others. Hiding it. Keeping it a secret. Genna Turned with him, shy and curious. They both had an easier time communicating their affection in wolf form. The honesty of scent and touch. Being human was complicated. Being a wolf was not. He groomed her, which was a surprisingly intimate experience. His nose ruffled her fur. She allowed his muzzle to travel along the soft fur of her underbelly and armpit. Not sexual. Only loving touch. The Egyptian cotton sheets were a high-enough thread count not to immediately tear under their claws as they dug at the bedding and curled up.

Quincy spent most of his time in the library. Genna spotted him twirling Troy down the ballroom in big waltzing steps as he sang 'Once Upon a Dream'. Both men laughing. Quincy had a bass operatic voice that could shake the chandeliers.

She liked them together. She liked them separately. She liked them in her bed. She wanted to keep them both instead of choosing one or the other. They loved the fairytale of the castle.

Cleopatra smiled more but stayed reserved. Genna learned through observation what Cleopatra would not say out loud. She loved the castle. Her favorite place had moved from the pool into the rose garden. She liked to wear kaftans with nothing underneath. The bright rainbow geometric patterns emphasized the swell of her curves. When she stopped wearing bras, let all the natural curves jiggle, Genna nearly broke her own nose on the edge of a tree. Naomi was in the garden too, braiding her hair or flat ironing it straight or whatever idea came into her mind that day. Cleopatra would sit and read. She did not mind being Naomi's favorite dress-up doll.

Naomi was the only fly in the ointment. Genna did not have sex with her and locked down her senses when the others did. Naomi's wind and skin magic was dangerous. The fragile truce worked as long as they avoided each other. Naomi stayed in Miss Bootsie's apartment sewing costumes for the McBride Halloween party. Her absence meant that Genna did not have to pretend she liked the woman. Naomi was an horrible inversion of Miss Bootsie and Katie. It was a strain to see Pipsy inspecting the castle interior through her eyes.

A little bark prompted Genna to look around.

Toto and Grim sat on their haunches. They were in the center of her office. One on either side of the desk. No little wiggle from Toto. No panting from Grim. They were silent and coiled.

This was bad news. The doors to her office were closed. Usually the dogs pretended they could not travel through walls and doors. Whenever the two dogs came to get her, something was dead or in bad shape.

"Okay. I'm coming." Genna quickly turned off her electronics and locked them in the desk. She hurried up the stairs to the bedroom. She walked through the closet to the hidden compartment in a false wall for her real work clothes.

She dressed quickly in heavy jean overalls with reinforced

knees, Vasque hiking boots with reinforced toes, a Black Lives Matter t-shirt, a black flannel turtleneck underneath, a padded waterproof LL Bean vest on top. She wrapped her hair in a vintage Mariano Rubinacci scarf. Another scarf around her neck. A third on her wrist.

She had literally hundreds of scarves because several women in the family had an obsession with scarves.

She put a wide brimmed leather hat with a drawstring on top of the scarf. She picked up a leather trench coat and thick black gloves on the way out of the mud room. This particular outfit was cobbled out of habit.

She tossed on a doctors bag filled with emergency supplies, a med-kit, a hand sanitizer bottle, a spray bottle of Florida water, and bundled herbs. She went to the kitchen and packed a lunchbox with three bottles of water, some cheese wrapped in wax, beef jerky, trail mix, rolls, jar of honey, apples, oranges, and cookies. Then hooked the lunchbox to the bag with a carabiner.

The dogs watched her impatiently. Genna knew that extra food had many uses. Not just for fuel but as a bribe. Several times, Genna had used the lunchbox to convince a frightened human lost in the forest to put down a gun in exchange for a meal. Empathy was a very powerful kind of magic.

Genna followed the dogs. She was surprised that they headed into the greenhouse instead of outside.

Water splashing prompted Genna to glance through the greenhouse into the pool room as she skirted the orchid garden. Quincy was bent over the edge of the pool. Troy was wrapped around him from behind. Their muscles were tense and tendons corded. Short, sharp movements sent cascades of water over the edge of the pool. Quincy's hand reached back to clamp on the back of Troy's neck. The other braced against the stone as he arched. Troy wrapped him in a bear hug. They spun around. Two titans wrestling. Their snarls of need echoed off the ceiling.

Genna was happy for them. She felt no jealousy.

She lengthened her stride, following the clicking nails of her dogs across the castle bridge to the garage. Past the sports room, the woodworking room, and into the largest section of the garage. Toto and Grim led her to a corner in the very back where Pirate strutted on the top of a car, clucking and flapping.

Today's patient was not a human. It was an animal. A big coywolf, curled on the hood of an old black Lexus that was part of her grandfather's estate. No one had gotten rid of it, out of sentiment. Genna was not sure if this made it better or worse.

She jerked in surprised as the coywolf raised her head. She knew this animal. The castle staff changed so often, she never bothered to remember names. Too many weird things happened in the forest. The animals stayed when the humans fled or disappeared. This coywolf was a familiar face.

On sunny days, the coywolf liked to sleep on Sekhmet's mounting block. She was fleet, able to outrun the dogs. No gun or trap could get her. Genna would see her while riding through the forest. She had not known coyotes could climb trees until she saw the coywolf up in the boughs, chewing the apples from a branch.

Her skin prickled. "What happened to you?"

The coywolf stretched her neck down the edge of the Lexus. She touched noses with Genna.

The piquant stench of animal, dirt, blood, and urine was a rush of smells. Magic was an undercurrent that was too fast to parse through. She felt darkness, like a river on a moonless night. The current flowing fast. A waterfall ahead. Sharp rocks at the bottom. The shore shrouded in mist. Not yet. Soon.

Genna tried to communicate in Old Growl but the coywolf turned her head away, lay down, and died with a soft sigh. Her fur sagged as life snuffed out.

Pirate cockadoodled a farewell was loud enough to echo off the vaulted warehouse ceiling. Grim and Toto howled. Genna joined in, her atonal coyote yodel raucous and real.

A door slammed. Grim, Pirate, and Toto immediately charged away, barking and squawking at intruders. Their job of alerting Genna was taken care of. The coywolf was now her responsibility.

Genna wiped her face, pushing grief aside to focus on the task at hand. The Lexus was the closest car to the side door that led to the alley of trash cans, compost bins, and animal graveyard. There was only one reason anything came to this corner of the garage. It was a quiet place to die.

The coywolf lay on the hood of the car like she wanted to be seen. Perhaps that was a stretch, but this was a deviation from normal patterns of behavior. Usually, Genna found corpses in the alley of trash cans outside not inside the garage.

That area seemed to attract death. Deer, boar, and rabbits would run all the way up the property before dying from a rifle wound or car impact. She might find Pirate pecking the eye out of a dead cat, or Toto dragging a dead possum, or Grim gnawing on a dead deer's leg. But none of her pets had touched the coywolf.

Genna reached into her medical kit and got a garbage bag. She used the thin plastic to trace the cooling body for damage. The wounds were big and deep from bites and claws. Not knives. No smell, bloat, or purple gums from poison. No bleeding eyes or blistered tongue from curses. And there was a smell. A heavy musk. It was familiar. Like a tickle in the back of her mind.

A deep purr by her foot. She put the bag over the coywolf. She crouched down as Schrodinger peeked out from under the Lexus. His yellow eyes were round and dilated like an owl's. The enormous Maine Coon cat had flattened himself under the Lexus.

"Hey, Schrodinger, how are you doing? Good to see you."

Schrodinger crept forward, squeezing his big fluffy self out. His fluffy tail was longer than Toto. He sniffed her hand and rubbed his head against the back of it. Then down her arm. Around her back. And up her arm. Momentarily circling her nose to tail. He purred like a thunderstorm. She petted him carefully, the lightest of touches. He flinched and retreated back under the Lexus. Genna stared at the blood on her gloves and along her coat.

Anger rippled through her.

Katie had not done this. Schrodinger was the closest thing she had to a pet. The one animal she never harmed. He would sit on the couch in the cottage if Katie or Genna didn't try to pet him.

No human had not done this. No animal she had encountered either. Was it Naomi? Or someone else using the upheaval to get close?

Something was wrong. Something bad was happening.

Genna studied the wounds again. She took a step back and let herself think. She ran her tongue over her teeth. Her nose finally pinpointed the smell on the coywolf.

Werewolves had attacked the coywolf but not a local pack. There must be a lot of them because it took a lot to turf Schrodinger out. They had taken control of the forest. Perhaps Grim, Toto, and Pirate had only been able to save the coywolf from this new enemy.

Had someone made an example of the coywolf? They wanted her to know the forest wasn't hers anymore?

It didn't matter. She would kill whoever or whatever was in the forest. This was her territory. She had to protect it.

"Genna? You in here?" Troy called while coming unerringly to the Lexus. The dogs were with him. Pirate had flown off somewhere else.

She lifted the coywolf, folding her away from his eyes. The coywolf was heavy. There was no denying that the Lexus was her mortuary car.

Genna carried the coywolf to the door. "Can you get the door for me?"

Thirty-Three

Troy blinked once at the garbage bag. His nostrils flared. The wolf close. Her tension fed his own. "What is that?"

"A friend." Genna glared at the door until Troy opened it to the alley of trash cans.

The mangled bodies of cats, possums, skunks, foxes, ravens, turkey vultures, and more crowded the alley. They were curled, nose to tail. Wings outstretched. Grim trotted down the alley with a dead porcupine. Not a whimper with the quills in his muzzle. Toto dragged a pale orange tabby.

Schrodinger shot past in a blur of fur. He bounded down the alley, undeterred by the ground covered by dead animals. He loped across the driveway into the rose garden.

Troy met Genna's grim gaze as he pulled a pair of black gloves out of his pocket and put them on. "These critters were chewed up and spat out. They were left alive just enough to crawl here. You can see where they came through the thicket over there." He pointed at the ivy and overgrown hedge. "Halloween is next week but this doesn't look like a prank. It looks like a warning. I think they want you to know that they're here."

"I know." Genna gulped a sob as she hefted the coywolf

higher. The coywolf's long neck lolled so her head bumped against Genna's shoulder. The lukewarm weight and wayward limbs strained the thin plastic. "I'll show you where to bury them. Make sure you stay on the stone path. The soil is too soft to support your weight."

"Sure."

Genna paused to meet his eyes. Troy straightened up. She was angry and sad about the coywolf so the wattage of her glare was high. "I'm serious. Don't leave the rocks. Don't touch the dirt with bare skin. Ever."

Troy nodded curtly. "Yes, ma'am."

She picked her way carefully through the bodies, standing on the balls of her feet. She minced down the length of the alley to the ivy-covered gate. Troy tried to help but Genna was used to doing this alone. She had personally installed a latch that could be triggered to swing wide with an elbow.

Today, the gate looked like the unhinged jaw of a snake. Genna walked from one smooth stone to the next. She had laid the stones herself after professional installations kept sinking under the ivy.

Miss Bootsie had explained that some things had to be done by herself. She called it 'laying on of hands.' As doctors, Genna's parents understood that well.

Genna set the coywolf down among the ivy, careful to touch only the plastic, not the dirt. Troy gathered the train of her coat, twisting it up away from the dirt, which was thoughtful. She would thank him once she said goodbye to the coywolf. She crumpled the plastic in one hand. She pushed her fingers into the fur, petting down the jaw and the neck. She sniffled, her lips trembling as tears wet her cheeks.

"I'm sorry," she whispered. "I'll miss you."

The coywolf sank into the ivy, revealing the tar pit under the dirt.

Genna stood up and spun around on the same stone. Troy let go of her coat. She smiled at him without showing teeth. He nodded and gently took the plastic bag. He retreated back down the stone path. She frowned as his broad back disappeared around the garage edge. She never had to explain with him. He understood without there being a conversation. He never said she was weird. Never gave her a side eye or scoffed like Quincy. Instead, he moved in sync, following her lead. Giving her space. He was there when she needed.

"This is your fault," Katie said, standing behind the ivy-covered trees.

"Get out of the graveyard," Genna said, not looking her way.

"I'm pregnant," Katie said. "It's yours."

Genna finally looked through the gray-green gloom. The mist swirled in a vaguely human shape. "I thought McBrides couldn't get pregnant. That's why you need brides to plant your eggs in someone else."

"Unless you are a boo hag. Then you have a fertile womb. That's what Miss Bootsie gave when I went to see her in the stable. That's the spell that killed her. Biting her was only to ease her suffering. To say thank you." Katie frowned. "She wanted our daughter to be a York."

"That doesn't explain what that has to do with me."

"Your big orgy in Chicago. All that sex magic. And then you made me swallow that bowling ball opal. It had a ton of fertility magic."

Genna was suddenly worried about the horseshoe crabs in that magic world. "You're a fucking bitch."

"You smell so good. Happy. Your dopamine levels are supposed to up for me. Not him. Your vasopressin is supposed to be mine to control. But I can't move your blood chemistry. Loving them made you immune to me. You've never smelled like that for anyone. You've never liked anyone before."

Genna stood on her toes, fighting the urge to stay on the rocks. The dirt looked soft. She was only a few steps away into the forest. It would be so easy.

"For the record, They love you back, Iffy. Like for real for real.

That's how I made our lovechild." Katie pressed her hand against her stomach. She swayed. Her hair was braided down. Her face was gaunt. "It's just that Pipsy's mad at me. She's never mad. She's sending in werewolves."

"The kitchen staff?"

"No, they're the real deal. You need to run. Get in the Falcon and go." Katie tugged on her braids. "I can't stop her. You know how pregnancy saps our strength. I'll be in the cottage but I can't do anything. I'm sorry."

"What about the truce? What about the pool room? It wasn't real?" Genna hated herself for the warble of insecurity.

"She wanted to keep you occupied. Your sex binge kept you out of our hair."

Genna crossed her arms, angry that she had allowed herself to relax. She shrugged dismissively.

Katie tugged harder on her braids. "You know what's crazy? Half of the town got pregnant. I know everyone in forest did."

Genna sucked on her lips. "That isn't my fault."

"Sweetwater chose you. You won, Iffy. I'm your bride. I'm a Bellwether bitch. I'm your trophy wife." Katie spread her hands. "I'm yours. I'm full and fertile. Sweetwater is too. Everything grows with abundance. It thrives with you as its new sovereign. You are the queen."

"What does that even mean?"

"I'll forsake my family. I'll shed my skin. I'll become a wolf. I'll have your daughters. I won't even eat them. Our daughters will be yours. Not mine. I'll do anything you want. I'll protect the Bellwether name. I give you my life. My body. I'm yours. Forever and ever. You defeated me. That's why Pipsy is sending the wolves. She thought that the sex binge would make you weak. Instead it made you strong enough to control us."

Genna pursed her lips. Amazing how that declaration was obsessively consistent. Winning didn't feel like winning. It felt like a punishment.

Then she thought about brunch. Of ordering Katie and Mimi

to leave and they did. Of holding Olympia at bay. Of turning her skin into dragon hardness and lightning when Pipsy coiled around her in the pool room. She had shrugged off Pipsy on her own turf like it was nothing. She had gotten stronger since Chicago.

"I like being your bride better. But never mind that now." Katie darted a look to the tree. She nervously tugged on her braids. "Pipsy wants to talk to you. Mimi's going to eat our baby. I have to hide in the cottage. It's the only place that's safe. Okay. Bye." Katie ran into the gray gloom like a carnivorous gazelle.

Cold mist obscured her vision. Grim the wolfhound put himself between Genna and the forest. A deep growl rattled her ears. His fur was warm like stone around a hearth fire. He pushed against Genna's hip moving her back down the stone path. She slid her numb fingers under his collar to hold on.

The shadows of the trees became an enormous black snake. Pipsy lowered her great wide head. The long black tongue flicking. She looked Genna in the eye. Her expression smooth as ice. A predatory sneer curved her lips. "Iphigenia Bellwether."

"Pipsy Montgomery," Genna said.

"You impregnated my granddaughter."

"She got herself pregnant."

"You have humiliated my family for the last time, Iphigenia Bellwether. You will die learning respect. You do not get to turn a McBride into a Bellwether bitch. You think you've won? There are plenty who will tear you apart. I have protected you. No longer."

"So I don't have your blessing?" Genna meant it as a joke.

"You have taken my heir!" Pipsy snarled. "You have ensnared her in your sexual spell. She loves nothing but you. How dare you steal her from me? How dare you take Sweetwater? You are not the queen. I am. You will die a thousand deaths. The werewolves are coming for you. When the moon is new. When the shadows are darkest. When the air is thin and clear. The werewolves will come and eat everything that you hold dear."

"You could say they'll be here on Halloween instead of spouting bad poetry."

Pipsy hissed like a steam train coming to a stop. Her eight fangs extended.

The trees howled. Loud. Terrible. Close. As if an army of werewolves stood behind the trees that lined the graveyard. There was movement in the mist. The reflection of eyes. The edge of fur. The snuffle of canine nostrils. Except they were bigger than normal sized werewolves. Allowing her to see them.

"No one will ever believe you," Pipsy said. "No one will save you. Not those cute little hunters you love. Not their parents. Not even that traitorous dragon girl. You are alone, Iphigenia. You will always be alone."

Genna held on to Grim's collar, afraid to lose her footing and stand in the dirt. She tried to be strong and defiant. Even witty. "I'm going to kill you, Pipsy."

"You can't." Pipsy became mist again.

Grim towed Genna back out of the graveyard. She only stepped on stone. Her teeth chattered.

She reached the gate. The trash-can alley was empty. She heard noise. She turned to see Troy and Quincy were also inside the graveyard, dumping straining garbage bags into the ivy edge of the forest. Quincy was a dark bulk behind Troy with more bags of dead animals. Toto barked, yapping at the mist. Her little face poked out of his jacket, straining the buttons.

Genna had walked right past them.

Grim tugged her onward. Away from the rotten death, clinging ivy, and cold mist. Down the brick alley. Out into the green lawn. There was no sunshine but the overcast gray sky was brighter. No howls, either. Only quiet. The breeze in the trees and the lush leaves.

He led her to the gardens, wending through the rose maze. The red blooms were so big, they looked like pillows she could rest her head against. Grim towed her up to the greenhouse. He waited patiently for her to open the door, then inside to the mudroom. He allowed her to wipe the mud off his paws. She took her muddy boots off and hung her coat up. She washed her hands in the vestibule bathroom. She walked barefoot into the kitchen to return the lunchbox.

They went up to the turret. He sat at the bedroom door on guard. Toto trotted up to join him on the landing, panting at the effort. Genna petted them both in thanks. Then put the medical bag and clothes back in the closet.

She washed her hair and scratched at her scalp. She cried in the shower and let the warm water drain her sorrow away. She hated the hitch in her breath. How her hands shook.

Pipsy had spoken with so much hatred that Genna felt as if she were drowning in a septic ocean. Her comeback felt insignificant.

She thought about Katie instead. Katie never braided her hair in plaits. Female snakes could choose if they wanted to get pregnant after intercourse. Katie had been waiting, planning, and Genna was incensed that she hadn't believed her.

What the hell was going to happen on Halloween?

Thirty-Four

THE NIGHT PASSED WITHOUT ANY BLOODSHED. GENNA did not sleep well. Troy opted for sleeping with Quincy. The next morning she wandered the castle and the property. She found Cleopatra in the rose maze.

Cleopatra looked up from her book. She was reading Octavia Butler's *Fledgling*. The copy was weathered and the binding creased. She wore a loose green and red kaftan that blended in with the roses. Sunlight dappled her skin. It turned her thick tight curls into coils of copper and brown. Schrodinger was asleep on the bench next to her. He lay on his side. Tail twitching. His head rested in Cleopatra's open palm on her lap.

Megan Thee Stallion sang on a bluetooth speaker. "*Even bad bitches have bad days too.*"

She was so beautiful and perfect and natural. As if she were supposed to be here.

Genna shook off that dangerous thought. No. That was the forest talking. Wanting to swallow up a dragon. All that magic was exactly Sweetwater's flavor. Another Night Skin. Another caretaker. Like Genna.

Cleopatra smiled at Genna. She waggled the book. "It's my favorite book."

Genna stared at Cleopatra. Ordinarily Genna would have talked all day about the author, Octavia Butler. Instead Genna thought of the howl in the graveyard. The dead animals. Schrodinger's horrible scars. She couldn't find Toto or Grim. Pirate hadn't crowed this morning. She had searched the greenhouse and his normal roosts. Not a feather.

She imagined finding Cleopatra's beautiful body mangled like the horses. Or holding her as she bled like Miss Bootsie. Or savaged like the coywolf. Or survived but haunted by tragedy like her mother.

She couldn't do it. Not one more person.

"Is everything okay?" Cleopatra said.

Troy, Quincy, and Naomi were already part of the forest. As if they had replaced her missing pets. Cleopatra was still free. Still standing in the sunshine instead of the shadows. She was a dream. Genna was a nightmare.

She could run but Cleopatra wouldn't. She would stay. She would fight. She would trust friends who were compromised. She was noble and kind and had bloomed like the flowers in the garden. Genna wanted her to stay.

No, Genna simply wanted her with all of the awkward vulnerability that came with it. Genna loved Cleopatra. She had no idea what to say.

Tears burned like lava down Genna's smooth face. "Will you come with me for a moment?"

Cleopatra inhaled sharply. Genna tried not to stare at the bounce of her cleavage. She stood up. Earnest. Her brown hands soft. She smiled demurely. "Sure, Genna."

Their hands threaded together. They walked through the rose garden. Past the apples trees. The other gardens. To the garage. The whisper of Cleopatra's silk. The scent of her. Genna led her to the garage, walked to the Mustang, and opened the passenger door. "Want a ride?"

Cleopatra simpered. Climbed in. Genna hurried to the drivers side. Turned the Mustang on so its loud roar echoed off the ceiling.

The garage door opened.

Troy and Quincy were walking up the driveway when Genna drove past. Cleopatra waved and posed. Laughing.

"Aw, come on!" Troy shouted, not entirely joking.

Cleopatra's laughter filled Genna with warmth. Her skin flushed hot. She beeped the horn. The Mustang bucked and expelled Naomi through the tail pipe like bad gas. She hit the ground and rolled to her feet, yelling with outraged. Quincy and Troy crouched to help her up. Genna smirked as she drove down the long slope.

"You really don't like Naomi," Cleopatra said.

"I wanted some time with you. I can't get that with her buzzing in my ear like a mosquito."

"She thinks you're going to steal me away."

"I don't care what she thinks."

Genna drove the pretty way. Cleopatra sat, a slight smile on her face. Erykah Badu sang *Didn't Cha Know* on the radio.

The forest was orange and red to brown but it was still warm. A light rain made things damp. The green of the pine was more pronounced. The mansions of the Heights were hidden by ancient mountains blanketed by trees and mist.

"You know the Mustang has a lot of special features," Genna said. "It's bulletproof. Open the trunk and you'll find a secret compartment that's big enough to sleep in. There's an air tank and a breathing mask. There are little compartments inside with cash, passports, and burner phone."

"You have a James Bond car. You should compare notes with Troy. His Bronco is like this." Cleopatra ran a hand along the leopard print ceiling. "I like yours better."

Genna put a small black bag on her lap. "This is the spare key. Wear it."

"Genna, what are you doing?"

"If you need to run, then run. If you need to hide, then hide. Don't die for this. You've got your own life. If you need permission, I'm giving it to you. Take it from one someone who knows what it's like to be crushed under the weight of *good girl* and *Black excellence*. Quincy's not the one."

"He's like me."

"He has the same magic. You think that's all you need but it's not enough."

"I'm sorry it's not working out with Troy."

"I'm not talking about Troy. I'm talking about you. Quincy doesn't see you. He's got a dream. That doesn't mean you have to keep playing that role. He's not a bad guy. He's just not your guy. He's in love. That's why he's here. Everything else doesn't matter."

"He's in love with you."

"He's in love with dream of himself as the dragon prince in the castle. He doesn't see any difference between you or me."

"This is about Naomi, isn't it?"

"Naomi is a part of Sweetwater, Cleopatra. She's got things to figure out. I'd hate for you to be collateral damage."

Cleopatra scowled at her. "You'll say anything. You can't see her. You don't know what she's been through. She's not bad. All vampires aren't bad."

"The McBrides call themselves vampires because they don't want people to know what they are. In Naomi's case, she's vulnerable because she actually believes the lies."

"You're paranoid. You didn't even try to get to know her. You just assumed."

"I know enough." This wasn't going well but Genna persisted. It was now or never. "We're both Black American princesses. We're both responsible good girls. I would've loved to be your friend. I mean that." She could not keep the wobble out of her voice. "I didn't have someone like you. I didn't have anyone but monsters, so I need you do to something for me. I need you to leave, because I can't. I've tried. Will you do that if you get a chance? Can you live and do what I can't? Keep going, okay? Don't stop. You need to let go or you'll drown too, Cleopatra."

"You don't get to say that to me. You should be asking for help not running away."

"If you were me, would you ask for help? Or would you save who you could?"

Cleopatra hunched and jabbed the radio off. "Stop the car. Naomi was right. You're out to get her."

"I don't give a damn about Naomi. I care about you!"

"Why?" It was more of a shout. "Troy loves you. He's never had a chance at love. Stop looking at me and focus on him. Can't you see how it's hurting him? You're breaking his heart. Why do you keep harassing me?"

"I'm not and never will be monogamous."

"No, you're scared. You love him. I know you do. This is exactly what happened in Chicago. You ran from him and jumped me. I don't want you, Genna. I still have the scar. I can still turn into a werewolf. That's your fault!"

"You can Turn into a werewolf?"

Silence.

Out of the corner of her eye Genna saw Cleopatra's skin change into fur. Her kaftan expanded and shifted as her body changed shape. Cleopatra's fur was gold, silver, and copper. She could blend into the autumn forest they drove past. She was a coywolf like Genna. Gold fur painted her body. Her breasts. Her fluffy tail. Her black afro had two golden ears peaking through the curls. Roses filled her curls. The forest had given her the ability to grow thorns and roses along her body. The scent of her filled the Mustang. "Can you undo it like you told him?"

"It's been like this since Chicago?"

"Yes, can you fix it? Naomi says I taste weird."

Genna's mind was blank. She thought about Schrodinger. She had never seen the cat sleep on anyone. Never seen him lay in sunlight. The signs were there. The feeling of connection.

"I didn't Turn you on purpose, Cleopatra. You're a Night

Skin. It happened because you attacked me. It was reactive bite. Troy's a hunter. I Turned him on purpose. With him it's like reversing polarities. I haven't changed you, only shown you how to wear a different skin. You're still you. You're not a werewolf anymore than you're a dragon. It's another manifestation of your magic. It's why the forest recognizes you."

"Then it is permanent." Cleopatra sniffled. She changed back into a human with ease, executing a flawless clothed Turn. She shoved the key back at Genna. "Take me to McBride Mansion. I've had enough of your hospitality."

"We're nearly there anyway."

They drove in silence. Cleopatra sat ramrod straight. Genna turned on the radio. The Temptations *Just My Imagination* was a melancholy refrain.

The trees arched over the white driveway like grasping hands ready to drag the Mustang into their dark green shadows. Genna pulled into the mansion's horseshoe driveway. She felt Pipsy rouse in the pool room. Katie was painting in her studio. Mimi was in her lair having sex with five handsome young brown-skinned men.

Naomi waited on the porch, tapping her foot. Genna wanted to punch her in the face. Instead she eased the Mustang to a halt.

Cleopatra shoved the door open. Slammed it. Stalked over to Naomi. Picked her up. Kissed her hard on the mouth. Naomi lifted them both up into the air.

The three McBrides watched. All the mansion windows felt like appraising eyes. Genna took a deep breath. Exhaled. Her chest felt tight. The key slid out of its bag. The long gold chain supple and strong. It was shaped like a crocodile biting its tail.

Genna sped back down the driveway. The Mustang snarled as she pressed on the gas. She drove back to the castle.

Schrodinger was in the garage when she drove in. He hopped into her lap when she opened the car, sniffing around. He was looking for Cleopatra. Ears flickering. Genna took the key and the necklace and looped it around his neck. "Keep an eye on Cleopatra for me. She's in danger."

Schrodinger rubbed his head against her hand. His teeth scraped her wrist. The prick of his claws through her jeans. He smacked her in the face with his tail as he jumped out of the Mustang. He trotted over to the door that lead to the graveyard door. He turned into a shadow as he slipped through.

Genna leaned back against the headrest. She closed her eyes and squeezed the steering wheel. She opened them to find Troy watching her. His head low. He wore a black *Bad Brains* t-shirt and smudged jeans low on his hips. A baseball cap turned backwards. He leaned on a wall in the mechanic's section. The Bronco's hood was lifted. She gave him a small smile that he did not return.

Instead the castle grounds were empty of any signature except his. "Where is Quincy?"

"I asked him to give us some space," Troy said. "He probably went to check on the girls."

"Great," Genna said, tired and sad. What was even the point of caring anymore? Everyone was so sure that the McBrides were harmless.

He walked over, wiping his hands on a black bandana. "Can I see under your hood?"

"Haven't you already?"

He looked down at the Mustang. "This is your car."

"Sure, Troy. You can look."

She watched him move around the car. Her vision filled with the designs on the hood as he lifted it to see the engine. "Your family aren't car people."

"Not really. Is the Mustang in terrible shape?" She pushed herself out of the seat. She wanted to watch him though she did not understand what he was doing.

"It only needs a little bit of a tune up."

She watched the muscles in his arm and his long back. "Your tattoos changed again."

His movements slowed down. He looked at the engine. He squeezed the metal edge of the Mustang. Then he pushed away to glare down at her. "You bit Cleopatra. I can smell it."

"That happened in Chicago. I just found out."

"How can you not know?"

"Because I've never bitten anyone before, Troy."

He scoffed. "You're a werewolf. Of course you have. You have to hunt. You have to eat. You act all nice but I've felt your hunger."

Genna didn't like this brittle jealousy. She took a deep breath against the anger. "Didn't we agree that we couldn't be serious? This is what it looks like, Troy."

"I know." He didn't shout but the cars and windows rattled around them like a train had passed by. "I didn't think you'd be so in control."

Genna gave him a long look. "Because werewolves have to be raging sex monsters?"

"Aren't they? I know I am." He tugged on his shirt. He pulled out the collar. He looked away. "Or I would be."

Genna raised both eyebrows. "What's wrong, Troy? Do you want me to take the collar off?" She invaded his space. "You want to lose control. You want to run and kill and fuck and tear? It's not fun, is it? All that power and potential with nowhere to go? You can feel it. How you're crawling out of your skin because it feels too tight? The hunger. The need. That's what it's like to be a werewolf."

"It's the same. I don't feel any different."

"Everywhere you go, there you are." She shoved him. Angry. Sad. Upset. Hating him. Afraid for Cleopatra and Quincy. Because she did care and he was jealous. She was trying. She had shown him everything and he had only found new things to kill.

His blue lightning eyes flared, spitting sparks. "Genna."

"If you don't want the collar anymore then take it off. You can. You always could." Her voice hitched. "I don't need you to fix my Mustang. It's not broken. It's not yours. We're opposites,

Troy. Wolf and hunter. The harder we try. The less it works. So stop getting jealous that I'm not waiting around for you to break my heart."

"You never gave us a chance."

"How can I? Your mom needs you."

"She's got people."

"No, she doesn't."

"I can't live for her, Genna. That's all I've been doing. I've hunted for her. I've been her weapon. I can't do it anymore." He rubbed a grubby hand over his hat. "I can't stay in that Waffle House. I can't be my dad. I can't bring him back from the dead."

"Then why is she making deals with vampires, Troy? Why does she hate werewolves so damn much? I thought your dad drowned in Hurricane Katrina."

"He did. He was saving Quincy from a rougarou."

"You should've told me." Genna unhooked the Mustang's hood. Troy winced as she slammed it shut.

"Be gentle with that."

"Do not tell me how to take care of my car!"

Troy grimaced. Stiffened. Nodded.

She stared down at Mustang's tanzanite purple and cobalt blue paint. Why the hell had she chosen a snake skin pattern? The scales looked exactly like Katie's. Why the hell hadn't she noticed it until now? There were snakes everywhere.

She stepped away. Angry. Tired. Sick of feeling emotions. Sick of being yanked one direction or another. Sick of all these people who wanted her to love them but with conditions and caveats. What she had wasn't enough. Or too much. Or they only wanted a sliver. Cleopatra didn't want her. Quincy and Troy did.

Lightning sparked between them. The smell of wolf. It used to make her happy. Now it only made her angry. Troy cautiously slid his hands over hers. She growled at him.

"Genna, talk to me."

"Much as I want to act like this doesn't mean anything, it does, okay? I need someone who gets it. Who chooses me.

Between you and Quincy, how can I trust you?" She shook her head. "Women aren't barbie dolls you can swap out for better models."

He gestured at the Mustang. "Can we go for a drive?"

She couldn't think of a reason to refuse. She snapped her fingers and pointed at the passenger seat, not caring if she was rude. Or she hurt his feelings.

Thirty-Five

GENNA DROVE ON THE HIGHWAY INSTEAD OF THROUGH the forest. The car radio was static, effected by Troy's electrical output. She followed the Ohio River. Humanity flowed past.

This drive was not so scenic. It was the middle of a gray day with all of the beauty of a sooty cinderblock. Shabby buildings. Abandoned factories. Beige siding. Small towns that huddled like maggots picking the last vitality from a place where once a steel mill thrived. The trees were only trees. The land were a husk. Its magic was sequestered, forgotten, or sold. The mountains were shaved bald and excavated. A mall sat on top of the crest of a strip-mined hill.

The Mustang idled at a red light.

"What did you want to talk about?" Genna said.

Silence.

She glared at the red light.

Troy did not move. Only stared at her.

The red light changed to green.

She drove onward into Pittsburgh, across the bridges through the traffic, and out the tunnel to the other side of the mountains. She passed suburbs built into mountains. She had no particular direction. Only forward.

She drove on the interstate. She waited for him to speak. To say something. Instead he sat and watched the world pass.

His hand drifted over to her thigh. She did not shove him off.

A half hour later, without preamble, Troy began to sing in a crisp clear baritone: *"Do I love you because you're beautiful? Or are you beautiful because I love you?"*

Genna sucked in a breath, feeling like she had a bucket of ice water dropped on her head.

It wasn't fair. She had to drive straight. Not skid into traffic. Guys were not supposed to be fans of fairytales too. Yet here he was, singing Prince Charming's song from Rogers & Hammerstein's *Cinderella*.

His voice filled the Mustang. Her thoughts. Her blood. Her mouth opened and the duet poured out. She had watched that *Cinderella* movie a thousand times. She loved the colors. The absurd happiness and earnestness. The color-blind casting was part of its charm. A fantastic musical world where everyone simply was.

Genna turned off into a small park. She stopped the Mustang and turned to him, fighting tears. "What is going on? If you're leaving then say that. It's okay to say goodbye."

Troy took off his watch. He slid it gently onto her hand. He cupped it as though in prayer. He kissed her knuckles. He pressed her palm against his cheek. "Goodbye, my queen."

Genna swallowed hard. She was fine. This is what she expected. "Goodbye."

Black tar seeped down his tear ducts, around the crease of his nose to his jaw.

Genna recoiled. "I told you not to touch the grave dirt!"

He shook his head but could not speak. More tar from his nostrils, outlining his lips, and the curve of his chin. Tar slid out of his ears, two more lines down his neck. These lines blended together, coated his tattoos, the swirled spirals on the belly. Tar formed like sticky rope ties knotted around his neck, shoulders, elbows, wrists, knees, and ankles. Tar soaked through his clothes.

Tendrils flowed down his spine and rib cage. Around his thighs. His fingers turned black.

Against her better judgment, Genna hesitantly reached for him but he evaded her touch. He melted into his own shadow. The tar slid up the passenger side head rest and into the back of the Mustang.

Naomi coalesced out of thin air. She sat in the middle of the back seat. She held a small handmade clay jar. The tar slid across the upholstery, up her skirts, and pushed itself into the jar. More tar went in than should have fit.

"Why did you do that to him?" Genna whispered.

"Because I can and he's my ken doll." Naomi took a pair of tweezers out of her pocket. She reached into the jar and extracted a large diamond stud earring and the silver necklace. The tar clung. She hissed, scolding. She jabbed the tar with the sharp ends of the tweezers. "Both of you need to stop. You had your fun and now you're done."

She dropped the diamond and necklace into a fabric bag. She shook the bag then she tossed it at Genna's head. Hard. Genna caught it with one hand.

Naomi scraped the tar off her tweezers. She corked the jar. The jar shrank to the size of a vial. She slid it into a pocket of her skirt.

"Start driving, Miss Daisy." Naomi peeled off Miss Bootsie's skin, revealing her true self with a flourish for the first time since they had met.

She looked like a frog pushed into a barbie doll mold. Everything was slightly off. Her eyes bulged as if trying to escape her perfectly symmetrical head. Her oversized mouth stretched too wide into her cheeks. Her sloped shoulders were dragged down by large veiny breasts shoved high in her blouse because of her steel boned corset. She had thin stringy brown hair and ashen brown skin sagging off her body like wet cardboard. Miss Bootsie's rotted skin stretched over her body like a misshapen onsie. Her hands were long with the tips rounded. Her painted claws were sharp and long.

Her beautiful clothing had a film of poisonous goo along the top. The fringes dripped. Genna knew that there were acid burns in the upholstery that would never come out. Naomi was that kind of petty.

Naomi moved like she had no bones inside her body. Different parts expanded and flexed, trying to find a correct shape. The corset kept her core in place. The rest of her bubbled and oozed inside of malleable flesh. Naomi was stuffed full of tumors, braided keloids, and curses. Magical cancer festered.

Genna focused on the road, nauseous.

"Like what you see?" Naomi flexed. There were tattoos. Same as Troy's but reversed. "You're disgusted, aren't you? I make you sick."

Naomi expanded and contracted like a fleshy accordion. She squelched and burbled and oozed. Parts of her were pus yellow and inflamed red and corpse gray. She was trying to be horrifying but Naomi looked exactly like Kyle. Same bad skin, same ooze, and same ribbit guttural croak.

Naomi's boo hag magic tried to warp stolen skin into a more pleasing shape but kept failing.

Genna parked the car again.

"What the fuck are you doing, bitch! Drive!"

"Sable couldn't teach you how to hold your shape. Consume and destroy doesn't translate well to boo hag magic."

"Don't talk about what you don't know, bitch. Sable's skin magic is as weak as wet tissue paper. I spent all of my life keeping them from falling apart."

"You ate what little there was left of their magic after Donnie."

"You don't know me. You don't know what I've been through. I'm going to scalp you and wear that pretty hair of yours, bitch." Naomi breathed on the back of Genna's neck. The tickle of long claws in her hair tested Genna's temper.

Troy's watch was heavy and warm on her wrist. The jewelry bag was made of skin that still moved and breathed. Genna could feel the double heartbeat as if Troy and Quincy had been turned into a pocket square of flesh. Genna slid the bag into a shadow in her pocket. It floated in the darkness. Barbed tendrils reached out like an octopus exploring a new cage. Naomi's spell found nothing to grab but more darkness and the inside of a smooth containment bubble.

"Nice of you to let him say goodbye before you make him forget," Genna said. "You didn't give Quincy that chance."

"Yeah, and he whined like a bitch about it too." Naomi sucked on her teeth. "What did you and Cleopatra talk about?"

"Why do you need to know?"

"You've got jokes." It was Donnie's smile. A leer of fury and greed. "They're not yours. They're mine. They've always been mine. Ever since they walked into my Waffle House. They're always going to be mine. You can have the castle, pretty pretty princess. You can have the money. The clothes. The name. The lights. You can't have what's mine."

"You have nothing to do with my money."

"You owe me."

"I owe you nothing. Though I will ask, if this was all your idea, why are you willing to part with Quincy? Not Troy or Cleopatra?"

"Quincy's annoying. His parents won't stop nagging about legacy. You were supposed to shut up and marry him. Then we could move into the castle. No problem. But no. You had to make things difficult. You had to call me by my name to my face."

"No, I bet it's because I know more about boo hag magic than you do."

Naomi squelched faster. "The fuck did you say to me?"

"You heard me."

Naomi used Cleopatra, Troy and Quincy to find her journals but Genna had encrypted and enchanted her field notes. Anyone who read the journals were compelled to add their knowledge into her notes then forget they had written anything. Genna had learned a lot by leaving a diary for Katie to read. Quincy and Cleopatra's extensive knowledge from the witch finder perspective fleshed out anything Naomi couldn't answer. Even now, Troy whispered secrets kept inside his watch, using the gold curse to transfer the knowledge.

Naomi had no idea what she was. She did have creative solutions. Witchy solutions. The extra enchantments Genna added to her field journal were specially tagged for boo hags.

Genna tugged on her wind catcher earrings, feeling the magic activate along her jaw. "We didn't talk about you, Naomi."

"Liar. You don't even have the decency say it to my face," Naomi scoffed, "You made wind catchers. Really, bitch? Wind catchers? You dragged me back to that shitty little cottage in the woods where that old hag burned my parent and me up? That hag said it was for our own good. She said I was a monster. She said that I was worse than a devil. I was McBride. That's what broke Sable. Not Donnie. It was her. We lost everything and then she scattered us to the wind. We survived. And here you are, crying for that old hag like she was somebody. You don't even have a picture of her. Neither you or Katie. I checked."

"Miss Bootsie burned up any photo or likeness we took." Genna tried hard to have something of Miss Bootsie's likeness. Katie tried to paint Miss Bootsie but they were always destroyed.

"Sure, that's convenient. Why I should believe you?"

"What do you want, Naomi?"

"I want you to stop getting in my way!"

"Did Tituba give you that tar?"

Naomi glared at her, smoothing her hand over her skirts. "You don't get to love Troy. You don't get to love Cleopatra. I was going to allow you to marry Quincy but Katie doesn't like it when you cheat on her. Don't make your bride feel insecure. She might forget she loves you and kill you."

"You're best friends now? That's nice."

"Oh, I'm going to kill her and eat her," Naomi said, flicking her hair over her shoulder. "She called me a toad."

"Aren't you?"

Another mean-eyed look. "It must be nice wearing all that beautiful skin the hag made you. It'd be a shame if someone ripped it off."

"If you could've, you would've."

"Fucking Troy." Her face smushed like playdough. "His bitch-ass ruins everything."

"What do you want, Naomi? Sympathy? You didn't want the cloak."

"You think I want to stay in this janky ass town longer than I have to?"

"Yes."

"Bitch, you don't know me! You're the ugly stepsister. I'm Cinderella. You're just some bitch who came in and stole my life." There was a lot of snapping fingers and head bobbing and fake treble in her voice. "What did you tell Cleopatra about me? You poisoned her against me, didn't you?"

"Why did you steal Cleopatra's baby and sell it to Katie?"

Naomi flicked her hand dismissively. "Oh please, Cleopatra lays eggs like a hen. I eat them so Quincy won't fertilize any. All I did was share a few with Pipsy. They haven't ever tasted eggs so good."

"Except Katie didn't eat the egg. She fertilized it."

"You spoiled everything."

Genna wanted to feel some kind of Black solidarity. She wanted to help Naomi find her place. Reclaim her home. Be the next vampire princess. Except Naomi was stupid. Not even the manipulatable kind. A dangerous clown filled with other people's ideas and a whole lot of self-loathing.

Genna rolled down the Mustang's window. "Hey Katie, can you do something about this bitch? She's annoying as hell."

"Don't ignore me!" Naomi screeched. Then yelped as she bit her own tongue. She wrestled her own face. Stripes of skin came off as she clawed at her lips. Blood dribbled and pitted her skirts. Miss Bootsie's skin disintegrated.

"Thank you," Genna said as the air coalesced in the passenger seat. Katie sat where Troy had, brushing her skirts off.

"Can you believe she thinks she's Cinderella?" Katie muttered.

"She's got the ego. Humble beginnings. Evil stepsisters. Who is Prince Charming in the story?"

Naomi writhed in the backseat, flailing against Genna and Katie's twinned power. Naomi leaked acidic tears. The smell of burning vinyl was getting on Genna's nerves.

"Look at this mess. I'll have to have the interior redone."

"She wants a ball. Her big debut to Sweetwater high society will be my Halloween party. It's such a pain in the ass!" Katie spun and hissed. "Stop kicking the seat! Be still. Be quiet, you miserable toad!"

Naomi froze mid-writhe. She slid sideways. Panting.

Katie took off her earrings and tossed them in the back seat. The threads wrapped around Naomi. She shuddered and fought as it wrapped her in a cocoon. Then she shrank down to the size of a fly. Katie slid into the back seat, her hip bumping into Genna who shoved it aside.

"Get your butt out of my face!"

Katie wiggled. "Want to spank it?"

"Katie, if your Manolos put a hole in my seat, I'm putting a hole in your head."

Katie turned back around, sliding into the passenger side. She snuggled against Genna. "You can put a hole in me anytime."

Genna scoffed. She started the car again. She opened the windows to get rid of Naomi's stench. "I can't believe she's Miss Bootsie's granddaughter."

"I can't believe we haven't figured out a way to kill the bitch."

Genna sighed. "The harder we try, the strong she gets. We need to change tactics."

"Do you have a plan?"

"I wish I did."

Katie frowned. "That's not like you."

Genna glared at the winding road. "I know, Katie. I know. Get off my tits."

To her surprise, Katie patted her on the thigh and offered her part of a cookie. "Here. Have a cookie. It's my last one."

Genna took a thoughtful bite of cookie. The half-melted chocolate was warm. The smell familiar. Like Katie. "Thanks."

"I was heading into town to get another batch of cookies as samples for the party. You might as well drive me." Katie opened the sun visor to check her makeup and hair. "Don't worry. We'll figure it out together."

Thirty-Six

KATIE ENJOYED THE DRIVE BACK TO SWEETWATER. SHE talked nonstop. Genna found herself relaxing into the familiar banter. Troy's watch thrummed on her wrist.

Katie waggled the earrings. They hummed with magic. "I love these."

"I'm glad they work."

The earrings separated, stretched, and tangled Naomi's power. One earring for boo hag magic. The other for McBride. Katie devoured the magic that held Naomi together.

"I can't believe that's Miss Bootsie's granddaughter. She's just so *ugh*." Katie huffed, sucking on the earrings.

Genna shook her head. "Naomi's an airhead. I've spent so much time trying to dig deep down and find something. There's nothing but hot air."

"I tried too but she's dumber than a bag of hair. Even Mimi thinks she's hopelessly boring."

"What about Kyle?"

"He's tried to eat her. They squabble like children. All bull-frog croaking and slapping. It's gross. Frog people. I can't believe I'm related to them."

"Why are you throwing Naomi a party that's bigger than yours was? Won't everyone think she's special?"

Katie gasped. "You mean, Mimi's right?"

"Even a broken watch is right twice a day."

"But I wanted to throw a party in the castle. You never let me do that."

"Tough shit. I caught Naomi with a measuring tape and making new drapes. She can put all that redecorating in the mansion. It needs a facelift anyway. Window treatments would go a long way."

"Naomi likes tassels," Katie said, disparagingly.

"I saw her wearing brown corduroy overalls," Genna said.

They both shuddered.

"And you wanted to give her a party at the castle."

"You're right. What was I thinking? I've got such pregnancy brain."

"Already blaming the baby."

Katie rubbed her belly. "Pregnancy is hard. I'm eating eight times as much. Your baby is so hungry."

"What's going on, Katie? Seriously?"

Katie lost her smile. Her hair curtained her face as she glared at Troy's watch. "You called him Prometheus. That's for us. You broke your promise."

Genna sucked on her teeth. "What do you want me to say? He tastes good."

"You have me."

"Oh stop being annoying. You feed and fuck who you want. It's a little late in the game to get jealous. I refuse to abide by arbitrary rules you tacked on after the fact. All I said was that I'd play with you. Not only you. I wanted some variety."

"You stopped playing with me."

"Tituba is trying to get me killed. The whole forest is overrun with hunters and finders. That is your fault."

"That's not my fault. It's Pipsy. She wanted this toad. Not me."

"Yeah, well now I've got hunters *and* werewolves because of you. So I can fuck who I want!" Genna glared at Katie who looked back at her neutrally.

"He sang to you, *Cinderella*. And I've got another frog I have to kiss."

"You've kissed Naomi? I thought Kyle forced himself on you and you stomped him."

Katie flicked her shoulders as though twitching off a fly. "Why did you think I started painting?"

"Katie, why haven't you killed him yet? He's sick even for a McBride."

"He's my big brother. He protected me from Mommy and Daddy and Daddy's friends. He fed me. I'm special."

The bickering faded into silence. Genna had always wondered what happened behind closed doors in the McBride mansion.

When they reached the town proper, Katie terrorized pedestrians by waving at them out of the Mustang's window. The humans froze or run like startled deer. Katie's pink hair floated in the breeze as she cackled with delight. Genna hid a smirk.

"All told, I don't think that Naomi's the real problem," Genna said, switching to a safer topic. "She got mojo but it's Sable, Camile, and Olympia that I'm worried about. If Olympia or any of them kill Pipsy, hunters and finders will take over Sweetwater."

"And you'll lose Prince Charming forever."

"You're banking on the idea that they won't kill you too. Olympia was a teenage mom. She could abort you herself. Sable might not be too stoked about another McBride in the family. Quincy's parents value their son too highly. Cleopatra's family hate you on principal."

"It's your baby. I'm your surrogate."

"Now you're hiding under my skirts after all of the shit you've put me through? I should kill you myself."

"But you won't. Otherwise you'll starve to death. You can't live without my blood, Iffy."

"I can, Katie. You're just convenient."

"But you came back to me. You forgave me."

"I came back to Sweetwater. I came back to the castle. I didn't come back to you. Yes, I should've ignored you instead of reestablishing contact but honestly, you're the only friend I have. It's sick and twisted and we bring out the worst in each other but who else do we have? I thought we were good until you started doing fuck shit again. That's why I had to find a new weapon. I couldn't trust you."

Katie gasped, her hand drifted up over her sternum. "You don't trust me?"

"You forced my hand bringing a baby into this. You crossed a line. The game is over." Genna shook her head as she drove into Sweetwater's single road downtown. "I didn't end it. You did."

"Iffy, come on."

"What, you'll kill the baby? Pretend you haven't told everyone you're carrying my baby? Get back into Pipsy's good graces when she's got Olympia as your stand-in? You overplayed your hand, Katie. I was the one ally you had. Now I have to choose. I get blamed for that life in your belly. I get all of the attention. I have to be a mother because you're an asshole!"

"Miss Bootsie wanted us to have a daughter."

Genna stomped on the break in front of Sweetwater Bakery. "Get the fuck out of my car."

Katie sniffled as tears dripped on her cheeks. "Iffy, don't be like this."

"I can hear your stomach. Go eat some salted toffee chocolate chip cookies and think about what you've done. I have to figure this shit out on my own. Again. Thanks for letting an army of werewolves I don't want to kill into my forest. I didn't have any issues with the local packs and now I have someone else biting my ass. What a wonderful Halloween treat. Now get out!"

Katie slunk out of the Mustang, head hung, snuffling pathetically. Her earrings swung as she slouched into the bakery.

"And don't slam my door!"

Katie closed the Mustang with the tiniest slide of the latch. She pressed her hands flat against the window. "Iffy, I want to be a mom. I wanted us to be together forever. That's all."

"No, you got jealous and wanted to trap me. Again. You know good and damn well that I wouldn't trust you to raise a baby right. So fuck you and fuck your crocodile tears."

Genna drove off. She nearly hit a kid who had stepped into the road. Genna stomped on the break, cussing as the tires squealed. A fresh bakers dozen of chocolate chip cookies bounced off the hood. The kid hugged a crumpled cardboard box hugged.

A lofted Jeep behind the Mustang honked.

The kid trembled. Eyes glazed. No sign of moving. It was trans kid that Genna had found in her hayloft years ago. The remaining hair on their half-shaved head fluffed in an ombre orange to purple halo. The sunlight in their hair lit them like a candle.

Genna got out, swearing to herself. The Jeep honked again. She pointed at the Jeep. "Either wait or go around!"

The trans kid scampered back onto the sidewalk and charged down the block. Their heavy boots slapped the ground. Their black and red plaid skirt flapped at the speed of their sprint. Their fishnet stockings flashed on coltish legs that were orange from too much fake suntan lotion. Their jewelry jangled and clanked. Their oversized coat had a howling wolf painted across the back.

Genna grimaced and checked the Mustang for damage. There were two intact cookies on the hood of the car. She decided that this was a sign. She felt bad for the kid. Did they know they were the forest's avatar? Or was the kid doomed to stagger from one seemingly random situation to the next with no idea the impact they had? They wanted their existence to matter. That desire had gotten them out of the woods. They should have been more specific.

The Jeep honked again. And revved its engine. Olympia was behind the wheel. She glared through the bulletproof glass.

Genna walked over to the Jeep and knocked on the window. She offered Olympia the cookie and ate the other. "Let's talk."

Slowly the window rolled down. Olympia scowled but took the cookie. "Did you hit that kid?"

"No, I didn't."

Olympia reached out to take the cookie. They ate in unfriendly silence. Troy really was the male version of his mother. He had the same features, same hair, and same expressions.

Genna dangled Naomi's skin bag in the window. "I'm not your enemy. Naomi did this to Troy and Quincy. She's out of control. If you kill Pipsy, you become the next Montgomery. You get the legacy. You also become the thing you kill. Focus on what's important."

Olympia took the skin bag. "You've got some nerve. You collared my son."

"Yes, I did. But I didn't use a spell to enchant him. You can check the silver and the diamond. They're tokens of affection. Not leashes." Reluctantly she handed over the stud earring and the silver collar.

Olympia took the jewelry and closed the window. She revved the Jeep's engine.

Genna walked back to the Mustang. She spotted the worried face of the trans kid peeking from the corner of the building like a nervous squirrel. "Do you need a ride or what?"

The kid darted to the Mustang and hopped in. Genna drove. Cypress Hill played '*I Ain't Going Out Like That*' on the radio.

The kid looked around the inside of the Mustang. "It looks like my bedroom."

"I guess we have similar tastes."

The kid flinched and hugged themselves. Their fists squeezed on their lap. "It's funny to run into you."

"Why's that?"

"Something happened to me in the forest. You said that I'd forget but I haven't."

"Why don't you tell me what's been going on?"

"My body keeps changing genders. I thought everyone became a boy when they hit puberty. But now I have boobs and my p-penis went away. My boobs are heavy. My bones hurt all the time. Then they started shrinking. And my clit is like a balloon. What's wrong with me?"

"You're a boo hag. That's a skin witch. Every boo hag goes through a metamorphic period when their body changes rapidly. Short, tall, dark, mid-tone, light, hairy, bald. You can call it gender fluid. You have to make up your mind. Choose a shape. Or don't. Though if you don't, you'll use up all your magic in transformation. There won't be enough magic to defend yourself from predators who'll try to take your skin and hurt you. If you're really unlucky, they'll plant their power in you like a jewel wasp lays her eggs inside of a spider."

The kid turned a dingy white. "How do you know all of this stuff?"

"I've seen it happen. Don't throw up. You're getting the answers you wanted."

"I don't want wasps planting eggs in me!"

"Then defend yourself. Get training. Learn how to control your shape. Otherwise you're either melting like a barbie doll in a microwave or inflating like balloon full of old pudding."

"Can't I stop it?"

"Of course you can. You're in control. You can become whatever you want. Though pretending you don't have magic won't make it go away. Or others not see that you're special. Pick somebody you want to look like. I picked Aaliyah."

"Who's that?"

"Google it. Ignorance isn't a flex." Genna stopped at a stop sign. "Now where am I taking you?"

"The library, please," the kid whispered.

Genna drove to the large stone temple with ionian columns on the front. "Take care."

The kid paused. Looked at Genna. "Are you okay?"

"When has that mattered?"

The kid frowned. They slid a metal cuff off of their wrist and handed it to Genna. "Here. Take this as payment for telling me the truth."

Genna read the inscription out loud. *'Smooth seas never made a skilled sailor.'*

"Thanks, kid."

"You know you're a legend at the Academy, right? They still talk about how you came out and didn't care what people thought. You and Katie made it possible for weird kids like me to be normal." The kid gestured at the cuff. "I made that myself. I know it's not much but I hope it helps you like you helped me."

Genna looked down. The tear escaped before she could hide it. She smirked. Nodded. "Thanks, kid."

"I always thought you're like the captain of the boat. You can see the rocks. You steer us where we need to go."

"That's one way of putting it."

The kid slid out of the Mustang. "Bye, Belle."

"What'd you call me?"

The kid frowned. "Belle? That's your name isn't it?"

"My name is Genna. My last name is Bellwether."

"Oh, well, everybody calls you Belle and that bitchy vampire the Bride." The kid tapped on the roof of the Mustang. Polite but impatient. "I have to go now."

"See you around. Your body will settle down. It just takes time and practice. You have to keep going."

"You too, okay? Eat the assholes that get in your way."

"Don't invite me to a good time." Genna winked.

The kid chortled then covered their mouth. "You're funny."

"I have my moments."

Genna drove away. A smile tugged at her cheeks. Belle wasn't the worst nickname. Predictable but not bad.

Katie was at the art gallery, talking to a slack-jawed crowd. Her dramatic gesticulations were practically Shakespearean. Genna beeped the Mustang's horn. Katie looked through the glass. She knocked people over in her haste to dance to the door.

"Iffeee! You came back!"

"Did you get the cookies?"

"Of course!"

A whey-faced girl still wearing her bakery apron and visor came over loaded down with several bags and boxes. Others had bouquets of flowers.

Katie shoved a bouquet in Genna's face. "I got spider mums, your favorite." She made a big show of putting them into the back seat. Along with clothing and shoe bags. Several hat and jewelry boxes.

To Katie's annoyance the wrapped painting didn't fit in the back of the trunk. "Make sure she gets this, understood?"

"Yes, Bride," the shop girl said dully. She held the passenger door open.

Katie flounced into the passenger seat. "And don't slam the door!"

The girl slowly shut the Mustang.

"Hurry up!" Katie hissed. She yanked on the door. "Absolutely useless."

"Don't spoil the mood," Genna said as she left the art gallery and drove up BackBone road.

"I'm in a great mood. You did a little retail therapy too, I see."

Genna moved her hand so Katie couldn't touch the cuff. "How long have they been calling us Belle and the Bride?"

"Since the engagement."

"Where am I taking all this?"

"To the mansion. You're *absolutely* right about the party. Naomi only needs a normal Halloween party. It's going to be a bloodbath anyway. Why worry about the thread count of the napkins?" Katie searched through the bags. She lifted a still warm box. The heavenly scent of freshly made salty toffee chocolate cookies increased. She lifted a cookie, hand underneath to catch any crumbs. "Open your mouth. Say aah!"

Genna opened her mouth. Katie kissed her, shoving her tongue down her throat. Genna bit her tongue off. Her mouth filled with blood. Katie yelped but sat back, humming in triumph as she ate the cookie. Genna chewed on her tongue. It tasted sweeter than chocolate.

"You did that on purpose." Genna grumpily took a cookie from the box.

"You're welcome, Iffy," Katie's teeth were red and brown from bloody chocolate. "No matter what you think, I'm on your side."

Thirty-Seven

It was Halloween and the McBride mansion was quiet. The grassy knoll on either side of the driveway was crowded with cars. Genna walked the perimeter and inspected the cars, taking photos of the license plates.

Jack-o-lanterns and human skulls were stacked into a corridor of free standing walls. Each were decorated, painted, beaded, covered in lace, lacquered, and carved. The pumpkins were plastic but the human skulls were real.

Genna explored every hallway. Outside the guarded doorway, the mansion was as cold and clean as a polished mausoleum. The hallways were completely empty. No one tried to break the glass windows. No one snuck past the skull walls searching for a bathroom or smoked on the porch, too drunk to stand. No one vomited on the plastic plants.

What happened inside was contained by pristine stone walls and polished white floors.

The door into the party felt like a crocodile's mouth waiting for the unwary to walk up its tongue. The McBride parties never stopped. There were magical doors that connected the mansion to various nightclubs around the world. Those who walked in could be from everywhere and nowhere. Not everyone who entered found the correct exit, if they left at all.

Genna took a deep breath, her fingers tracing the edge of her cloak. She had turned the fur black side up. She pulled the hood over her head. Her curls were wrapped into a black Ferragamo silk scarf in the deep interior. She wore careful ambergris perfume that negated her scent. Her black leather pants were skin tight. Her black silk corset with a sweet heart peekaboo collar with silver embroidery across the slats with black pearls on top. Her thigh-high metallic black boots were custom instead of name brand. Her hands were covered in black gloves that reached to the elbow. She wore silver fingernail claw rings on each digit attached to bracelets by fine silver chains. Her face was hidden by a clay wolf's mask. The black muzzle was smooth.

She stepped through the door. She shivered as the spell hovering in the doorway slid over her skin and marked her as a welcomed guest.

'*About Damn Time*' by Lizzo blared from the sound system, except there was an atonal twang. The normal festive ebullience was replaced by fetid intensity. The flute was a screech of a dying bird clawing out of its cage.

Her magic ignited defensively. Her eyes glowed like twin flames. Streamers of smoke drifted out of strategic vent holes on the mask. The billowing smoke looked like fur and swallowed her scent. Her magic ate the light and her presence. She looked like a walking shadow.

The warehouse-sized nightclub was crowded with costumed carnality. Desire had peeled off its skin of civility. Everyone was feral, urgent, and uninhibited.

The tables were forested with empty liquor bottles. The walls trickled condensation between giant mirrors. The whirling glittery lights painted intertwined bodies in pinks, blues, and greens. The carnage and death was hidden by enchanted fog machines.

To the left, around the curved edge of the front desk, was the dance floor. It was pure bedlam. Monsters and humans danced and gyrated. The crowd of costumers milled around the dance floor or turned down connecting hallways to the kinky play rooms, the curtained beds, the row of glory holes, the saddle-shaped swings where anyone could lie in and get penetrated. The hallways were clogged with those who stopped waiting for a curtained bed and picked the nearest available surface. Their hands reached out in invitation to anyone who passed too close, tracing shoulders and hips.

On the second floor balcony there were two illuminated performances. The first bed was a Black cowboy riding a stable of enthusiastic White women wearing pony-play leathers, hooves, and butt-plug tails. He swung his Stetson over his head as though riding a bull at a rodeo while he penetrated a blonde filly from behind. His oiled brown muscles were slick in the dance light. The flex of his butt cheeks encouraged a few eager smacks from onlookers.

On the second bed was an Asian-American woman. Her flowing red kimono flapped like butterfly wings. Her long black hair was bunched in a man's fist. Her head busily bobbed on the cock in her mouth while two incredibly well-endowed men pene-trated her from behind and below.

The rapt audience on the first floor were uncomfortably enthusiastic. There were bouncers at the bottom of the stairs to keep peons from joining in. Not even the girl-on-girl perfor-mances in lofted cages hanging from the ceiling had this much attention.

Genna kept walking, careful not to get too close to anyone.

The Cowboy and the Geisha were iconic monster porn actors that Genna had seen perform before at McBride parties. They had fangs. Genna could see them reflecting bright in the blacklight.

Katie and Cleopatra were kissing passionately in the back corner of the second floor. Cleopatra wore a white corset with her breasts out, a white veil over her afro, stockings with no crotch. Katie was dressed like Elvira, complete with beehive hair and slinky black dress. They were supposed to be hidden by the sex acts but Genna could see them from the angle she stood on the first floor.

Cleopatra cupped Katie's jaw. Her head arched back as Katie sank her teeth into her neck. A possessive hand was in Katie's hair. The other hand was firm on her pregnant belly. They gyrated together over the desiccated corpse in a minister's robe and collar.

Kyle held Naomi, his long frog tongue sliming her neck, shoulder, and into her cleavage. Naomi kicked and squirmed, twisting like a caught marlin in his grip. She shouted threats and tried to get to Cleopatra and Katie. It was Naomi's reaction that focused Genna's attention but she was too far away to do anything about it. Kyle flipped on a glowing sign that flashed 'Just Married' over the couple.

Genna had hoped that Cleopatra would leave the forest, leave everything and simply driving off. She had already packed the Mustang for Cleopatra. She stuffed gemstones and money and everything else she could think of into purses and bags. But that Cleopatra was a dream in sunshine and roses. The real Cleopatra had been a vampire's bride for nearly twenty years. Genna did not have what she wanted. Katie did.

Genna waited to feel jealous or sad. Instead, she felt nothing but vaguely disappointed.

Her view was obscured by a porn performer shoving his dick down the Geisha's throat then reeling back, holding his crotch and screaming. The Geisha leapt after him, her claws on her hands and feet extending to full length. They hit the corner of the bed and landed on the floor. Meanwhile the second man writhed, curled into a fetal position. The other men stumbled back, pointing and shouting. Only to get pounced on by monstrous onlookers. The orgy became a feeding frenzy. The Geisha lifted her head, transforming into a vixen with silver white fur and nine tails. Her fox scream was like a sonic bludgeon. More howls rose around the room mixed with the wretched shrieks of humans. People scrambled over each other, attempting to run in every direction.

The Cowboy was on his feet. He transformed. Shoulders spreading. Back widening. Muscles building on top of each other. Swelling like his skin was a bag of heated popcorn. His pants ripped down the seams. The rags of his shirt trapped around his armpits before they split. His fur jutted out of his body like enthusiastic grass. His ears scuttled up the side of his head like ambitious mollusks circumnavigating a brain coral. His short afro straightened into layers of brown fur. More hair grew out of smooth brown skin. His tail unfurled, long and hairless like a rat's, then puffed with fur. The werewolf howled. The pony girls were alive long enough to whinny and try to run in their hooves before he pounced.

Big Dawgs by Hanumankind and Kalmi blared from the speakers in the ceiling.

An eerie warbling scream attracted Genna's attention. There was nothing but empty space between Genna and the werewolf eating a man dressed as a Harry Potter while he was still alive. The wizard sounded like a baby bunny caught by a cat. His scream ended with a wet crunch. The slop of wet gristle and septic stink of unspooling intestines mixed with the cherry-sugar smell of spilled Red Bull.

Even though Genna called herself a werewolf she felt no connection to the monster snarling at her. Werewolves registered as food to eat same as vampires. Still, Genna could appreciate werewolves.

She kept moving and watched as if this were an animal documentary. The slaughterhouse screams were like birdsong. She could hear who died fighting and who died scared.

Werewolves were majestic. Their fur were sleek blurs of moment. It was easier to track when they pounced on a fleeing human than when they hid in the shadows of furniture. Their impossibly big mouths were crowded with long, sharp teeth.

One werewolf put a blonde woman's entire head in his mouth. His jaws slammed together as he whipped her up into the air. Her legs and arms flailed limply. Her back was broken.

It wasn't like the movies. Only constant movement. The werewolves leapt and pounced. They bit and ripped. Blood and dismembered parts looked unreal in the black light. The smell of carnage mixed with the reek of wild animal, perfume, and cocktails.

Many humans were too intoxicated to react. They snorted lines of white powder on the mirrored tables while werewolves dragged their neighbors behind the couch. Others were too busy fighting to get a drink at the crowded bars to notice until it was too late.

The vampires stayed in human shape, which meant they got pounced on by werewolves too. This turned into a fight.

The concussive blast and ratchet of gunfire was slightly muffled by the walls. Hunters fought monsters.

Still the costume party continued. The party was so crowded that the violence was swallowed by the crush of people.

Spells in the music enchanted the ear to only hear the rhythm and not the screams. Magic turned real fur into mascot costumes. To dismiss the wet underfoot the partiers slipped on as spilled drinks and broken glass instead of blood and bone. The air was sweet instead of charnel. Death matches were just dance battles. Gunfire were merely champagne corks exploding.

The sound system pumped out *Closer* by Nine Inch Nails, accompanied by the thump and rattle of plastic speakers. The disco ball still spun across corpses, dancing humans, and the feasting monsters.

Monsters leapt and pounced. They were strange. No longer human-shaped. Genna could smell the Deep Magic as the permanent residents of the forest were lured by the carnage. They feasted.

Men with swords and guns shot anyone in range. The human-shaped werewolves dove among the crowd, blending in. Victims died as they were shoved in front. The real scrum of battle momentarily overtook the dancing.

The animal monsters ignored bullets. Except for the hunter

with a double-barrel shotgun that exploded the head of a human man when the werewolf dodged with superhuman speed. But she moved too fast, and slipped, her feet kicking, her claws scrabbling on cement like a dog taking a corner in a hallway too sharp. The shotgun exploded her head and chest, too. The hunter pulled out an ax but missed the human-shaped werewolf behind him until she ripped his throat out. The man swung, yelling. His elbow went into the werewolf's face, then chop to the ribs with his full weight. They both went down. The werewolf got up, his head hanging from her jaws by a broken spinal cord.

A third group of monsters were in beast mode. Were-panthers and were-grizzlies were among the carnage. The panthers leapt down from the catwalk and landed on their prey.

The grizzlies smacked humans and vampires into the mirrors with their great paws. The grizzlies were terrifyingly huge in this crowded space. They made the mind gibber in denial. A paw across the head broke the neck but not the skin. The dead man's head bounced like a bowling ball in a rubber bag. The weight dragged the rest of the body into a haphazard spin as it fell.

Someone threw a flaming bottle of whiskey. Then vodka. Then a barrage from the bar. The bartenders, busboys, and people trapped behind the bar were galvanized by hysteria and the hunters. They saw humans fighting back. Even the human-shaped monsters were an inspiration. Chairs and knives and even a blunt katana were yanked weapons off of corpses. They died fighting.

There was a group of humans on the third floor. A few of the men with weapons had stripped off their clothing, checking their bodies with rough hands. Men and women sobbed and covered their genitals, cringing from their touch. A blonde woman hid at the back of the group and was dragged forward. Her arm was wrenched high. Her bicep was bloody. She shook her head, sobbing, and was stabbed mid-plea. A man with an ax swung down on the felled body. Her blond hair bounced like a mop. Then a man swung a sledgehammer. The tresses soaked up the blood, skull, and bits of brain.

The men went back to strip-searching the rescued humans. Two men hiding bloody wounds across the side and leg were also beheaded. The second man charged with wildly swinging fists. He was perforated by three different types of long knife. Then beheaded. Then smashed into a pulp.

A female were-grizzly looked around, chewing on an arm. She met Genna's gaze. Both poised for a fight then Genna moved on and the grizzly went back to eating.

The monsters did not bother Genna or any of the eating ones. A few watched. Big ears flicking. Nostrils flaring. Gaze steady with heads low. No attempt to steal food. The ones that watched were female. Their breasts were hidden under thick chest fur. A brown werewolf noticed Genna and carried a dead human by the neck over to another werewolf, a dappled brown and gray male. She tossed the corpse. The dappled male pounced on the new corpse, ripping out the belly, thigh, and armpit with hungry abandon. The she-wolf grunted in satisfaction as she retreated to resume watching.

Genna felt Troy before she spotted him. He was shirtless, covered in blood. The blacklight painted his bare skin. He glowed like an angry opal. He grappled a werewolf, slashing and stabbing with his sword. He dodged bites. Kicked the monster in the jaw. His size was half of the werewolf's, but when he slashed, the monster howled. He ducked under the werewolf's arm, wrenched it around, and broke it at the elbow.

Quincy was scaled. His dreadlocks were a solid cape of black moss covered. Anything that jumped on his back sank through as if they had landed in an algae covered swamp.

Troy and Quincy fought the monsters. They were mauled, healed, and kept fighting. They laughed with manic glee and howled with in savage triumph, roaring their dominance as they crushed the skulls. The glisten of spinal columns ripped out of black flak jackets.

Werewolves crawled away, dragging the ripped remains of their legs, streamers of tendons and bones trailing behind them leaving smears. Troy and Quincy beheaded them and kept on killing.

Genna slunk along the wall, amazed but unwilling to be drawn in.

The dance floor had its own enchantment. Anyone on the glowing tiles were protected. But they had to keep dancing, even if their fur and clothes were on fire. They danced until they died. Their twitching corpses were shunted to the edge to be grabbed and eaten by onlookers. If any onlooker got too close to the tiles, their bodies started to jerk and gyrate as they joined the dance and replaced the dead.

The humans had established strongholds on the second floor, the stairs, and behind the bar. An endlessly shifting rank of monsters attempted to breach the fortifications. Troy had not chosen the stairs. He had been herded there, like the rest of men. A werewolf paced and threatened the base of the stairs to catch anyone who tried to jump down to the first floor.

The monsters gobbling humans were thinner and smaller than the ones fighting on the stairs. Nearly half their size. Their fur was not the same bristled ruff. Almost soft. Their muzzles and ears were stubbier. Their tails were smaller. Their movements lacked the balletic elegance.

Genna had an epiphany.

These were newly Turned werewolves on their first hunt. The werewolves were making babies. The pack elders kept the humans at bay so the bitten could transform. Werewolves Turned anyone they could pounce on. The panthers and grizzlies killed before they could Turn.

Genna had wondered where monsters were made. If there were dens somewhere or did random people on the street get grabbed? It made terrible sense that McBride parties were a prime Turning ground. Instead of birthing litters of werewolves, they made more monsters through their highly contagious bite. It was a fast gestation. They could immediately feed that monstrous hunger, the same way a baby bird breaking free of its egg was fed.

It took an extreme amount of energy to survive the first Turn. There was plenty to eat at a McBride party.

The McBride mansion was an epicenter. A safe space for monsters to be monstrous. It was like the pole in the glenn. Death and sex were intertwined.

Genna took a deep breath. She navigated the party to exit the same door she entered. She needed to get back to the castle. It was tempting to move through shadows but that would open a door into the castle. She had to walk through the forest.

She knew the werewolves followed her into the forest. They were scouts from the party. They slunk among the trees. Perhaps it was stupid to lead them to the castle but Genna was tired of running.

Thirty-Eight

A HOWL DRIFTED IN THROUGH THE CURVED BAY window. Genna paused as she took off her corset then hurried the rest of the way to the tower's top still wearing her costume. She paced the perimeter of the castle ramparts, which had the best view of the stables and their surrounding pastures.

The sky was a bruised gunmetal grey. The wind was too cold for the autumn. Or even a Pittsburgh winter. The chill wind promised an ice storm. The temperature dropped as the thunderstorm circled the castle property. The clouds were full of Naomi's rage.

A whinny. The distant figures of her horses plunging and bucking. The herd formation in both wings of the pasture was already defensive and restless. Humans on horseback and ATVs attempted to wrangle them back to the stables. The white and black shapes of dogs running along the forest edge, lunging and barking at the forest.

There were no messages from the stable but they were notorious for not telling her anything. Equestrians would be focused on protecting the horses. Also, most of the stablehands were as bored and wealthy as she was. They had no real concept of danger. They were more likely to deny than act.

The animals were more honest, sounding the alarm.

The howl made her shiver. It was the sound of the Wilderness.

Genna had found the part of Mongolia that was the Wilderness with a capital W. The Wilderness was different from the Old Night. Sweetwater Forest contained an abundance of game and clear running water. It was safe. It was a sanctuary. The Wilderness thrived on scarcity. Everything was harder, from the scrub brush to the shaggy ponies to the humans.

Genna remembered a night when she heard howls like this. She had paid for the 'full immersion' training package. The camp was so far away from any city that everyone had to chip in for everything.

The training camp was a flurry of activity. Genna ran with her translator to get to her horses, not understanding the language but wanting to be safe. She thought she wanted it. That it would make her tougher and better at riding. Instead, Genna realized how spoiled and ill equipped she was to survive in the Wilderness.

They had falcons to catch prey. They had dogs. But everyone and everything had a job. She was miserably useless. Slow at everything but riding.

"You are a princess," the translator said. "You pay us to protect you."

When the wolves howled, the campsite rallied. Genna was shocked to watch several genuine wolves get shot.

"Those are wolves!" Genna had exclaimed, horrified by the bodies they carried in on poles and immediately started skinning. "They're endangered. You can't do that."

The translator gave her the kind of look reserved for foolish Americans who should not be wasting her time and breathing her air. She was as short and nice as homemade apple pie right up until the howling began. The music and dancing around the campfire had been fun. Now the translator was as hard as steel and as pugnacious as her shaggy pony. A wall had slammed down between them. Playtime was over. This was life and death. No hesitation.

"You protect your home from the wolf or the wolf eats your home." Then, in case Genna did not understand, the translator tugged on the hem of Genna's cloak. "Isn't this wolf fur too?"

The translator made Genna go with the cleanup crew to deal with the sheep that the wolves had grabbed.

Genna had come back to America grateful for working toilets and determined to never go that deep into the Wilderness again.

Looking back, Genna realized that all of those people in the Mongolian camp were Night Skins. They welcomed and cared for Genna. They healed her wounded heart by treating her simply. They had magic too. She was just a sad and spoiled princess. They taught her without ever explaining. If she went back there would be no record of those people or that camp. She found them because she needed them.

More howls joined in with the first.

That camp in Mongolia had been a place like Sweetwater. A sanctuary that needed protecting. Her castle was in real danger.

The one thing she *knew* was how often people came onto her property believing that there would be no consequences because she was Black and female. The dogs barked then, too, but not like this. Never this squealing high danger, torn between their training and the instinct to run.

The Wilderness was in the forest. The Old Night was quiet, not wanting to get involved unless it was mortally necessary.

Another howl in the icy wind that ruffled her hair and rippled her cloak. Genna knew the howl because it was the same kind she made. There was a direwolf in the forest.

Grimly, she pulled her phone out and called her parents on the emergency line. She said the code phrase that signified mortal peril.

"Someone's attacking the castle," she said.

"Don't be ridiculous, Iphigenia," her mother said.

"I've contacted the security team but I'm getting a voicemail. The dogs are going crazy. I've locked everything up. I—I wanted you to know that I love you."

"Iphigenia, you need to calm down."

A howl, like it was right outside the window, the enemy looking in, as if able to see her antics through stone, curtains, and shutters. "Got to go— By the way, I'm engaged to Cleopatra— love you—Bye!"

"Cleopatra?" Her mother shouted.

She hung up as her mother demanded more information. She grimaced. She loved Troy but that would not get her mother out of bed. Saying Quincy would get a pleased but neutral response. Her mother had set Genna and Cleopatra together at brunch. Her mother wanted to be right.

Cleopatra would probably forgive her. Probably. If she survived. If she didn't, Cleopatra got all of the honor and respect and wealth she could want. She would probably run Genna's businesses better than she ever could. She would raise Katie's baby. Quincy, Troy, and Naomi would be a part of her life. But the castle was in good hands. Even if Genna never told her the truth.

Now that Genna had publicly claimed Cleopatra, Katie would have to tell everyone that she had married Cleopatra. The scandal would bring media attention that Pipsy would want to suppress.

Genna forced herself to take a deep breath.

In, *two, three, four.* Hold, *two, three, four.* Out, *two, three, four.* Hold, *two, three, four.*

Her mind whirled like a hamster in a runaway wheel. She flipped her cloak red side up to take a moment to think. Her parents were alerted. Her security team were unnervingly silent the one time she needed them. She was alone. No mice scurrying in the walls. No birds flying through the rafters. They hid in their roosts and holes listening to the howls.

Now what?

The forest looked like an open mouth with straight brown teeth.

She needed to put the castle in full lockdown. That had to be done manually.

She locked the roof door. She hurried down to the security room and pulled levers. Shudders ran through the castle. The artwork on the walls in their glass cases were pulled into the walls. Then those inner walls slid down into the sealed vault. The figurines sank down into their plinths. Which sank into the floor. The shutters slid down across the library walls, sealing the books and the carved wood. Then another wall, heavy stone set on top of the shelves.

She watched through the security cameras to confirm that the art went to the vault and the books were inside waterproof and fireproof boxes. It was not perfect storage. If things were already missing, they would not be in the vault. However, it got the majority of her collection.

She pulled the curtains shut and the reinforced metal and shutters on the windows. She clamped the doors shut. She turned on all of the security lights.

Perhaps it was a crazy level of paranoia, but Genna had watched enough movies about robbers breaking into vaults to add boobytraps and at least make an effort of protecting her treasures. There was still plenty to steal, but she would not lose historically precious things out of neglect.

Her great-grandmother probably hadn't been sorry either. Spitting defiance at the enemy. Not ashamed or hiding her wealth.

Genna ran to her office. She quickly took her precious stone falcon figurines off of their shelves and put them in their travel cases, setting them in black foam. She went to her closet and stuffed her jewelry in bags. Some had been taken out of the vault for research or to wear. She had not put them back. Now she had to keep them with her. Sweat prickled her scalp. She carefully navigated the steps down to the armory. She shoved the figurine cases and purses into a lockbox.

Hurry. Hurry. Hurry.

The howl was all around her. It was hard to think.

The hallways echoed with the thud of her boots. She ran through the Good Room to make sure everything had gone down to the vault. The room sealed with the antique furniture in it. The furs were sealed in the turret walls.

Genna ran faster.

She went to a closet where her Mongolian riding clothes hung in a travel bag. She carried the dress bag down to the armory. Once she locked everything up, then she would suit up.

She ran back up to her office, hefted the giant opal, and carried it down to the pool room her Birkin. She carefully lowered it into the basin below the waterfall. The water churned a glitter blue for a moment then went back to normal. She used the Birkin to scoop up random jewelry, electronics, and important documents as she ran from room to room. The castle was so damn big. So many rooms to check.

The chandeliers looked lonely and out of place surrounded by smooth gray cement. Genna had decided not to worry about those back when she remodeled the castle. They were too cumbersome to save.

What else? What else?

Sweat in her armpits and down her back. This was not a drill. The dogs were scared. The howls filled her thoughts. She fumbled and dropped her bags. She scrambled to scoop spilled jewelry back into their handbags. Her stomach clenched. She wanted to throw up. She kept moving.

Usually she would be packing things into the Mustang. It was surreal to focus on battening down the hatches instead of gathering things to run.

She clattered to the armory. She put the Birkin and other loaded purses on a bench by the dress bag.

She searched the security cameras again. Still nothing. No perimeter breach. No strange cars. Motion sensors had always had a difficult time discerning plants waving in the wind and someone sneaking on foot. The property was simply too damn big.

This was her land. Her responsibility. She ran along the outer hallways checking and locking doors and windows to make sure every portal was firmly sealed.

She could not hear the howling this deep in the castle, but she still moved quickly. Her Black Beauties, her Bouviers and her Akitas were military-trained and did not scare easy. The working dogs and horses were farm-raised and well-bred. The other untrained horses were wild cards but they followed the herd. The donkeys were bloody minded murderers when given half a chance. She trusted her senses. Nothing had come onto the property yet but the enemy was closing in.

She put on an armored reinforced jacket with a thick turtle-neck-like collar that cupped her ears and the base of her neck. It was tailor-made body armor. The good kind. It had been an impulse buy and sat in her closet until now. It did not impinge upon her movements, either. She wrapped extra padding to her ankles, calves, forearms, and the back of her knees. She put a bulletproof vest on under her cloak. It was definitely too much padding but paranoia held full sway. It was easy to imagine sharp jaws grabbing her arm, dragging her through iced grass.

Genna unzipped the dress bag. The smell of Mongolia filled her nostrils. The hunting clothes were a heavy long coat, pleated skirt, and boots. Each pleat had metal slats sewn into the panel and embroidered with flowers and wolves. Sheepskin lined the inside.

The translator had made it for Genna and given it to her as a farewell gift. She rubbed the patterns. It fit perfectly. She had been afraid that the extra armor underneath would get in the way. Instead, the entire ensemble fit together like they had always meant to be. That was the magic.

Genna silently thanked the translator for her pugnacious presence. That tough old bitch had been a friend when Genna needed one. She had encouraged Genna's determination.

Genna smoothed the protective flaps down her chest and over her arms. Her heartbeat slowed. The extra weight helped calm her nerves. The panic was there but it was easier to think. She had trained for this.

Genna practice-rolled down the hallway, got up, punched the air, jumped. She took her rings off and put them in a small drawstring velvet pouch, then into the pocket in her skirt. She strapped on leather archery gloves and bracers.

Then she went into the armory to choose her weapons.

Genna went down to the gun safe for her elephant gun. She laid out the enormous rifle on the long table. She began to take it apart.

The elephant gun was inlaid with mother-of-pearl and filigreed. It looked ridiculous, but one of the loopholes Genna found in the 'ladylike' activities was she could get away with sports as long as they looked as girly as possible. It might not be pink, but every piece in her armory looked like it was made of lace and would fall apart in expensive filigreed pieces when fired. Genna fired them during regular monthly practice. They were well made by a female gunsmith who understood the commission. The decoration was part of the illusion. The other guns were not a high enough caliber.

An AK-47 and the like were not great for horseback. She needed accuracy and stopping power.

She put the elephant gun back together. Genna loaded three bandoliers with extra rounds.

She strung her hunting bow. She changed the practice arrowheads for metal ones. She grabbed a bundle of arrows, filling her biggest quiver that was designed to fit on a horse blanket. She checked her short bow. The strings. She practiced a shot, adjusted the bow, and put it on.

The family had hundreds of decorative weapons. Swords, guns, knives, shields, and holsters. Some were still sharp. Some were rusted into their scabbards. Genna had learned how to use them enough to correctly assess which arms dealers were honest and which had no idea what they were doing. She was not an expert but with practice came confidence.

She sharpened her favorite calvary saber, sheathed it, and strapped it across her back. She put a hunting knife in her belt. The hunting knife made her feel ill. She was in real trouble if she was close enough to use it.

What did she have? What did she miss?

She forced herself to make a mental checklist. To breathe.

Genna stuffed her gun carry permit in her pocket and a large billfold of cash into a pocket on the inner lining of her riding jacket. She left the expert marksman plaque on the wall. Everyone believed it was fake at worst and a conversation starter at best.

She grabbed a pair of protective goggles.

Hurry. Hurry. Hurry.

Her helmet. Where the hell was her riding helmet?

Genna looked around. It had to be down in the stable. Maybe the tack room? All that she had here was the decorative helmet from Mongolia that she had stitched. It would have to do.

The Mongolian helmet had a nose guard, chin strap, and cheek guards. There was a tall Mohawk of braided cowrie shells, strips of beaded leather, and Sneakers' horse hair down the ridge. The leather exterior was sewn in a swirled pattern. It was not nearly as pretty as the rest. Genna had made it herself during the training camp, in the long, tedious stretches of time when there was nothing to do but sit and sew and listen to the camp women talk. Her fingers would ache as she fought the thick leather. The translator instructed her on how to make sure it fit on her helmet. She smacked her on the head several times to make sure nothing fell off. The helmet had been approved by the tent community.

Genna had not worn it since Mongolia. It was too embarrassing. No, it was a war helmet. She had not needed it until now.

Except her head felt bare. The anxious sweat had frizzed her hair. Genna twisted the sides of her hair into a crown and braided it down her back. She grabbed a cotton bandana and bundled her braid into it. She knotted it tight and stuffed the helmet on top. She banged it a few times. It stayed in place. She let the chin strap loose.

Genna concentrated. The air shimmered. She Turned into a coywolf and then back again. She swayed, panting as she checked herself. Armor, helmet, and clothes were intact. Finally, a Clothed Turn worked!

The elephant gun went in carrying case. She added a few more arrows into the quiver. She strapped on the bandoliers and a belt full of bullets. She rolled extra arrow bundles into a horse blanket and strapped that on too.

She forced herself to stop in the kitchen to gobble down a cup of water, a hasty ham, cheese, and mustard biscuit sandwich. She grabbed some granola bars, a water bottle, then to the bathroom linen closet for a first aid kit. She hooked it to her bandolier. She needed to pee. Her medical bag was still up in its special close in the tower. She didn't stop.

She walked around the castle, checking every door and the security room. There were no signs of break-ins or attempts. Yet. No perimeter alarms triggered, either. All of the outdoor lights were on, decorative and security. She tried to contact the security team again. Genna looked at her phone. No signal. The castle and the property ran on solar power. There were also generators. She had been so busy rushing around, she missed the attempt to cut the power.

The howling continued.

She walked quickly to the bridge to get a better view. The castle was lit. The stable was a little pool of light. The rest of the property was unlit. The forest was dark. The howls by the forest was next to the stable not the castle.

There was an empty spot where the Mustang had been. Cleopatra had taken it after all. This caused a pang in Genna's stomach. She jogged through the garage, snatching the keys from the wall for her grandfather's Lexus because it felt right.

The Lexus snarled to life. She kept the helmet on but put weapons in the backseat, needing to do a few adjustments to sit down. She was unable to sit comfortably with all of the armor on.

Hurry. Hurry. Hurry.

The garage door opened at the Lexus's approach. The driveway was empty. Nothing tried to stop her driving down the little path from the garage to the stable.

She spotted two figures walking out from behind the garage. It was Troy and Quincy in full hunter and finder regalia. Their paramilitary best. She was happy to see them.

Genna squeezed the steering wheel. She stopped. Reversed. "What are you doing here?"

Troy and Quincy raised their eyebrows when they saw how she was dressed as she rolled the window down.

"Are you going to spare Katie McBride because she's carrying your child?" She demanded.

They tried to hide it. The flex of their lips were enough of an affirmative.

"She's got our kid," Quincy said.

"I know you both wanted to marry me but if I marry Cleopatra then she and the baby can be near the forest. The child will be a boo hag."

"Genna, don't talk like that," Quincy said.

"My queen," Troy said, stepping in front of him. "Allow us to protect you."

Genna focused on Troy. She didn't know what to say to him. She half-spoke and half-sang lines from the musical *South Pacific*. "*Some enchanted evening. When you find your true love. When you feel him call you across crowded room. And somehow you know. You know even then.*"

Troy sparkled like a diamond firework. He rushed forward. He kissed her through the window. She held onto him, clawing up his armored sleeves. Her helmet fell off to bounce on the passenger seat and onto the floor. Her hair was a mess. Their tongues jockeyed as their mouths mashed together bruisingly hard. Lightning zinged back and forth as their magic was frantic and desperate. Sweat evaporated off her skin.

It was too soon. Too late. Too much. How could she meet him now at the end of everything?

She pulled away. He held on, trying to pull her through the window. She peeled his fingers off of the front of her jacket. She needed to use her real strength, nearly breaking a few fingers in the process.

"Let me go."

Troy cradled his hand. Quincy gripped his shoulder, pulling him back. His voice was raw. "Genna, what are you doing?"

"You need to tell Galveston and Roanoke to give Sweetwater a pass. Full amnesty. No hunting. No witch finding. This is a sanctuary space. You protect us from the zealots, vigilantes, psychotics, and your own crew."

They nodded. Nearly in unison.

"We've already done it," Quincy said.

"We're staying," Troy said, throatily. "If you're okay with that."

Genna clamped down on a tremble of relief. She nodded brusquely. "Then I need you to be bait for your parents. Go into the woods. Fight Olympia. She's got the bling I gave you. Get it back. Put it on. Use it to find the castle."

"Mom isn't a monster," Troy said.

"Pipsy's good at exploiting human weakness. Your mom is lonely, ambitious, and fed-up with the bullshit. She blames herself for your brothers and stepmom dying. Things have slipped from her control. We're all going to pay for that."

"We're are going to attack Pipsy tonight. It's Sable's revenge," Quincy said. "We've been planning it for a while. There might be some stranglers that come your way."

"That's why we came here to warn you," Troy said. "But you'd already locked the castle down. Nice security system."

"Whichever of your parents kills Pipsy will become a Montgomery," Genna said, "You need to be careful. There's a whole lot of power that goes behind that name."

"You're part of our family now," Quincy said, "We'll be parents together. You'll help us raise our child."

Genna shook her head. He was focusing on the wrong thing.

A howl pulled her attention back to the stables. "I need to protect my horses."

She closed the window and drove forward. The white fences of the paddocks on either side of the lane and the pasture grass beyond them was empty. Shifting shadows in the forest were obscured by hedge growth.

The Lexus bumped and shimmied as she went down the long, sloped lane to the stable. She shook off residual emotions and focused.

She had to save her horses.

Thirty-Nine

Genna pulled under the lit garage awning crowded with muddy SUVS, sedans, trucks, and other vehicles used by the stable. She grabbed her things, expecting something to jump out and grab her. Nothing did.

The horses were kicking their stalls and neighing. The dogs barked in their kennels.

The senior and junior staff were still on site, even though it was late. The farrier strode out to greet her, frowning severely. He was three times her age, didn't believe in texting, didn't like people, but was better with animals than anyone she'd ever met. The look he gave her ensemble was not complimentary. There were a few wearing Halloween scarves, but only Genna was dressed up. "What are you doing here? Shouldn't you be off at at Halloween party or something?"

It was a mental adjustment to talk to humans. Their faces seemed too pink and doughy, like puffed pastries with a bad attitude. "There are wolves in the forest."

"Those are wild dogs not wolves," the farrier scoffed, "Don't worry your pretty head about it."

She gritted her teeth. Only she got stared at instead of a respectful greeting. "But you know about them?"

"A pack of wild dogs got into the Farrows' stable and killed a bunch of the horses. It was a goddamn bloodbath."

"When was this?"

"Last week. We combed through the forest. Bupkis. I thought they'd moved on. I guess they're back for more."

"Are they rabid?"

"The vet doesn't think so. Some wild dogs are just born mean and get meaner."

"That's why you did locked up the dogs and horses?"

He sneered at her. "Look, I know you think that fancy training means something, but it won't do you a lick of good against a pack of wild dogs. All you'll do is get good horses hurt."

"Lady Belle?" a stable hand said, shocked. "What's she doing here?"

Howls in the forest. Genna's skin clenched. Tingles ran along her body. The werewolves were far too close. The horses whinnied, rearing and bucking in their stalls. The dogs barked, hurling themselves against the kennels. Scratching. Jumping on hind legs. Ignoring the humans trying to shush them with threats. Someone had needles, trying to get the dogs tranquilized.

"You need to get inside. It's not safe." The farrier patted her on the shoulder in an attempt to take her rifle.

Movement along the edge of the tree line. Something leaped over the pasture fence. Another slid under. Genna smacked the farrier's hand away, lined up her rifle, and fired when she saw light reflecting off of a pair of eyes. A yelp. Shadows scrambled back the way they came.

She turned to the farrier. "Don't you ever tell me how to run my stable! This is my castle and these are my goddamn horses. You don't pay for a goddamn cent. I *trained* them for this. Get my goddamn saddle and I'll get Sneakers before he kicks down the door. I want the horses and the dogs suited up by the time I finish with Sneakers, now!"

"But they might get hurt," a stablehand whined, her ponytail windblown.

Obviously, they mistook the horses attempting to kick their way through the walls and doors as fear not rage.

Genna whistled, a sharp command of *Pay attention!*

The dogs and the horses stopped their frenzying. They answered the command with quivering stillness. The stable hands turned around, staring at the horses like they had been betrayed.

"What the fuck?" the farrier said. "What'd you do to them?"

"What I trained them to do. Get the armor. Get them ready." Genna jerked a thumb toward the still whinnying and screeching side of the renters' stable. "You assholes take care of the other horses. The rest of you jackasses, remember your goddamn training! Who do you think can better handle what's out there? Us or a bunch of pissed-off and above all *trained* horses and dogs?"

"You can't be serious. It's all a joke," the farrier said.

"You think this is the first time I've had to deal with wild dogs? Hiding won't work. We've got to get out and fight!"

"You don't know what you're talking about."

Genna smacked him hard enough to knock him into the nearest stall wall. She grabbed his vest and roared in his face. "Wake to fuck up! This is happening! Do what I say now!"

He stared in mute horror at the ember light in her eyes and the sharpness of her teeth. There were plenty of rumors about Genna but her strength and rage six inches from his nose scared him worse than the howling outside.

Sneakers stomped and whinnied, impatiently kicking the half stall door. He demanded that she let him out right the fuck now.

Genna shoved the farrier away and hurried to the stall. "I know. I know. Back up so I can get you out," Genna said to the horse, grabbing his halter off the hook. He put his face down so she could snap it on. She had to push him back so she could unlock the door.

The farrier sagged. Several stablehands rushed to check on him and glared after her. He batted them away. "Get off me."

"You can't do this," another stablehand mumbled.

"Shut your bitch-ass up and get out of my way." Genna stormed over to the tack room.

Her saddle was different from the rest. It was decorated with tassels, bells, and little embroidered mirrors. She grabbed the halter and a few other things. Sneakers stamped impatiently as she cinched the saddle on. Then she added the underbelly protectors and neck straps. She unrolled the horse blanket and arranged the bow, arrows, and gun holster.

"This is crazy," a stablehand said loudly, glaring at Genna. "She can't do this!."

"Shut up and do it," the farrier said, spitting blood on the ground. "She's right. We need to turn the horses loose or they'll break their own legs."

"It was bullshit!"

"Horses doesn't know that. Dogs don't either. Look at this shit." The farrier waved expansively. "It's Halloween. There're wild dogs howling like—like—like fucking *werewolves* out there! She's dressed like the Red Riding Hood had a roadtrip through Africa. Why the fuck shouldn't the horses think they're Lancelot's noble steeds? The Farrows went to fucking Bali after those dogs killed their horses. They needed a spiritual cleanse or whatever. They left me to clean up the goddamn mess. It was the worst thing I've ever seen. If the princess thinks she can shoot those mutts, then she can go right on ahead."

"I'm not riding out there," a stablehand crossed her arms.

"Yeah, you are. Mommy Dearest will have my hide if anything happens to her princess."

"She shot that dog like it was nothing," another stablehand said. "What about the Bouvies?"

The farrier sucked and spat on the ground again. "Did you forget the cop training? They were war dogs in both world wars. A Bouvie bit Hitler. Do your job. Get them suited them up."

More mutters along the lines of *crazy bitch*, but everyone got to work. The stablehands complained, but their movements had smoothed out in purpose. Genna could be weird. They could be sane and beleaguered staff of an eccentric billionaire and put bells on all of the horses and dogs.

Genna kept cinching and fastening on armor. Sneakers stood like he had been molded out of bronze. The gear was not actually armor. Only decorative tassels, bells, and straps collected from traveling the world. She had it customized for Sneakers from bridle to belly band. The metallic sound of the bells and the weight helped Genna and the horse get into the proper mindset. The only time she used this saddle and gear was for warhorse training. It might be in her mind, but right now, as the howling got closer, as her stomach clenched at the reality of going out into the dark with a gun and no plan, and sweat slicked down the small of her back, the sound of bells calmed her.

Bibi whinnied. Genna whispered in her ear via the shadows. To lead the herd. To protect the land. She felt Schrodinger brush against her thoughts. He had not stopped watching Cleopatra's back. He would keep her safe now. Troy and Quincy were in the forest.

Grim, Toto, and Pirate were angry but were trapped inside the cottage. Katie had locked them in. The forest did not want its guardians involved. Schrodinger and the Mustang were in the cottage's garage. Genna was relieved. "Thanks for telling me."

The cat padded into the shadows to the cottage.

She stroked Sneakers along his thick withers. The smell of a freshly made stall. New sawdust. The pervasive smell of hay, urine, manure, and horse. She whispered to herself like a prayer, gilding the truth with a story instead of terror. She was a Black American Princess. There were werewolves in the forest. She needed to protect the things she loved. Her castle. Her horses.

Her trusty steed stomped his mighty hooves. He was ready. This was what they had been training for. She was glad she had taken him to Mongolia. Yes, he had been absurdly big, compared to the sturdy local horses, but her mother was right. Learning to ride on your own horse had built a trust that anchored her now.

She did not feel brave. She felt angry and scared and nauseous and extremely out of her depth. But she had to do something. She was doing right. However ridiculous.

"We should call animal control," a stablehand said.

Animal control would not get there in time. Maybe they would arrive as one horse got bitten. They would think it was a win instead of soul-destroying.

She had to do it. No one else would. Not these handwringing ninnies who wanted someone else to come in and do it. Who trusted a uniform more than their own instincts, while conversely believing they were superior. She was not like them. She was going to save everything.

Ten Bouviers trotted down the lane with two handlers holding thick leashes. Their curly coats packed into attack vests, neck protectors, and eye guards.

The Akita handlers came over. Also dressed. Their ears flicked at the howling. Tensed. Ready. A few barks and prancing, but that was nerves.

The farm dogs came with them. They were muddy and already pissed off to be wearing bite guards and bells but game. They scratched at the eye shields, shaking their heads, distracted.

"Take the eye guards off," Genna said, reaching down to free the nearest Bouvier. "They won't be able to see if they get mud on them. Trust the dogs."

The handlers glared. "Their eyes might get scratched."

"Take them off." Genna snapped her fingers. The eye shields undid themselves and fell to the ground.

Meanwhile, the farrier tried to check and tightened Sneakers' gear but recoiled when the warhorse tried to bite him. He was driven further back by stomped hooves and the clash of bells. He whinnied a warning, half-rearing. Genna had not tied Sneakers down. The farrier and the stablehands were forced to retreat.

Genna strode over to the dogs who stiffened to attention at her whistled command. She checked their armor. She ignored the wittering comments from the stablehands, who were red-faced with anxiety. The dogs were calmer than the humans. They focused on Genna. She was their pack leader. Her scent was determined.

"You go and see about the puppies and the others," Genna said.

"These are my fucking dogs—"

Genna snapped her fingers. Hard. Glared at the woman. "*No.*"

"If you—"

"*No!*"

The farrier walked over, giving her a way to back down. "Go see about the puppies."

"This is bullshit!" The stablehand still retreated. The others squeezed the leashes but unclipped them and followed her back to the kennels.

The farrier crouched, threaded his fingers together. Genna jumped without his help and swung across the saddle. Her skirts flared, revealing her armored pants. The farrier stared at her as she fluffed and adjusted her skirts. She made sure the quiver, bow, and the gun were easy to grab. She arranged the reins so they were out of the way.

Genna buckled the neck guard. She strapped on her helmet. The clasps snapped shut. She pushed the helmet low over her forehead. She tightened the helmet again until it felt like it was choking.

There was assault rifle gunfire out in the woods. Troy and Quincy had shown Genna their guns on lazy days in the gun range. They let her shoot them too. She knew their power. She hoped they were all right.

She had to set aside the tangled feelings about Cleopatra. Could she have handled Naomi better? Had she created an enemy when there had been an uncomfortable ally?

Troy and Quincy were focused on driving their parents away from the castle.

Pipsy had made Genna into her heir too. Now she was here to kill Genna, acknowledging that Genna had become a real threat.

The truth was that Katie wasn't evil. Katie was a monster, exactly as she was made and trained to be. She had no ambition beyond making brides because that was her entire purpose. She was a princess no one wanted to rescue. Pipsy made Katie and sent her out into the world to devour as much as she could. Now that Katie was ripe, Pipsy would eat her as she had eaten all of her heirs.

Mimi was a bitter husk. Kyle had been stripped for parts. Naomi and Sable were her heirs too. Miss Bootsie had saved the forest severing their connection.

Katie locking Toto, Pirate, and Grim in the cottage was a small gesture but it proved to Genna that she wasn't on Pipsy's side. There had to be a way to separate Katie from Pipsy. How did this all work together?

She had to let all of that go.

Two stablehands fussed over their horses but Sneakers raised his head, bulged a challenge. She whistled absently to the dogs and the horses. He shifted, half-reared; she quieted him with a squeeze of her thighs.

Genna fit the thumb ring onto her right hand. She was already focused beyond the brightly lit edge of the grass and pasture. Her hands traveled along the bundles of arrows, confirming their placement. She simulated how she'd grab an arrow and fire. She moved the saber. Undid the safety tie. She would use a rifle first but wanted to be ready.

The farrier tried to check the straps and cinch the saddle tighter but got zapped by electrical sparks. Then had to dodge a kick from Sneakers.

The farrier backed up to the stable door. He stared up at Genna. The transformation was subtle. The set of her face. The way she squared her shoulders and settled into the saddle. The way Sneakers flicked his tail and pranced so his bells jangled. His head high. His wavy black hair brushed her front while she checked her weapons again. His aggressive refusal to allow anyone close.

She no longer looked silly. She looked exactly like a noble princess on her warhorse, weapons ready and charging into battle. There was no fear. Only lethal determination. The farrier felt like a stupid old man too hidebound to know when to get out of somebody's way.

"You actually know what you're doing, don't you, princess?" the farrier said, in lieu of an apology. He held the stable door. "Go get them, princess. You shoot the fuck out of those fuckers. Don't worry about us. I'll send the rest along. I won't let you down."

Perhaps he expected her to sneer down at him, her lips curled in derision or blush prettily, embarrassed, as she took the rifle out of its holster. Genna did not hear him. She was listening to the howls. The farrier didn't matter. She could see the wolves loping along the edge of the field. Too many to count.

She whistled to the dogs and squeezed her thighs. Sneakers trotted forward into the darkness.

The farrier hastily closed the door. Then rushed to get the rest of the horses and dogs ready. The stablehands had stopped moving until he yelled at them.

Forty

IT WAS SURPRISINGLY EASY TO SEE AWAY FROM THE floodlights.

She saw eyes in the woods. The McBrides had come to watch.

Pipsy Montgomery lounged on a throne built on a tiered platform ten feet from the property line. She wore the same dress *My Fair Lady* pinstripes and ruffles she had worn to the engagement party. The same oversized hat and tired petticoats.

Naomi was on her left. Katie was on her right. They sat on lower stools. Pipsy had them leashed by IVs in their necks. Sable, Kyle, and Mimi were on the lowest part of the stage, cadaverously gray. The revenants formed a deep human wall.

Her other vampires wore dresses and ruffles as if they were on their way to the Kentucky Derby. Straw boater hats and bow ties for the men. Large flora bonnets for the women. They had come to watch the massacre.

Genna raised her gun. Thirty years of grief and rage and hate and fear pressured into diamond hard focus. Sneakers reared, whinnying his challenge while his great hooves boxed the air.

Pipsy smiled at Genna, taking a moment to savor the blood dripping from Katie's IV. "Why, Iphigenia Bellwether, you think that little gun is going to kill me?"

Sneakers slammed his hooves on the ground at the same moment that Genna fired. The recoil in her shoulder pushed down through her body.

The bullet hit Pipsy at the same moment a bolt of lightning struck. Pipsy gasped and toppled off of her throne, shrieking as her dress caught fire. Lightning flooded every veins. She transformed into a giant snake. Her weight broke the platform into splinters of cheap wood and burning muslin. Her scales were blackened and shedding to reveal raw flesh underneath. Her eyes were blinded, cataract gray. Her teeth snapped at the air and sprayed acid that melted nearby trees and revenants.

Mimi and Katie fell over, writhing and burning. Naomi and Sable whirled into air. Kyle oozed to put out his own flames. The vampires and revenants screeched as they disintegrated into burnt embers.

The McBride Mansion was aflame. Pipsy's minions in Sweetwater and beyond collapsed, clutching their hearts as their blood burned and their synapses misfired. Electrical fires ripped through the power grid. Pittsburgh and the areas not connected to a backup generator went dark.

Katie was the first to get back on her feet. She pounced on Pipsy with teeth and claws. Mimi, Sable, Naomi, and Kyle dogpiled the writhing charred snake. They ripped and tore at each other. Pipsy tried to eat them. Katie ripped her jaw off. Pipsy went down and did not get up again.

Meanwhile the revenants burned, running and shrieking. The light of their burning bodies momentarily illuminated the forest full of shifting furred bodies as werewolves flooded the pasture. Each werewolf was a huge beast. Their brown-gray fur blended in with the churned muddy grass.

The werewolves circled and barked at Sneakers. Their teeth were bared. They clawed up the dirt. They ran in opposite directions and tried to back Sneakers against the pasture fences and into the trees.

Her dogs drove the werewolves away from the stables. They

fought the werewolves in concerted units. Protecting the pasture had been their job for years. The dogs were faster than the were-wolves, not wasting time with transformation. Tangles of fights dotted the pasture.

Sneakers bugled his challenge. The werewolves attacked, but Genna and Sneakers moved as one mind and one big pissed off body. Every thought had smoothed out into purpose. Years of practice had her able to trust her horse without the reins. Genna held on as he bucked and kicked and stomped. Gravity was a mere suggestion. Her gun was at the ready. Her stomach was tense. The reinforced clothes shored up her strength as he twisted and leapt, free and wild. He reared. She held on. He leaped, she was ready. He tripped on a patch of mud or a gopher hole, and she shifted her weight to help him stand again.

Genna shot at any eyes reflected in the light. She loaded quick. She shot another werewolf coming up from behind. She shot any werewolf that got too close, the power of each bullet exploded on impact.

Old monsters ran out of the forest for the first time in centuries, freed from Pipsy's control. There were better things to eat less dangerous than Genna. But others ran for the horses because they were closer. To them, Genna was simply a girl with a gun. She shot the old monsters too. The lightning punched down, illuminating them for a moment before they burned fast and bright. Their death painted the forest in stark light as they ran back into the trees.

Sneakers was transcendent. He bit a werewolf and flung it up into the air. Genna shot it twice as it pinwheeled, squealing, through the air. Sneakers pirouetted and kicked it sideways. Bells jangled like a backbeat to their war dance.

Genna ran out of bullets faster than she hoped. A werewolf came at her ankle, teeth snapping at her skirts. She swung the rifle like a polo stick, clocking it right in the jaw. Sneakers landed with both feet on the werewolf. The strangled yelp was lost in a thunder of stomps.

She stowed the rifle and grabbed her bow and arrow in one smooth motion. She fired with more accuracy. She aimed for eyes. The werewolves looked like pincushions, but there was more of them, always more.

Genna's dogs did their best to keep the werewolves away from Sneakers. His black coat was slick with blood and sweat. His bells jangled and sparked as lightning jumped off the metal to electrocute a werewolf that bit his ankle. Genna shot the werewolf down its throat when it reared back with a blistered mouth.

When Genna ran out of arrows, she stowed the bow and unsheathed her calvary saber. She had to be more careful with the saber. Sneakers was tall. If she leaned down too far, she might fall or haul on the reins, messing with his movements. Instead, she sat, sword poised to chop or stab. Her long cloak and skirts caught a few misses instead of cutting herself or the horse.

A thunder of hooves behind her. The farrier had finally let the horses and the rest of the dogs out of left the stable in a solid stream. Bibi led the herd, her own Mongolian war gear ringing at she galloped. Groundhogs and small rodents fled their holes, escaping the earthquake as hundreds of hooves churned the ground. The riders were in the front, fanning outward, screaming bloody murder, firing wildly, and driving the werewolves and dogs before them. Bullets whizzed past Genna. The jangle of bells was a cacophonous wave of sound.

The werewolves sprinted to get out of the way, many back into the forest. They leapt over the charred remains of the remnants and scrambled over the platform. The McBrides were a tangle of hunger, ripping and fighting each other to eat more of Pipsy while she tried to shake them off.

The horses emptied the pasture. Sneakers raced to join them. His muscles moved like oiled pistons, pounding into the ground, throwing Genna forward. She stowed the bow and focused on steering. Even with her experience, her entire focus was holding on tight. She leaned on Sneakers, guiding him and the herd in a wide circle, giving the werewolves a way out if any were smart enough to retreat. Not all did. Many attacked and were trampled.

The herd had transformed into a full-blown stampede. A few stablehands fell off and were trampled. She kept ahead, goading Sneakers to run faster, steering him away from the forest to the trail between the pasture fence and the trees, up towards the castle. They needed to check the rest of the property for stray werewolves.

The herd narrowed down into twos and threes. They charged up the long slope. Sure enough, there were more werewolves trying to break into the castle. She must have walked right over them on her way to the garage. The herd trampled them as they pounded the gardens into the broken branches. The perfume of herbs and flowers were a welcome change to blood and dogs.

The herd ran past the nine mansions. Through the farmland. Along the secondary buildings and storage warehouses. Werewolves fled or were trampled. None got close enough to kill with the saber. She led the herd back down the hill towards the stable.

A single howl drifted out of the forest. A deeper bass menace. Power rolled over the pasture in a cold rush of a breeze that whipped past fast enough to yank their manes and tails straight. The dogs yelped and the horses squealed with fear and lost their rhythm. The stampede broke apart. The dogs fled.

Genna held onto Sneakers as the arctic chill turned her sweat into ice. It was like being swept up in a tsunami of freezing water. Her skin prickled with familiarity. Her nose and ears told her that it was the direwolf she had heard while in the castle.

Sneakers slowed in the pasture, his ears up and nostrils blowing. The herd clustered behind him. He pawed the suddenly frozen ground, chipping blades of frosted grass. He was not afraid of this new enemy. Steam rose from his sides. Fire banked in his flaming eyes. Smoke in his mane. His magic reacted to the direwolf.

The wind was colder than cold. It clawed at her lungs. Hoarfrost dusted Sneakers as his flame was snuffed out. He shivered.

His mane was edged in icicles. The blood from his wounds and sweat of exertion hardened painfully. Her lips were chapped. The churned mud below crackled under hoof and turned sharp.

Then the breeze stopped. The trees stilled. The forest took an indrawn breath.

The direwolf padded out of the forest. He was impossibly big. His ears were the same height as the tree tops. His gigantic proportions made no sense. Gravity should have slowed down his movements but instead he was as light on his paws as a dancer. His fur was silverly white and pale blue like snow on the top of an iceberg. He reared back, his muscles shunting into shape. He was humanoid and lupine mixed together. His claws were like black sickles. Even in this gloom she could see that he was a male.

The direwolf roared. It sounded so loud that Genna felt like she had been ripped open. Katie, the other McBrides, and the werewolves who had paused to watch their direwolf's arrival fled into the woods.

The direwolf attacked Pipsy's remains, ripping the snake into bits and gulping down the pieces. His throat expanded to fit each mouthful. He roared as he chewed. He licked the ground. He beat the platform to pieces with his mighty fists.

The herd huddled together, afraid to move. Sneakers was stiff and quivering.

Genna had no more bullets. No more arrows. The saber in her hand felt like a metal toothpick. She felt very small and very alone. She had already poured her everything out into the bullet that fried Pipsy. Now there was nothing left. Only an exhausted woman on a tired black horse. She rubbed Sneakers along his neck, using her body warmth to melt the ice crusting his mane. He relaxed at her touch and tossed his head. Genna smiled at her noble steed.

That was the thing about death. You were alive until it happened. No warning. No ability to dodge or change.

Forty-One

GENNA HAD NEVER SEEN ANOTHER DIREWOLF LIKE HIM before. The Old Night was made of moonless shadows. She was scary but familiar. This direwolf was an enemy and here to kill her. Magic snowed off of him. The trees crackled as they froze. Their leaves fell so there was nothing to obscure his silvery bulk as he chewed the last of Pipsy's bones.

Pipsy had protected her from the direwolf. She kept him outside of the forest. Now Pipsy wasn't here to keep him at bay.

Genna knew she should be scared. Nothing had gone according to plan. She hadn't killed Pipsy with her supercharged bullet, only winged her enough for Katie to get the jump on her. The damn werewolves had not died when she shot them. Now here was this asshole. The Big Bad Wolf had watched and waited while Red Riding Hood tired herself out doing the dirty work. Now he expected to eat her horses.

She could smell the herd's ripe fear. The heat of life blooming bright on this cold windswept pasture. The stable felt far away and no safety either. The forest was full of werewolves.

If this were a cowboy movie, this was that moment of truth when the hero gunslinger squared off against her true enemy. No more running. No more distractions. It was High Noon on this moonless night. And Genna was pissed off.

Fuck this guy. Fuck his army of werewolves. Fuck his ice magic. Fuck his ugly red dick that he waggled at her when he reared back to howl. She was going to kill him.

She lifted her sword and stabbed at the sky as rage eclipsed thought. She hauled on Sneakers, spurring him into a rear. He punched at the air, dancing on his hind legs, whinnying his own challenge as Genna screamed. *"Stay out!"*

Her chest was hot. The snarled command tore at her throat. "I will kill you! You will never get what you want here. I won't let you! You will never touch a hair on their heads. They are mine and mine alone! This castle is mine. These animals are mine. *Never come here again!"*

Lightning filled the sky with a theatrical purple flash spidering across the forest and pasture. She pointed the sword at the forest. Her jewelry stuffed in her pockets clashed together, humming with gold curse magic. The metal in her clothes spat sparks from wild magic. Her cloak fluffed and flared back in a gust of wind with boo hag magic.

The forest answered her rage. Her power spread out. The castle was her crown. The forest and the castle grounds were the folds of her dress. The nine mansions and onsite buildings were ornamental jewelry. The billowing smoke in her hair braided with purple lightning. The herd echoed Sneakers, whinnying and stomping. Bibi jockeyed the herd into defensive formation. The castle dogs closed ranks, baying their threats.

Another crack of lightning. Magic chased up her saber. It became the cottage's kitchen knife. A weapon she knew how to use. It was coated in Katie's blue blood. Her blood. The cloak flashed red.

The truth of her magic poured up through the ground, the power of it roaring like a tide of fire, the certainty of actions. In the whole wide world, this place, this castle, the pastures, the forest, and the animals inside it were hers. Nothing and no one got to be there.

The forest was there. The Old Night shook off the film of ice and howled as Genna howled. Sweetwater rallied. Old things. Nameless things. Elemental. All of it fighting to protect their territory.

Sneakers slammed down onto his front legs. It caused a shock-wave, a force field speeding outward in front. Genna's magic became a direwolf made of wildfire and lightning. Her wrath poured out beyond the forest. The horses and dogs became part of that wildfire. The thunder of their hooves broke the land apart. Their speed was an explosion, covering every inch of ground with hoof prints. Power caught everything hostile up like leaves in snow.

The werwolves yelped and ran with their tails between their legs. They hid behind the ice direwolf.

In the forest, the monster hunters and witch finders were at war with the werewolves and vampires. Troy and Quincy valiantly kept their own people away from the castle. The sudden fire caused Olympia, Camille, and Reginald to throw up shields but were knocked aside. Magic washed over Troy and Quincy, healing and enhancing. The lightning wolf and the nightmares stampeded across the Heights. Down Backbone. Into Sweetwater. The fire devoured every werewolf, vampire, and monster that had escaped the woods.

The ground bucked. A portion of the mountain collapsed. Hundreds of thousands of tons of rock and dirt swept over the highway, across the railroad tracks, and down into the Ohio River. The landslide effectively cut Sweetwater off from Pittsburgh and the world at large. The narrow two lane Sweetwater bridge did not break but it changed. Lightning jumped along the spires and down into the stone and lattice of the bridge. Cars and phones died. The Ohio River shimmered for a moment, like light reflected off of an oil spill.

In an airfield, Genna's plane transformed into a silver and

white falcon. It flapped up into the night, winging for the forest. The other planes melted into smoking husks.

The lightning rebounded off of the town border. It raced back through Sweetwater. The fires caused by exploding electronics were snuffed out. The burned victims were healed. Those crushed under collapsed masonry were remade as the buildings rebuilt themselves. Babies were born. The sick healed. Animals howled. People changed as secrets in their blood woke up.

Genna spread her hand out. She erected an invisible force field around the property line. She knew where it ended. Not legally but where she believed it did. Right at the edge of the golf course and where the trees became grass on the other side of the forest in every direction. Everything inside of that, the small river, the hills, the forest, was hers. It caged the ice direwolf inside with her too.

Katie was there, hiding in the trees. Her skin was flushed from drinking Pipsy's power. Katie shrieked as she was incinerated. She fled the wildfire and dove into the cottage.

The forest grew, expanding fast to accommodate all the power. Things crushed between trees. Roots leapt like anacondas from the soil. The creek became a river. Waterfalls born.

The silver direwolf watched it all. Mist rose from his fur. His pervasive chill spread into the forest. It doused the flaming werewolves. They climbed back to their feet, shaken and furious. His muzzle was smooth. His ears were up. His fur was fluffed. His tail was bushy. Genna knew that look. He wasn't intimidated by her firepower, he was aroused.

He howled, a gross sexual come-on folded in with his challenge. He spoke Old Growl, the ancient language of direwolves. He told her what he was going to do to her and how he was going to do it.

Genna was revolted. She pointed the knife at him and snarled in Old Growl. *"Come and get it."*

The thunder echoed her animosity overheard. The storm overheard was swollen with their warring hot and cold magic.

He charged out of the forest. One moment still. The next

barreling down on her. Given the time between each stride, she had seconds before he pounced.

She spun Sneakers and he kicked, both hooves out, full-power into the direwolf's shoulder, diverting all of his forward momentum sideways. Sneakers spun. His muscled hip caught the direwolf across the jaw and neck, a strategic strike that knocked him off course. Then Sneakers skidded him in the throat. Then his front hooves skidded under him on a patch of ice.

Genna was still thrusting forward down the long pink interior of the direwolf's mouth. She intended to pierce his brain through the back of his mouth. Then his jagged yellow teeth closed on Genna's forearm.

Pain. Bright and brittle agony. The mangled remains of her arm was crushed inside the armored plating sleeve. The torque of her shoulder. The wet pop of her bones as they broke before the skin did. The sleeve created wrinkles in the wrong place. The faintest message from her fingers that her hand was still clamped around the knife which was stuck in his soft pallet but not enough to penetrate. The furry wall of his lips and the cold wet his nose smushed against her face.

Sneakers kept spinning, twisting and bucking. His powerful shoulders slewed him sideways. His teeth clamped down on a wayward hairy front leg. He yanked the direwolf under, stomping up the exposed belly, kicking and biting the direwolf's soft underbelly, trampling his nuts. The direwolf roared and fought the warhorse.

Genna was flicked into the air. There was a long terrible moment when her feet were pointed at the sky, her knees still bent, her posture still perfect as if she were riding the clouds and lightning. The blur of mud, silver fur, and she slammed into the ground. then brand-new agony in the base of her spine as two thousand pounds of pissed-off stallion stomped her left thigh into the direwolf's belly. The skin of her arm tried to rip free of her torso. Her pelvis was crushed. Her hips popped. She was kicked off the direwolf. The sharp jab of frozen mud.

Movement around her as big paws and hooves dug at the ground.

Genna lay where she landed like a broken porcelain marionette. Her face was covered in blood, still protected by her helmet. Her arm was oozing pulp. Her leg was bent the wrong way. Her torso was a balloon full of broken bones. Blood filled the wrong places. Her armored corsetry had provided minimal protection. Pain was her world.

Sneakers bugled his outrage, squalling pain as the direwolf's back claws ripped open his belly. The slop of intestines splashed hot on her face. A bunch of werewolves swarmed over Sneakers, smaller than the direwolf. They pulled him down. Their teeth clamped onto his throat, his haunches, his legs. More, always more. Sneakers fought them all. The direwolf ate the werewolves while he tried to gore Sneakers.

Then a blinding light. The direwolf bellowed. The stink of burning fur. Burnt werewolves littered the ground. Their heads separated from their bodies.

Troy stood over Genna, howling with rage. He was made of blue lightning. A sword in one hand and a lasso made of lightning in the other. Quincy hauled the direwolf in the opposite direction. He was on his Clydesdale's back, the horse pulling the hogtied direwolf between the two opposing ropes. Troy hacked and cut. The direwolf's body was now in hacked chunks. A front leg hung off by a few furred strips. His back legs were not working. Spine was caved in. His magic steamed off of him as the lasso crushed him down to his physical body. He was smaller than his first appearance. Still big at a warhorse but no longer fantastical.

The rest of the herd attacked the direwolf. Bibi, the appaloosa, and the Clydesdale stomped and kicked while the other horses kept the werewolves at back. The dogs attacked, darting in and out to bite. Quincy kept the lasso tight, hauling backwards.

Troy put his hand on Genna's chest. She was filled with the raging ocean of his love, his fear, his rage, and his despair.

"Live!" Troy commanded. "You must live!"

If that first time in Chicago felt like a waterfall. This was a Category 5 hurricane as Quincy added his own earth and water magic.

Genna screamed, as weird, slurping, inverted agony poured through her broken body. She curled and uncurled, thrashing as her shattered bones leapt back together. Her blood returned to reknit veins. Her tendons regrew like wild vines twisting back together. Lightning jumped between them as Troy gave her more and more. The mounting block was a nexus of lightning, arcing between them.

Sneakers staggered to his feet as magic wrapped around him. His guts recoiled into his belly. His mane dripped with blood. His big hooves splayed to keep himself standing. Troy and Quincy's magic covered the horses and dogs, lifting them up and sweeping away from the pasture to shove them into the stables and seal the door shut. They added a wall of mud on top and surrounded the stable with protective power.

Then the direwolf healed in a burst of arctic air. That momentary distraction of saving Genna and Sneakers was his opportunity to break free of the lightning lassos.

Troy and Quincy fell back. Their fronts were covered with a sheet of ice. The direwolf launched at them like an iced torpedo. Troy stabbed the direwolf in the mouth as Genna had stabbed. Only he dodged and chopped at the direwolf's neck, intending to behead. The direwolf bit his side with teeth coated in icicles. Troy bellowed but kept stabbing. The direwolf transformed, rearing up like a bear as his paws became hands. His claws ripped open Troy's back and broke his arms.

Quincy was behind the direwolf, swinging at his legs and the base of his tail with a double-headed ax. The direwolf threw Troy aside. Quincy gathered his magic to pull water into his control. Troy healed as he spun through the air and attacked the direwolf again with bolts of blue lightning.

Quincy's swing was stopped by two furred bodies. A were-grizzly's tree-trunk hand smacked Quincy in the head while a werewolf grabbed his ankle and ran the opposite direction. Quincy slammed to the ground and was dragged away into the forest. He turned into a swamp dragon. The grizzly and werewolf sank into the sudden quagmire. Quincy slashed and bit his attackers. Then erupted out of the swamp, jaws out, and grabbed the direwolf again, trying to drag him under.

Cleopatra landed on the silver direwolf in a blur of golden magic. She was a dragon. She used Quincy's swamp magic to create a funnel as her wings pumped. The direwolf's howl of challenge was cut off as she stabbed him in the throat with her spear shaped tail. Quincy held his other side, twisting his limbs. They dragged him into the swamp, holding him splayed on his back.

Troy became a red direwolf of blood and lightning. He bit through the direwolf's hamstrings and gutted him.

Expect the direwolf healed as quickly as he was injured. He froze Cleopatra and Quincy in their own swamp. They bellowed as their blood turned to ice. Their dragon scales fell off.

Troy dodged the direwolf's teeth. His lightning crackled across the direwolf's ice fur. It freed Quincy and Cleopatra from their swamp. Cleopatra, Troy and Quincy's magic roared out in a hurricane. Waves of mud and lightning engulfed the werewolves and coated the direwolf.

But the direwolf shook his attackers off. He turned everything into ice. The trees burst from the drop in temperature. The land cracked. Grass turned into blades of ice. He encased the three hunters in an iceberg.

Sweetwater screamed as it froze.

The mud washed over Genna too. She felt as raw and vulnerable as a shucked oyster. Nothing but gooey skin. A ragged red and black cloak. Her human body had healed but she was too weak to move. There was no wolf. No fire magic. Nothing but a woman in a muddy dress.

The silver direwolf had skillfully snuffed out her magic. Everything that Troy and Quincy had poured into her had passed through instead of staying.

Genna watched him attack Troy, Quincy, and Cleopatra with blurry eyes. Their magic wasn't working. The negation of their power was too effective.

Again she tried to Turn into a wolf. Into fire. Into anything. All she could do was bleed.

It wasn't ice magic. It was a containment spell. The direwolf was using magic, *human* magic nullifying their power.

Troy screamed as the direwolf chewed into the avalanche. Quincy and Cleopatra moaned.

Genna concentrated, wiping mud off her face. Under her cold skin was a whole lot of hellfire mad. Under the ice was still her Sweetwater. The direwolf had come to take her territory and she was still alive. He thought he had won. That was why he was focused on killing a bunch of monster hunters and witch finders.

The hyperthermic chill ebbed as she lit her own candle. The ground softened under her. The ice melted from her bloody ragged clothes.

The fur cloak gave its last magic to transform her into a coywolf. Small and ragged but herself. The ashes of the cloak blended with her black and gray fur.

She pushed herself to her feet. She shook herself off. Her fur fluffed. Her ears pressed back against her skull. Her tail puffed. She growled as she paced toward the direwolf. She howled an insult in Old Growl, a sweet song of derision. It was the human equivalent of, "Is that the best you can do, you weak-ass bitch-baby?"

It was a stupid tactic, all swagger and no muscle behind it, but amazingly it worked. The direwolf spun and snarled an avalanche of predictable masculine fury. Troy, Quincy, and Cleopatra were forgotten. He was furious. She was supposed to be dead.

Genna laughed like a coyote, interrupting his sleeting storm of curses. She pawed the ground, head up, chest puffed with dominant arrogance. She was a queen. This was her land, she proclaimed. He was nothing but a pathetic bully. She howled a challenge.

The direwolf attacked with a roar, no longer elegant but wild with fury. Slobbering on himself. Blood foaming between his teeth.

She spotted the hilt of the kitchen knife still inside his mouth, sunk into the soft pallet like a splinter.

He charged, his mouth opened wide to swallow her whole. The same move he used the first time and again on Troy. He howled for her death. His hatred was sharp and cold.

Genna dodged his bite and launched upward. She unleashed her magic in a volcanic eruption narrowed to a tight angry stream. She hit him through the throat right where the knife had penetrated. She pierced his brain with her fire and diamond sharp teeth and the knife's forged steel. A superheat blast of power melted his ice into steam and flood water.

The direwolf collapsed into water. Instantly dead.

Genna landed in a large puddle that once was a direwolf. She was in her human form and holding a kitchen knife. Her clothes had also sewn themselves back together. She surveyed the pasture, ready to kill anything and anyone.

It began to rain.

GENNA STOOD IN THE RAIN. THE MIST SPREAD AROUND her and roiled off of her skin. For a moment the mist resembled a white dress and the rain in her wild curls looked like diamonds.

Bellwether castle sparkled like a freshly polished gemstone. The grass grew lush. The fruit plumped. The gardens sprouted anew. The wounds of the battle were smoothed over by mud.

Genna spotted enormous frogs swimming along the flash flood. Naomi, Sable, and Kyle surfed the last dregs of the direwolf's hostile magic out of the pasture. A creek formed down the trail mouth into the forest like a dark, gaping throat guzzling in the water from Genna's land. The water ate its way through the trees. The bodies were swept away. Their ashes became part of the mud and left nothing but silence of rain.

The grass turned yellow across the McBride Mansion. The leaves rotted off the trees and fell under the onslaught of rain. Small things died inside the trees. The trees split and toppled, exposing their rotten roots. Brittle branches dropped, breaking smaller growth. Sap became fuzzy green rot. The rot spread through the mansion, lapping and sucking what it could not immediately eat. The last of the revenants died. The humans in cages died. Their bodies rotted off the bones. Gray fungus and black mold spread between the tiles and across the walls. Most of the mansion was stone, but the furniture became spongy with rot. Katie's paintings molded off the walls. The ceiling cracked then caved in. The pool congealed into fetid brown sludge with a scum of algae bloom softening the stone. The mansion rotted like a dead tooth. Mud and rain and moss covered the land. The secret lairs dissolved under the deluge. The road cratered. The ground eroded under the porch. The floodwater gouged out the foundations, revealing bones buried in the ground. McBride Mansion collapsed into rusted rebar at the bottom of a widening sinkhole.

The water pushed bones out of the ground. They swept into the forest, flowed along the flash flood, and scraped bark off the trees. The bones became a part of the bracken clogging creek beds. They lined the slick slopes of mud, like teeth lining the inside of a snapping turtle's throat.

The frogs escaped the forest with the water that poured out through the Heights, down Backbone, and swallowed Sweetwater proper. It flooded the country club and overflowed every pool, fountain, and pond. The damp and wet suppressed the fires still burning. The water flowed down into the Ohio River. It caused several smaller mudslides.

Naomi, Sable, and Kyle nabbed anyone they could as they swam in the malevolent flood water. They did not go gently and dragged who they could grab by their ankles and shove them into their big mouths. The malevolent water buried humans in mud, swallowed screams, and trapped many inside of buildings to drown while they tried to breathe against the ceiling. The water emptied into the Sweetwater cemetery. It washed around Miss Bootsie's mausoleum. The ground crumbled in the cemetery.

Two black oak trees erupted from the muddy water on either side of Miss Bootsie's mausoleum. The branches reached up. Some of the branches intertwined like praying fingers. Others clawed beseeching at the sky. Many branches spread outward. Some planted themselves back into the ground, shielding the building below. It cast the mausoleum in shadows as the forest remembered when there had been no manicured lawn and uniform lines of headstones. The trees drank the malevolent water.

The bones settled into the cemetery wall. It created a dam. The finer bones moved to the edge of the cemetery. The wall built slower, spreading wider. It created a protection against the wild magic from the forest. The last of the direwolf's death spell dissipated in the rain. Leaves, bracken, and dirt thickened the screen until only sweet water filtered through.

Kyle cut himself as he hopped over the headstones. Naomi and Sable lingered for a moment, dragging their hands along the rough bark of the twinned trees.

"Goodbye Mama," Sable croaked.

"Ciao, Grams," Naomi said, "Nice wearing you."

Then they hopped past the bones piling up around the mausoleum.

Naomi and Sable caught up with Kyle as he dove into the Ohio River on a slipstream by the Sweetwater bridge. The landslide still dumped dirt and rock into the water. They had to swim carefully to get down river. Only to swim right into a golden net. They tried to break free as they were pulled into a boat by a dark-skinned woman in a white dress and white headscarf.

There were gold bangles on Tituba's wrists all the way up to her elbows. Gold earrings pulled down her earlobes. Gold around her neck. A belt of woven gold. Gold around her ankles of her bare feet. Gold rings on her toes. Gold in her teeth. Gold piercings through her nose and eyebrows.

Kyle attacked and was skewered on a pole. Naomi fought and thrashed as she was trussed up then was stuffed into a cage. Tituba grabbed Sable by the shoulder. The frog skin sloughed off like mud. "It's over."

Sable down on a wicker chair in the back of the boat with an exhausted slump. A trembling grip on Tituba's wrist. "I just want to get back to the Waffle House with my daughter."

"The Waffle House is gone, Sable," Tituba said. "There's no going back."

Sable stared up at Tituba, haggard and angry. Then noticed Genna watching in the mist. Sable stood up, gathering handfuls of hurricane magic. "Get away from us, you bitch!"

Tituba dissipating her spell. "None of that now. Iphigenia Bellwether is no threat to you."

"What do you mean? Did you see what she did to Naomi? You can't trust her!"

"I can trust that she wants you out of Sweetwater as much as you want to leave. Now help me with this frog." Tituba smirked at Genna as she and Sable skewered Kyle a second time and put him on a spit. "We're having frog legs for dinner to celebrate your triumph, Miss Iphigenia. You've done well."

"So we're square?" Genna demanded. "No more gold curse bullshit?"

"You will have a beautiful daughter. Aaliyah will be just like you. Naomi will make her a beautiful dress."

"What about them?" Genna nodded at Naomi and Sable. "Do we have a problem?"

"Don't you worry about me and mine," Tituba said. "We're going home."

Then mist shrouded the boat. Genna sneezed. The magic faded. The river emptied of anything but muddy water.

The rain increased. Genna was alone in the pasture, far away from the Ohio River. She wanted to sit down but forced her legs to keep moving. She walked towards the creek.

Troy, Quincy, and Cleopatra pushed themselves out of the mud, climbing up the steep slope and into the pasture. They staggered over and hugged Genna, too exhausted for caution, words, or balance. She was kissed. Throughly and sloppily with mouths filled with mud. She wiggled at Cleopatra's tight hug.

"I'm sorry! I'm so sorry!" Cleopatra sobbed. "You were right!"

"It's alright. You're okay." Genna hugged her as their knees gave out. They slipped. Fell together. Splashed in mud.

"Ow," Genna said, squashed under Cleopatra until she rolled off.

Troy grabbed Genna the moment she sat up. He caged her inside of his arms and knees. He rocked in place. His forehead against her scalp. He shook slightly. She petted his cheek. Troy exhaled shakily. He petted Genna and kissed her face. "Thanks for saving us."

"That was amazing," Quincy said. Since Troy would not let Genna go, Quincy hugged him too. Cleopatra settled for holding onto Genna's ankle. She flopped back.

"Christ, I need a bath," Cleopatra muttered.

"I thought you loved mud," Genna said.

"There's mud and there's mud," Cleopatra said.

"Oh I'm hurt," Quincy moaned, massaging his shoulder. "My neck. My back. My neck and my back."

The others chuckled at the *Friday* reference. None of them tried to get up. The rain only spread the mud more evenly. It tasted a little salty, like tears. Genna squinted up, relieved to be alive.

Sneakers plodded over. He splashed them with more mud and ignored their annoyed but half-hearted yells. He lipped at Genna's hair. He nickered, demanding to know why Genna did not have the sense to come out of the rain. Bibi, Troy's Appaloosa, and Quincy's Clydesdale added to the investigation. The rest of the herd ranged around them. The dogs yipped and shook themselves.

The rain had defused the mud protection over the stable. The dogs woofed happily. Their wounds were healed.

Genna did a headcount. It was a miracle. Her horses and her dogs had all survived.

Sneakers lowered his head so Genna could curl her fingers in his mane. He lifted her to her feet. He walked her slowly. Bibi helped Cleopatra. Troy and Quincy slung their arms across each other and their horses' shoulders. They wobbled towards the stable.

Genna stared at the castle. "Let's go to the stable. I'm not ready to test my knees on that slope."

"You ain't lying," Quincy said.

Bibi and Sneakers led them into stable. Genna took a moment to put her hand on the mounting block. She felt a pulse of warmth. Hot. Healing. A little strength returned to her legs. The last of the direwolf's chill touch was absorbed. The enemy was defeated. Genna sat down on the mounting block. She needed a moment. More magic warmed her from the inside.

Troy, Quincy, and Cleopatra also touched the mounting block. They inhaled sharply as Sekhmet snarled. Troy whistled.

Quincy nudged Cleopatra. "Told you."

She scoffed at him, cranky, as she twisted her hair into a loose braided crown. "I don't want to hear it."

"I wonder if I should've talked to the direwolf," Genna said.

"That's just the survivor's guilt talking," Cleopatra said.

"That direwolf was a wolf king," Troy said. "He would've eaten you up and moved on."

"He was sent here. Pipsy used the werewolves as cannon fodder."

"Do you want werewolves in your castle?" Quincy said.

"No, but I could've reached out."

"Just because you're both direwolves doesn't mean he gets you," Cleopatra said.

Genna rubbed the edge of the mounting block. Sneakers lipped at her hair, and pushed his big nose against her neck. Genna hugged Sneakers. "Well done."

Sneakers bumped her chest. They had both done well. She stood up. They made their way down to the locked stable door.

Troy brushed Genna's hand. For once his eyes had lost their blue glow. "You did what you did. You trusted your gut. You didn't hesitate."

"I had to keep the horses safe." Genna threaded her fingers with his. "I couldn't let him eat you three."

She leaned briefly against his chest. He tucked his nose against her ear. The tickle of his breath. She looked around the castle grounds. The werewolves were gone. Everything was fine. Her people were safe. It was over. She had won.

"I'm so glad you're okay," she said, a warble of insecurity. Troy hugged her tighter.

"Thanks to you," Cleopatra said.

Quincy smirked. "What did you say to him that made him drop us?"

Genna shrugged. "It doesn't translate well."

They walked into the stable via the far end. The door unlocked itself and slid open. She touched every stall, making sure each horse food and brushed down. The dogs got back to their kennels safely. Troy, Quincy, and Cleopatra helped her towel them off.

The tedious normalcy of chores helped her anchor back into her body. She measured out grain. She took extra time to groom Sneakers down. She checked his hooves. She combed out his tail and his mane. She gave him an abundance of treats. Sneakers nickered, his eyelashes fluttering. His ears flicking. He was drowsy, relaxing into her hands.

She caught sight of her reflection in the tack room bathroom. She stared at herself. She looked like herself. Muddy. Tired. But otherwise unchanged.

Genna hastily washed her hands and dabbed her face relatively clean. She wondered where the saddle went. Her helmet, gun, bow, and saber were lost in the flood and fight. They had served their purpose.

She looked up the hayloft to find it full of cats and dogs who had been put there by the stablehands. The rafters rustled with birds. Pirate patrolled the hayloft, he squawked at her imperiously. She spotted her silver falcon keeping the great horned owls from eating the other raptors.

Troy, Quincy, and Cleopatra met her in the juncture between the stables and the apartments.

"All of the humans are in Naomi's spot," Cleopatra pointed at the barricaded door.

The stablehands hid in Miss Bootsie's apartment. Genna could hear *Beauty & the Beast* blaring from the television. The volume was turned up to its highest setting, rattling the plastic speakers. Lit candles of all shapes and sizes covered every flat surface in front of the door. The apartment hallway smelled like burnt popcorn.

"We could leave them in there?" Quincy suggested.

"No, they're still my staff." Genna sighed. "I'll tell them that the coast is clear."

The humans yelped and scrambled away when the door opened itself for Genna. The barricades of furniture and nailed wood removed itself.

"It's okay," Genna said, trying to shout above the screams.

Cleopatra yanked Genna backwards into the stable. Troy and Quincy charged forward. Two blurs of movement.

Muffled thunder of gunfire.

Cleopatra slammed Genna against a wall, wrapped around her, scales and wings blocked the light. The hard impact against the wall, the full weight of a protective dragon on Genna's already fragile body made her black out.

SCREAMS WOKE GENNA UP. SHE WAS ON MISS BOOTSIE'S bed in her apartment. She was naked and sticky from the ointments Quincy dabbed on her body. She felt like a dragonfly that had hit the windshield of a speeding semi-truck. It hurt to blink.

And Quincy was a werewolf the size of a grizzly bear. His fur was black and brown.

"You're a werewolf?" She whispered.

"Yep." His little shrug failed to hide his nervousness. The constant micro-movements of his ears and fur implied that he was genuinely afraid of her now.

Genna tried to sit up. She paused to groan through clenched teeth. Quincy stopped her with a firm hand and helped her lie back down. "Hey, take it easy."

She looked around, her tired eyes focusing.

Miss Bootsie's apartment looked like a slaughterhouse kill floor. Bodies littered the floor. Hacked limbs still held rifles and handguns. There were bullet holes and shotgun blasts along the walls and doors. Motes of couch stuffing and clothing soaked puddles of blood. Impact craters turned the floor into an obstacle course.

The shelves of VHS tapes had melted together. All of the

furniture were blackened. Only the cracked glass screen remained of the television. Its electronics inside were melted into slag. The vinyl record player and microwave were smashed apart.

Someone in the bathroom was alive enough to scream. Those screams had woken Genna up. His gargled begging was interrupted by heavy impact. Several times.

"What's going on?" Genna asked. "Is that the farrier?"

"Cleopatra is asking questions," Quincy said. Another nervous glance at Genna. "She's upset."

"Was I shot?" Genna said, searching her body but finding smooth skin.

"It was whiplash. Cleopatra is the fastest and strongest of us. She squeezed you a little too tight and moved a little too quick to get you out of harms way. When you hit the wall, you kind of...burst."

"She's got a great ass too," Genna said, trying to minimize her own pain. She tried to get comfortable but the bed was too soft. She wished she was laying on the floor. Blood and all.

She brushed Quincy's furred wrist. He smelled like her pack. "What happened? Did I bite you?"

"You were hurt. You needed to feed." He brushed her forehead, implying that a whole lot else was wrong but was spoonfeeding her truths. "Here."

He spread what smelled like Vics VaporRub on her forehead. It tingled her skin. Genna remembered.

Gunfire and shouting. Cleopatra's panicked voice as Genna lay in her arms. Troy, Quincy, and Cleopatra arguing while their hurricane magic whirled around her, creating a vortex. Then Old Night grabbed them all teeth first. Shadows filled the apartment and devoured their defensive spells.

The Old Night curled around Genna with fur soft as smoke. The black direwolf was big and bloody. Her wounds were recently healed. She had been hurt by the silver direwolf. She licked Genna all over with a motherly tongue. Only instead of saliva, Genna was bathed in pure wild magic. It hurt but it was a good pain. A healing pain. Full of complicated grief and love. Genna was hungry like a newborn. Her body burst open, shedding its skin. She transformed from wolf to woman to dragon to coyote, growing another skin, again and again.

Then brown muscled flesh was pressed against her mouth. She bit down on Quincy's shoulder. She forgot everything but eating. She ripped tendons and muscles. She slurped, gobbled, growled and dug down into his chest to get his liver. Quincy's broad hands squeezed her back until she winced and snarled. The Old Night fed her using Quincy as a funnel. The forest gave back. Troy and Cleopatra were there too. They strengthened her, cemented the bonds of her pack as the Old Night made them into direwolves.

Genna caught Quincy's hand, pushing it away from her face. "I'm sorry."

"I was starting to feel left out," Quincy said, unwilling to admit his fear. "I was worried. Cleopatra's talking to farrier. He knows the most. He was in on it."

Between the grunting and sloppy sounds of someone being disjointed while still alive and her body shrieking, victory felt more like a punishment. "In on what?"

"Naomi glamoured your stablehands. They were supposed to let you get eaten by the direwolf. The farrier tried to cut your saddle but Sneakers stopped him."

Genna vaguely remembered Sneakers trying to kick the farrier. She thought it was just nerves not sabotage. "Where's Troy?"

"He loves you very much." Quincy had a drowning look as he squinted at the broken and burnt ceiling. "You didn't tell your parents that you're engaged to Cleopatra, did you?"

Genna blinked. "Why?"

"Naomi lost her shit when she heard you two were engaged," Katie said, very pregnant as she waddled in through a door that had not existed until she opened the wall. Through the door

Genna saw the interior of the cottage. Grim, Toto, and Schrodinger slunk in after Katie as though dragged by leashes.

"What the hell? Did you make a door?" Genna sat up fast. She froze with pain.

Katie flapped her hands. "Relax, I'm a York now. Not a McBride."

Katie peeled her face. She revealed yellow fur underneath. Then she smoothed her skin back over like putty. "See? I can't turn into a snake anymore. I'm a wolf."

"You shed your skin."

"I'm a boo hag and everything. The baby's a boo hag too."

Katie had changed her look. Her hair was now a dusky lavender instead of champagne pink. She had brushed her hair with Genna's comb. She used her flatiron to style her gentle curls. Purple lipstick. A black lace dress with diagonal sleeves. She dabbed on Genna's makeup that was too dark for her complexion. The black dress was one of Genna's favorite articles of clothing in her extensive wardrobe. She wore platinum jewelry. She stacked pearls, howlite, moonstones, white opals, and white diamonds bracelets on top of each other. She added finger cuffs to her already long, sharp nails, now painted a matte black.

Genna inched back to lean against the wall next to Miss Bootsie's bed. Talking to Katie helped her focus. "You're wearing my stuff."

"New me. New look. I'm a gorgeous wolf too," Katie said, "You left your bug-out bag in the Lexus."

"So while I was fighting for my life, you were giving yourself a makeover," Genna said.

"I am the witchiest witch." Katie smiled at herself, pleased. "I look *fabulous.*"

"That doesn't mean you should use my hairbrush." Genna closed her eyes.

"The mansion is a shithole now." Katie giggled. "It happened exactly like you said. Your plan worked, Iffy."

"Did it?" Genna pinched the bridge of her nose. "How so?"

"When you told everybody that you were engaged to Cleopatra, Naomi lost her shit. She tried to kill your family, your three favorite fuck toys, and their families. She glamoured everyone in the castle to kill you. I stopped her." She smiled at Quincy. "Thanks for catching the bullets. Naomi stole them from Olympia's armory. They're full of nasty shit."

"Wait a minute, you were in on it? So it was all a trick? You were playing us?" Quincy said, with the edge of a growl. "That's a fucked up thing to do to Cleopatra. What about me?"

"What about you?" She glared.

He dropped his eyes to the jars of ointment. "What about Troy? He loves you."

"Oh, my god. Are you hearing this guy? He's such a dumbass. This isn't about love." Katie said to Quincy. "Iffy did what she did because of *politics*, you dumbass. Don't you know anything about anything?"

Quincy snarled. Katie snarled back. Genna creakily pushed herself. Quincy grabbed her to help her sit. "You need to stay still."

"I'm good." Genna had no intention of laying in the bed that Miss Bootsie had died in.

"Why'd you tell your folks you were marrying Cleopatra?" Quincy said.

"I thought I was going to die. I wanted them to save her if I couldn't."

"Save her? She's fine." He gestured at the bathroom. "She's kicking ass and taking names like she always does."

Katie snapped her fingers. "Hey, dumbass. Naomi planted her power in Cleopatra. She was eating her alive from the inside and none of you noticed."

"You should've told us," Quincy muttered to Genna.

"Oh yeah right. You were glamoured too, dumbass," Katie said. "Just be grateful Iffy save your sorry asses instead of bitching like a little bitch."

"You know what, bitch? Go fuck yourself."

"Stop flirting," Genna said.

"I'm not flirting!" Quincy exclaimed, aghast.

"But she is," Genna gave Katie a look. "Enough."

Katie flicked her hair over her shoulder, rolling her eyes. "Anyway, Naomi's on the run."

"I know."

"But did you know that you're the new queen of the werewolves since you killed White Fang?"

"His name was White Fang?" Genna repeated.

Katie grinned. "Iffy, you really need to get out more. Even I knew who he was."

"But White Fang? That's so basic."

"Look, he's a direwolf. He doesn't have to be smart. He has the power of deep winter. He's super old. What else would they call him? And you know he's stupid. That's why he lost his shit when you laughed at him."

Quincy looked at Genna. "Is that what you did?"

She shrugged and her back spasmed. "What about the vampires? Are there pockets of resistance?"

"Most of them are dead," Katie said, "Anyone left won't fuck with the new Montgomery. Way to consolidate power."

"But I didn't kill Pipsy!"

"Oh, but you did. You took her power." Katie made her fingers into guns and shot at the ceiling. "Pew. Pew."

"No one's going to believe that's true. What about the direwolf. And you?"

"I couldn't close the deal. The direwolf ate what was left but you killed him, so boom, there you go. And I got it on camera and everything. Or at least until you melted my camera equipment."

Genna rubbed her temples. Her skin felt too tight. Her head felt like it was about to explode. "This can't be happening."

"Believe it. This is really about brunch."

Genna inhaled sharply. "But that was months ago!"

Katie grinned. "Pipsy's been scrambling ever since."

"Wait a minute, how can Genna be a witch, and the queen of vampires and werewolves?" Quincy demanded.

"Because she's Iphigenia Bellwether."

"So?"

Katie cocked her head. "Wow, you really don't know anything, do you? Do you think it was just dumb luck that she killed a direwolf?"

"I was there!"

"So what are you talking about?"

"This is bullshit!" Genna shouted then started coughing.

Spasms wracked her body. She bent over, clutching the quilt as she fought to take a breath. Quincy and Katie were arguing, smacking each other away from the bed. Genna tried to breathe. Her skin split, opening in seams along the contours of her muscles. She bled worse as she coughed. Her bones tried to flip into lupine form.

A deafening crack, flash, and room shaking impact of blue lightning burst through the door. Quincy and Katie were knocked on their butts against the far wall.

Troy materialized in the middle of the room. He strode over to the bed, picked Genna up and hugged her tight. He draped a fur cloak around her body. It was warm and calming. Also hiding her naked body. Its weight calmed her. She was worried it had been destroyed. No, it was different cloak. It contained fur that matched Troy, Quincy, Cleopatra, and Katie's pelts along with her own. It hummed with magic. The pin was the boulder opal. She felt its oceanic hum. So much magic contained in the cloak. He pressed his hand against her chest and filled her with magic.

The coughing eased. Her skin healed. The blood evaporated. It was like that moment in the battle only now she could focus on Troy.

He set Genna down on the floor. He tucked the cloak more firmly around her body, pulling her arms through the arm holes.

He wore the silver wolf collar. She tottered to get her feet back. She was restored. The cloak warmed his body.

"Did you make this cloak?"

"Not exactly."

Genna traced the silver necklace, relieved. "You know that you and me are still—"

He gripped her hands. "Forever, Iphigenia."

"I love you, Achilles." She stood up on her tiptoes and kissed him. She tasted blood magic on his tongue.

He gently straightened away. She sank back to her feet. They locked their emotions back behind their eyes. They became what they needed to be. A queen talking to her faithful knight, pouring cement into the foundation of those defined structures with light touches. Perhaps it was inevitable. Troy was a sword. Genna was a sword master. Both were honed sharp by their own experiences. It was a relief to break the cycle of violence by accepting the past instead of erasing it. They could move forward together towards a common goal. They could love and be loved.

"You get what I did with Cleopatra, right?" Genna said, urgently.

Troy nodded. "Cleopatra was the lynchpin and she was exposed. We dropped the ball."

"Naomi and Sable have been working with Tituba. I saw them escape in a boat. They killed and ate Kyle." She glanced at Katie.

"He had it coming." Katie dusted herself off, straightening her dress.

"Naomi bit a lot of your people. This was a setup." Troy said, gesturing at the room's devastation.

"She knows. I told her," Quincy said.

Troy glanced at Quincy. "It wasn't just Genna. Naomi wanted all of us dead, Quincy. Not just the crew but Galveston and Roanoke. Shelly was Naomi's puppet. Sable's been pulling the strings since we walked into the Waffle House. They used the hurricane to funnel prey into their lair."

Quincy straightened up. "That means—what about my parents? Are they? Did she?" He could not finish his sentence.

"They're okay. Mom got them away from Sable."

"What about Memphis?" Cleopatra stood in the doorway of the bathroom. She wiped her hands on a towel. Fury turned her face into a remote mask. "What about my family?"

"Your family are under Bellwether protection. Beyond that, it's too soon to say." Troy smirked at Genna. "You saw Naomi coming a mile away, didn't you?"

"This isn't my first rodeo," Genna said.

Grim trotted out of the cottage. The dog rubbed against Genna, licking her hand, but he was focused on Troy. He woofed a command to follow. Troy stepped towards the dog. Genna was surprised.

"What's this?"

"I need to borrow Grim and the Gray horse," Troy said. "They're part of the Wild Hunt. They can walk places I can't tread even as a wolf."

"Why?"

"Naomi and Sable cracked things wide open. The Ghost Riders are in the sky."

It was code for something. Cleopatra and Quincy quietly swore.

"Is it that bad?" Cleopatra squeezed the bloody towel in her fists. "Naomi really let them out?"

"Someone should watch your back," Quincy said.

"No, you stay here. Help Cleopatra find out what's what."

Cleopatra nodded. She looked aged. "Don't worry. We'll get them back."

"I don't think we will," Troy said softly. "But I can kill a few before they get too far. The trail is fresh. But it'll have to be my way."

Cleopatra and Quincy exhaled. They nodded. "Happy hunting."

He nodded as he settled his black stetson lower on his forehead. Otherness carved his face. Blue lightning ignited in his eyes. His tattoos slithered along his skin. He became the Lone Ranger, the Man in Black, Achilles the warrior king, the Viking, and every other iteration of a lethal man on a mission.

Genna's nipples were hard. "Come back to me."

Troy swayed. He looked down at her as if from a great distance. He had already gone into hunter mode. She had surprised him. He loomed over Genna. "You want that?"

She stepped closer, not afraid. "Kill what you've got to kill but don't take any unnecessary risks. This is not a suicide mission. I want you to come back to me."

He stroked her cheek. He traced her knuckles and kissed them. "Yes, my queen."

Grim woofed again, already at the door. Troy strode out of the apartment and into the stable. His long leather duster flapped like wet vultures wings. Grim was at his side. The Appaloosa was already saddled and waiting. He mounted up and rode out into the rain. Grim swelled to his true size as he padded with him. A great shaggy grim hound. A blinding flash of light made Genna blink then they were gone.

Other horses and dogs pawed restlessly in their stalls. Fire was in their eyes. Smoke drifted from their nostrils. But they stayed. Guarding the stable.

Genna blinked the sun spots out of her eyes.

"Iffy, I need to talk to you," Katie said, breaking the moment with a hammer. "In private."

Genna nodded. "Yeah, in a minute."

"Hey, do you mind if we use this place to ask questions?" Cleopatra said. "Troy brought me a few more people. This may take a while to get some answers."

"Cleopatra," Genna said, then stopped, not sure what to say. "I know that we're not—you don't have to—it was just a ploy."

"I know," Cleopatra said. "But thank you for saving my family."

"Yeah, thanks," Quincy said.

"You're welcome." Genna fidgeted. "I'm sorry."

"How did you know that Troy was a Ghost Rider?" Quincy demanded, his fur rippling.

"How could she do this to me?" Cleopatra exclaimed. "I thought we were family. Not prey! After everything we'd done done for her! And she was working with Tituba!"

Quincy strode over to Cleopatra, gripping her shoulders. "Hey, Naomi did this to all of us."

Cleopatra squeeze the towel in her hands. "Still I love her. Was that just a trick?"

"We'll get through this." Quincy pressed his forehead against hers.

They looked as if their insides had been scraped by an ice cream scoop. The room was too small for their rage. There were livid wounds from bullet holes on their skin that had gone untreated. They had taken bullets for Genna. She would not forget that.

She felt bad for them. They were confused by the depth of their pain. They had done what they always did on a hunt. The sexy fun was just a way to pass the time while they fought the good fight. They liked Genna enough to invite her into their circle. There was not supposed to be a grand conspiracy at the heart of their crew.

Naomi had ripped out their connections at the roots to destroy not punish. It was cruel and effective. She wanted them to suffer so she could feed on their pain.

Genna creakily minced towards the magic door. "I'll be in the cottage. Call if you need me."

Quincy and Cleopatra broke their hug. They nodded without looking her way. They wouldn't call. Genna could feel it in the fur cloak. Neither wanted to be a werewolf. That was how Troy had made a cloak. Genna could keep them here, trap them with obligations and skin magic but she let them go instead.

Quincy shifted back into his human form. Cleopatra rubbed her arm. The cloak felt heavy.

Genna knew that tomorrow she would wake up to find both of them halfway to Memphis, Tennessee. They were done with Sweetwater. They would shed this place like they shed their skin.

At least they wouldn't take the Mustang.

Forty-Four

Genna escorted Katie through the magic door to the cottage. She noticed that Katie wore Miss Bootsie's mustard seed necklace and shoved her, hard.

"Be nice to me,' Katie said as she staggered. "I'm pregnant."

"Oh, shut up." Genna closed the door firmly. The door sealed into a wall, closing off access to Miss Bootsie's apartment. Genna exhaled with relief.

The cottage was a mess but intact. *Sleeping Beauty* played on the television.

Genna's suitcases and bug-out bags were also rifled through. Katie had tried on several outfits without bothering to clean things up. Jewelry spilled out of their travel bags. Makeup lay open to dry out.

The kitchen counter and the floor surrounding the pull-out couch were crowded with buckets full of body parts. A skin of coagulation had settled across the hairy meat.

"What is this?" Genna demanded. "*Who* is this?"

"The stablehands and your staff," Katie said, "I was hungry. It wasn't like those hunters would eat them. That's why I used the door to the apartment to carry the leftovers out of the way."

"So that's how you kept getting in."

Katie grimaced. "Don't be mad, Iffy. I know you haven't eaten any humans since they came to the castle."

Genna's traitorous stomach squelched in agreement. "And my stuff?"

"I needed an outfit."

Genna took off the fur cloak and hung it from a hook on the wall. Her skin ached but Troy's healing hummed in her skin. She went to the bathroom to wash her face. She mechanically did her own makeup and closed the makeup. She brushed her hair. Her reflection was remote and beautiful but her eyes were brown. No fire in the pupils. Burn out.

She grabbed some underwear, a sports bra, and a t-shirt dress to shrug on. Then packed her bags. She slid on jewelry that was within reach. She found Troy's gold watch and her ring in a white cotton drawstring bag.

Tituba left the watch and ring behind. She stared at them but did not put them on.

Katie picked up a leg and started chewing. Her cheeks distended like a carnivorous chipmunk. "It's really weird to chew instead of suck."

Genna went into the kitchen. She poured herself a glass of water. She searched and found a lone jug of apple cider in the cooler. She guzzled it empty. She waited to feel something but she was just glad for the quiet.

Katie sat on the couch. "Ooh, my feet hurt." She started gnawing meat and cracking bone.

Genna leaned against the kitchen counter, watching the Disney movie from there.

"Maleficent reminds me of you, Iffy."

Genna wiped dribbles of cider off of her chin. "That's the nicest thing you've ever said to me, Katie. What's going on with you?"

"I'm in a good mood. Mimi's dead. Sable chopped off her head. Kyle swam off with Naomi. Sable's gone."

"Kyle's dead too. Tituba ate him."

"You know he tried to kill Pipsy?" Katie bounced on the pullout couch, drumming her feet against the mattress as she laughed. "You should've seen him gumming on her tail. He tried so hard but he couldn't break through her scales. Pathetic!"

"I guess he was sick of being the frog in a nest of vipers. Who really killed Pipsy?"

"I already told you."

"So that wasn't just to fuck with Quincy?"

Katie flipped her hair and rolled her eyes. "You did most of the work frying her up with that lightning bolt. That really hurt, by the way. It's a good thing that Aaliyah likes the taste. She ate it all up." Katie affectionately patted her belly. "Aaliyah even took your lightning from everyone else. She wouldn't share. She's just like her mommy! Aren't you? Yes, you are! You liked all that nummy nummy lightning, didn't you?"

Genna was mildly disgusted by the fluting baby talk. She thought about the Old Night filling her with magic. Tituba had already told her the baby's name.

Genna opened the drawer and stared at the kitchen knife resting in its stand. She traced the metal. "I can't believed I killed that direwolf."

"Not just any direwolf. You killed White Fang the wolf king. That makes you the queen bitch of the Appalachian Trail."

"So you weren't lying." Genna groaned. "I thought the werewolf hollers were independently governed packs too busy fighting each other to bother with the outside civilization."

"The Pandemic was a busy time for werewolves. Lots of dead bodies. Lots of people walking the Appalachian Trail. The humans moving to the sticks pushed the packs out of their hollers and onto the streets. No one asks questions if people disappear anymore. White Fang consolidated the packs. You killed all of his pack leaders and cronies last night. Sweetwater is about to be to be busy busy busy."

Genna slammed the drawer shut, annoyed. "Why did White Fang come here? Since when do direwolves work for vampires?

He should've known better. I haven't messed with the werewolves at all."

"He wanted you. Without Pipsy claiming you then it's open season. Werewolves aren't civilized like us. It doesn't matter that you Turned the hunters, the packs would still try to take the castle."

"So killing White Fang was the only option."

"You did what you had to do."

Genna found the keys to the Mustang next to a row of candles. Their shapes had changed into wolves and dragons. No more snakes. "I can't believe you shed your skin."

"It was the only way I could get into the cottage. A vampire Turning into a wolf is more on brand anyway."

"But you're still the Bride. Others will think you're the new Montgomery."

"That is their mistake."

"You're the last McBride."

Katie's smile slipped off her face. Anger flashed. "My last name is York."

Genna stopped swinging the keys. "You changed your name?"

It wasn't simply the skin or the name. Katie *was* different. Genna did not entirely understand what a McBride was, or a York, or what the cottage meant to Katie.

It was suicidal to be empathetic to a vampire but perhaps as a werewolf, Katie was feeling the loss of her family. Katie was pack now. The wolf under her skin was real and deferential. Genna was the leader. She needed to change how she treated Katie.

Genna walked into the garage. The Mustang filled most of the space. She saw Schrodinger, Toto, and Pirate hiding in the back seat. She stroked the hood, relieved to see them safe.

She opened a closet in the garage's back wall and pulled out a sealed box. She pulled out a large thin wooden box. She opened the taped sides and slid the painting free of its bubble wrap. The cottage sprouted a hook and extra wall space with a special light overhead. She hung the familiar painting on the wall.

Katie's pale teenage self hanging front a pole. The leering eagle. Genna self-consciously straightened the edge of the gold leaf frame so the rococo gleamed in the light. "I've always called this one: *The Torture of Katie McBride.*"

Katie rubbed her swollen belly, focused on painted herself. "I thought I'd lost that painting forever."

"I took it. I thought you knew."

"I wanted it to be you but they all hated that painting so much. I thought they'd burned it."

Kyle had taken it off the art gallery wall right in the middle of the exhibition. He had the gallery owner wrap it up. Genna switched boxes while Kyle was back in the gallery grabbing another painting. Then she ran out of the gallery's service door carrying the painting.

It had been a long run up Backbone Road. She tried to stay off the streets and keep to the hedges. She kept expecting someone to notice or comment. She ran through the forest and straight to Miss Bootsie's cottage. She stuffed the painting into the garage closet, too ashamed to unwrap it.

Miss Bootsie had been in the living room, reading in her rocking chair. Genna had been so focused on hiding the painting that she didn't notice the boo hag until after she barricaded the closet door. "What are you doing, honey child?"

"I don't know what you're talking about." Genna had said, blushing with embarrassment.

"You need to start accepting yourself, honey child. That eagle needs to eat. You do too."

"I don't like her. It's just a painting."

"Like ain't got nothing to do with it. You are what you are. Do what must be done. You keep holding back then you will lose control and eat someone you do care about. Seducing Katie McBride will get her away from her family and under your thumb. You have to use what you've got."

"I don't want to be a monster."

"But you are a monster, honey child."

Genna had cried, on her knees, her face pressed into Miss Bootsie's lap. Genna still remembered those soft hands patting her back.

Miss Bootsie put on *Sleeping Beauty* that night too. She pointed at Maleficent. "That dragon queen knows how to keep her power inside of her skin. She saves it for when the time is right. But she also knows who to eat and who to keep."

Now, decades later, Genna stared at the painting instead of Katie. "You've got a gift, Katie. You should keep painting."

Katie hiccuped. Her face became blotchy with emotion. "Iffy, I think you're my best friend. I'm sorry about everything. I'm sorry I'm so shitty. I'm sorry I got pregnant but now I love my baby. Please don't leave me."

Hormonal Katie was a new mountain to climb. "Are you still adjusting to the messy emotions of being a mammal?"

"You don't think we're best friends?"

"I've given up on defining what we are. You're a pain in my ass but I like you more than I like your half-sister."

"I'm so relieved!" Katie sobbed.

Genna rifled through the buckets and settled on a severed ribcage. She turned the movie back on and sat down on the couch. She was exhausted. She wasn't ready to go back to the castle. Or deal with consequences of success.

They watched *Sleeping Beauty.* They munched on body parts. They cracked the bones with their molars. They licked the marrow. The cottage and the cloak absorbed the excess.

Genna could taste the magical signature of who killed each person. She learned the difference in strike patterns between Troy, Quincy, and Cleopatra. Also the amount of damage. Cleopatra ripped, focused on pain. Quincy bludgeoned and crushed. Even the ones Troy did not kill had been cooked by lightning. His strikes were so clean and strong that he sheered through solid muscle and bone, cauterizing along the way.

Genna stroked the edge of a bone that still hummed with

Troy's magic. She wondered what her strike patterned looked like. Katie noticed that Genna only ate Troy's kills.

"I'm sorry I fucked with Troy." Katie rubbed her belly. "I won't do it again."

Genna snapped the femur in half. "You better not."

Katie blushed. "Did you know that all of this drama happened because Miss Bootsie knew Pipsy's big secret?"

"You mean that Pipsy is Black but passing as White?" Genna said as she dragged a new bucket of parts over.

"How did you know?"

"I figured it out when I looked up your ancestry. Passing as White was pretty common thing back in the day. Pipsy absolutely would exploit colorism. Either way, she's a vampire first."

"That means I'm Black too."

"Yes, it does. How does that make you feel?"

"The same," Katie shrugged. "I'm me."

Genna smirked. Katie was Katie.

"You know, Pipsy tried to eat me?" Katie said while nibbling the fingers off of a hand.

"I told you so."

"I know. You warned me she would but I didn't listen. What's really crazy is that I didn't even fight her. I just stood there. I couldn't move." Katie patted her belly. "Aaliyah saved me. My stomach turned into this big ball of lightning. Like you do when you're mad. It burned up my skin. That's when I went from snake to wolf the first time. Pipsy spat me out." Katie picked up Genna hand. "Here. Feel this. The baby's been kicking. She lights up whenever you're around."

"Kicking? Isn't it too soon? How fast is your gestation?" Genna felt a pulse against her palm. Her lightning reached down. The ball of lightning inside reached out. Katie whimpered, uncomfortably as Genna fed the fetus lightning.

"You see? I wasn't lying. She's yours," Katie said.

Genna pulled her hand away but she still felt connected. "And

Troy's, Quincy's, Cleopatra's, Miss Bootsie's, and yours. That baby has a grab-bag of magical signatures."

"She's yours," Katie repeated. "After I have her, I won't be involved in raising her."

"Nice try but you're a mom now. Not a surrogate." Genna poked her in the belly. "You're going to raise her in the cottage because it's safer here than anywhere outside of the forest. You can't be Mimi."

"Fine, but I'm not changing diapers."

"Yes, you will. You'll love her more than you love anything. Even yourself."

"You will too."

Genna did not feel love. It was more complicated than that. The Old Night filled her blood with strength and maternal acceptance. The lightning created images. Genna saw a black wolf nuzzling a newborn. She saw a little girl with light brown skin and wild black curls running through the woods wearing a long red cloak. It could have been a memory. It could be Aaliyah.

Good or bad, Aaliyah was hers. Genna had a feeling the town would call her Baby Belle.

When *Sleeping Beauty* movie ended, Genna got up and ejected the VHS tape. "What do you want to watch next?"

"How about *Sister Act*?"

Genna nodded somberly. She took the cloak off the hook and spread it across her knees like a blanket. Neither ate anything as they watched the movie. They sat straight up, their hands neatly in their laps, ankles crossed. As Miss Bootsie had taught them. Genna petted the fur cloak. Katie fiddled with the mustard seed necklace and pet her belly. Tears wet their faces.

Genna found two embroidered and lavender scented handkerchiefs in a side drawer and passed one to Katie while she dabbed her eyes.

"I miss her," Katie said.

"Me too," Genna said, blowing her nose.

"Do you think Naomi will come back?"

"I can't worry about that right now."

"You're right. We've got funerals to plan. And a wedding. And a baby shower. And a christening. I guess you don't want an engagement party?"

"I meant the war between monsters and humans that's going on in Sweetwater right now," Genna said dryly. "You know, the one we started by creating a power vacuum?"

"Nah, there won't be a war because you're the power. The queen is dead. Long live the queen. You know that the real negotiations happen on the golf course and at a party. There's better lighting and better food. Why do you think Pipsy had those parties at her house?"

"She loved the carnage."

"Well, yeah, but that's how she could meet friends and influence people."

"Okay, Dale Carnegie."

"Look at how much you accomplished during that brunch. You got Olympia Billson the Huntress and Camille Snodgrass the Book Wyrm to break bread with a werewolf princess and a vampire princess. The best part was how you let everyone talk. You didn't force it. You sat there at the head of the table as the queen of Sweetwater. No one died. I hired a bunch of photographers." Katie flicked her hand at the door. "There won't be any news about tonight. Sweetwater is already yours. That's why Pipsy was so desperate to kill you. She couldn't undo in the shadows what you did in broad daylight."

Genna chewed at bone. Katie as an ally was a different kind of trouble. "I'd like to see those photos."

"Don't worry, you looked great."

"I am *not* having them at the castle." Genna said, knowing it was inevitable.

"Your castle is perfect." Katie giggled while Genna groaned. Katie clapped her hands together. "I love party planning. No one ever appreciates the work I put into it. Maybe I should do it professionally."

A slow evil smile bloomed on Genna's lips. "You could plan the Sweetwater weddings. You could call your company *Always a McBride.*"

Katie tittered. "Oooh, that's perfect!"

They finished the movie.

Outside it stormed as Troy, Quincy, and Cleopatra raged through Sweetwater. Their howls were in the wind and the slashing rain. Hale bounced off the cottage roof.

"Iffy?"

"Yeah?"

"You can't marry Cleopatra because I made her my bride."

"When was that?"

"At the Halloween party. Naomi was so angry."

"Does Cleopatra remember?"

"Of course she does. I've learned from my mistakes. It's legal and everything."

As Genna anticipated, announcing her engagement to Cleopatra prompted Katie's swift action. "So you're married to the mother of your child?"

"I had a hell of a time sharking Cleopatra away from your parents. They've gotten vicious. Don't be mad at me, okay? I'll give you anything you want in exchange."

Genna hid a smile. "You'll need to have an official wedding."

"I want it during Pipsy's funeral so we can dance on her grave."

"That's a little tacky, Katie."

"You need to stop thinking like a human and start thinking like a direwolf queen. All hail Black Belle, the queen of Sweetwater. Devourer of enemies."

"I am what I need to be," Genna said, unnerved by Katie's little nod of pride. "Now, will you tell me what's really on your mind? This Perky McPerkison cheerleader barbie act makes my skin crawl."

Katie stopped smiling. She fiddled with the femur in her hands. "I thought you were going to die."

Genna took a deep breath. She stared out the window at the storm. A part of her still sat on Sneakers in the pasture facing down the direwolf. Winning felt like a delusion. That terrible finality was hard to shake. She was glad to be alive.

"I'm glad you didn't die," Katie continued, "It was all my fault. You fell in love with Troy and I got jealous. It's so stupid. I was stupid. I knew Naomi enchanted your stablehands. I told her how to do it. I didn't think it'd work. I'm so used to you winning that I didn't think you could lose."

"You're a bitch, Katie." In a weird way, Naomi and the stablehands' betrayal balanced the scales but Genna wasn't about to let Katie off the hook.

Katie clutched her wrist and sniffled. "I'm sorry, okay? You can have as many chewtoys as you want. I promise I won't get jealous. I'm sorry. Can you forgive me?"

Genna glared out the window, simmering with aggression. The forest swayed beyond the clearing. The rain had turned into a sleet. It was not Halloween in Pittsburgh without an ice storm.

Katie scooted closer, petting Genna's thigh. "Iffy? I apologized. Now you have to forgive me. Say that you forgive me."

Fury sharpened Genna's cheekbones and her teeth strained her gums. She grabbed Katie's face, squeezing the hinge bones of her jaw. She spoke carefully to avoid a lisp. "No, Katie, I don't forgive you. If you pull this shit again, I'll kill you."

Katie sucked in a breath as she leaned into Genna's hand, exposing her throat in pure submission. "I can live with that."

Acknowledgments

There are many people that need to be thanked. To protect their identities I will speak in generalizations.

To my beloved: I don't just lycanthrope you, I love you.

To my family: I descend from giants. Thank you for teaching me how to trace my roots. I love you.

To my friends: Thank you for your support and sharing your lives with me.

To my writing partners and mentors: Thank you for listening instead of rolling your eyes when I change the entire plot line for the billionth time.

To the lonely angry people out there who read because that's the only freedom they have: Be the dream of yourself. Ride your nightmares.

You are all treasured members of my pack.

www.ingramcontent.com/pod-product-compliance
Lightning Source LLC
Chambersburg PA
CBHW020322010826

48973CB00005B/1088